W9-CCT-879

"AN A-PLUS FIRST NOVEL."
—*The Philadelphia Inquirer*

Debut author Sheldon Siegel bursts into the legal thriller arena with a riveting courtroom drama, exposing the world of big-time law firms and lawyers in a fresh, sharp-witted, wonderfully sardonic page-turner.

Meet Mike Daley. Ex-priest. Ex–public defender. And as of yesterday, ex-partner in one of San Francisco's most prominent law firms. Today he's out on his own, setting up practice on the wrong side of town. Then his best friend and former colleague is charged with a brutal double murder, and Daley is instantly catapulted into a high-profile investigation involving the prestigious law firm that just booted him. As he prepares his case, Daley uncovers the firm's dirtiest secrets. It doesn't take long for him to discover that in this trial, ambition, friendship, greed, and long-standing grudges will play just as important a role as truth and justice.

Brilliantly paced, crackling with energy and suspense, *Special Circumstances* reminds us why we love to hate lawyers—but can't get enough of courtroom drama when it's done this well.

"A poignant, feisty tale . . . characters so finely drawn you can almost smell their fear and desperation. The dialogue is taut and tangy." —*USA Today*

"By the time the whole circus ends up in the courtroom, the hurtling plot threatens to rip paper cuts into readers' hands." —*San Francisco Chronicle*

SPECIAL CIRCUMSTANCES

a novel by

Sheldon Siegel

BANTAM BOOKS
New York Toronto London Sydney Auckland

This edition contains the complete text
of the original hardcover edition.
NOT ONE WORD HAS BEEN OMITTED.

SPECIAL CIRCUMSTANCES

A Bantam Book

PUBLISHING HISTORY

Bantam hardcover edition / February 2000
Bantam mass market edition / July 2001

ISBN 0-553-58192-9

Published simultaneously in the United States and Canada

Bantam Books are published by Bantam Books, a division of
Random House, Inc. Its trademark, consisting of the words
"Bantam Books" and the portrayal of a rooster, is Registered
in U.S. Patent and Trademark Office and in other
countries. Marca Registrada.
Bantam Books, 1540 Broadway, New York, New York 10036.

PRINTED IN THE UNITED STATES OF AMERICA

OPM   10 9 8 7 6 5 4 3 2 1

For Linda, Alan, Stephen and Charlotte

SPECIAL
CIRCUMSTANCES

1
A LICENSE TO PRINT MONEY

"Founded in 1929 and headquartered in San Francisco, Simpson and Gates is the largest full-service law firm based west of the Mississippi. With over nine hundred attorneys in eighteen offices on four continents, Simpson and Gates is recognized as an international leader in the legal profession."
—SIMPSON AND GATES ATTORNEY RECRUITING BROCHURE.

"For three hundred and fifty dollars an hour, I'd bite the heads off live chickens."
—J. ROBERT HOLMES JR., CHAIRMAN, SIMPSON AND GATES CORPORATE DEPARTMENT. WELCOMING REMARKS TO NEW ATTORNEYS.

For the last twenty years or so, being a partner in a big corporate law firm has been like having a license to print money. At my firm, Simpson and Gates, we've had a license to print *a lot* of money.

At six-fifteen in the evening of Tuesday, December 30, the printing press is running at full speed forty-eight floors above California Street in downtown San Francisco in what our executive committee modestly likes to call our world headquarters. Our 320 attorneys are housed in opulent offices on eight floors at the top of the Bank of America Building, a fifty-two-story bronze edifice that takes up almost an entire city block and is the tallest and ugliest testimonial to unimaginative architecture in the city skyline.

Our two-story rosewood-paneled reception area is about the size of a basketball court. A reception desk that is longer than a city bus sits at the south end of the forty-eighth floor, and I can see the Golden Gate Bridge, Alcatraz Island and Sausalito through the glass-enclosed conference room on the north wall. The gray carpet, overstuffed leather chairs and antique coffee tables create the ambiance of a classic men's club, which is entirely appropriate since most of our attorneys and clients are white, male and Republican.

Even in the evening of the customarily quiet week between Christmas and New Year's, our reception area is buzzing with a higher level of activity than most businesses see in the middle of the day. Then again, most businesses aren't the largest and most profitable law firm on the West Coast.

Tomorrow is my last day with the firm and I am trying to shove my way through three hundred attorneys, clients, politicians and other hangers-on who have gathered for one of our insufferable cocktail parties. I hate this stuff. I guess it's appropriate I have to walk the gauntlet one last time.

In the spirit of the holiday season, everybody is dressed in festive dark gray business suits, starched monogrammed white shirts and red power ties. A string quartet plays classical music in front of the blinking lights of our tired-looking twenty-foot Christmas tree. The suits have gathered to drink chardonnay, eat hors d'oeuvres and pay tribute to my soon-to-be ex-partner, Prentice Marshall Gates III, the son of our late founding partner Prentice Marshall Gates II. Prentice III, one of many lawyers in our firm with roman numerals behind his name, is known as Skipper. He is also sailing out of the firm tomorrow. The circumstances of our respective departures are, shall I say, somewhat different.

After my five years as an underproductive partner in our white-collar criminal defense department, our executive committee asked me to leave. I was, in short, fired. Although the request was polite, I was told that if I didn't leave voluntarily, they would invoke Article Seven of our partnership agreement, which states, and I quote, that "a Partner of the

Firm may be terminated by the Firm upon the affirmative vote of two-thirds ($2/3$) of the Partners of the Firm, at a duly called and held meeting of the Partners of the Firm." In the last three years, fourteen of my partners have been Article Sevened. I have graciously agreed to resign. On Monday, I'll open the law offices of Michael J. Daley, criminal defense attorney, in a subleased office in a walk-up building in the not-so-trendy part of San Francisco's South of Market area. Welcome to the modern practice of law.

Skipper's story is a little different. After thirty years as an underproductive partner in our real estate department, he spent three million dollars of the money he inherited from his father to win a mean-spirited race for district attorney of San Francisco, even though he hasn't set foot in a courtroom in over twenty years. My partners are thrilled. They have never complained about his arrogance, sloppy work and condescending attitude. Hell, the same could be said about most of my partners. What they can't live with is his four-hundred-thousand-dollar draw. He has been living off his father's reputation for years. That's why all the power partners are here. They want to give him a big send-off. More importantly, they want to be sure he doesn't change his mind.

The temperature is about ninety degrees and it smells more like a locker room than a law firm. I nod to the mayor, shake hands with two of my former colleagues from the San Francisco Public Defender's Office and carefully avoid eye contact with Skipper, who is working the room. I overhear him say the DA's office is his first step toward becoming attorney general and, ultimately, governor.

In your dreams, Skipper.

I'm trying to get to our reception desk to pick up a settlement agreement. Ordinarily, such a document would be brought to me by one of our many in-house messengers. Tonight, I'm on my own because the kids who work in our mailroom aren't allowed to come to the front desk when the VIPs are around. I sample skewered shrimp provided by a tuxedoed waiter and elbow my way to the desk, where four evening-shift receptionists operate telephone consoles that have more buttons than a 747. I lean over the polished counter and politely ask Cindi Harris if she has an envelope for me.

"Let me look, Mr. Daley," she replies. She's a twenty-two-year-old part-time art student from Modesto with long black hair, a prim nose and a radiant smile. She has confided to me that she would like to become an artist, a stock-car driver or the wife of a rich attorney. I have it on good authority that a couple of my partners have already taken her out for a test drive.

A few years ago, our executive committee hired a consultant to spruce up our image. It's hard to believe, but many people seem to perceive our firm as stuffy. For a hundred thousand dollars, our consultant expressed concern that our middle-aged receptionists did not look "perky" enough to convey the appropriate image of a law firm of our stature. In addition, he was mortified that we had two receptionists who were members of the male gender.

At a meeting that everyone adamantly denies ever took place, our executive committee concluded that our clients—the white, middle-aged men who run the banks, insurance companies, defense contractors and conglomerates that we represent—would be more comfortable if our receptionists were younger, female, attractive and, above all, perkier. As a result, our middle-aged female and male receptionists were reassigned to less-visible duties. We hired Cindi because she fit the profile recommended by our consultant. Although she's incapable of taking a phone message, she looks like a model for Victoria's Secret. S&G isn't known as a hotbed of progressive thinking.

Don't get me wrong. As a divorced forty-five-year-old, I

have nothing against attractive young women. I do have a problem when a firm adopts a policy of reassigning older women and men to less-visible positions just because they aren't attractive enough. For one thing, it's illegal. For another thing, it's wrong. That's another reason I got fired. Getting a reputation as the "house liberal" at S&G isn't great for your career.

Cindi's search turns up empty. "I'm sorry, Mr. Daley," she says, batting her eyes. She flashes an uncomfortable smile and looks like she's afraid I may yell at her. While such wariness is generally advisable at S&G, it shows she doesn't know me very well. Jimmy Carter was in the White House the last time I yelled at anybody. "Let me look again," she says.

I spy a manila envelope with my name on it sitting in front of her. "I think that may be it."

Big smile. "Oh, good," she says.

Success. I take the envelope. "By the way, have you seen my secretary?"

Deer in the headlights. "What's her name again?"

"Doris."

"Ah, yes." Long pause. "Dooooris." Longer pause. "What does she look like?"

I opt for the path of least resistance. "It's okay, Cindi. I'll find her."

I start to walk away. She grabs my arm. I turn and look into her perplexed eyes. "Mr. Daley," she says, "are you really leaving? I mean, well, you're one of the nice guys. I mean, for a lawyer. I thought partners never leave."

Cindi, I'm leaving because I have more in common with the kids who push the mail carts than I do with my partners. I was fired because my piddly book of business isn't big enough.

I summon my best sincere face, look her right in her puppy eyes and make believe I am pouring out my heart. "I've been here for five years. I'm getting too old for a big firm. I've decided to try it on my own. Besides, I want more time for Grace." My ex-wife has custody of our six-year-old daughter, but we get along pretty well and Grace stays with me every other weekend.

Her eyes get larger. "Somebody said you might go back to the public defender's office."

I frown. I worked as a San Francisco PD for seven years before I joined S&G. The *State Bar Journal* once proclaimed I was the best PD in Northern California. Before I went to law school, I was a priest for three years. "Actually, I'm going to share office space with another attorney." Without an ounce of conviction, I add, "It'll be fun." I leave out the fact I'm subleasing from my ex-wife.

"Good luck, Mr. Daley."

"Thanks, Cindi." It's a little scary when you talk to people at work in the same tone of voice you use with your first-grade daughter. It's even scarier to think I'll probably miss Cindi more than I'll miss any of my partners. Then again, she didn't fire me.

I know one thing for certain. I'll sure miss the regular paychecks.

I begin to push my way toward the conference room in search of Doris when I'm confronted by the six-foot-six-inch frame of Skipper Gates, who flashes the plastic three-million-dollar smile that graces fading campaign posters that are still nailed to power poles across the city. He is inhaling a glass of wine. "Michael," he slurs, "so good to see you."

I don't want to deal with this right now.

At fifty-eight, his tanned face is chiseled out of solid rock, with a Roman nose, high forehead and graceful mane of silver hair. His charcoal-gray double-breasted Brioni suit, Egyptian-cotton white shirt and striped tie add dignity to his rugged features. He looks like he is ready to assume his rightful place on Mount Rushmore next to George Washington.

As an attorney, he's careless, lazy and unimaginative. As a human being, he's greedy, condescending and an unapologetic philanderer. As a politician, however, he's the real deal. Even when he's half tanked and there's a piece of shrimp hanging from his chin, he exudes charisma, wealth and, above all, style. It must be some sort of birthright of those born into privilege. As one of four children of a San Francisco cop, privilege is something I know very little about.

He squeezes my hand and pulls me uncomfortably close. "I can't believe you're leaving," he says. His baritone has the affected quality of a man who spent his youth in boarding schools and his adulthood in country clubs. As he shouts into my ear, his breath confirms he could launch his forty-foot sailboat with the chardonnay he's consumed tonight.

His speech is touching. It's also utter bullshit. Instinctively, I begin evasive maneuvers. I pound him a little too hard on his back and dislodge the shrimp from his chin. "Who knows?" I say. "Maybe we'll get to work on a case together."

He tilts his head back and laughs too loudly. "You bet."

I go for the quick tweak. "Skipper, you *are* going to try cases, right?" District attorneys in big cities are political, ceremonial and administrative lawyers. They don't go to court. The assistant DAs try cases. If the ADA wins, the DA takes credit. If the ADA loses, the DA deflects blame. The San Francisco DA has tried only a handful of cases since the fifties.

He turns up the voltage. Like many politicians, he can speak and grin simultaneously. He hides behind the protective cocoon of his favorite sound bite. "Skipper Gates's administration is going to be different," he says. "The DA is supposed to be a law-enforcement officer, not a social worker. Skipper Gates is going to try cases. Skipper Gates is going to put the bad guys away."

And Mike Daley thinks you sound like a pompous ass.

He sees the mayor and staggers away. I wish you smooth sailing, Skipper. The political waters in the city tend to be choppy, even for well-connected operators like you. Things may be different when your daddy's name isn't on the door.

A moment later, I find my secretary, Doris Fontaine, who is standing just outside our power conference room, or "PCR." Doris is a dignified fifty-six-year-old with serious blue eyes, carefully coiffed gray hair and the quiet confidence of a consummate professional. If she had been born twenty years later, she would have gone to law school and become a partner here.

"Thanks for everything, Doris," I say. "I'll miss you."

"I'll never get another one like you, Mikey," she replies.

I hate it when she calls me Mikey. She does it all the time. She absentmindedly fingers the reading glasses that hang from a small gold chain around her neck. She reminds me of Sister Eunice, my kindergarten teacher at St. Peter's. She looks at the chaos in the PCR through the heavy glass door and shakes her head.

The PCR houses an eighty-foot rosewood table with a marble top, matching credenza and fifty chairs, a closed-circuit television system connecting our eighteen offices and a museum-quality collection of Currier and Ives lithographs. Six presidents, eight governors and countless local politicians have solicited campaign funds in this very room. Thirty expandable aluminum racks holding hundreds of carefully labeled manila folders containing legal documents cover the table. The room is littered with paper, coffee cups, half-eaten sandwiches, legal pads and cellular phones. It looks like mission control before a space shuttle launch. The grim faces of the fifty people scattered in small groups in the PCR are in contrast to the forced smiles at Skipper's party outside. Nobody is admiring the lithographs.

"How is Bob's deal going?" I ask.

"Not so well," she replies. Doris. Ever the diplomat. She's worked for Bob Holmes, the head of our corporate department, for about twenty years. In every law firm, there's one individual with a huge book of business and an even bigger ego whose sole purpose is to make everyone else miserable. Bob is our resident nine-hundred-pound gorilla. His eight-million-dollar book of business lets him do pretty much whatever he wants. For the most part, he's content to sit on our executive committee, torture his associates and whine. Last year he took home a million three hundred thousand. Not bad for a short kid from the wrong side of the tracks in Wilkes-Barre. Although my partners find it difficult to agree on anything, they're willing to acknowledge that Bob is a flaming asshole.

Whenever a big deal is coming down at S&G, the PCR is the stage and Bob plays the lead. At the moment, he's screaming into a cellular phone. He hasn't slept in three days, and it shows. He's in his late forties, but with his five-seven frame holding 230 pounds, his puffy red face and jowls make him look at least sixty. Although some of us remember when his hair was gray, it's now dyed an unnatural shade of orange-brown that he combs over an expanding bald spot. On his best days, he storms through our office with a pained expression suggesting he's battling a perpetual case of hemorrhoids. Tonight the grimace is even more pronounced.

I share Doris with Bob and a first-year associate named Donna Williams, who spends all of her waking hours in our library preparing memoranda on esoteric legal issues. It may seem odd that a heavy hitter like Bob has to share a secretary. However, by executive committee fiat, every attorney (including immortals) must share a secretary with two others. This means Bob gets ninety-nine percent of Doris's time, I get one percent and Donna gets nothing. From the firm's perspective, this allocation is entirely appropriate. Bob runs the firm, I'm on my way out the door and Donna is irrelevant.

"Doris, can you still take the day off tomorrow?" I ask.

She sighs. "Doesn't look good. I was hoping I'd get some time with Jenny." She's a single mom. Never been married. Her daughter is a senior at Stanford.

"I saw her earlier today," I say. "Sounded like she had a cold."

"You know how it is. Spend your whole life worrying about your kids."

Don't I know. "Any chance you got my bills out?" Ordinarily, I don't sweat administrative details like bills and time sheets. However, if my bills don't go out on time, the firm will withhold my paycheck. It's our only absolute rule. No bills—no paycheck—no exceptions. You don't become the biggest law firm in California if you aren't careful about money. Doris has long been convinced my lackadaisical attitude would do irreparable harm to S&G's finely tuned money machine.

"I got them into the last mail run," she says.

Relief. "You're still the best. Are you sure you won't come work for me?"

"You can't afford me, Mikey."

The door to the PCR opens and a blast of stale air hits me. Joel Friedman, a harried-looking corporate associate, steps outside. His collar is unbuttoned and the bags under his eyes extend halfway down his cheeks. "Doris," he says, "are you going to be here for a while?"

"Just for a few more minutes," she replies.

Joel is sort of a Jewish Ward Cleaver. He's an excellent attorney with a terrific wife and twin six-year-old boys. He's thirty-eight, a trim five-nine. His father is the rabbi at Temple Beth Sholom in the Richmond District. Joel left the yeshiva after two years and went to my alma mater, UC Berkeley's Boalt Law School. He graduated second in his class and joined S&G seven years ago. His brown hair is graying, the bald spot he tries to hide is getting larger and his tortoiseshell glasses give him a rabbinical look which, in the circumstances, is entirely appropriate. In Yiddish, he would be described as a mensch, which means an honorable man. He's also my best friend.

"Is your deal going to close?" I ask. He's up for partner this year. If his deal closes, he's a shoo-in. He modestly describes his job as thanklessly walking behind Bob Holmes and sweeping up the debris. In reality, he does all the work and Bob takes the credit. Frankly, he's the last line of defense between Bob and our malpractice carrier.

"It's all fucked up," he says. Like many attorneys, he holds the misguided belief that he's more convincing if he peppers his speech with four-letter words. Very unbecoming for the rabbi's son. He nods in the direction of our client, Vince Russo, an oily-looking man about Joel's age who has jammed his Jabba the Hutt torso into the chair at the table next to Holmes. "The closing depends on him," he says. "He's supposed to be selling his father's business, but he's having second thoughts. He thinks he can get a higher price if he can line up another buyer."

I've never had the pleasure of meeting Russo. From what I've read, he's run his father's real-estate investment conglomerate into the ground. "Why doesn't he pull out?" I ask.

"His creditors will force him into bankruptcy. He's jerked them around since his father died. They aren't going to wait around for another year or two."

I gaze at the frenzy in the PCR. "Looks like you could use some help."

"As usual, I'm not getting much." He glances at Diana Kennedy, a glamorous twenty-nine-year-old associate with deep blue eyes, stylish blond hair and a beautiful figure that reflects a lot of time at the gym. She's the only person in the room who looks presentable. She always does. She's a rising star. "Things might go a little faster if Diana would focus a little more on work," he says.

Doris looks away. If you believe the firm's gossipmongers, Bob Holmes and Diana Kennedy have been sleeping together for the last year or so. I don't know for sure.

"To top everything off," Joel says, "Beth showed up an hour ago and served Bob with divorce papers."

I grin. Beth is Bob's soon-to-be-fourth ex-wife. It's twisted, but I silently rejoice at his latest marital failure. I'm sorry I won't be around to witness the fallout. His last divorce was spectacular.

Instinctively, Doris comes to Bob's defense. "She could have waited," she says indignantly. It's funny. Bob has been treating Doris like dirt for about twenty years. They fight like cats and dogs all day, yet she's always the first to defend him.

I opt to change the subject. "Why doesn't Bob get Russo to take his chances in bankruptcy?"

Joel's eyes twinkle. "Because we won't get paid. Do you know how much Russo owes us?"

I shake my head. "A million bucks?"

"Try fifteen million." I'm stunned. His grin widens. "If you're going to start your own firm, you should learn a little more about this financial stuff. We're doing this deal for a contingency fee. We get paid only if it closes. It's in the escrow instructions. We get twelve million at the closing."

"I thought you said he owes us fifteen."

"He does."

"But you said we're getting only twelve."

"We are."

I'm confused. "Who gets the other three?"

"Guess."

I shake my head. "Who gets it?" I demand.

Doris nods knowingly. "Bob does," she replies calmly.

"No way," I say. "He can't siphon off a three-million-dollar personal gratuity. It's against firm policy. The fees belong to the firm. Some of that money belongs to *me*."

Joel laughs. "It's been approved by the executive committee. That's why Bob will pull every string to get this deal to close."

As he says the word "close," we see Russo's eyes getting as big as manhole covers and his face turning bright crimson. "Stand back," Joel says. "Mount Russo is about to erupt."

Russo clumsily squeezes out of his chair on the second try and storms toward us. He slams his three-hundred-pound frame against the glass door. When he's halfway out, he turns around and faces the roomful of apprehensive eyes. "Another forty *fucking* million?" he shrieks. "How the *fuck* am I supposed to afford another forty *fucking* million? Why the *fuck* do I pay you *fucking* lawyers?"

The party outside goes silent. Skipper looks mortified. Russo waddles off down the hall.

I look at Joel and Doris. "What was that all about?" I ask.

Doris shrugs and says she has to go back to work.

Joel winks. "I'm not entirely sure," he deadpans, "but it seems there's been a modest reduction in the purchase price. It's such a pleasure working with our highly sophisticated, state-of-the-art corporate clients." He arches his eyebrows. "I think we could use a glass of wine."

2
"WE MAY HAVE A LITTLE PROBLEM WITH THE CLOSING"

"People think being administrative partner is a boring, thankless job. I disagree. The administrative partner is the glue that holds the firm together as an institution."
—SIMPSON AND GATES ADMINISTRATIVE PARTNER CHARLES STERN.
WELCOMING REMARKS TO NEW ATTORNEYS.

A few minutes later, I am sitting in a sterile conference room on the forty-fifth floor, where my partner, Charles Stern, has called a meeting of our associates. For the last ten years, Charles has held the boring, thankless job of serving as our administrative partner, a position for which he is uniquely suited. A terminally morose tax attorney, his unnaturally pasty complexion, pronounced widow's peak and emaciated physique make him look considerably older than fifty-five. He views the Internal Revenue Code as akin to the Bible. He always refers to it as the Good Book. Likewise, he calls the 1986 Tax Act the Satanic Verses, because it took away many of his favorite tax-avoidance schemes. At S&G, we call what he does creative tax planning. Out there in the real world, most people would say he helps his clients engage in varying degrees of tax fraud.

In addition to his modest tax practice, he devotes most of

his time to serving on virtually every firm committee, thereby bringing order to the chaos that would ensue without his steady hand. He has also appointed himself as the financial conscience of the firm, and reviews each and every expense report and check request before any of our hard-earned cash goes out the door. He handles personnel matters and insists on being present when anyone is fired. He seems to take particular pleasure in this aspect of his job. He's known as the Grim Reaper.

Except for light reading of the *Daily Tax Report*, the only joy in his life seems to be the production of an endless stream of memos on every imaginable administrative subject, and some that are unimaginable. My life would be a hollow, empty shell without at least one missive every day about procedures, time sheets and expense reimbursements.

He insists that everyone call him Charles. Not Charlie. Not Chuck. Charles. An unseemly annual hazing ritual takes place when Bob Holmes sends an unsuspecting new associate to visit "Charlie." Last year, I had to intervene to prevent Stern from firing an associate on her third day.

A couple of years ago, in a meeting with the associates, my mouth shifted into gear while my brain was still idling, and I sarcastically dubbed him Chuckles. Naturally, everyone now refers to him by that name.

I have been invited to the meeting because I have served as the liaison partner for five years and Chuckles wants to make a presentation to the associates. As liaison partner, I have had the joyous task of addressing the concerns of our associates. It's the second-most-thankless job at the firm, behind administrative partner. The title of liaison partner goes to the most junior partner who doesn't have the practice or the balls to say no. If there's a shoe with dog shit on it, I seem to be wearing it.

Everybody hates the liaison partner. With good reason, I might add. The associates hate me because they think I'm a toady for the partners. They're right. The partners hate me because starting salaries are more than one hundred twenty-five thousand dollars. Nice piece of change for a kid right out of law school. In fairness to yours truly, our salaries are the same as every other big firm in the city. The managing partners of the big firms get together every year to decide how much money the new attorneys will make. In other industries, this would be called price-fixing. It's not fair to blame me because the managing partners have had a collective brain cramp for the last ten years and decided to grossly overpay baby lawyers. Then again, nobody said life is supposed to be fair.

Our offices are hooked up by conference telephone call, so this meeting is a bad sign. Good news is communicated by closed-circuit television. The lack of refreshments is even more ominous. We're incapable of holding a meeting without an assortment of sodas, bottled water, cheese, crackers and fruit. On extraordinarily festive occasions, we get cookies.

Of the fifty associates, only five are women and just one is black. Although Chuckles doesn't know it, the black associate has accepted a job at another firm, and will give notice after he gets his bonus tomorrow. The seating is always the same. Chuckles sits at one end of the table and everybody else (including me) sits as far away from him as possible. He looks somewhat sad and lonely at the other end of the table. He clears his throat. Joel slides into the seat to my immediate right.

"May I have your attention, please?" Chuckles says. He's wearing his gray Men's Wearhouse suit and his blue polka-dot tie has a stranglehold around his neck. The room becomes silent. He glances uncomfortably over the top of his reading glasses. He looks my way and his thin lips contort to form the pained expression that suggests he's trying to smile. I fear he'll cackle at me. He takes off his reading glasses with uncharacteristic animation and says, "Before we start, I want to thank Mike Daley for his hard work on associate issues."

Relief, followed by acute embarrassment. "As you know," he continues, "Mike's last day is tomorrow. On behalf of everybody in this room, I want to wish Mike the very best."

My face is red and my neck is burning. I nod politely and smile as the associates dutifully pat their hands together in quiet applause.

He puts his reading glasses back on. His eyes never leave his legal pad. "The partners asked me to update you on certain issues considered by the executive committee. After discussion with our consultant, we have made some important decisions. I want to assure you we have reviewed these issues very carefully and acted fairly and in the best interests of the firm as an institution."

I just love it when he refers to the firm as an institution. I can't help myself and I grin. I've placed a legal pad between Joel and me. I jot a note that says, "Hold on to your wallet."

Stern's eyes are still glued to his notes. "Effective immediately," he drones, "associates will be considered for election to the partnership after eight and a half years at the firm, instead of seven years, as is current policy." He looks up for a fraction of a second to see if an insurrection is brewing.

Joel writes "Bullshit" on the pad and interrupts him. "Excuse me, Charles," he says. "May we assume that those of us who are up for partner this year will be grandfathered in under the old rules, and that we will be considered this year?"

Chuckles closes the small lizardlike slits he uses for eyes. He takes off his glasses and furrows his brow. "Joel," he says slowly, "did Bob talk to you?"

"Nope."

Long pause. He twirls the glasses. The telltale "oh shit" expression. "Joel," he implores, "let's talk about this after the meeting." It's fun to watch Chuckles tap-dance.

Joel's eyes light up. He barks in his best lawyerly "don't fuck with me" voice, "I think we should talk about this right now. Am I up for partner or not?"

Chuckles sighs. "You're not. And Bob was supposed to talk to you about it."

Chuckles usually doesn't have to face the music from the associates. Joel isn't backing off. "Well, he didn't," he snaps. "This stinks. We *will* talk after the meeting. Before we do, maybe you should explain why the associates shouldn't have their resumes out on the street tomorrow morning."

We've always had great finesse with these touchy-feely human-relations issues.

On go the glasses. Chuckles finds his place and continues reading. "In addition, the firm will not be in a position to pay associate bonuses this year."

There's an audible gasp. He looks up at dumbfounded faces. The more-senior associates are expecting bonuses in excess of thirty thousand dollars. He's astute enough to realize he's in trouble. He makes the correct move and returns to the script. "I want to assure you these decisions were made after careful deliberation and represent the unanimous view of the executive committee as to what is fair and what constitutes the best interests of the firm as an institution."

At times like this, I've tried to defuse the tension with a wisecrack. Tonight, I figure it's time for Chuckles to start getting used to working without a net. I write another note to Joel that says, "Now, the explanation."

"By way of explanation," Chuckles says, "the partners wanted me to make it clear that these decisions were not made for economic reasons. The financial health of the firm is excellent."

Bad move. If we're doing so great, it means the partners have decided to keep more money for themselves. I don't necessarily have a problem with this because it means my last draw check will be a little bigger. On the other hand, if we aren't doing great, he's lying. Either way, the associates are getting screwed. And they know it.

"With respect to the partnership track," he says, "we have decided it would be beneficial to give each associate additional time to work with as many partners as possible."

Right. It's not like we're just pulling up the ladder.

"With respect to bonuses," he continues, "we have expended substantial sums to upgrade our computers, a decision made in response to concerns expressed by our younger attorneys. We believe it is in the firm's long-term financial interests to pay for our new equipment as soon as possible. We realize this may not be the most popular decision, but we believe the computer enhancement is in the best interests of the firm as an institution."

Especially if the associates pay for it.

The associates turn toward Joel, who has been their spokesman for the last few years. He takes the cue. He writes a note that says, "Watch this." He stands, looks at Chuckles and says, "You realize, Charles, that what you just said is complete and utter bullshit?" Without waiting for a response, he pushes his chair back and calmly walks out of the room.

Chuckles looks over the top of his reading glasses. Sensing the mood is not good, he asks for questions. He pauses for at least a full second before he gathers his notes and practically sprints from the room. The meeting lasted less than five minutes.

When I return to my office a few minutes later, the gruff voice of Arthur Patton, our managing partner and chairman of the three-man star chamber we call our executive committee, or X-Com, summons me from my voice mail. As usual, he never wastes a word. "Michael, Arthur Patton. Come to the executive conference room ASAP." It would never occur to him that I may not be available.

I walk downstairs to our "executive" conference room, which is located on the north wall of the forty-sixth floor in an office that once belonged to Skipper's father. When he died, a catfight broke out. Skipper laid claim to the office by birthright. Bob Holmes said he was entitled to it because he had the biggest book of business. Arthur Patton said he should get it just because he's Patton. After three weeks of backbiting, Chuckles Stern implemented what is now known as the Great Compromise, and the office was converted into a conference room. My suggestion of a "one potato, two potato" marathon was dismissed.

The room has a marble conference table, ten black leather chairs and a view of the Golden Gate Bridge. Portraits of our founding partners hang on the west wall and portraits of our current X-Com—Patton, Chuckles and Holmes—hang on the east wall. Patton and Chuckles look unhappy as they sit beneath the smiling pictures of themselves. Mercifully, Holmes is nowhere to be found. The usual assortment of cheese and fruit is on a silver platter.

On December 30 of each year, X-Com meets to give themselves a collective pat on the back and to determine "the Estimate," which is their best guess of firm profits for the year. More importantly, they allocate each partner's percentage interest in the profits of the firm, or "points," for the upcoming year. The Estimate will be announced with great ceremony at a partners' meeting at eight o'clock tomorrow morning. I've always thought we could streamline the process by putting a tote board like the one they have on the Jerry Lewis telethon in our reception area. This suggestion has not been well received over the years. At the meeting, each partner will receive a check and a memo indicating the partner's points. Theoretically, everybody will begin the new year in a good mood. Unless you're like me, and your points have been reduced in each of the last four years.

I'm not sure why I've been summoned on the night of all nights. I'm pretty sure they can't fire me again. I take a seat beneath the portraits of Leland Simpson and Skipper's dad. They grimace at me. I feel like I'm surrounded. Patton glares at me and growls, "I wanted to discuss your departure."

Uh-oh.

Patton's huge bald head, Nixon-like jowls and Brezhnev-like eyebrows overwhelm the rest of his tiny face. His red suspenders strain to hold his ample gut. At sixty-two, his gravel baritone is commanding, but its forcefulness has been tempered by forty years of cigars and single-malt scotch. At times, he's capable of playing the role of the genial grandfather. Last year, he was Santa at our Christmas party. The next day, he fired his secretary because there was one typo in an eighty-page brief. That's part of his charm. On any given day, you never know if you'll get the puppy or the pit bull.

In law-firm-lingo, he handles complex civil litigation. Of course, I've never met a lawyer who admits he handles litigation that's anything less than "complex." In reality, he represents defense contractors who get sued when their bombers don't fly. To Art, every case is a holy war of attrition. He showers the other side with paper. Fortunately, his clients have the resources to wear down their opponents. He responds to every letter with his own version that rearranges the facts in his favor. He follows up every phone call with a letter that bears only passing resemblance to the matters that were discussed. Around the firm, he's known as the Smiling Assassin. He's one mean son of a bitch.

He stares over my right shoulder. He begins with the

grandfatherly tone. "I know we have had our disagreements, but I would like to think we can work things out and remain friends."

As if. I look right through him and remain silent. Let him talk. Don't react.

His condescending smirk makes its first appearance. "Here is our proposal. If anyone asks, we will portray your departure as voluntary. We will say you left to pursue a different direction. You will agree not to say anything bad about us. We will return your capital contribution tomorrow." Upon election to the partnership, every partner must make a capital contribution to the firm. The amount depends on the number of points you have. Baby partners like me contribute seventy-five thousand dollars. The power partners like Patton have ponied up about a quarter of a million bucks.

"That's it?"

"That's it. Except for one thing. As a matter of good practice, we want you to sign a full release of the firm. We ask all departing partners. Just housekeeping."

"That's it?"

He nods. "That's it."

Keep the tone measured. "Let me see if I have this straight. I won't piss on you, and you won't piss on me. That's fair. And that's the way it will work because we're smart enough not to say shitty things about each other. San Francisco is a small town. And you will pay me back my capital."

"Yes."

"Good. Because our partnership agreement says you have to pay me back whether or not I agree to say nice things about you and even if I don't sign your release. I have no intention of suing you, but if I change my mind, I don't want you waving a release in my face."

Gotcha. If I were in his shoes, I'd ask for the release. If

he were in mine, he'd say no. I'm glad Joel showed me the section in our partnership agreement that says they have to return my capital.

He shifts to the half grin. "We figured you might say that," he says. "We are prepared to make a one-time offer of twenty thousand dollars for your cooperation. Take it or leave it."

Visions of paying off my Visa bill and a year of rent dance in my head. "Not enough," I say. "Make it a hundred and we may have something to talk about."

Chuckles shakes his head. "Too much, Mike. No can do."

Patton trots out his "mad dog" persona for a preemptive strike, if only for effect. His act loses some of its impact when you've seen it as many times as I have. "Look," he says, "if it had been up to me, I would have thrown your sorry ass out of here at least two years ago."

For an instant, I think Leland Simpson's picture is going to spring to life. "Yeah," he'd say, "I would have thrown your sorry ass out of here at least *three* years ago."

Patton isn't finished. His bald dome turns red. "Use your head for once and take the fucking money," he bellows. I'm told he can actually make his head explode.

I place my fingertips together in my best Mother Teresa imitation. "Arthur," I say slowly, "if you're going to lose your temper, you're going to have to go to your office and take a time-out." I've been waiting five years to say that to him. I stand and walk toward the door, where I turn and face them. "Gentlemen, I'll see you in the morning. I wouldn't want to miss the reading of the Estimate."

When I arrive at the office at seven the next morning, I have voice-mail messages from five associates who are furious about the decision on bonuses. Three ask me to be a refer-

ence. As always, the first person I see is Anna Sharansky, a
Soviet refugee who begins every day by brewing enough
Peet's coffee to fill the sixty coffeepots placed around the
firm. S&G spends over a hundred thousand dollars a year
on coffee. We exchange pleasantries. She never complains.
I'll miss her.

At seven-forty-five, I walk to a sparsely furnished conference room on the forty-sixth floor to get a seat for the reading of the Estimate. The ceremony usually takes place in
the PCR. We have moved downstairs because Bob Holmes
won't move the closing documents for Russo's deal. It smells
like a French pastry shop. Croissants, muffins, scones and
fruit are lined up in neat rows on silver platters. Anna has
filled the coffeepots and set out the bone china bearing the
S&G logo. In the center of the table sit ninety envelopes,
each with a partner's name on it. They look like seating
assignments at a wedding.

By 7:55, the room is full. I pour myself a cup of coffee
and take a croissant with the sterling-silver tongs. The blue
sky frames the Golden Gate Bridge. Several partners wish
me well. Let the exercises begin.

Patton always wears his tuxedo to the reading of the Estimate. He seems to think this lends a festive mood to the
occasion. I think he looks like a maitre d'. At precisely eight
o'clock, he makes his grand entrance, his face glowing. For
Patton, this is what it's all about. For fifteen minutes a year,
we look like everything our recruiting brochure says we are:
a big, collegial family of highly trained professionals who
admire, respect and trust one another. He beams from the
head of the table. We clap politely. "Thank you for coming
at this early hour," he says. "I know how hard it is for some
of you to get here when you've been out partying all night."
Forced laughter. "I want to get Bob Holmes down here to
report on Vince Russo's deal. We will start in just a couple
of minutes."

He asks Chuckles to find Bob. Chuckles seems pleased he won't have a speaking role today, and he darts out. The sound of clinking china resumes. Several partners take calls on their cellular phones. I focus on the envelope in the middle of the table that bears my name.

Ten minutes pass. Chuckles and Joel appear outside the glass door. Chuckles looks more gaunt than usual. Joel looks distraught. Chuckles opens the door and says in a barely audible voice, "Art, can I see you outside for a minute?"

The room goes silent. Patton motions Chuckles in. Chuckles tries to convince him to step outside. After a moment's hesitation, Chuckles comes in and whispers into Patton's ear. Patton's eyes get larger. I hear him mutter, "Jesus."

Patton faces nobody in particular, strokes his jowls and says, "It is my unhappy responsibility to make a sad announcement. Bob Holmes and Diana Kennedy were found dead in Bob's office a few minutes ago. I have no other information. The police have been called."

We sit in stunned silence.

"Obviously," he continues, "we may have a little problem with the closing of the Russo deal. Any discussion of the firm's results for this year would be premature and out of place. I will provide further information later today. Meeting adjourned."

More silence.

After a moment, I hear Patton whisper to Chuckles, "He couldn't have fucking killed himself. We're completely fucked. He had a fiduciary duty to us to close the deal."

Leave it to Arthur Patton to try to explain a man's death by citing a legal doctrine.

As always, Chuckles is more sanguine. He says to Patton, "I suspect Bob wasn't thinking about his fiduciary duties last night."

Without another word, we file out, pausing only briefly to pick up our envelopes.

3

"HE KEPT A LOADED GUN
AT HIS DESK"

"The managing partner of Simpson and Gates has issued a
statement to reassure the firm's clients that the situation is
completely under control."

—KCBS NEWS RADIO. WEDNESDAY, DECEMBER 31. 8:40 A.M.

By eight-thirty, all hell has broken loose. Every thirty seconds or so, a man's voice announces on the emergency in-
tercom that there has been an incident and we shouldn't use
the elevators. Word spreads quickly and people gather in
small groups in the corridors.

My office is on the forty-seventh floor, between Joel's
small office and Bob's palatial northwest corner. Joel is talking loudly into the phone as I walk past his doorway. He's
trying to find Vince Russo. A policeman is unrolling yellow
tape outside Bob's office.

I walk into my office and sit down. The room is empty of
my stuff except for a few last boxes and my coffee cup with
Grace's picture on it. I listen to the sirens forty-seven floors
below. It sounds as though every police car and fire engine
in the city is heading toward our building.

Doris walks in a few minutes later. "Is it true?" she asks.

"It's true. Patton said Bob and Diana are dead. Chuckles and Joel broke up the partners' meeting. I don't know any details."

Tears well up in her eyes. "I can't believe it," she cries.

I give her a hug. She starts sobbing into my shoulder. "It'll be all right," I say feebly.

"It finally got to him. The divorce, the deal, the money. I knew something would happen. And Diana, too. Why Diana?"

"These things happen for a reason." As I say it, I realize this line from my religious training never rang very true. It was one of the reasons I ended up leaving the priesthood. I had a lot of trouble saying the party line toward the end. She wipes her eyes and sits down.

We're silent for a moment and I absentmindedly turn on my computer. It's funny how you revert to habit. I have two E-mail messages. The second message, which I open first, is from Patton, advising that there will be an emergency meeting in the reception area at nine o'clock. The other is from Bob Holmes. It was sent at 1:20 this morning. I get chills. "Look at this," I say.

Doris comes around behind my desk and reads over my shoulder. Bob's final words are concise. *"To everyone. I am genuinely sorry for the pain I have inflicted. I hope you will find it in your heart to forgive me. I cannot go on. I wish you all the best. Bob."*

"Jesus," I say. "An E-mail suicide note. This is weird, even for Bob." I get a sour feeling in my stomach. His body is still in the office next door.

My phone rings and I pick up. "Mickey, I'm watching TV." My mother is at home in the Sunset District. "They said somebody got shot at your office. Are you okay?"

"I'm fine, Ma. Don't worry."

"Thank God, Mickey. Did you know them?"

"Yeah, Ma, I knew them."

"Mickey, be careful."

"I will. I'll call you back a little later, okay?" I hang up and paw through my boxes until I find the five-inch black-and-white TV I kept under my desk to watch sports. I turn to Channel 4 and play with the antenna until I make out a fuzzy reporter standing in the plaza outside the California Street entrance to our building. She's in front of the huge black polished-granite sculpture designed by Masayuki Nagare that the late Herb Caen, the immortal *San Francisco Chronicle* columnist, dubbed the Banker's Heart.

"This is Rita Roberts. We are live in San Francisco, where police are reporting an incident in the offices of Simpson and Gates, the city's largest law firm. Details are sketchy, but it appears that two Simpson and Gates attorneys have been killed by gunshots. Newly elected San Francisco District Attorney Prentice Gates III was a partner at the firm. Mr. Gates and the mayor were in the firm's office last night. We don't know whether the incident has anything to do with Mr. Gates or the mayor. Moments ago, a spokesman told us that the mayor left the Simpson and Gates suite about nine o'clock last night and arrived at his office this morning at his usual time. We haven't been able to confirm the whereabouts of Mr. Gates. Rita Roberts for News-Center 4."

I'm turning down the sound when a young Asian policeman knocks on my open door and politely says, "I'm Officer Chinn. We're asking everyone to return to their desk."

"We understand," I say. He nods and walks down the hall. Doris looks offended. "He's just following procedure," I explain. "He's supposed to secure the scene and wait for help." In reality he's also supposed to separate us so we can't compare stories. She heads out the door.

———

My phone keeps ringing. My younger brother, Pete, a former San Francisco cop who works as a private investigator, gets through on the first try. "You okay, Mick? I heard it on the box."

"I'm fine."

"You talked to Ma?"

"Yeah. Told her I'm okay. Mind giving her a call? She'll feel better if she hears from you."

"No problem, Mick. Gotta go. I'm working. I'll see you this weekend." I pity the poor unfaithful husband he's tailing. What he lacks in finesse he makes up for in tenacity.

"*Qué pasa*, Miguel? You all right?" My ex-wife. Rosita Carmela Fernandez doesn't speak Spanish, except to me. "I heard it on the radio." She grew up in the Hispanic enclave in the Mission District. Her dad was a carpenter. Her mom babysits Grace whenever Rosie's in trial. Rosie was the first member of her family to go to college. She worked her way through San Francisco State and Hastings law school. We used to work together at the PD's office. We were married for about three years. We were a lot better at trying cases than we were at being married.

"I'm fine, Rosie."

"Good. I was worried my new tenant wasn't going to move in."

That was part of the problem when we were married. Among other things, Rosie is good at keeping track of money. I'm not. She's also very organized. Let's just say I'm more flexible. It used to drive her nuts. We got along great right until the time we got married. Then all of my faults came to light. After a couple of years of ceaseless sniping, we finally split up. It was right after Grace turned one. Once the divorce messiness was really over, we started to get along a lot better. Go figure. "I'm moving in just the way we planned," I say.

"Good man. I'll call you later. *Adios.*"

Rosie, you're the best ex-wife a man could have. Damn shame we couldn't stand living together.

Joel pokes his head in while I'm on the phone with my baby sister, Mary, a first-grade teacher in L.A. His hair is disheveled. His eyes are puffy. I motion him to sit down. I say good-bye to Mary.

"Long night, Mike," he says in a hoarse whisper.

I pick up a rubber band. "What can I say?"

"I've never seen a dead body before. We Jewish folks don't do open caskets." He pauses for a moment to compose himself and says, "He practically blew the side of his head off." He looks out the window. "We finished negotiations about nine o'clock and we gave the documents to the word processors. Diana and I went to Harrington's for a quick bite. She went home. I got back around eleven-fifteen. We finished signing papers by twelve-thirty. Everybody was leaving. I went down to the lunchroom for a Coke. I read documents for two or three hours and I took a nap down there. I got up around six and went back to my office. It was quiet. I thought Bob had gone home. Next thing I knew, it was eight o'clock and Chuckles asked me for the keys to Bob's office. That's when we found them."

I swallow the lump in my throat. "Did Russo kill the deal?" As I say it, I realize that my choice of words could have been more discreet.

"I don't know. I can't find him. He was here when we signed the papers. He said he was going back to the Ritz. He stays there when he doesn't want to drive all the way down to his house in Hillsborough. He wasn't sure if he'd authorize the wire transfers to close the deal. He said he was going to sleep on it. He said he might have to go to his backup plan."

"What's that?"

"A flying leap off the Golden Gate Bridge."

"I see."

"I called his hotel. They said he didn't sleep in his bed last night." He sighs. "I just can't believe Bob killed himself, even if Vince decided to pull out. Bob's seen deals go south before."

"The police are going to want to talk to you. I'll drive you home when you're done."

"Thanks, Mike."

This is going to be tough on Joel.

At five after nine, Arthur Patton is still wearing his tuxedo when he convenes an all-hands meeting in the main reception area. Thankfully, somebody's had the good judgment to turn off the lights on the Christmas tree. Patton asks for quiet and says, "As many of you are aware, we have had a great tragedy. Bob Holmes and Diana Kennedy were found dead in Bob's office this morning. The police have indicated they died of gunshot wounds. Bob's wounds may have been self-inflicted.

"This is Inspector Roosevelt Johnson of the SFPD, who is in charge of the investigation. I would ask each of you to assist the police. Our office is now closed until Monday, and you are free to go home as soon as the police say you may do so."

Roosevelt Johnson was my father's first partner. Every time I see him, I think of my dad. I've known Roosevelt since I was a kid. He worked his way up the ranks and made homicide inspector. Dad stayed on the street. Although

Roosevelt is in his early sixties, at about six-four and maybe
235 pounds, he still looks like he can play linebacker at Cal.
His dark brown skin, gray mustache, bald head and gold
wire-rimmed glasses command the attention of everyone in
the room.

His eloquent baritone is captivating. "Ladies and gentlemen," he says, "I promise we will get you home as soon as
we can. We would like to obtain a statement from each of
you. For those of you who didn't see or hear anything, I
would ask you to write a note to that effect and give it to one
of our officers. I would appreciate it if you would return to
your office or workstation. I must ask you not to discuss this
matter with one another until we have talked to you. Please
stay away from the area around the offices of Mr. Holmes
and Ms. Kennedy so we may gather evidence. I apologize in
advance for the inconvenience and I thank you for your
cooperation."

Doris raises her hand. "Inspector, can you give us any
information about the circumstances surrounding Bob's and
Diana's deaths?"

"We are beginning to gather evidence. It appears they
were victims of gunshot wounds."

"Were the wounds self-inflicted?"

"We don't know yet. A handgun was found at the scene.
We will provide additional information as soon as possible."

At ten o'clock, I'm on the phone when a subdued Chuckles
Stern walks into my office. I hold my thumb and forefinger
about a quarter of an inch apart, signaling I'll only be a
minute. He sits down. I reassure my mother for the third
time today and hang up.

"I can't believe it," he says. I wonder why he's come to see
me. Then I realize he has nobody else to talk to. "I haven't
seen so much blood since I was in the service," he says.

To Chuckles, the service usually means the IRS. I'm surprised when I realize he's talking about the armed service. "You were in the service, Charles?"

"Vietnam. Marines. I've got a bum shoulder to show for it."

I never would have figured. Although it's entirely inappropriate, I find myself imagining Chuckles and his platoon lobbing copies of the Internal Revenue Code toward the Vietcong. "I lost a brother over there, Charles," I say. "Near the end of the war."

"I didn't know that," he replies.

I pause. My brother Tommy's death was one of the big reasons why I became a priest. My family was very seriously Catholic. I was better at it than either of my brothers. Although the church had a lot of rules, it was a truly spiritual place for me while I was growing up. Then I became a priest and the spirituality disappeared. I decide it may not be a great time to discuss my participation in the antiwar protests on the Berkeley campus.

He looks out the window. "I know we have other things on our minds," he says, "but I wanted to let you know we decided to let bygones be bygones and just give you your capital back. We aren't going to insist that you sign a release." He pulls a check out of his jacket pocket and hands it to me.

"Thanks, Charles. That's very decent of you." My mind races. Why are they doing this? I add, for the record, "I think you made the right decision."

"Sometimes you make decisions just because it's the right thing to do," he says.

And sometimes you fire your partners because their book of business isn't big enough. I expect him to leave, but he doesn't. There's an uncomfortable silence. "So," I say, "you knew Bob for a long time. Do you have any idea what this is all about?"

"I don't know. We weren't close. I'm not sure he had any close friends."

The same could be said about you, Chuckles. I hold back.

He continues. "Art knew him the best. They used to talk about stocks. They invested in a restaurant together. That fancy place in Palo Alto. Bob called it his private black hole for money. Bob and I just used to talk about firm business. He was having his biggest year ever. I can't believe he'd kill himself the night before his big deal was supposed to close. Confidentially, he was going to get a big bonus today."

I feign mild surprise. Joel was right. "I didn't realize that, Charles."

"That's why it doesn't make sense. You know Bob. Or knew him, I guess. He'd never turn down a paycheck. Maybe it was the divorce." He pauses. "You heard he used his own gun."

Huh? "He had a gun?"

"Yeah."

"He brought a gun to the office?"

"He *kept* it at the office, Mike. At his desk. Jesus, I thought everyone knew."

No, not everyone knew. "Loaded?" I ask.

"Yep."

"What the hell for?"

"Don't be naive. You were here when that lunatic killed all those people at 101 California."

In July of 1993, a crazed former client walked into the offices of a prominent San Francisco law firm and opened fire with an arsenal of semiautomatic weapons. He killed eight people and wounded a dozen others before he killed himself. The firm closed its doors two years later. "I knew some people over there," I say. "Good lawyers. Nice people."

"Ever since, every big firm has put in a security system.

We spent almost a hundred grand on ours. Each reception-ist has a panic button. If they see trouble, they punch it. The doors lock and a red light goes on in personnel and at the security desk. Thank goodness we've never had to use it."

"Brave new world."

"No kidding. After the incident at 101 Cal, Bob said he wasn't going to let the same thing happen to him. He kept a loaded gun at his desk. He didn't make a big deal about it." He pauses. "We'd like to try to keep it out of the papers, if we can."

"Not a bad idea." What's next? Metal detectors? I can just see the headlines. *"Prominent San Francisco Attorney Kills Himself with Loaded Piece He Kept at His Desk."*

"Anyway," he continues, "we have a problem. We were counting on the fees from the Russo deal to make our year-end numbers. Some of the partners won't be happy with the results now."

There's the Chuckles I know and love. Two hours after he finds his partner's body, he's already worried about his draw. As Art Patton likes to say, we shouldn't dwell on the negative.

"What a mess," I say.

"Art's beside himself. I think he may retire and move to Napa full-time. I'm thinking about getting out. I don't know if the firm can survive."

He isn't very convincing when he's being melodramatic. "I'm sure the firm will survive."

"I gotta run, Mike."

"Those police inspectors are really pushy, Mike." Doris is back in my office at ten-fifteen. "They treated me like a criminal," she says.

"Take it easy. I did my five minutes with Officer Chinn. He was okay."

"Maybe to you. The cop I talked to acted like I was a murder suspect."

"I know this is tough. They're just trying to do their job."

"They were rude. And they asked a lot of questions about Diana's personal life."

"Like what?"

"Like whether she was sleeping with Bob."

"Was she?"

She frowns. "It's none of your business. And it sure as hell is none of theirs."

I look her in the eyes. "Doris, this thing is tough on all of us. Give yourself a little space."

She starts to cry. I get up and put my arm around her. "It's such a waste," she says.

4
THE LEGEND

"When I started working Homicide, there was no such thing as affirmative action. I'm not saying it was right. It's just the way it was."

—INSPECTOR ROOSEVELT JOHNSON.
SAN FRANCISCO CHRONICLE. JULY 14, 1998.

At ten-thirty I'm at my desk watching Skipper being interviewed on TV. He briefly mentions the shootings and moves straight into his campaign speech. I'm turning down the sound when Roosevelt Johnson's familiar baritone resonates off the walls. "Hello, Michael," he says. "I didn't realize you worked at this firm." He takes up the entire doorway. "This is a pretty far cry from the PD's office."

"It's been a long time, Roosevelt."

We shake hands. He's a legend. He and his partner, Marcus Banks, are the SFPD's most senior homicide team. They handle all the high-profile cases. He closes my door. "How's your mama?" he asks.

"She has good days and bad days. On good days she's ornery. On bad days, she doesn't say much. She's in the early stages of Alzheimer's. It's not going to get better, but we're hoping it won't get a lot worse too soon. She's still living at home. Pete's living with her. He never moved out."

"Things have been tough."

Tell me about it. "Mom and Dad were never really the same after Tommy died." My older brother was one of the last MIAs in Vietnam. They never found his body. He was an all-city quarterback at St. Ignatius and all-conference at Cal. Tommy had another year of eligibility. He could have gotten deferred. He volunteered for the Marines. I tried to talk him out of it, but Dad told him it was the right thing to do. He never forgave me for trying to talk Tommy out of going, and he never forgave himself when Tommy died. Then he got sick. Roosevelt knows the story. My dad worked his ass off for thirty years for his city pension. He died five years ago, about a year after Grace was born. At least he got to see his first grandchild.

"It's hard to bury your children, Mike," he says. He knows. His son was nineteen when he was killed in a drive-by shooting near Candlestick Park. "Did you decide to become a priest after Tommy died?" he asks.

"In part." Unlike most of my friends, I loved going to church when I was a kid. It gave me time with my mom and dad. It gave structure to my life. And it had lots of rules. I was always good at rules. It wasn't until I was in college that I started asking the hard questions about the rules. I'll never forget the look of pride on my dad's face when I told him I was going to the seminary. And I'll never forget the look of disdain when I told him I was leaving the priesthood to become a lawyer. He hated lawyers. "When Tommy died," I say, "I went to the church to try to find some answers."

"What happened?"

I dodge the question. "It didn't have the answers I was looking for." He looks uncomfortable. "Don't worry, Roosevelt. I didn't do anything terrible. It just didn't work out." I don't really want to explain that the concept of celibacy is a whole lot easier in theory than in practice. And all the rules that were so meaningful when I was a kid seemed hopelessly out of touch by the time I was a priest. It was the post-Watergate era, and traditional Catholicism felt prehistoric. It's tough to try to get people to abide by rules that you question.

"Why did you end up in law school?" he asks.

"Why not? You think the church has an outplacement program for downsized priests? I figured I might be able to make a living helping people who got screwed. Lawyers get to do a lot of things nobody else can do. Besides, I didn't have any better ideas." This is clearly more than he'd bargained for. I decide to change the subject. "How's your family?"

"Janet has good days and bad days, too. Arthritis. My daughter is working OB-GYN at San Francisco General. My granddaughter is at UCLA Law School. With my luck, she'll end up a public defender like you did."

"She'll probably end up at some Wall Street firm making a hundred thou a year."

He chuckles. "How are Rosie and the baby?"

"Complicated subject. Rosie and I split up about a year after Grace was born. We were on each other for a couple of years. We couldn't figure out a way to work out the little stuff. And if you can't deal with the little stuff, you can't deal with the big stuff. Things got better after we split up. Grace is in first grade. She lives with Rosie, but I'm a couple of blocks away. She stays with me every other weekend."

He changes the subject quickly. "How did you end up in a fancy-dancy place like this?"

"I needed the money. We were getting divorced. The firm was starting a white-collar criminal defense practice. They needed a criminal defense attorney. I was the best guy at the PD's office, so they hired me. They made me a partner. Doubled my salary."

He glances around my stripped office. "I take it you're leaving?"

"It didn't work out. The big-time white-collar practice didn't happen. The guy with the big book of business left after a year. I started bringing in some DUI and robbery cases. The firm didn't like it. Firms like S and G don't like to have real crooks roaming around the office. It scares the corporate clients away." I pause. "Today's my last day. I'm going out on my own. I'm renting some space on Mission."

"Sounds pretty good."

"I hope so. Rosie's my landlord."

He grins. "You've always had a flair." He turns serious and I sense the social portion of our conversation is coming to an end. "I know we didn't always see eye to eye when you were at the PD's office," he says. "I'd like to think it was because we were on opposite sides of a few cases."

"Roosevelt," I say with conviction, "we worked different sides of the same screwed-up system. There's always some tension."

He looks right at me. "Let me ask you for a favor," he says. "I'd like your help in sorting out this case. Off the record, if you'd like. Professional courtesy."

He's savvy. He's listening to every word I say. He's watching every move I make. "I'll do anything I can to help you," I tell him.

"Great. I'd appreciate it if you'd keep our discussion confidential for the time being."

"Of course."

He skims his notes. "So far, we know Holmes and Kennedy died of gunshot wounds. His to the head, hers to the chest. His wound looks self-inflicted. Your colleagues Charles Stern and Joel Friedman found the bodies and a Smith and Wesson thirty-eight-caliber revolver on the floor. Friedman said he last saw Holmes about twelve-thirty this morning. He had dinner with Kennedy about ten last night.

He said she went home from the restaurant. We don't know when she came back. Our people are dusting the office and the gun. If I had to guess, it looks like he killed her and then killed himself. We've seen the E-mail message that was sent from his computer. But it's too soon to tell. You know me. I do it by the numbers."

"I know. Have you been able to impart your way of thinking upon your partner?"

He looks troubled. "Marcus is a good cop," he says emphatically. "Sometimes he doesn't handle things the way I would. He's kept his nose clean the last few years." He pauses. "What can you tell me about Holmes? Was anything bothering him? Was anybody pissed off at him?"

"A lot was bothering him. And everybody in the city was pissed off at him."

He raises his eyebrows. I tell him what I know about Bob. How my partners hated his guts. About his acrimonious divorces. About the divorce papers his wife served on him last night.

"Anybody else mad at him?"

"He was working on a big deal. Everybody was unhappy. There was quite a scene last night. His client, Vince Russo, was screaming at him. I presume it isn't going to close now." I ponder how much I can and should tell Roosevelt about Joel's description of the deal.

"I heard Russo seems to have dropped off the face of the earth," he says. "What's his story?"

I describe how Russo inherited his father's business and it went to hell. I explain that Russo's creditors were forcing him to sell the business. "I hear he's a tough guy to like," I say.

He knows more than he's letting on. "Where does Ms. Kennedy fit in?"

"She was Bob's star associate and a real go-getter. She was on the fast track."

"What about their personal relationship? Anything out of the ordinary? Any hanky-panky?"

"Purely professional, as far as I know. But some people think there was more to it."

"Were they sleeping together?"

"Don't know." I answer too quickly and he gives me a skeptical look. I raise my right hand like a Boy Scout. "Honest, Roosevelt. If there were something I promised to keep quiet, I'd tell you that much. The fact is, I just don't know."

"Was she sleeping with anybody else?" He's boring in now.

"I don't know. She was single. She didn't have a steady boyfriend. She always had a date for the Christmas party. I'm not tuned in to firm gossip."

"Fair enough. Who *is* tuned in?"

Before I can catch myself, I blurt out, "Joel."

He chuckles. "I figured that out already. There are still a few instincts left in this old carcass."

"Did you ask him?" I'm as curious as the next guy.

"Yeah. He said he wasn't sure. He's heard the rumors. Who else should I talk to?"

"Charles Stern knows about the firm's finances. Arthur Patton is the managing partner."

"I've talked to them. They think Holmes wouldn't have killed himself. Patton said Holmes was up for a big bonus."

"I've heard that."

"What about his secretary?"

"Doris? She's a gem. She can give you the skinny on Bob's divorces. She's very discreet, though. And very protective of him." I add, "By the way, if you get any dirt on his divorces, I'll buy you a dinner at any restaurant in town to hear about it."

"You got a deal. What about Mr. Gates?"

I laugh. "Our district attorney? He wore out his welcome years ago. Between us, they couldn't wait to get him out the door."

"Doesn't surprise me." He wipes his glasses. "Mike, do you think Holmes was the kind of guy who would kill himself?"

"I don't know," I answer. "A few days ago, I would have said no way. On the other hand, his deal may have been cratering. His wife served him with divorce papers. Now, I'm not sure."

"I'll call you when I have a better handle on things."

I'm sure he will. "Let me know if there's anything else I can do."

"Say hi to your mama."

Joel is standing in my doorway at twelve-thirty. "You ready to get out of here?" he asks.

"Let's hit it." I pick up my coffee mug. As we walk out my door I see a female police officer standing by the door to Bob's office. A team from the coroner's office is inside. "Did you ever find Russo?" I ask Joel, as he opens the double doors to our elevator lobby.

"Nope. Never showed up. Never called. We had a ten o'clock deadline for the wire transfers. We didn't make it. The buyer's attorney said he'd call me Monday. As far as he's concerned, the deal is off. I guess we'll deal with bankruptcy if and when Vince surfaces."

We reach the lobby and head down the escalators toward the garage, which is two levels below ground. We stop on the intermediate level so I can drop off announcements for my new office in our mailroom, which is in a windowless suite next to the entrance to the health club. In a cost-saving move a few years ago, we moved our mailroom, copy center and accounting department to this subterranean vault everyone calls the Catacomb. I feel sorry for these poor people who never see the daylight.

I bang on the heavy steel door. In view of today's events, our usual jokes about Bela Lugosi answering don't seem funny. Virginia Wallace, the officious, utterly intimidating manager of our accounting department, opens the door. A ghoulish, gray-haired woman of indeterminate age, she started as a file clerk about thirty years ago. She's clawed her way up the ladder and runs the entire "backroom" without the slightest hint of finesse. I've always been terrified of her. True to form, she's waiting to see if any of our clients send us any money before the stroke of midnight and our fiscal year turns into a pumpkin.

"Hi, Virginia," I say politely. "You holding up okay?"

She looks bored. In fact, she always looks bored. "As well as can be expected."

"Good. Can you do me a favor and leave these envelopes for the guys in the mailroom? I was hoping they might be able to get these out to the post office in the last run today."

Big sigh. "Just this once, because it's your last day."

"Thanks, Virginia." I solemnly swear I'll never impose upon you again.

I look over her shoulder and see Mark Jenkins, our head delivery person, getting out of the freight elevator that connects the Catacomb with our main offices upstairs. I've always liked Mark, an articulate young black man from Hunter's Point who's worked his way out of the projects and spends his days riding up and down the freight elevator and putting up with Virginia's shit. He's finishing up at San Francisco State this year. I'm hopeful he'll be able to find something better suited to his talents when he graduates. Mark agrees to send out my announcements and I wish him well. Virginia glares.

The steel door slams and Joel and I head to the garage.

With a little coaxing, my nine-year-old Corolla turns over, I pay eighteen bucks to the Asian teenager with monster headphones in the booth, and we head west up the hill on Pine. The street is littered with paper. It's New Year's Eve. In San Francisco, the people who don't work in hermetically sealed high-rises traditionally toss their obsolete calendar pages out their windows. The city pays a fortune in overtime to clean up the mess.

Traffic is relatively light as we drive in silence past the Ritz and the back of the Stanford Court toward Joel's house in the Richmond District. When we reach Van Ness, he says, "I can't believe it. Yesterday, I was getting ready to close a huge deal and to celebrate my election as a partner. Today, two people are dead, the deal is off and my career is in limbo."

"You'll be all right," I say. "They need you to service Bob's clients."

"I guess. I still can't figure it out. He waits another day and he gets three million bucks."

"There's got to be more to it."

"The cops sure think so."

"They're just doing their jobs."

"Spoken like the son of a cop. The head guy, Johnson, thinks there's more to it than suicide."

"I know Johnson. He's a good man."

We drive in silence across Fillmore Street through a neighborhood that once was known as the Western Addition, but with gentrification was rechristened Lower Pacific Heights. We pass the dim sum restaurants on Clement Street. Joel says, "I know Bob was going through another divorce and this deal was all fucked up. But I don't see him killing himself. And I don't see him taking Diana with him."

"Johnson asked me if Bob and Diana were sleeping together. You know anything?"

"Not really. I've heard the same stuff everybody's heard."

"Just between us," I say. "You think they were getting it on?"

"It wouldn't surprise me."

"Well, while we're speculating, let's suppose they were sleeping together. And she decided to break up with him. And Vince told Bob the deal's off. And Bob was really pissed off about the divorce. Maybe you've got a scenario where he decided to end it."

"Maybe," he says, "but I just can't see it. Bob's been through it before. He's been divorced three times. He's seen deals go down in flames."

"You think somebody killed him?"

He shrugs. "Russo really wanted out of the deal. For that matter, so did the buyer."

"Why?"

"Continental Capital Corporation is the fourth-largest public company in the world. Their young mergers-and-acquisitions stud, Jack Frazier, convinced them to buy Vince's business. Frazier's one of those young MBAs who figured this deal was the next step up the ladder. He convinced the suits at CCC to pay nine hundred million for a company that's worth a lot less. By the time Golden Boy Frazier figured out he was buying a proverbial pig in a poke, it was too late. The boys at headquarters in Stamford won't be happy."

"Why didn't they pull out?"

"They wanted to, but they couldn't."

"Why not?"

"Do you know what a breakup fee is?"

I shake my head.

"It's a payment a buyer has to make to a seller if the buyer backs out of a deal for no reason. It's supposed to keep the buyer serious and cover the seller's legal fees and costs if the deal craters."

"Why didn't CCC pay the fee and walk?"

"Because the fee is fifty million dollars. It's a lot of money for nothing, even for a big outfit like CCC. If they paid it, Frazier would be working on one of CCC's oil rigs off the coast of Siberia by the end of the week. There was no breakup fee if Vince killed the deal. Frazier's been trying to get Vince to pull the plug for the last two weeks."

"What about the guy from the mayor's office, Dan Morris? What was he doing there?"

"You'll never believe this. When it looked like Vince's business was going down in flames, the mayor appointed one of those blue-ribbon task forces. He didn't want three thousand jobs moving to CCC's western headquarters in Dallas. Bad politics. It's one thing for the Niners to lose a game to the Cowboys every once in a while. It's another thing for three thousand jobs to go to the land of Ross Perot. So the mayor got CCC to agree to keep Russo International's headquarters here by providing a hundred million in financing. Pretty slick. If the deal closes, the mayor can take credit for saving a bunch of jobs."

"So the city wanted the deal to close, even if nobody else did."

"Actually," he says, "they didn't want the deal to close either." He glances at his watch. "It turns out the city didn't have the money to make the loan. Cash-flow problems. The city was going to have to borrow the money at loan-shark rates. The mayor figured it out last night. He decided he'd rather lose the jobs. He figures the voters will forget about the jobs, but they'll never forgive a budget deficit. He sent his political fixer over here to kill the deal, but make it look like somebody else's fault. The city was going to use tax dollars to finance the acquisition by an international conglomerate in a deal that was so screwed up, nobody, including our own client, wanted it to close."

"Looks like everybody is going to get their wish," I say.

"Looks that way," he replies.

As always, the weather in the Richmond District is cooler and cloudier than downtown. We pass Park Presidio Boulevard and drive past Temple Beth Sholom, where Joel's father holds court, so to speak. I turn right onto Sixteenth Avenue and drive halfway up the block of tightly packed bungalows. I stop in front of Joel's modest gray house, around the corner from his father's.

"Happy New Year," he says as he gets out. "I'll talk to you next week."

I think to myself, I hope you still have a career.

5

THE LAW OFFICES OF
MICHAEL J. DALEY, ESQ.

"Michael J. Daley, formerly of the San Francisco Public Defender's Office and formerly a partner at Simpson and Gates, announces the opening of the law offices of Michael J. Daley, Esq., at 553 Mission Street, San Francisco, California. Mr. Daley will continue to specialize in criminal defense practice in state and federal court."

—*SAN FRANCISCO LEGAL JOURNAL.* MONDAY, JANUARY 5.

"Now," I say to Rosie, "all I need are a couple of paying clients, a secretary, a functional telephone and a working computer, and I'm on my way back to the big time." She chuckles as I unpack boxes at nine-fifteen in the morning on Monday, January 5. Looks like the grand opening of the law offices of Michael J. Daley, Esq., is going to be somewhat less than auspicious.

My new office is in the basement of the small two-story 1920s building on Mission Street, down the block from the Transbay bus terminal. I'm renting space from the law offices of Rosita C. Fernandez. It was a fashionable neighborhood seventy years ago. After decades of neglect, the sprawl of downtown San Francisco has given the area new life. Nevertheless, by six in the evening, there seems to be a regular gathering of homeless people in front of the building. I look up at the side of a Chinese restaurant called

Lucky Corner No. 2 through the heavy metal bars that protect my small window. The name is misleading. The restaurant isn't located on a corner. We'll see whether it will be lucky for me. At least I know where I can get a fast lunch.

"Give it time," Rosie says. "We had to move a lot of files to set this up."

"This was your file room?"

"Yeah. It looks much nicer now. Rolanda can help you get settled."

"Thanks." I look at the metal desk, mismatched chairs and stained file cabinet. "I didn't bring much. Just my computer, some books and a few files."

"Good. Rent is due the first of the month."

I'm already beginning to feel like we're married again. It was much more fun when we were first dating and we didn't worry about rent, car payments and, later, diapers. We had started going out when we worked at the PD's office. Rosie was spinning out of a bad marriage. I was coming off a long-term relationship with a law school classmate. We found each other on the rebound. I think she liked me because I was funny. I liked her because she was direct. And Lord knows, we knew each other's work schedules. "You won't need to remind me. And my highly generous former partners gave me a seventy-five-thousand-dollar check for my capital and a five-thousand-dollar bonus on my way out the door."

Rosie gives me the "okay" sign.

"Any decent places to get a bite around here?" I ask her.

"Chinese place next door isn't bad. Noah's Bagels on the corner is pretty good. We don't get out very much." After a brief pause, she asks, "Any more on the incident at S and G?"

Interesting choice of words. I guess "incident" sounds better than "suicides," "shootings" or the more generic "tragedy." "Not much. I haven't talked to Roosevelt since Wednesday."

"I saw your pal Skipper Gates on the tube. He seems to think there's more to it."

"He's trying to keep his name in the papers. He's called a press conference at nine-thirty. Want to watch?"

"Sure."

I find my TV and turn it on. The picture isn't bad, but the reception was better at the top of the Bank of America Building. I can make out the faces of Skipper and Roosevelt standing in a briefing room.

"This is Rita Roberts of NewsCenter 4 reporting live from San Francisco police headquarters. San Francisco District Attorney Prentice Gates and Homicide Inspector Roosevelt Johnson are about to begin a press briefing concerning the incident at the Simpson and Gates law firm last week, where two attorneys were killed. Mr. Gates will speak first."

"Incident" does seem to be the word of choice. Skipper and Roosevelt are standing behind a table on which the obligatory assortment of evidence is laid out in clear plastic bags: some bullet casings, a computer keyboard, a telephone answering machine and some computer printouts. Skipper steps to the microphone. The lights go on and he's ready. He works without notes.

"I want to thank you for coming this morning," he begins. "My first day on the job and already I have a major case. As you know, sometime between the hours of eleven-thirty P.M. on Tuesday, December thirtieth, and eight A.M. on Wednesday, December thirty-first, my friend and former partner, Bob Holmes, and my former associate, Diana Kennedy, were killed by gunshots. We are in the process of investigating this tragedy and we will have further details for you as they become available. I will now call upon Inspector Roosevelt Johnson, who is in charge of the investigation."

Roosevelt steps to the microphone. He plays his cards close to the vest. "Ladies and gentlemen," he says, "we are continuing our investigation. We are reviewing the evidence. We will have more for you as the situation develops."

Skipper returns to the microphone. He doesn't realize he's smiling. "I want to thank you all for coming. We have time for just a few questions."

The first question comes from the silver-haired anchor of Channel 5 *Eyewitness News*. "Mr. Gates, is it true the gun belonged to Mr. Holmes?"

Skipper glances at Roosevelt. "Yes," Skipper says. "It was registered to Mr. Holmes."

"How did the gun get to the S and G office?"

The last thing Skipper wants to do is admit his partner kept a loaded piece at his desk. He takes the offensive. "The way any gun gets anywhere. Somebody carried it to the office."

Not a bad response. I'm convinced.

"One of the lawyers at the firm said Holmes kept a loaded gun at his desk. Is it true?"

"You have good sources. I would like to talk to that person." Laughter. "The answer, by the way, is I don't know. But we are looking into it."

Roosevelt moves to the front again. "We are checking everything out."

Skipper looks annoyed. "Obviously," he says, "we wouldn't want to encourage people to keep concealed weapons at their desks."

The serious-looking woman from Channel 7 shouts, "We understand there was a suicide note."

Skipper says, "We have no comment."

"Are you treating this case as a homicide or a suicide?"

Roosevelt steps forward. "Ms. Kennedy's death almost certainly appears to be a homicide. The investigation is ongoing."

The pretty blonde from Channel 2 who used to work at NBC pushes her way to the front. "Mr. Gates, what's your gut feeling? Was it a suicide?"

Roosevelt tries to intercept Skipper before he gets to the microphone. Skipper pushes him back. "Young lady," he says, "Bob Holmes was my partner and my friend. I must rely on the SFPD and experienced homicide investigators like Inspector Johnson. They will gather the evidence and I will ultimately decide whether there is any basis to prosecute anyone. That's all I have for today."

I turn off the TV. "Well, what do you think?" Rosie asks.

"Not a bad performance for his first press conference."

"No, dummy. Not Skipper. The killings. What do you think?"

"They're not telling the whole story. They're holding stuff back."

"Like what?"

"Like Vince Russo. He hasn't been found. His name wasn't even mentioned. There was nothing about the deal. There was nothing about the divorce."

Rosie shrugs. "I'm due in court in twenty minutes. I'll see you later."

"Jesus, Mikey, I know you said you were going small-time, but this is ridiculous." At twelve-fifteen the same day, Doris is getting her first look at my new office.

"Do you like it?"

"This isn't an office, it's a closet." She gives me a hug. "What's that smell?"

"I think it's moo shu pork." Rosie warned me. It seems my office starts to smell like the Chinese place next door by midmorning.

"You'll get used to it, Mikey."

"I hope so."

"How's Grace?"

"Fine. And Jenny?"

"So-so. Boyfriend trouble. You know how it is."

"I wish."

"You will."

We exchange small talk. She tells me things are starting to calm down at S&G. She's been reassigned to another attorney for the time being. She says she's going to take a few weeks off for a trip to the Bahamas. "I brought you something, Mikey," she says. She opens a shopping bag, takes out a small plant and gives it to me. "I thought you might like something to brighten up your office."

"Thanks. It could use a little help."

"So I see." She looks at Grace's picture. "I was hoping you'd do me a favor."

"Anything."

She takes a manila envelope out of her purse and hands it to me. "Open it," she says.

I find a check made out to me for a hundred dollars. On the memo line, it says "retainer." There is a letter that says she's retaining the law office of Michael J. Daley to represent her on all legal matters. There is a copy of her will.

"Doris," I begin.

She interrupts me. "Mikey," she says, "how many clients do you have?"

I look down.

"I thought so," she says. "Well, now you have one."

"Look, Doris, I can't . . ."

"Yes, you can. This isn't charity. I need you to review my will."

"Doris," I say, "I'm sure there are people at S and G who could help you."

She holds up her hand. "If I wanted somebody at the firm to represent me, I wouldn't be here. How long did we work together?"

"About five years."

"And how many arguments did we have?"

"A few."

"And how many of those arguments did I win?"

"All of them."

"And I'm going to win this one, too." She smiles. "You don't have to cash the check."

"If it's okay with you, I think I'll frame it."

"That's fine. The law offices of Michael J. Daley are now officially open for business."

"Can I buy you lunch?"

"Absolutely. The moo shu pork smells pretty good."

6

"A GREAT HUMANITARIAN"

"**HOLMES, John Robert, Jr.,** died December 31, at age 48. Beloved husband of Elizabeth, father of seven. A respected partner at the international law firm of Simpson and Gates. Services will be held at Grace Cathedral, San Francisco, on Tuesday, January 6, at 10:00 A.M. Donations in his memory may be made to the Legal Community Against Violence."

—OBITUARY NOTICE, *SAN FRANCISCO CHRONICLE.*

TUESDAY, JANUARY 6.

"Did you read Bob's obit, Mike? Jesus, you'd have thought he was fucking Mother Teresa." Arthur Patton is talking to me on a misty morning as Rosie and I stand waiting for Joel on the front steps of the city's magnificent Grace Cathedral, which sits atop Nob Hill. His second trophy wife, Shari, a one-time model and former S&G receptionist, smiles politely. She's certainly come a long way since she was a giggly nineteen-year-old working our phones four years ago. From her appearance, you would never have a hint that she and Art are going through a nasty divorce.

I lean over and say just loud enough so Rosie and the two of them can hear me, "Well, Art, I guess it depends on how you're using the word 'fucking' in this context."

Rosie stifles a chuckle. Shari keeps smiling. Art ignores me. They walk inside.

"They never knew what hit them," Rosie says.

Bob had told me a few months ago he wanted a funeral just like Princess Di's, except Bruce Springsteen would sing "Born to Run" instead of Elton John singing "Candle in the Wind." As it turns out, the funeral Beth Holmes has arranged isn't far from Bob's wish.

The front steps of Grace look like the Academy Awards. The TV cameras, minicams and A-team reporters are here. The service itself is going to be filmed. Two traffic copters hover overhead. Some people are here just to see the celebrities. Everybody is dressed to the teeth. A thousand people are expected.

Rosie is being a good sport. Funerals are difficult in the best of circumstances. Funerals for assholes in your ex-husband's former law firm are really tough. Even during the darkest times of our marriage and divorce, we always went to funerals together. It's our unspoken pact. We wait for Doris to arrive.

I've never really been very good about funerals. It goes back to my days as a priest. When you're the low priest on the totem pole, you tend to get a lot of funeral duty. I remember doing five of them in one day for people I'd never met. I felt bad for the families. I did my standard spiel, said a few words to the families and left. Tough gig, funerals.

The paparazzi remain at a respectful distance and I have naive hopes this will not turn into a circus. Then Skipper's black Lincoln arrives and the feeding frenzy begins. The cameramen jockey for position as the reporters shove microphones into his face. His long-suffering wife, Natalie, a well-known society matron, looks embarrassed. Skipper mouths appropriate sentiments about attending his partner's funeral and says the DA's office is working day and night to solve the case. To his credit, Skipper seems to be resisting the urge to turn Bob's funeral into a press conference.

My former partners file past without saying much. Chuckles tries to ignore me, but his wife stops to chat. I've always liked Ellen. For the life of me, I can't figure out how an outgoing interior decorator who serves on the symphony and opera boards has managed to stay married to Chuckles for thirty-two years. Maybe she's a closet tax-code junkie.

Doris arrives with her daughter, Jenny. I hug them and they shake hands with Rosie. Jenny's pretty face is pale and she looks sad in her dark dress. She's taking this harder than I would have thought. Doris never warmed up to Rosie. It goes back to the bad old days after we got divorced. Things were pretty acrimonious between us when I first started working at the Simpson firm. We had a big fight over custody. Big mistake on my part. If I had a chance to do anything over again, I would have let Rosie have custody from the beginning. It's amazing how otherwise rational people can turn into jerks when emotions run amok. We finally called a truce when Rosie's mom and my mom got together and told us we were going to screw up Grace's entire life if we didn't stop acting like idiots. I'm glad we listened to them.

"Pretty rough time, Doris," I say.

"You got that right."

I turn to Jenny. "How are things at Stanford?"

"One more semester to go."

"Are you still thinking about law school?"

"I'm not sure. I applied to UCLA, Hastings and Boalt. We'll see. I have a lot on my mind."

I'd like to be twenty-two again just to see what it feels like to have a lot on my mind.

Joel and Naomi Friedman arrive by cab and join us. Joel has been asked to speak and he looks nervous. Naomi is a petite brunette with curly hair and dark features who teaches nursery school at the Jewish Community Center. She's a ball of fire. Perfect for Joel.

We head in and pay our brief respects to Bob's widow, Beth, and her three children, ages two to five, all of whom are sitting in the front row. The second row is reserved for Bob's three ex-wives and their current spouses and significant others and Bob's four children from his previous marriages.

The Simpson and Gates contingent occupies about twenty rows on the left side of the cathedral as you face the front. We take our seats opposite them on the right side. I'm not in the mood to visit with my former colleagues today. The back of the house is packed. The legal community has turned out. So have the politicians and the upper crust of Pacific Heights. Somber organ music emanates from the front of the cathedral. I never had a chance to work such a big crowd when I was a priest.

At ten-fifteen, the organist plays a loud chord, signaling the service is about to begin. A young minister welcomes us and says a few perfunctory words about Bob's life and career. He clearly never met him. He introduces Art Patton, who tries to appear respectful, but looks like David Letterman preparing to deliver a monologue as he saunters to the front. Rosie is thinking the same thing and she whispers to me, "He thinks it's the firm Christmas party."

"Thank you for coming," Art says. "Bob would have been pleased to see such a large turnout. It's sad that it takes a great tragedy to bring us together. I hope we will have a chance to meet on a happier occasion." His eyes gleam. He takes a deep breath. It's hard to look somber with a smirk plastered on your face. "Bob Holmes was a great lawyer and my best friend."

Murmurs from the S&G section. Art's taking some license. He and Bob coexisted, but it's a stretch to say they were friends, let alone great friends. Some people think they hated each other's guts.

"He was also a great humanitarian."

Someone in the S&G section laughs out loud.

"It's appropriate that we gather here to celebrate his life

and pay our respects to his memory." He describes Bob's humble beginnings in Wilkes-Barre, his education at Penn and Harvard Law School, his admission to the partnership at the age of thirty-two. He says Bob was a loving father, but doesn't linger on the subject of his four marriages. Bob's eldest son once told me that the children from his first three marriages stopped speaking to him several years ago.

After a brief description of Bob's achievements, he introduces Joel, who walks slowly to the lectern, a faraway look in his eyes.

"My name is Joel Friedman. Bob Holmes was my colleague, my mentor and my friend. This is the most difficult thing I've ever had to do."

Easy, Joel.

"Bob taught me how to be a lawyer. He taught me how to handle difficult situations. And, despite what some people may think, he taught me how important it is to treat everyone with respect. He was a fine man whose legacy is in this room. He leaves his family, colleagues and friends with memories of a man who worked hard, loved his family and loved his job. I will miss him."

Well done. He steps away from the podium to compose himself. The minister comforts him.

Skipper's up next. Rosie whispers, "This should be a beaut."

Skipper does his best to look serious. He faces the television camera and says, "I knew Bob for twenty-two years. He was one of the finest lawyers I've ever met. More than anyone else, Bob built Simpson and Gates into a powerhouse." He pauses. "More importantly, I want to say a few words about Bob, the man. Bob was sometimes difficult to get along with. That's the price you pay for dealing with genius. He never demanded more from his colleagues than he expected from himself. Yes, he was a perfectionist. Yes, he was driven. Yes, he screamed at times. It was never out of malice. He simply wanted to be the best he could be, and he expected the same from his colleagues."

More coughing from the S&G section. Rosie whispers, "This is really getting thick."

"It is tragic Bob won't have an opportunity to see his children grow up. It is sad he won't have a chance to fulfill his dreams. A great life. Cut short." He stops to wipe away a tear that isn't there. "The legacy he leaves us is great. In his honor, I promise to each of you, and to Bob, that I will not rest until I find out the true circumstances surrounding his death. It is my solemn pledge."

Doris nudges me and whispers, "For God's sake, he's making a campaign speech at a funeral."

Skipper finishes his remarks with a tribute to Bob's distinguished record as a husband and as a father, which brings audible laughter from several members of the firm. Two of Bob's college friends say a few words about his life's achievements. A neighbor reads a poem. The minister reads two psalms and a small choir sings "Amazing Grace." Finally, the organist plays "Born to Run." At eleven-thirty, we begin to file out.

The TV cameras jockey for the standard shot of the pallbearers bringing the casket down the steps. Bob would have loved the fact that the pallbearers include Skipper, the two surviving members of X-Com and three of his partners. When we reach the bottom of the steps, I gaze around and my eyes meet those of Roosevelt Johnson, who is standing on the sidewalk, a respectful distance away. He is looking discreetly through the crowd. It is common practice for a homicide inspector to show up at the funeral of the subject of his investigation, but somehow, I didn't expect to see him today.

Joel and Naomi find us and we watch the pallbearers

load the casket into the hearse. I say good-bye to Doris and
Jenny. Skipper's Lincoln pulls up behind the hearse and the
reporters surround him.

"Mr. Gates," a reporter calls out, "any new information
on the case?"

Skipper elects to take the high road. "This is an inappropriate time to discuss the investigation," he says. "I will talk
to you at the office." The hearse pulls away and begins the
long drive to the town of Colma, just south of the city,
where San Franciscans bury their dead.

You won't find Bill's Place in *Gourmet* magazine. Housed in
an old building at Twenty-fifth and Clement, it was a diner
before diners became fashionable and it served "comfort
food" four decades before food critics coined the term. The
long counters, huge chandeliers and Formica tables are a
throwback to simpler times. The waitresses have hair in varying shades of blue and orange and call their customers
"honey." It's the best place in the city to take screaming
children for hamburgers and milk shakes. It may never be
the subject of an American Express commercial, but it's
been one of my favorite places since my dad took me here
when I was a kid.

Naomi Friedman is eating a french fry. "Mike, I'm worried about Joel," she says. Joel is in the men's room. Naomi
takes off her red-framed glasses. Rosie, Joel, Naomi and I are
eating a quick lunch before we head south on the 280 freeway to Colma for our second funeral of the day. Diana's
funeral is going to be a graveside affair for immediate family
and friends. I've been asked to say a few words.

"What's the problem?" I ask.

"He was at police headquarters all day Sunday. They
asked him a lot of questions."

Rosie and I glance at each other. I take a bite out of my

cheeseburger. "I'm sure they're just trying to be thorough," I say. "This is a high-profile case."

Joel returns and there's an uncomfortable silence. "What?" he asks.

"Nothing," Naomi says.

"Come on," he says.

"All right," Naomi says. "I was just telling them about your glorious afternoon Sunday."

"I already told you. It's nothing to worry about."

She gives him a sharp look. "It's a lot to worry about. Why are they so interested in talking to you for so long?"

I sense annoyance. They've been through this already and Joel doesn't want to replay it in front of Rosie and me. He picks up his hamburger, turns to me and says, "I don't know how you can eat this stuff. It'll kill you."

"My grandfather ate this stuff every day of his life for eighty-seven years."

"Imagine how long he would have lived if he had taken better care of himself."

Naomi is annoyed. "Can you guys stop it for a minute? This is serious. Mike, why do you think they're giving Joel the third degree?"

Joel answers her. "They're just trying to figure out what happened. That's it. Nothing more to it. Jesus, it's not like I'm a suspect. Two people are dead and the cops are just doing their job. They said they'd probably declare it a suicide in the next couple of days."

Naomi scowls. "What about Vince Russo?" she asks.

"No word yet," Joel says.

"Did the cops tell you anything more about what happened?" I ask.

"Not much. The bullets came from Bob's gun."

Naomi loses interest in her french fries. "Do we have to talk about this at lunch?"

"Sorry," I say. "I'm just trying to figure out why they're so interested in talking to Joel." I turn toward him. "Which cop did you talk to?"

"Your buddy, Roosevelt Johnson, and his partner, Marcus Banks."

"Johnson's a good man."

He shifts in his chair. "He's a very suspicious man. And his partner isn't a nice guy."

"Marcus got himself into some trouble a few years ago. He's a little heavy-handed. He beat a confession out of a white man for the murder of a black prostitute. Turns out the guy really did it, but they had to turn him loose because they had nothing besides the coerced confession. A week later, the guy woke up dead."

"Oops."

"Don't underestimate them, Joel. They're the best on the force."

Rosie has heard enough. "Can we change the subject now?"

Naomi looks relieved.

"You know, Mike," Joel says, "my dad is doing the service for Diana."

"I didn't know she was Jewish."

"Yeah. Well, sort of. She grew up in our neighborhood and went to our temple. Except back then, her name was Debbie Fink, her hair was dark brown, her nose was longer than mine and she weighed about two hundred and fifty pounds."

"What happened to Debbie Fink?"

"The way I understand the story, between her senior year in college and her first year in law school, she spent a summer at a fat farm, had her hair dyed and got her nose fixed. Lord knows what else she had taken in. Her personal trainer was a guy named Billy Kennedy. They were married for about six months. By the time she finished her first year in law school, they were divorced. But the remake stuck. Debbie Fink became Diana Kennedy."

"Sounds like quite a transformation."

"More like a rebirth. She had lots of secrets."

"Does anybody else know about this?"

"Everybody at the firm . . . except you, of course."

I look at Naomi and she nods. Rosie tosses her head back and laughs. "I just figured out what we're going to inscribe on your tombstone," she says. " 'Michael Daley. Priest. Lawyer. He was always the last to know.' "

Naomi chuckles. We pay the bill and drive southbound through Golden Gate Park to Nineteenth Avenue. It's about twenty minutes to Colma.

It's drizzling when we reach the old Jewish cemetery at three o'clock. The crowd numbers only about thirty, and we stand under umbrellas on an artificial-turf mat next to the gravesite. Joel's father is wearing a beige overcoat and is standing under a black umbrella. Standing next to him is a woman I assume is Diana's mother.

We greet him. I've known Rabbi Neil Friedman for years. He's an older, huskier version of Joel, with an eloquent, stained-glass voice with the hint of a New York accent. "Michael, I haven't seen you in a while," he says. He's polite, but somewhat distant. He introduces us to Diana's mother, Ruth Fink. Joel told us Diana's father died when Diana was in her teens. Mrs. Fink is also polite, but brief.

Doris and Jenny Fontaine join us. Skipper, Arthur Patton and Charles Stern arrive as the service is beginning. A television cameraman stands about a hundred yards away, by the gate to the cemetery. No reporters or minicams this afternoon.

As Rabbi Friedman begins the service, I notice Roosevelt Johnson standing next to the gate. He nods to me. The rain becomes heavier and Mrs. Fink loses her composure. The rabbi intones the kaddish, the Jewish prayer of mourning.

It's been a helluva week.

7

"I'VE GOT TO GO BE A LAWYER FOR A COUPLE OF HOURS"

"We are looking forward to the new year with great optimism."

—SIMPSON AND GATES MANAGING PARTNER ARTHUR PATTON.
SAN FRANCISCO LEGAL JOURNAL. FRIDAY, JANUARY 9.

"The firm is starting to implode, Mike. Twenty labor lawyers announced they're leaving. They're talking about staff layoffs and big cutbacks." Joel is describing the state of the firm three days later, at six o'clock on Friday evening. We're having a beer on his back porch as a light mist falls on the small houses built back-to-back in the Richmond District. This is his going-away party for me from S&G. Rosie and Grace and my mom are here. So are Doris and Jenny Fontaine, and Wendy Hogan, a part-time tax attorney at S&G, and her six-year-old son, Danny. Joel's parents are supposed to stop by on their way to temple for Friday-night services.

"That's fast," I reply. "Sounds like I got out just in time."

"The firm must be in worse shape financially than anybody let on. I guess we really needed the cash from Vince Russo's deal. I've heard First Bank may foreclose on our equipment loans. They may hit up the partners. It may turn out to be a good thing I didn't make partner."

"Joint-and-several liability is a nasty thing when you've got a bunch of creditors out there." Although most states now permit law firms to be organized as "professional corporations" or "limited-liability partnerships," many firms, S&G among them, are still set up as general partnerships, which means each partner is fully responsible for firm debts even if the partner didn't sign the papers or incur the debt on behalf of the firm. It's an anachronism. Professional-service firms are the only large businesses still organized as partnerships. General Motors wouldn't be structured in a similar way.

"I heard they found Vince Russo's car," I say.

"They found his car, keys and wallet in the parking lot at the Vista Point at the north end of the Golden Gate Bridge. They think he may have jumped. Nobody saw him."

"Any chance he's still alive?"

He shrugs. "No body has turned up. He could have planted the car and driven away in another one. He could have walked to Sausalito and taken a cab. Hell, somebody could have picked him up and driven him to the airport. It wouldn't surprise me if he's in a warm climate sipping a fruity drink by the beach."

"Did he stash any cash?"

"He probably had some money in a foreign bank account."

My mom walks out from the kitchen. "Hello, Joel," she says. She's having a good night. "Have things settled down at the office?"

"Nice to see you, Mrs. Daley. Things have quieted down. We're hoping things will get back to normal in a few weeks."

Joel's son Alan marches outside with the bravado of a six-year-old and gives my mom a big hug. Little kids can spot a grandmother a hundred yards away. He is holding a piece of challah in his right hand. "Uncle Mike," he says, "Mommy says it's time for you and Daddy to come inside for dinner."

"Are you sure, Alan?"

Still clutching the challah, he points his index finger toward me for emphasis. "Uncle Mike, Mommy says you and Daddy have to come in right now, or you'll have to take a time-out."

"Okay," I say. "Tell Mommy we'll be right there. Oh, Alan? Can I sit next to you?"

He smiles. "Sorry, Uncle Mike. I always sit next to Daddy."

A large oak table overwhelms the small dining room. Alan and his twin brother, Stephen, are impressively well-behaved as they sit quietly on opposite sides of the table, at right angles to their father. Joel sits at the head. Grace sits between Rosie and me with our backs toward the windows. My mom is next to me. Doris and Jenny are across from me. Naomi sits at the foot of the table.

Wendy Hogan is next to Doris. Her son, Danny, sits next to her. Wendy and her husband split up a couple of years ago. She went through the mother of all custody battles. I can relate. She keeps her sad brown eyes hidden behind large wire-rimmed glasses. Her frizzy hair and mousy demeanor belie the fact that she's an absolute terror in negotiations with the IRS. I like her. We divorced, recovering Catholics have a lot in common. And S&G has treated her like shit for the past five years. Someday, I'm going to summon the courage to ask her out. She's a little gun-shy around men these days. She looks serious and says to me, "I think I may get laid off."

"No way," I say. "There will be nobody left to do the work."

"Every department is making a 'hit list.' They won't keep any of us part-timers. My billables aren't good enough."

She may be right. She works four days a week, but she's paid only about 60 percent of what a full-time associate makes. According to the firm, if a lawyer works four days a week, you still have to pay rent and a secretary five days a week. As a result, it's unfair for the firm to pay the attorney a straight prorated salary. Most people think it's just another way to screw the part-timers.

Rosie pipes up. "Don't worry, Wendy. The economy is good. You'll find something."

"It doesn't make things easier. Whenever my finances change, Andy's lurking, trying to figure out ways to break up our custody and child-support deal."

Danny frowns. He's a good kid. He's watched his parents fight over custody his entire life. I don't say it out loud, but I'm betting he's on his way to years of therapy.

The kids finish first and they wander to the small den in the back of the house to do what children do these days—watch videos and play computer games. As we're clearing the table, there's a knock at the door. Joel looks up. "Mom and Dad are here."

Alan comes bouncing down the hall. "Grandma and Grandpa!" he shrieks with six-year-old glee. He runs through the dining room and down the interior stairs to open the door. His brother is a step behind him. Naomi smiles. A moment later, Alan comes back up the stairs, a troubled look on his face. "Daddy, there's a policeman downstairs. He wants to talk to you."

What the hell? Joel freezes. Naomi looks alarmed.

"Okay, Alan," he says. "Daddy will go down and see what this is all about. Don't worry."

Alan goes over to his mother and grabs her hand. Joel walks downstairs.

A moment later, we hear loud talking at the bottom of the stairs. Rosie goes to the living room in the front of the house and looks out the windows. I follow her. She turns to me and says, "This doesn't look good."

I look out and see two police cars parked in the small driveway. My stomach tightens. There are four policemen. One is having a heated discussion with Joel.

Grace comes up to us. "Is something wrong, Daddy?" she asks.

"No, sweetie," I lie, trying to keep my voice calm. "I don't think so. It looks like the policemen want to talk to Uncle Joel for a few minutes. I'll go downstairs to find out what's going on." She moves closer to Rosie.

I reach the bottom of the stairs and open the heavy wooden door. I'm stunned to see a middle-aged policeman, whose face I remember, but whose name escapes me, putting handcuffs on Joel.

"You have the right to remain silent."

This is bullshit. "Excuse me. May I ask what's going on?" I try to keep my tone nonconfrontational. It's important to remember the guys with the uniforms have the guns.

"You have the right to an attorney."

The policeman looks at me. "Please step back, sir. This matter does not concern you."

"Anything you say can be used against you in a court of law."

What the fuck is this all about? "Officer, Mr. Friedman's wife asked me to find out what's going on."

"If you cannot afford an attorney, one will be appointed for you."

Naomi is coming out the door as the policeman says, "Mr. Friedman is being arrested for the murders of Robert

Holmes and Diana Kennedy. We have a warrant for his arrest and we're taking him into custody. Please step aside."

Un-fucking-believable. Skipper's pulling a publicity stunt.

Naomi screams. Joel tries to calm her down. "It's okay. We'll get this straightened out."

Although Naomi doesn't realize it, her kids have followed her. They start to cry. "Naomi," I say calmly, "let me handle this. Why don't you take the kids back up?"

She nods and takes them upstairs. She returns without them a moment later.

Joel is trying to reason with the policeman when a black Lincoln drives up and Skipper steps out. The pieces are starting to fit together. "It's under control," he says to nobody in particular. He turns to Joel. "Well, young man, I knew you had a temper, but I didn't think you'd kill two people."

A white Channel 4 minivan pulls up behind Skipper's car. Rita Roberts and her cameraman leap out.

Joel is furious. "Are you out of your fucking mind, Skipper? You think I'd kill two people because I didn't make partner?"

"There's a lot more to it, and you know it. You'll have your day in court."

I try to interject before things deteriorate further. I address the policeman. I point to the handcuffs. "Officer, do you really need those? Mr. Friedman is a respected attorney. He's not a threat."

The cop shrugs. I see the name D'Augustino on his nameplate. "Standard procedure, sir."

I take Skipper aside. "What kind of stunt are you trying to pull here?"

His expression is condescending. "Look who's here. My favorite ex-partner. The one who just got fired. And with good reason. Always spend your free time with murderers?"

It's hard for me to believe what I'm hearing. I clench my

teeth. "For God's sake, Skipper, if you wanted to arrest him, you could have called. He would have surrendered without all the theatrics. He's not exactly a flight risk."

"Bullshit, Mike. You don't know the half of it."

"And I suppose you called the TV stations to make sure they were here in time for your collar?"

"I don't know anything about that. They must have heard it on the police band."

Now it's my turn. "Bullshit, Skipper."

"Fuck you. This doesn't have anything to do with you, so stay out of it."

Through sheer willpower, I don't retort. Joel is in enough trouble without my getting into hand-to-hand combat with Skipper on the front steps of Joel's house.

At that moment, Joel's mother and father arrive. They look startled at the sight. Joel's mother, Mollie, a heavyset woman, has a knack for saying the right thing or deciding to stay mum. She usually elects to remain silent. It keeps her out of trouble with the congregants. Joel's father keeps his face impassive as he asks politely, "Is there a problem, Officer?"

Skipper steps up. "Rabbi, I'm sorry I'm the one who has to tell you, but your son is under arrest for the murder of two people."

The rabbi looks stunned. He takes a step back. "There's been a mistake."

"I'm afraid there's no mistake, Rabbi. Now, if you'll excuse us."

Rabbi and Mrs. Friedman huddle with Naomi, who is standing behind me. I turn around to look at them and say, "I'll figure out what's going on. You guys stay put."

The uniforms push Joel toward one of the squad cars. "For God's sake," I say, "take off the handcuffs."

Skipper can't resist. "Bob and Diana would have wished he'd been in handcuffs the night he killed them."

Asshole.

One of the uniforms says they're taking him to the Hall of Justice. Before they put him in the car, I say to him, "Joel, I'll be right behind you. Be cooperative and above all, don't talk to anyone. These people are not your friends. Nobody down there is your friend. Got it?"

He nods, but I see him biting back panic. "You've got to take care of this, Mike."

"I will. Right now, you've got to do what I say."

The uniform shoves me out of the way. "Who the hell are you, anyway?" he asks. I resist the urge to shove him back.

Joel answers. "He's my lawyer. I'm not saying a word to you assholes unless he's present."

I summon my best authoritative tone. "May I have your attention, please?" I turn and look directly into Rita Roberts's camera. My voice is shaking. "My name is Michael Daley. I am Mr. Friedman's attorney. I have instructed Mr. Friedman not to talk to any of you outside of my presence. Rabbi and Mrs. Friedman are witnesses." I turn to Skipper. "If you talk to my client, I'll have you brought up before the state bar."

He turns away. My little speech was just beamed live to households all over the Bay Area. A media star is born.

The two police cars pull away and head down Sixteenth. The Lincoln follows. I turn to Rabbi and Mrs. Friedman. "Let's go in. We have a problem."

Upstairs, Naomi has sent the children to watch TV under my mother's watchful eye. Naomi, Rosie, Wendy, Doris, Jenny and I gather in the living room with Rabbi and Mrs. Friedman.

"What happens now?" Naomi asks.

"I'll go down to the Hall of Justice and ask for bail. He may have to spend the night. They arrested him late on a

Friday because it's tough to find a judge right before the weekend."

Rosie looks at me. "You'd better get down there right away."

"He didn't do it, Mike," Naomi implores.

"I know. I'll call you as soon as I can." I ask Rosie to call Pete to take my mother home. She agrees.

I walk to the back of the house where the kids are gathered with my mother. I give Grace a hug. "Daddy has to go out for a while," I explain. "You're going to have to stay with Mommy tonight."

"Okay," she says. Then she adds, "Is Uncle Joel in trouble?"

The wisdom of a six year old. "Yeah, sweetie. But it's a big mistake. Daddy is going downtown to straighten it out. You look after Mommy and Grandma, okay?"

"I will, Daddy. I love you."

"I love you, too."

I turn to my mother. For the first time in five years, her eyes are truly clear. Before I can say anything, she says, "They arrested him."

"Yeah."

I see the look that I saw so many times when my dad got a call at home from his sergeant. It's the look of a policeman's wife. For a moment, she's thirty years younger and her blue eyes are steel. "Do what you have to do to help him, Michael."

"Yes, Mama. Right now, I've got to go be a lawyer for a couple of hours."

"I know. You take good care of him."

"I will. Pete's going to come over and take you home."

"I'll be up late, Michael. Would you please call me when you know what's going on?"

"Of course." After all these years, Margaret Murphy Daley is still the wife of a cop.

8

THE HALL OF JUSTICE

"The Hall of Justice is an incredibly expensive homeless shelter, detox center and drug-treatment center, and an utterly inept way to handle social problems."

—DIRECTOR OF INMATE RELEASE PROGRAM.
SAN FRANCISCO EXAMINER.

In San Francisco, the DA's office, criminal courts and city jail are located in a Stalinesque seven-story structure at Seventh and Bryant that is modestly known as the Hall of Justice. Although a new fifty-million-dollar jail wing was added in the early nineties, the Hall hasn't lost any of its original charm. The new jail was built to ease overcrowding in the system, which has been under a federal court consent decree since the eighties because of poor conditions. The north wall of the new jail practically touches the 101 freeway, and prisoners sleep less than fifty feet from the slow lane.

At seven-thirty, the traffic on Van Ness is heavy as I weave southbound through a driving rain. Surprisingly, I find a parking place on Seventh between two squad cars. I grab my briefcase from the trunk and try to look lawyerly in my jeans and long-sleeved polo shirt.

I'm soaked as I run up the front steps of the Hall and

explain to the guard at the metal detector that I'm here to
see my client, Mr. Friedman. He motions me through and I
detour around the tortoise-slow Depression-era elevators and
head for the stairs.

In October of 1996, a new intake center was opened in
the new wing of the Hall. County Jail 9, as the intake center
is known, is a far cry from the chaos that reigned at the
raucous old booking center on the sixth floor of the old
Hall, which at times seemed more like an overcrowded zoo
on a busy night. The old jail is now used primarily for high-
security housing and prisoner classification. The intake area
was the last part of the new facility to come on-line.

The booking hub is antiseptic clean. In contrast to traditional "linear" jails, which have cells lining a central corridor, the holding cells in the new booking center are
arranged in a circle around a deputies' workstation. The
prisoners are housed in well-lighted cells behind glass doors.
When the doors are shut, the place is relatively quiet. There
are no heavy, clanking iron cell doors or shouts of inmates.
As always, the usual parade of humanity is awaiting processing.

Whenever I'm in the Hall, I think of my dad. I always
expect to see him walking down the corridors, his bearing
erect, his chest out, a cigarette hanging from his lips. He was
so proud that he was a cop. He put the bad guys away.

Although the Hall serves as the city jail, for historic bureaucratic reasons, it's actually run by the County Sheriff's
Department. I survey the sheriff's deputies working behind
the desk and I recognize the pockmarked face and thick
mustache of Sergeant Philip Ramos. I'm thankful I had the
foresight to get some business cards printed. "Good evening,
Sergeant Ramos," I say, handing him my state bar card and
my driver's license.

The heavyset man looks at my card, then surveys me up
and down. About ten years ago, Phil Ramos found himself

on the wrong side of a gang fight. A bullet wound in his left thigh moved him behind a desk. He's never been happy about it. He's a good, tough cop. "Mike Daley," he says. "I thought you moved downtown. May I assume your visit this evening is not entirely social?"

"That would be correct."

"And may I ask which one of our guests will have the pleasure of your company?"

"Joel Friedman. They just brought him in."

He types on his computer. "Excuse me, Mr. Big Time. A murder rap. He's being processed. Gonna be a few minutes." He picks up his phone and asks someone to bring Joel to the holding room adjacent to his desk. "Do me a favor and keep it short. They haven't finished booking him." He looks at his computer screen. "What's this about?" he asks.

"You heard about the shootings last week at the Simpson and Gates firm?"

"Yeah."

"I worked there. Friedman still works there. Skipper's trying to pin the shootings on him."

He's surprised. "I thought it was a suicide."

"There's something else going on. Skipper's calling the shots. There's no way this guy did it."

He gives me the "I've heard it a million times" look. "Sometimes people do stupid things," he says. "I just process them. Roosevelt wouldn't have charged him if he didn't have a solid case."

"Do me a favor, Phil. I don't know if we'll be able to get a judge to set bail tonight. If he has to stay the night, put him in his own cell, okay? If you put him in with everybody, he'll get eaten alive."

He scowls. "I'll try. We have a full house. Fridays are always busy. I'll see what I can do."

"Thanks, Phil."

Two deputies lead Joel into the holding room behind the intake desk. I used to meet with my clients in similar rooms when I was a PD. The lucky ones got five minutes of my time. I didn't create the system. I'd try to come up with a workable deal and move to the next case. I did the best I could. Joel keeps his head down. Intake isn't fun. First you get fingerprinted. Then you have a medical interview. In some cases, you get strip-searched. Finally, you're issued an orange jumpsuit and you're assigned to a cell.

Ramos presses a button and the door opens to let me into the room. The deputies have taken off Joel's handcuffs. He slumps into a chair. I ask the deputies to wait outside. The larger one tells me we have ten minutes.

Joel's eyes are tired. "You've got to get me out of here," he says. His voice is desperate.

"We need to talk fast. First, I'm going to try to find a judge to set bail. I don't know if I'll be able to find one at this hour on a Friday night."

"You can't let them keep me here."

"I know the desk sergeant. He's going to get you your own cell." I don't know this for sure, but I'm hoping Ramos will keep his word. "Don't talk to anybody. Everybody here will lie about you. They'll say you confessed to something. Even the ones you don't talk to will lie. Got it?"

"Got it."

"Good. They're going to finish your paperwork and they'll probably take you to a holding cell."

"What am I gonna tell Naomi and the kids?"

"I'll take care of that. We'll take this one step at a time. Rosie's there and so are your mom and dad. We'll get through this. Right now, you've got to stay calm and be smart. You got it?"

"Yeah." There's panic in his voice.

The deputy opens the door. "Time to go," he says. "We need to finish his paperwork."

"Just one more minute," I say. He steps back outside. "Joel, one other thing. I'll do everything I can to help you if you want me to represent you. But I don't want you to feel obligated to hire me as your lawyer. You don't have to tell me tonight. But you're going to have to decide soon."

He looks me in the eye. "I wouldn't trust anybody else. You're the man."

"Good. Now do what these nice deputies say. I'll take care of everything else."

He looks back at me as they lead him out the door. He mouths the word "Thanks."

At ten-fifteen, I'm at the pay phone in the lobby of the Hall. I should have brought my cellular. I dial Joel and Naomi's number. Rosie answers.

"It's Mike."

"No bail," she says.

"That's right. How did you know?"

"We saw it on the news. Fucking Skipper got in front of the cameras and said he's charging Joel with first-degree murder."

"The duty judge wouldn't set bail."

"I figured. I didn't think they'd let him out tonight." If it's first-degree, they may not set bail at all. "Here's Naomi."

"Hi, Mike." Her voice cracks.

"Look, Naomi, I just talked to Joel. He's doing okay." A small lie. "I know the desk sergeant. He's going to put Joel in his own cell. He'll be all right for the night."

"What am I supposed to tell the boys?"

I pause. What *is* she supposed to tell the boys? "The legal system works slowly, so we have to stay calm." Easy for me to say. People hate it when their lawyer tells them their only choice is to be patient. "I'll be right over," I say. "Have Rosie screen any calls. And don't talk to the press."

"Whatever you say."

The kids are asleep at eleven-thirty when Rosie, Naomi and I sit down in the dining room where we'd been eating Naomi's chicken a few hours earlier. The minicams left after the eleven o'clock news programs ended. Rabbi and Mrs. Friedman just went home. Pete picked up my mom an hour ago.

Naomi turns her puffy red eyes toward me. "What do we do now?" she asks.

I take her hand. "I'll talk to another judge. It would help if you have access to some money."

"We'll find it. They said on the news they may not grant bail."

I look at Rosie. If Skipper goes for special circumstances (that is, the death penalty), there will be no bail. Not even for a pillar of the legal community. Not even for the rabbi's son. "Naomi," Rosie says, "sometimes they don't set bail. It depends on the charge."

Naomi is holding back tears. "What's next? You guys are the lawyers."

"He'll probably be arraigned on Monday," I reply. We lawyers often forget how Byzantine the legal system sounds to civilians. "We go to court and formal charges are read. Joel pleads not guilty. It takes about five minutes. Then I'll go have a big fight with the DA."

"And if they don't drop the charges?"

Rosie and I glance at each other, and I say quietly, "We'll get ready to go to trial, if we have to."

"I see." It's sinking in. Naomi pauses, then asks, "When will that be?"

"Technically, we can demand a trial within sixty days,

but almost everybody agrees to a delay so they have more time to prepare." She's starting to lose it. "One other thing," I say. "You and Joel may decide to let somebody else handle the case. If you do, I'll understand." Rosie looks at me as if I've lost my mind.

Naomi shrugs. "I'll talk it over with Joel. I'm sure he'll want you. I do."

"Thanks, Naomi. I'd better get going."

I carry Grace to Rosie's car. She's getting heavy. "Rosie," I say, "mind if I stop by for a few minutes on my way home?"

"You were reading my mind."

"Just business tonight. I seem to have a murder case to prepare for."

"Absolutely."

I smile at her. "How do you think George Costanza would describe us?"

"I believe the term is 'crisis sex,' with a few doses of 'sympathy sex' and 'guilt sex' thrown in."

"One of these days, you're going to find a guy you really like and we're going to have to shut this down."

"I know. But, for the time being, this works all right for me."

"Me too. I'll see you at home."

9
LARKSPUR

"You're moving to Larkspur? Marin County? You're kidding, right? You can't move to Marin. You're a city boy, Mike. The fresh air will kill you."

—JOEL FRIEDMAN.

Rosie and I live about three blocks from each other in Marin County in a little suburb called Larkspur, which is about ten miles north of the Golden Gate Bridge. Larkspur's eleven thousand residents live in small, well-tended houses on the flatlands between the 101 freeway and the base of Mount Tamalpais. In Marin, the single folks live in Sausalito, the artists and writers live in Mill Valley, the nouveau riche live in Tiburon and the old money live in Ross. The few working stiffs tend to congregate in Larkspur and its sister city, Corte Madera, although housing prices are getting so high that only the truly affluent will be living there soon.

Moving to Marin was one of our many compromises. It's a move we never would have made if Grace hadn't been born. If it had been up to me, we'd have moved back to Berkeley. If Rosie had had her way, we wouldn't have left the city. Kids change things. A lot. The scary thing is I like where we are. Maybe you don't have to make a political statement with every aspect of your life.

It's a few minutes after midnight now and I've just crossed the Golden Gate Bridge. The Corolla strains up the Waldo Grade toward the tunnel above Sausalito. If it weren't raining so hard, I'd have a great view of the city out my right window.

As usual, I'm listening to KCBS, the all-news station. Joel is a hot topic. "In tonight's headlines, Joel Mark Friedman was arrested for the murder of two prominent attorneys at the Simpson and Gates law firm."

Randy Long, my mentor at the PD's office, used to say you know your client is in really big trouble when they use all three of his names on the news.

"District Attorney Prentice Gates will hold a press conference Saturday morning to discuss the case. KCBS will cover it live. KCBS news time is twelve-ten." I switch the station to jazz.

I take Paradise Drive west past the upscale Corte Madera mall. I head north on Magnolia, Larkspur's main street. A mile later, I turn right onto a side street called Alexander Avenue, and pull into the narrow driveway of Number 8, across from the Twin Cities Little League field. Because of its proximity to the ballpark, it's known as the hey-batter-batter house. Rosie has been renting the tiny white bungalow since Grace started school last year. Many homes in Larkspur were built as temporary housing after the 1906 earthquake. Some have been remodeled, but most are still quite small. Rosie's was built in 1925 for a local school-teacher, who paid twenty-five hundred dollars for it. Today, the seven-hundred-square-foot house would set you back at least six hundred thousand.

The light's on. Rosie is watching the rebroadcast of the late news. I knock quietly on the door and let myself in. It's a good sign when your ex-wife lets you have your own key. It wasn't always the case when we were in the middle of our divorce. Her dark eyes light up. She holds a finger to her lips and motions me into the living room. Grace is asleep.

"Joel's the lead story."

"So I gather. I was listening to it on the radio."

"They got your little speech in front of his house on camera."

"Great."

"They got another shot of you walking out of the Hall."

"Nike will be calling tomorrow to offer me a sneaker contract. The 'Air Daley' line."

She smiles. She's heard this one before. "They said you had no comment."

"That would be correct."

"You could have said he was innocent."

"I know. I want to save my best lines for my interview with Ted Koppel."

"Probably smart."

"I hope so."

We stare at the TV. NewsCenter 4 loves to send its mini-cams all over the Bay Area to do live "team coverage," even when it makes no sense to do so. Why TV news directors think we want to see their reporters catching pneumonia escapes me. I guess if you have the fancy toys, you might as well use them. Rita Roberts is standing in the pouring rain on the dark, empty street in front of Joel's house. As she gets soaked, they show videotape of the arrest a few hours earlier. They show my speech to the cops and a brief interview with Skipper. The second reporter, a tall man with beautiful dark hair and a cleft chin, is getting drenched on the dark, empty street in front of the Hall. They show videotape of Joel being escorted into the building. Then they show me hustling up the front steps of the Hall.

Rosie shuts off the TV. "Joel has a big problem."

"Tell me about it. What else did they say on the news?"

"The basics. The usual blather about incontrovertible evidence placing Joel at the scene. Inconsistencies in his story. They claim he's been uncooperative and tried to flee." She pauses. "Oh, one more thing. One station quoted 'reliable sources' saying Joel was having an affair with Diana."

"I see. Who was saying all that?"

"They didn't say, but it has to be Skipper. It's a DA's wet dream. First week on the job and he's got a high-profile murder case." Rosie has such a delicate way with words.

"Did they interview Roosevelt?"

"Briefly. He didn't say much. He just said they have solid evidence."

I look at the fire in the small fireplace. "Joel's got a big problem."

She grins. The dancing light reflects off her dark eyes. "My little rainmaker. First week on the job and you have already landed a high-profile murder case. Not bad."

"It's a standard marketing technique," I say. "You go to dinner at your best friend's house and hope he gets arrested for murder sometime between the salad and the entree. All those marketing seminars at S and G finally paid off."

She turns serious. "First things first. You're going to do this by the book. I have a standard form of retainer letter on my laptop here. We're going to put one together for you right now. Joel has to sign a retainer letter. And you have to talk to him about what this is going to cost."

I swallow. "I know."

She takes my hand. "I know you hate this stuff. But you've got to take care of business. You're going to have to take this case all the way to the finish line, Mike. I don't want to hear you ever again suggest to Joel or Naomi that they hire another lawyer. This is your case. Period. And if you're going to be the attorney of record, you have to get a retainer letter."

"I will." She's right, of course. Rosie used to lecture me a lot when we were married. More often than not, she had good reason.

"Good. Then I think you should spend tomorrow with your buddy, Joel."

"I'm going to spend as much time as I can with him. Unless I can pull a rabbit out of my hat, he isn't going anywhere any time soon."

At one-fifteen, I arrive at my second-story one-bedroom apartment in an eight-unit walk-up building just behind the fire station in downtown Larkspur. I climb up the short flight of steps, find the afternoon paper and fumble for my keys in the dark. The building is vintage fifties, and it's showing its age. My apartment consists of a small living room, an even smaller bedroom, a dining area big enough for a dinette set and a kitchen big enough for one. It's enough for me, but cramped when Grace stays here. The furniture is basic cheap Scandinavian teak, with a few book-cases built of bricks and boards. The only indication of modern technology is a computer in the corner of my bedroom, a Mitsubishi nineteen-inch TV and a small compact-disc player. Forty-five years old and I'm still living like a college student. It's the price you pay when you have alimony, child support and an ex-wife who wants nice stuff for our daughter. Although Rosie probably doesn't need the money from me, she's absolutely right in demanding it. Given my propensity for frittering it away, it's better that I have a legal obligation to pay it to her. It doesn't help that I have a sixty-eight-year-old mother who isn't in the greatest of health.

I grab a Diet Dr Pepper from the fridge and I look at my reflection in the small mirror in the kitchen. My thick light brown hair is matted to the top of my head. There are a few flecks of gray in the sideburns. The crow's-feet around my eyes remind me that I'm no longer in my thirties. My face is a little more rounded than it used to be. I still have the lean legs and torso of a cross-country runner. Rosie says I look like the consummate middle-aged Irishman—a combination of boiled potatoes and beer. I realize that I'm beginning to look more and more like my dad.

There are two messages on the answering machine. The first one surprises me. "Mike, this is Roosevelt Johnson. I'd appreciate it if you would call me as soon as you can." I jot down his phone number.

The second message is from Rabbi Friedman. "Michael, please call me on Saturday afternoon after services. There are a few things I'd like to discuss with you."

I tilt my head back and close my eyes. I wonder if Rabbi Friedman is calling to ask why Joel is still in jail.

Let the second-guessing begin.

10

"FIRST, YOU HAVE TO TELL
ME EVERYTHING"

"In our top story this morning, District Attorney Prentice
Gates said attorney Joel Mark Friedman will be charged with
first-degree murder in the shootings of two colleagues."

—*NEWSCENTER 4 DAYBREAK.* SATURDAY, JANUARY 10.

"Did you find a judge yet, Mike? When the hell am I getting out of here?" At eight-thirty the next morning, Joel's
unshaven face has a look of desperation. The small, gray
interview room is stuffy.

"Not yet. Rosie's calling in some favors. The duty judge
said we'd have to wait till Monday."

"Shit."

"It's an old trick. They haul you in on Friday night so
you have to spend the weekend in the clink. They think it'll
soften you up."

He looks incredulous. "Soften me up for what? They
think I'm gonna confess to something?"

"I assume you have nothing to confess to."

"You got that right."

"Good. First things first. How did you make it through
the night?"

"Like any other night at a fine hotel."

"I'm serious, Joel. Did they give you your own cell?"

"For a couple of hours. Then they ran out of space so they put a guy in with me who was arrested for beating a prostitute. The cops said he wasn't dangerous. He scared the hell out of me."

Swell. Thanks a lot, Sergeant Ramos.

"So, what happens next?" he asks in a dejected tone.

"First, you have to tell me everything. Then you have to tell me what you told the police. You can leave out the part where you got arrested last night. I was there for that. Then I'll find a judge who's willing to set bail. And I'll have a little talk with Inspector Johnson. And with Skipper."

"I don't trust either of them."

"You shouldn't. The only person you should trust is me."

He gives me a weak smile. "I know. Do I get to talk to the judge anytime soon?"

Corporate attorneys haven't the slightest idea how the criminal justice system works. It's probably better that way. "For one thing, Joel, you don't talk to the judge. I do. For another thing, on Monday, we'll go to court for an arraignment. They'll charge you. You'll plead not guilty. Don't get cute. Just say it clear and fast. The judge will schedule a preliminary hearing. That's it. It's as exciting as watching grass grow."

"Can you get me out of here on Monday?"

"Maybe. If we can't get a judge over the weekend, we'll ask the judge at the arraignment."

"What are the chances of bail?"

"Depends on the charge. You're booked on suspicion of murder. If they go murder one, bail may be tough." I don't add that if they ask for the death penalty, there's no way.

He's crushed. It's a shock when somebody first says aloud you're being charged with murder.

"I need to know all the details from you so I can do my

job. I need the story straight. Don't embellish it. Don't sugarcoat it. Just tell me everything that happened." This is standard defense attorney jargon. I don't want to ask him flat out if he did it. If he did, and he lies to me, I've got perjury problems. I'm not supposed to let him lie. It happens all the time, of course, but I try to avoid it. If he didn't do it, which I assume, and, coincidentally, I believe, I need his story to put together his defense.

He figures out where this is heading. "I want to get this right out on the table," he says. "I didn't do it. And it is absolutely imperative not only that I be found not guilty, but also that I am fully exonerated. Are we clear on that?"

I pause to collect my thoughts. This part of a defense lawyer's speech is always the most difficult. "Joel, I need you to understand a few things. First, I believe you. I don't think you're capable of killing two people. I've known you for a long time and I'm a very good judge of people."

I get the hint of a smile.

"But," I continue, "my job is to give you the best defense I can. I'll give you all the support I can, twenty-four hours a day. But I don't do absolutions anymore. My job is to try to get you off. I'll do everything I can to do just that. If you need more than that, you'll probably need to go to your rabbi, or at least to another lawyer." I know it sounds harsh. But, it's the truth. My job is to be Johnnie Cochran. I'll play all the cards I have within the scope of the State Bar Rules of Professional Conduct to get him off.

He looks away.

"You can still find another lawyer, you know," I say.

His eyes turn to brown steel. "No. I want you to be my lawyer." He glances at the top of the table. "One more thing," he says. "How much do you think this is going to cost?"

I pause. "If we go to trial, at least a hundred thousand—probably more. If we need a lot of experts, double it.

If you want fancy jury consultants and mock trials, figure a quarter of a million."

"Jesus. I thought corporate lawyers were expensive."

"You know how it is. Trials have a life of their own. And Grace has to eat."

"I know." He takes a sip of coffee. "What's your billing rate?"

I stop cold. The fact is, I haven't decided. I didn't think I'd have a client so soon. "One-eighty an hour," I mumble. Then I add quickly, "Plus expenses."

"Weren't you two-eighty at S and G?"

"Yeah. It's amazing what you can do if you keep your overhead down. I guess you can think of me as the legal profession's equivalent of the Kmart Blue Light Special."

"One-eighty it is. How big a retainer do you want?"

I swallow. Here goes. "Let's say twenty thousand."

He doesn't blink. I'm relieved. "All right," he says. "And if you get me off on Monday?"

"Your money will be cheerfully refunded and you can buy me lunch at Bill's."

"It's a deal. Naomi will get you a check. We may need to borrow some money."

"I understand. Your credit is good."

"All right, Counselor, where do we start?"

"From the beginning. Tell me everything that happened, minute by minute, on the evening of December thirtieth."

Joel is working on his second cup of coffee. "Right after the meeting with Chuckles," he says, "I went back to the PCR and reviewed the final documents."

"That was around seven-fifteen?"

"Right. We were waiting for a call from CCC's board in

Stamford. They were meeting to approve the deal. We got the go-ahead around eight-thirty."

"So at eight-thirty, the deal was still on track?"

"Yeah. Except, of course, for Vince. He was waffling. He said he wasn't sure he'd close. Nobody really knew if he would go forward."

"Who else was working on the deal?"

"Bob, Diana and the usual army of secretaries and paralegals. The young punk, Jack Frazier, from CCC. His lawyer, Martin Glass. Dan Morris, the political fixer. Ed Ehrlich from the city attorney's office." He pauses to think. "Yeah, that's everybody."

"Who else was around?"

"The word processors and a couple of file clerks. And some of the people from Skipper's party."

"Like who?"

"Like the mayor. He stopped by for a few minutes and talked to Morris privately. I think the mayor reamed him out. He looked like shit when he came back."

"Was Doris around?"

"No. She went home around eight."

I remember saying good night to Doris. "That's right."

"A few of the partners were there. Patton stopped by. Chuckles was around. I talked to him after the meeting with the associates. Gave him a little more shit. You have to keep them honest."

"I know." I pause. "Were you really surprised by the decision to extend the partner track?"

"Not entirely. I'd heard about it. Still, they didn't handle it right. Bob should have told me."

He's right, of course. On the other hand, it's hard to tell whether his speech to Chuckles at the associates' meeting was genuine or an act.

"Then what happened?"

"We gave some documents to the word processors around nine-thirty and we all went out to eat. Diana and I went to Harrington's. We finished around ten-fifteen. She went home. I came back upstairs. She lives just over in Golden Gateway." The Golden Gateway apartments are a high-rise complex a couple of blocks north of the Embarcadero Center towers. It's a five-minute walk from downtown. "Bob took Vince to Tadich's and Frazier and Morris went to Aqua. I think the mayor went with them. He's a regular there, you know." Tadich Grill opened in 1849 and serves traditional fish in a long, wood-paneled dining room on California Street. On a good night, you can get a private booth and a great piece of petrale sole. Aqua is two doors down and about a hundred and fifty years removed from Tadich's. It appears regularly in trendy food magazines. I've eaten there only once. The crab cakes are out of this world.

Joel stands and stretches his legs. "I got back first. Everybody else got back by eleven and we signed all the papers by twelve-fifteen. I had a few cleanup things to go through, so I went back to my office. We agreed to meet at eight-thirty the next morning for the closing. I worked on the escrow instructions in my office and gave the mark-up to word processing. I went to Bob's office around twelve-thirty to see what was going on. He was arguing with Vince, so I poked my head in and told him we were all ready. We barely said three words."

"So by twelve-thirty, the deal was set to close."

"Right. Except everything depended on Vince. He had to give the final go-ahead on Wednesday morning to authorize the wire transfers."

"And at twelve-thirty, he still wasn't prepared to close?"

"He said he had to sleep on it. He wasn't sure. I went to my office, got my closing checklist and went down to the lunchroom for a soda."

"You were ready to close?"

"Yeah. In big deals like this, you sign all the documents the day before. The closing is usually a nonevent. Everybody drinks coffee until you get confirmation of the wire transfers."

"What did you do in the lunchroom?"

"I went through the checklist. I pushed three chairs together and went to sleep. I woke up around six and went back to my office. I knocked on Bob's door, but it was locked. I figured he'd gone home. I went back to my office. I was there until a little after eight, when Chuckles came by and asked me if I had the keys to Bob's office."

"Did you?"

"No. But I knew where Doris kept an extra set."

"So the two of you let yourselves in and you found them."

"Right."

A few minutes later, I take a drink of water from a Styrofoam cup. "What happened when you found them?" I ask.

Joel hesitates.

"It's okay," I say. "You can tell me."

"I got sick. I . . . well . . . threw up."

"Right there?"

"No. I made it to the bathroom."

"I see."

"Chuckles was calling nine-one-one when I got back. Bob was on the floor. It looked like he shot himself in the temple. Diana was against the wall next to the door. Her clothes were all full of blood, and there was blood on the wall behind her. She was sitting down on the floor and . . . her eyes were still open. It looked like she was calling out for help."

This isn't getting any easier. "Where was the gun?"

"On the floor next to his chair. It must have fallen out of his hand. It looked like he fell out of his chair."

I know I'll be able to confirm this from the police reports and the photos. "What did you do?"

"Something stupid, in retrospect. I picked up the gun and took out the bullets."

My first impulse is to scream, "YOU DID WHAT?" But after years in this game, I've learned to keep the tone matter-of-fact. "Why did you pick up the gun?"

He scratches his ear. "I've shot Bob's gun at the range. He was real proud of it. Made everybody do it once or twice. Sort of a rite of passage."

"But why did you pick it up?"

"I wanted to make sure it didn't go off. It's a fussy revolver, Mike. The trigger was very sensitive and once it went off in my hand before it was supposed to. The bullet landed about halfway down the range."

"I see." I'm trying not to show it, but this part of Joel's story is sounding a little forced. "So you unloaded the gun?"

"Yes. I wanted to be sure it didn't go off." It's the second time he's mentioned it. "I put the gun down on the desk. I put the bullets and the shells next to it."

Swell. "I trust you told the police Bob kept a loaded gun at his desk."

"Yep. They were amazed."

"It's pretty surprising."

"Not if you knew Bob."

"Then what?"

"That's it. We came downstairs to your meeting and we told Art." A look of recognition appears on his face. "I bet they found my fingerprints on the gun."

"Sounds like a good bet." My mind is racing. There has to be more. He has an explanation for his fingerprints on the gun. I decide to probe a little more. "What haven't you told me?"

"Nothing. That's it. They know I was there. They probably have my fingerprints on the gun. And they seem to think I was really pissed off at Bob about the partner-election stuff."

"What have the police told you?"

"You told me not to talk to them."

"Good boy."

"So what do we do now?"

"I'll go see Roosevelt and Skipper. If this is all they've got, then we're in good shape."

I get up to leave. He says, "Mike, you've got to get me out of here. Promise me you'll come back later and tell me what you find out."

I hear the panic in his voice. "I will," I assure him.

"If Joel is telling the truth, they've got nothing, Rosie." At eleven-thirty, I'm back in my satellite office at the pay phones on the first floor of the Hall. "He admits he was there all night. He admits he found Bob and Diana. That much we knew. And he picked up the gun. So now I know how they may have found his fingerprints on it."

"That's it?"

"That's it."

Silence on the other end of the phone. "Well," she says, "Skipper said a whole lot more at his press conference."

"Like what?"

"Like they have a witness at Harrington's who says Joel and Diana were fighting at dinner. And they have a custodian at the building who says he heard Joel and Bob arguing loudly at around one o'clock."

Shit. "Did he hear gunshots?"

"They're not saying."

"Anything else?"

"They looked at the telephone records. Seems a call was placed from Joel's phone line to Diana's apartment at about ten to one in the morning. They think he lured her back to the office."

Great. I ask her if Skipper said anything else.

"Yeah. He said he's going to charge Joel with first-degree murder and he may ask for special circumstances."

Swell. "I'll talk to you later." I head for my car. I want to get to Roosevelt Johnson as soon as I can to get the full story on the evidence. And I want to talk to the coroner and the evidence technicians right away. I begin to outline our requests for access to the evidence in my head. Either Joel neglected to tell me a few important details or his story has some gaping holes in it. Or maybe he's flat-out lying.

11

"YOUR FRIEND IS IN
VERY SERIOUS TROUBLE"

"We're going to charge him with first-degree murder. As long as I'm the DA, we're going to be very aggressive prosecuting violent crimes."

— SKIPPER GATES. PRESS CONFERENCE. SATURDAY, JANUARY 10.

At twelve-thirty on Saturday afternoon, Roosevelt Johnson and I are sitting in a cramped red-vinyl booth in a coffee shop called JT's at the corner of Nineteenth and Taraval, a couple of blocks from his house in the Sunset District. He's eating scrambled eggs and toast. I'm nursing a cup of decidedly ungourmet coffee. "I tried to reach you yesterday," he says.

"I didn't get the message till I got home late last night. Thanks for trying."

"I didn't like the way it was handled. I know he's your friend. And I didn't realize you'd be representing him."

Neither did I. "Of course, Roosevelt. Thanks."

"Sometimes things don't work out so well." He pauses. "Especially when somebody else is calling the shots." He uses his toast to push his eggs onto his fork. He's doing me a favor. I'll have to let him make the first move. "Your friend is in very serious trouble, Mike." His gravel voice sounds tired. "We're off the record, now, understood?"

"Understood."

"Good." He spreads some jelly on his toast. He leans forward so nobody can hear us. "Holmes and Kennedy were killed by shots fired from Holmes's gun. She died from two shots to the chest. He died from one shot to the head. Your guy's fingerprints were on the gun. There were three spent shells and three unused bullets. His fingerprints were on those too."

"All that shows is he picked up the gun. He told you so. It doesn't prove he killed anyone."

He pushes his glasses up to the top of his nose and wipes his mustache with his napkin. I take the cue. Shut the fuck up, Mike. He'll tell me what he can. This isn't the time for me to start pleading Joel's case. "There's more," he says.

I'm trying to remain professional, if not nonchalant. I play with my coffee cup. I hold my palms up—the universal symbol for "So what have you got?"

He clears his throat. "Seems he and Holmes had a big fight. We aren't sure what it was about. The night janitor said they were screaming at each other. Friedman stormed out of Holmes's office."

"They could have been talking about business."

"I know. I understand Holmes was a screamer and Friedman doesn't like to take shit from anybody. They may have been engaged in lawyerly discourse. Or it may have been something more."

"Like what?"

"One of your partners said Friedman was pissed off about not making partner."

"Who told you that?"

"In due time." He finishes his coffee. "Was he pissed off about not making partner?"

Reflexively, I shrug. He looks through me. He knows I

know. I know he's going to find out. "Off the record, Roosevelt, you'll find that he was, in fact, pissed off about not making partner."

"You're not violating any confidences. I already knew that. He told me so."

The game's begun. He's testing me. "You think he killed him because he didn't make partner? Come on, Roosevelt."

Another cold stare. "You know a guy named Rick Cinelli?"

"Yeah. The bartender at Harrington's." He knows more about what's going on at our firm than most of the partners do.

"Friedman and Kennedy had dinner there," he says. "Cinelli says they got into a big fight and she left. She didn't touch her dinner."

I'm beginning to see where this is going. "They were probably talking business. She wasn't a great legal technician. She probably screwed something up and he laid into her."

I get the "nice try" look. "All I know is what Cinelli told me. He said they had a big fight. He didn't know what it was about."

Great.

Then he adds, "You know, I don't try the cases. I don't even decide whether to prosecute. I just gather the evidence."

His point is, of course, well taken. "I understand. Anything else?" Inside, I cringe. I half expect him to say he has another janitor who found Joel standing over Bob's body.

"Just one other thing. We're trying to figure out why she came back to the office."

I don't say it out loud, but I've been wondering the same thing.

He continues. "We checked the S and G phone records

and we found a two-minute phone call was placed from
Friedman's private line at twelve-fifty-one A.M."

"Let me guess. Somebody called Diana's apartment from
Joel's phone."

"Right." He eats another piece of toast. "We're looking
into it. You might want to ask him about it."

I lean back. None of this is news to me. I don't want him
to see me sweat. I have to play it carefully. Roosevelt is very
good. I don't want to invite speculation about whether Joel
may have tried to lure her to the office. I try to change the
subject. "Do you have the coroner's report yet?"

He finishes his eggs and takes a bite of toast. "Not final."

I don't want to push too far. "Thanks for your help. I
know you're sticking your neck out."

"You're family. Even if you're a defense lawyer. Besides,
you'll get all of this stuff anyway."

He's right. In a few weeks, Skipper will have to present
enough evidence at a preliminary hearing to show cause for
holding Joel over for trial. He'll undoubtedly use everything
Roosevelt has described so far. This isn't looking good for a
quick dismissal.

Joel is incredulous. "Now they're saying I threatened her at
Harrington's and I lured her back two hours later to murder
her?" At two o'clock on Saturday afternoon, I'm giving Joel a
report on my meeting with Roosevelt. "What'll they dream
up next? That I was sleeping with her?"

I take a drink of water. "I think they're full of shit. I just
don't want any more surprises. I'm meeting with Skipper in
twenty-five minutes and I don't want to hear about any more
arguments at restaurants, any more fights in the office and/
or more threats. Am I clear?"

"Yes." He takes off his glasses and rubs his eyes. "What
do you need to know?"

"I need to know everything that happened that night. Good, bad or otherwise. For starters, did you and Diana have an argument at Harrington's?"

"I wouldn't call it an argument."

"What would you call it?" I'm not up for cat and mouse now.

"A discussion."

"A discussion?"

"Yes, a discussion."

"Joel, I don't have time for this. Did you have a fight with Diana at Harrington's?"

"All right. Yes."

"What was it about?"

"She didn't finish our escrow instructions and a couple of closing certificates. We gave her a couple of simple things to do, and she didn't do them. She wasn't a very careful lawyer."

"That's what you guys were fighting about?"

"Of course."

"Good." I regain my composure and realize I've just congratulated him for making an ass of himself in a public place—for a perfectly valid reason. "All right," I continue, "let me ask you something else. Was there ever any hanky-panky between you and Diana?"

"Are you asking me if I ever slept with her?"

"In a word, yes."

"All right. The answer, in a word, is no."

"Good." If you're lying to me, I'll rip your lungs out. "Did you call her that night?"

"Yes."

"It would have helped if you had told me. Why did you call her?"

"Bob told me to call her and get her back to the office.

He wanted to talk to her about her closing documents." He pauses. "And I think he just wanted to talk to her."

I stop for a moment. "Why?"

"I don't know. They talked a lot."

"Were they sleeping together?"

"I don't know."

"Did you think so?"

He looks away. "Maybe . . . probably." He stands up. "All right. Yes. At least I think so."

"Did you and Bob have a fight that night?"

"I wouldn't call it a fight."

"Dammit, Joel. What were you and Bob arguing about?"

"What do you think? The little shit didn't have the guts to tell me the firm was going to defer all the people who were up for partner this year. I told him what I thought."

"Well, it seems one of the custodians heard you."

He closes his eyes. "Great," he murmurs. "So what are they saying? I threatened him?"

"That seems to be the jump in logic they're making."

"And I threatened Diana at Harrington's and lured her back, just so I could kill her?"

"Yeah."

"Well, that's a bunch of bullshit. You think I'd kill Bob and ruin my life because they didn't make me a partner? You think I'd kill Diana because she didn't finish a set of escrow instructions on time? This is fucking preposterous."

He's right, of course. But only if he's telling the truth.

"I'm going to meet with Skipper," I say.

"I expect you to get this thing dismissed by the end of the day."

NFC. No fucking chance.

12

"NICE OFFICE, SKIPPER"

"We are going to upgrade our facilities and computers. The San Francisco District Attorney's Office will be state of the art."

—Skipper Gates. Acceptance speech.

The only thing state of the art about the San Francisco District Attorney's Office is the remodeled suite that now belongs to Skipper Gates. The ADAs sit in cramped offices behind metal desks with dented olive-green file cabinets. The lucky ones get their own offices. The real lucky ones get windows looking out at the bail-bond shops across Bryant Street.

On the other hand, as soon as the election results were in, Skipper began tearing up half the third floor at the Hall to make some major capital improvements. His office has been expanded and he's built a large area for press conferences. The space allocated to the ADAs has shrunk and now only three senior ADAs have their own offices. The remodeling hasn't been met with a great deal of enthusiasm among the rank and file.

On Saturday afternoon, Skipper's office is a sea of splendor. He's dressed in khaki pants and a light blue polo shirt. He props his feet on his desk. I decline a Perrier from his new wet bar.

"Nice office, Skipper," I say. "I don't recall the hardwood floors and paneling when your predecessor occupied this space."

"Thanks. I'm glad you like it. We're trying to upgrade the image of the office." He's a master at accepting compliments, even when they're given facetiously.

Upgrading is one thing. Ostentatious is another. Hardwood floors, oak paneling, overstuffed chairs and an antique desk are more than an upgrade. I must admit the large photo of himself shaking hands with the mayor and the governor that he's hung behind his desk is very flattering.

"Skipper, if you don't mind my asking, don't you think this might be a little bit much?"

He laughs. "It's okay. The remodeling's being done on my nickel. It's very important to me to work where I'm comfortable."

"Don't you think the new press room is a little overdone?"

"Nonsense. I'm the district attorney. That makes me the chief law-enforcement officer in the city. If you're going to act the part, you've got to look the part."

I feel like quoting the old Billy Crystal "Fernando" routine on *Saturday Night Live*: "You look mahvalous, Skipper, simply mahvalous."

Sitting quietly in one of the overstuffed chairs and observing this banal exchange is a trim, middle-aged man with short gray hair and thick glasses. Bill McNulty, the ADA in charge of homicide cases, is a native San Franciscan and a career prosecutor. He thought his number had come up last year for the DA job. There were only two problems. First, there isn't a single ounce of charisma anywhere in Bill's body. Put him in front of a TV camera and he makes

Richard Nixon look photogenic. Second, Skipper tossed his hat into the ring and outspent Bill by about ten to one. Skipper annihilated him in the election in a vicious negative campaign. For twenty-six years, McNulty has been on a mission from God to put the bad guys away. He's good at it. What he lacks in charm, he makes up for by being careful, hard-nosed and meticulous. He has a reputation as a fighter and his nickname around the Hall is Bill McNasty.

"Mike," Skipper says, "I'm sure you've met Bill McNulty."

"We've worked on several cases over the years." I turn to McNulty. "Nice to see you again."

He nods and grimaces. A man of few words.

"Are you the ADA assigned to this case?"

He nods again.

"Good." Bad, actually. McNasty's good. He's tough. He's tenacious. And he's probably prosecuted about fifty murder cases. He's won most of them. Skipper has made an astute choice for help on his first big case.

McNulty looks at me. "The arraignment is scheduled for ten o'clock on Monday. We'll see you there." He starts to get up.

"Wait a minute, Bill. I thought we might take a few minutes to talk about this."

He gives me an impatient expression. "What's there to talk about? The next step is the arraignment. I assume your guy will plead not guilty and we're on our way."

Skipper holds up his hand. "I've just put Bill on this case," he says. "He's understandably reluctant to talk to you before he's been through the file. Isn't that right, Bill?"

McNasty scowls. I can't tell if he's pissed off about being here, being put on this case or having to suck up to Skipper. Probably all of the above.

"Well," Skipper continues, "maybe I can answer a few questions for you. And by the way, I'm sorry about all the hoopla last night. We didn't know you were going to be there. We sure as hell didn't know his kids and parents were going to be there."

Right. Where the hell did you think his kids would be at seven o'clock on a Friday night?

"Skipper," I say, "maybe you could just tell me what you've got in mind. You can't be serious about charging Joel based upon the skimpy evidence you've got so far."

His face turns solemn and he folds his arms. "You bet your ass."

I look at McNulty, who is completely still. He has a good poker face. I turn back to Skipper. "Maybe you can enlighten me. What evidence?" I want to find out everything that I can. And I don't want to give them anything else.

"You can't expect me to tip my hand," Skipper says. "All in due time."

McNulty looks pained. "You're going to have to tell him sooner or later. Now, tell him what you've got, or I will."

This is beginning to sound a little too rehearsed for my taste. "Well, Skipper?" I say.

"All right," he says. "We know he was there at the time of the murders."

"Alleged murders," I correct him.

Eye roll. "Alleged murders. He was the only one there. He knew where the gun was. He knew how to use it. He'd used it at the range. So we've got opportunity."

"Fine, Skipper," I say. "We know he was there. He told you so. And we all know about the gun. So what?" I'm tempted to ask Skipper where he was, but I let it go.

"There's the physical evidence. His fingerprints were on the gun, the spent shells and the unused bullets. So, we've got direct contact with the murder weapon."

"Not good enough," I say. "It shows he disarmed the gun. He told you that. He did it for the safety of the others in the firm. You aren't close to probable cause, let alone a conviction." Actually, he zoomed past probable cause a few minutes ago and he's about a quarter of the way to a conviction, but he doesn't have to hear that from me.

Skipper scratches the bottom of his chin and takes a drink of Perrier. I wonder if Perrier has ever found its way into this building before. "Then, of course, we have the question of motive."

I sit back in my chair and lock my fingers behind my head. I realize the chair is nicer than anything I have at home. This should be a gem. "And what motive have you concocted, Skipper?"

"Actually, he has motive in both cases. Let's talk about Diana first. He was really pissed off at her. They got into a big screaming match at Harrington's. The bartender saw it. She tossed a drink at him and stormed out."

"They were fighting about work. She fucked up some closing documents. It doesn't mean he killed her."

"That's what your guy is telling you. She went home, had a drink and went to bed. Then around twelve-fifty, after he had a chance to stew about it a little, he called her up and lured her back to the office. He waited for her, then he blasted her. Right there in Bob's office."

"You're dreaming, Skipper. What makes you think he called her?" I know what's coming.

"We have the phone records. A call was placed from his private line at the office to her apartment at twelve-fifty-one. The call lasted two minutes. She showed up at the office fifteen minutes later at about one-ten. We got the time of her arrival from the building security cameras."

This is getting interesting. At least the timing of things is becoming clear. I make a mental note to ask for all of the security tapes. "Assuming your phone records are right," I say, "I'll grant you that a call may have been placed from Joel's phone. But it doesn't show he made the call. Even if he did, he was undoubtedly calling to ask her to come to the office to help with the closing." I'm kind of enjoying the cat-and-mouse aspect of this. It's been a while.

He smiles confidently. "That's where you're wrong. We know exactly what he said to her in that telephone conversation. And it wasn't anything close to the way you described it."

"How's that, Skipper? Are you listening in on Joel's calls? Or did you bug his phone?"

"You see, the entire conversation was taped on Diana's answering machine."

Uh-oh.

The condescending smirk. "We got this yesterday. She must have been asleep and didn't pick up her phone until the answering machine started taping. She didn't erase the message when she left."

I'm getting a bad feeling about this.

McNulty stands up. "While we're being so open about our evidence, let me play something for you." He walks over to Skipper's desk, takes out a small cassette player and presses the start button.

Beep. "*Wednesday. December thirty-first. Twelve-fifty-one* A.M." *Beep.*

"*Pick up, Diana. God dammit.*"

"*Hello?*"

"*Diana, it's Joel. I was talking to Bob. We need you to come down here right away. We've got a bunch of things to go over for the closing. We really need you to get your ass down here right now.*"

"*Joel? What time is it?*"

"*About ten to one.*"

"*I'm exhausted. Can't it wait until morning?*"

"*No. It can't wait. I've got to see you now.*"

"*I don't want to deal with this right now.*"

"*You have to. I need to see you right now. Bob wants to*

resolve this stuff right now. ASAP. So get your tight little ass over here right away."

"Fuck you. You're a piece of shit."

"Fuck you too, you little tramp. If you're going to treat me like shit, I'll treat you like shit. Now get your ass over here or I'll come over there and get you myself."

"All right, asshole. I'll be right over. But this is the last time. We're finished. You understand? You can find another lackey to push around."

"I wouldn't have it any other way, you bitch."

Beep.

Skipper is triumphant. "Sounds to me like they were talking about a lot more than business."

I strain to sound incredulous. "That's it? That's what this is all about? A late-night telephone call where he tells her to come back to work? From that you get murder? You're dreaming. This isn't an old episode of *L.A. Law*, you know."

Out of the corner of my eye, I think I can see McNulty nod, but I'm not sure.

Skipper becomes more strident. "No," he says, "that's not it. Let me play something else for you." He fusses with the cassette player until he becomes frustrated and McNulty steps in and pushes the right button. I recognize the sound of our voice-mail prompts.

"Bob, Joel. I just found out about the new policy on partner elections. I came by your office, but you were with Vince. I want to tell you something. I think this whole thing stinks. You could have told me. You should have told me, but, as usual, you didn't have the balls. I'll get you for this, you little prick. I'm not gonna take this shit lying down. Call me right away."

I try to look skeptical. "I suppose you're going to say this represents a threat?"

"Damn right," Skipper snaps. "It speaks for itself."

I turn to McNulty. "Bill, you know there's no way this will ever add up to a conviction."

McNulty gives Skipper an inquisitive look. Skipper nods. "What?" I ask.

McNulty turns to me. "There's something else. It seems that your boy was having an affair with Diana Kennedy. We have a witness who is prepared to testify he saw the two of them in the same room at your last firm retreat. Let's just say that she wasn't fully clothed."

"No way."

"Yes way," Skipper says. "And that's what ties it all together. Kennedy was sleeping with Friedman. She pulled the plug on him and told him she was sleeping with Holmes. That's what led to the fight at Harrington's. He came back and confronted Holmes. That's what led to the phone call to her home."

"You're dreaming. Joel wasn't sleeping with her. You can't prove it."

McNulty speaks up. "Yes we can. We've got a witness. There's only one other living person who can rebut his testimony."

"And that would be Joel."

"And that would be correct."

"And who is this honest soul who will step forward and swear my client is an adulterer?"

McNulty stops. "I can't tell you."

"You mean you won't tell me."

"All right. I won't tell you. Not now, at least. Not until I have to."

I turn to Skipper. "Are you prepared to tell me?"

"No. We're only obligated to give you evidence that would exculpate your client. All the evidence we've given you so far points directly toward a conviction."

The key witness has to be an attorney at S&G. I have no idea who it is, but I will find out. "Skipper," I say, "you've got some shaky circumstantial stuff here, but nothing close to a case."

McNulty looks at me. "There's one more thing."

At this point, I'm wondering how many more things. I'm prepared for almost anything.

"She was pregnant."

Shit.

"And before you ask, we don't know who the father is. But we'll find out."

This is going to get messy. "Look," I say, "there's a lot of hard evidence this was a suicide, pure and simple. He shot himself with his own gun. He left a suicide note. Before you embarrass yourself on Monday, don't you think you ought to wait for the coroner's report?"

Skipper looks amused. "We got a preview. The cause of Bob's death will be a gunshot wound. But there is evidence that somebody hit him on the head before the shots were fired."

"In other words," I say, "you're saying somebody tried to make it look like a suicide?"

"Right."

"What about the suicide note, the E-mail?"

"Joel's fingerprints are on Bob's keyboard."

What? How the hell did Joel's fingerprints get on Bob's keyboard? "So? He could have used Bob's keyboard any-time. It still doesn't show he typed the E-mail."

Skipper takes a drink of his Perrier. "Look, Mike, it's against my better judgment," he says, "and Bill is going to kill me for saying it, but I'm prepared to discuss a plea bargain."

"What?"

"You heard me. I'm prepared to discuss a plea bargain. I'll go down to second-degree and recommend a lenient sentence if he admits to it."

Second-degree means at least fifteen years in jail. "Bull-shit. You've got no case."

"You're wrong. We do have a case. I'm going to try it myself."

"You're crazy."

Skipper's eyes gleam. "Tell him we're going to charge him with first-degree murder. We're considering special circumstances. If he's willing to save the taxpayers the cost of a trial, we'll agree to a plea of second-degree with a recommendation of fifteen years. We'll take the death penalty off the table. Our offer is open until the arraignment on Monday. You have an ethical obligation to convey it to your client."

"I won't recommend it. Not in a million years."

"I know you're a little rusty. Bill is my right hand on this case. He hasn't had a chance to study the file in detail, but he's damn sure we've got a strong case. A very strong case. Right, Bill?"

McNulty nods. I can't tell if he's sincere or just trying to appease his boss.

I turn to McNulty. "You're thinking about going for the death penalty in a circumstantial case in San Francisco? Have you lost your mind?"

He doesn't answer.

I leave.

13
"I HAVE TO CONSIDER
WHAT'S BEST FOR MY SON"

"Joel Mark Friedman will be arraigned on Monday for the alleged double murder of two colleagues. District Attorney Prentice Gates says he may seek the death penalty. In an unusual twist, Gates says he will try the case himself."

—KCBS NEWS RADIO. SATURDAY, JANUARY 10.

At three-thirty the same day, I'm at the pay phone in the lobby of the Hall. "Hello, Rabbi Friedman," I say.

He gets right down to business. "How are things going with Joel's case?" he asks.

"As well as can be expected." I describe my meetings with Joel and Skipper, judiciously leaving out any references to Joel's alleged infidelities or Skipper's plea bargain proposal. "It looks like they're going to charge Joel with murder on Monday."

Silence.

"We're doing everything we can. It's going to take some time."

He clears his throat. "That's what I wanted to talk to you about. I was talking to a couple of my congregants after services last night. A number of lawyers are members of the temple."

"I know." Probably half your board of directors.

"This is difficult, so forgive me for being blunt. A couple of members of my congregation whose judgment I respect suggested you may not be the right person to handle this case for my son."

It feels like a piece of sharp glass going straight through my stomach. Thankfully, he can't see my grimace. "Excuse me, but why did they say that?"

He's choosing his words carefully. "One of my congregants said you haven't spent a lot of time in court the last few years. He said you may be a little rusty after your tenure at the Simpson firm."

He's right, of course. "I defended over a hundred murder trials when I was at the PD's office. I've been defending white-collar criminals at the Simpson firm for the last five years. I'm completely current on the law." I'm trying not to sound too defensive.

He gathers his thoughts. "Another attorney suggested that you may have been something of a renegade at the public defender's office."

It's true. My bosses thought I took too many cases to trial. That's bad for business in the PD's office. The supervisors are paid for disposing of cases quickly, not necessarily winning them. "I took a lot of cases to trial when I was at the PD's office. That's what PDs get paid for. I won some cases others would have lost. I won some cases others would have pled out." And, in fairness, I probably lost a few that could have been pled out. "That's what you want from a defense lawyer. You want somebody who will go to bat for your client."

Silence. "I have to consider what's best for my son. I'll talk to him about it."

"I understand your concerns. This is a very important decision. It's up to Joel. If he wants to hire another lawyer, I'll be disappointed, but I'll understand." And Rosie will kill me.

He pauses. "Maybe there's an alternative. How would you feel about having another lawyer assist you?"

"What do you have in mind?" I ask slowly.

"I thought that maybe one of the lawyers from my congregation could help you. I know you don't have a lot of lawyers in your new firm."

This is delicate. "I'm always happy to have help. I figured Rosie would sit second chair. We were a great team at the PD's office."

"I see."

"We criminal defense lawyers get a little protective about our territory. I'd be happy to consider having someone else involved, but only with the understanding that I'd make the final decisions."

Silence. "I understand." He clears his throat. "Michael, let me discuss it with Joel."

Joel is less than enthusiastic about the possibility of a plea bargain when I explain Skipper's proposal to him at five o'clock the same day. "Plead guilty to second-degree murder? You've got to be fucking kidding me. No way. No fucking way. Tell Skipper to go fuck himself."

"I didn't say you should take it. I just said that they offered it, and I have an obligation to tell you about it. I'm not recommending it to you."

He regains his composure. "Fine. I'm instructing you to reject the plea bargain."

"Good."

"What did you find out from Skipper?"

This isn't going to be easy. I tell him about the phone calls, the bartender at Harrington's and the phone messages to Diana and Bob.

"Doesn't mean anything," he says. "It shows we were working on a deal. Nothing else."

"I agree with you." I watch him carefully. "There's something else. Diana was pregnant."

He looks down. "I know," he says quietly.

"Come again?"

"I know she was pregnant."

"How did you know?"

"How do you think I knew? She told me."

"When?"

"About three weeks ago."

"Did you tell anyone?"

"Of course not. She asked me not to tell anyone." He looks me in the eye. "When people tell me something in confidence, I don't repeat it. Do you know how many people have told me they're looking for a new job? I listen to them. And I keep my mouth shut. I didn't ask to be the father confessor for the entire firm. It just seems to have worked out that way."

I look right at him. "Joel," I say quietly, "you know I've got to ask."

"The answer is no, I'm not the father. Unless, of course there was some sort of immaculate conception. You Catholics are big on that stuff. We don't buy into it."

I look at the ceiling. This isn't going to get any easier. "There's more," I say.

"What else? Yesterday, I was just a garden-variety killer. Today I'm also an adulterer. Tomorrow, I'll be a sex offender and a child molester, too."

"They have a witness who saw you and Diana together in your room at Silverado at the firm retreat last year. He says she didn't have any clothes on."

"Patton," he murmurs. "He saw Diana in my room." He goes on, "There was a party in Patton's room. Art was drunk. He tried to put the moves on Diana. She blew him off. She went back to her room. He followed her. Depending on who's telling the story, either he asked her nicely to sleep with him, or he attacked her. At about two in the morning, there was banging on my door. Diana came rushing in. She said Patton tried to rape her. Two minutes later, he showed up. He said he heard some noise. He saw Diana."

"He set you up."

"Yeah. If Diana pursued it, Art could say she was in my room with me. He was protecting himself. And he was protecting the firm from a sexual-harassment suit."

Great. "Can anybody else corroborate any of this?"

"Probably not."

"Diana never pursued it?"

"There was an investigation. As far as I know, she didn't push it. She didn't want to torpedo her career."

"You think Patton is the father?"

"I don't know. It could've been Patton. It could've been Bob. Hell, it could've been anybody."

This is serious. The only person who can contradict Patton's account of the events of that night is Joel. And he isn't going up on the stand unless we're desperate. "Does Naomi know about this?"

"No," he says quietly. "And she doesn't need to know."

"It's going to come up," I tell him. "I'd rather she heard it from you."

"I'll talk to her."

I hope so.

"What else did you find out from Skipper?" he asks.

"They think Bob was sleeping with Diana."

"I've heard that one many times."

"And they seem to think you were, too."

"Great. Only two people know the truth—Diana and me. Diana is dead. That leaves me. And I presume you don't want me to testify."

"That's right."

"So I'm fucked."

Reality is at hand. "It doesn't look like we'll be able to get the charges dropped on Monday."

"What's the prognosis on bail?"

"Not great. If Skipper charges you with first-degree, bail will be tough, but not unheard of. If he goes for special circumstances, bail's out."

He turns white. My bedside manner lacked finesse. "The death penalty," he whispers.

"We have to be prepared for it. Skipper was talking about it. He may not decide until after the arraignment."

"Dammit."

I pause to let him get his bearings. "One other thing. I talked to your father. Seems he's gotten a few suggestions that I may need a little help on this case."

"Do you?"

"Yeah. I thought I'd handle it with Rosie. We were a good team at the PD's office." I explain that murder trials in California are divided into two phases. The first involves a determination of guilt or innocence. If there's a guilty verdict, the trial moves to the so-called penalty phase, where the jury decides whether to impose the death penalty. It's customary for the penalty phase to be handled by a different attorney, so the jury gets to see a new face. In addition, when all else fails, the penalty-phase attorney argues that the trial attorney was incompetent. If the trial attorney handles the penalty phase, the trial attorney may be put in the uncomfortable position of having to argue that he screwed up. The penalty-phase attorney is known as Keenan counsel. I tell him I'll handle the trial phase and Rosie will be Keenan counsel.

He stops to ponder for a moment, then he says, "I want to think about it. I know you and Rosie are good. I want to be sure you have enough firepower. My dad's pretty well-connected."

"I know."

"I'll let you know in the next day or so."

"He wants to hire another lawyer as co-counsel?" Rosie is slicing pizza in her small kitchen later the same evening. Grace is watching TV in the living room.

"Yeah. I'm beginning to see why Joel needed some space from his dad."

"He's worried, Mike."

"I know."

"You're going to need some help on this. Probably lots of help."

"I know that, too."

"What did you have in mind?"

"I figured I'd take the lead and use Pete as the primary investigator."

"Keep it in the family. I like that."

"He's good, Rosie."

"I know. What about Keenan counsel?"

"I took the liberty of recommending you. I hope it was okay. Joel deserves the best."

"I thought you'd never ask." She smiles. "One question. Do I have to marry you again?"

"Nope. No more mixing business and pleasure."

"It's a deal."

"Great. I'll check with Joel." I pause. "And his father, I suppose."

"So I gather."

"One other thing—I get to make all the final decisions in the trial phase."

"Of course."

Joel's lucky. He's just hired the best defense team from the San Francisco PD's office in the last twenty years. Of course, he's also hired two people who reenacted the War of the Roses only five short years ago. We're a mixed bag. And the arraignment is in just two days.

14

"NOTHING EVER HAPPENS
AT AN ARRAIGNMENT"

"Plea bargaining isn't just a part of the criminal-justice system—it IS the system."

—CRIMINAL DEFENSE ATTORNEY AND ADJUNCT PROFESSOR OF LAW
MORTON R. GOLDBERG. CONTINUING LEGAL EDUCATION SEMINAR.
MARCH 30, 1982.

Two days later. Monday, January 12. The television coverage for every arraignment begins essentially the same way. First, there's footage of an unshaven, handcuffed, jumpsuit-clad defendant being led into court looking guilty as hell. Next they show a clip of a grim-looking prosecutor (almost always a middle-aged white male) marching into court with his minions, uttering platitudes about the strength of his case and his faith in the criminal-justice system. Finally, the scene shifts to the front steps of the courthouse, where a smarmy-looking defense attorney boldly proclaims his client's innocence and castigates the DA for bringing trumped-up charges against a pillar of the community.

At nine-thirty in the morning, the smarmy-looking defense attorney standing in the drizzle on the front steps of the Hall of Justice is me.

I don't particularly care for this sideshow. I'd just as soon avoid becoming a media star. On the other hand, in our TV culture, you try to make points whenever you can with what we attorneys like to call the potential-juror pool.

An army of reporters and cameramen fight for space. It's a great day for the hair-spray industry. With Naomi standing to my left and Rosie to my right, I look directly into the cameras and say, "Ladies and gentlemen, we are shocked and dismayed Mr. Gates has chosen to proceed with these unsubstantiated charges. We are certain Mr. Friedman will be fully exonerated."

We push our way through the throng of shouting reporters.

"Mr. Daley, is it true your client has been offered a plea bargain?"

"Mr. Daley, is it true your client is going to plead guilty?"

"Mr. Daley, is it true your client tried to commit suicide last night?"

"Mr. Daley, is it true your client was having an affair with Diana Kennedy?"

"Mr. Daley? Mr. Daley? Mr. Daley?"

I run interference for Naomi and Rosie elbows Rita Roberts and her Channel 4 microphone.

"Is it always going to be like this?" Naomi asks.

"Probably for a while," I reply.

We head toward the elevators. I turn to Naomi. "Rosie will take you to the courtroom. I'm going to see Joel."

"Can I talk to you about something for a minute, Mike?" Joel and I are sitting in the holding area just behind the courtroom a few minutes before the arraignment is supposed to start.

I don't want any surprises today. "Of course, Joel." It's

not like either of us is going anywhere with two sheriff's deputies standing just outside the door.

"I was talking to my dad," he says. My ears begin to buzz. "He thinks it might be a good idea if we get you some help."

I knew this was coming. "As I told you on Saturday, I was figuring I'd take the lead and Rosie would sit second chair. Pete will be our lead investigator." I add halfheartedly, "Of course, we'll do it however you'd like."

He rubs his chin. "You know Mort Goldberg? He's the president of the temple."

Oy. Mort Goldberg. Mort the Sport. Smart. Shrewd. Well-connected in the Jewish community. In his day, he was one of the more successful criminal defense lawyers in town. He taught criminal procedure and evidence at Hastings for years. Unfortunately, his day ended about twenty years ago. These days, he spends most of his time cutting deals on drunk-driving cases.

"I've met him. He's been at it for years. Solid reputation." There's no point pissing on him.

"Dad and I thought Mort might be able to help. Do the research. Maybe take a few witnesses."

Look over my shoulder. Second-guess every decision I make. Sounds great. "Let me be honest. He's what we defense lawyers call a pleader. He's not a trial guy. He's a plea-bargain guy."

"Is he good at strategy?"

"Yes, but he's not a strong trial lawyer."

"That's why we have you, right?" He leans back in his chair. "I've given this a lot of thought. I want him involved. I thought he could help at the arraignment. He's waiting outside."

Jesus. "He's here?"

"Yeah. And he's available today."

"Joel, nothing ever happens at an arraignment. You plead not guilty and you sit down."

"I know, but I need to get bail. You have to get me out of here."

"The arraignment starts in five minutes. We can't start talking strategy now."

"I understand. Let me bring him in. I'll tell him he's just going to be an observer today."

"Fine." It's a done deal; what else can I say?

He motions to the deputies and they bring in Mort and Joel's father. Mort is a stocky sixty-three-year-old with a large, bald head and thick aviator-style glasses. A natural back-slapper, he shakes hands with Joel and greets me like we've been pals for years. Give him credit. He's an operator.

"Joel," he says, "don't worry about a thing. Mike and I will have you out of here by noon."

Rabbi Friedman beams. Temple board meetings must be a riot.

Mort turns to me. "Glad we'll finally have a chance to work together. I always admired your work at the PD's office. If I knew you were going to leave, I'd have asked you to work for me."

Smooth. Always start with flattery.

"We're due in court in about thirty seconds," I reply.

In California, criminal arraignments used to be handled in municipal court. In a court reorganization a few years ago, the muni courts were consolidated with the superior courts. As a result, arraignments are now conducted in superior court. Judge Samuel Levin is a dour bureaucrat who's in his late fifties. He's worked his way from traffic court down the hall to superior court in his twenty-some years on the bench. He spent the early part of his career defending insurance companies, which gave him tremendous skill in the art of expedience. He's not really a judge. He's more like a legal-system processor. Now semiretired, he doesn't sit through long trials anymore. He's found a home hearing motions and setting bail. He keeps the wheels of justice turning. We won't see him again after today. It's probably just as well.

The courtroom is packed. Reporters fill the jury box. The roar is deafening. Lawyers and police mill around. We aren't the only arraignment on the calendar this morning, but we're the biggest media event. We rise as Levin enters. The case is called. Skipper and I state our appearances.

Levin wastes no time. "Mr. Daley, does your client understand the charges?"

"Yes, Your Honor."

"May we dispense with a formal reading?"

"Yes, Your Honor."

He turns to Joel. "On the charge of murder in the first degree, how do you plead?"

I nod to Joel, who stands and says in a clear voice, "Not guilty, Your Honor."

Levin looks at me. "By statute, I am required to set a preliminary hearing within sixty days." The preliminary hearing is also held in superior court. At the prelim, the prosecution must show that there is "probable cause" to believe Joel committed a crime. Joel can accelerate the process by demanding that the prelim be held within ten days. Most defendants choose to "waive time," which means they give up their right to require the prelim within ten days. Ordinarily, the defense loses little by waiving time, because it gives them additional time to prepare or, in many cases, cut a deal with the DA.

"Mr. Friedman," I say, "chooses not to waive time."

Levin looks at me over the top of his reading glasses. His face turns somewhat more dour than usual. "May I ask why you believe it would be in your client's best interest to proceed so quickly?"

"My client's life has been severely and needlessly interrupted by these outrageous charges. We are prepared to proceed with his defense as soon as possible so that we may clear his name."

He grimaces. He's about to punt this matter to another judge, anyway. Then, after the prelim, we'll move to the slightly more grand surroundings in one of the trial courts upstairs. Levin looks at his calendar. He consults with his clerk. They have a somewhat heated discussion for a few moments. "The preliminary hearing will be one week from tomorrow in Judge Kenneth Brown's courtroom." Brown is a former prosecutor. Not a great draw for our side. Levin turns to Skipper. "Mr. Gates, I trust you're prepared to move forward next week?"

"Let me check my calendar, Your Honor," he replies.

"Mr. Gates," he snaps, "you are supposed to check your calendar before you enter my courtroom. I will assume you'll be there." He turns to me. "Mr. Daley, are you prepared to proceed?"

"Yes, Your Honor."

"See you next week." He raises his gavel and starts to stand.

"Your Honor," I say, "we would like to discuss bail."

He shuffles his papers. "Do I understand, Mr. Daley, that no bail has been set in this case?"

"That's correct, Your Honor. We request that bail be set for Mr. Friedman. He is a respected member of the community and he is hardly a flight risk."

Skipper is up like a shot. "Your Honor, the people oppose bail. The defendant is charged with first-degree murder. We may ask for special circumstances. He is dangerous and bail should not be granted."

Levin's jowls wiggle as he looks first at Skipper and then at me. "Your Honor," I say, "Mr. Friedman is an attorney with one of the most respected law firms in the city. He has lived here his entire life and has significant community and family ties. He is clearly entitled to bail."

"Your Honor," Skipper says, "we are considering special circumstances. It would be highly unusual for bail to be set in a capital case. Highly unusual."

Levin looks at his bench book. He hasn't had a capital case in front of him in some time.

"With all due respect, Your Honor," I say, "the state has not added special circumstances. As a result, at this point, this is not a capital case. The judge has discretion to set bail in this case."

Levin continues to flip through the penal code. Without looking up, he says, "Mr. Daley, let me give you some advice. I realize you haven't been in my courtroom in a while. When I hear the words 'With all due respect, Your Honor,' I interpret them to mean, 'You doddering old fool, Your Honor.' Now, let's try to come up with some authority on this subject, okay?"

Touchy, aren't we? Before I can respond, for some inexplicable reason, Skipper starts talking. He's prepared a speech and he's going to make it. "Your Honor," he says, "the defendant is, in fact, a flight risk. The weekend before he was arrested, he and his wife left town."

"One moment, Your Honor," I say. I turn to Joel. He whispers that he and Naomi did, in fact, drive up to Mendocino the weekend before he was arrested. He says they needed time to talk. "Your Honor," I say, "Mr. Friedman and his wife took a drive up the coast for a day. That hardly constitutes flight. He wasn't a suspect at the time."

Levin isn't listening. He looks at Skipper. "Mr. Gates, isn't there some statutory authority?"

Skipper shrugs and turns to McNulty, who stands and says, "Your Honor, Section twelve-seventy-five point five of the penal code says 'a defendant charged with a capital offense punishable by death cannot be admitted to bail when the proof of his guilt is evident or the presumption of guilt is great.' " McNulty recites the code section from memory. Impressive.

Levin looks pleased and he nods. "That's it. I knew there was something on this."

"But, Your Honor," I say, "this is not a capital offense." At least not yet. "The proof of guilt is not evident and the presumption of guilt is not great in this case." I can recite penal code sections, too.

He looks skeptical. "Mr. Daley," he says, "we can argue all day about whether the proof is evident and the presumption is great. I'm not going to take the court's time for that."

I see what's coming. "Your Honor," I begin.

He cuts me off. "Mr. Daley, the law is clear. The proof is evident enough for me."

And you have an early tee-off time. He's about to pound his gavel when I hear a distinctive nasal voice from behind me. "Your Honor, may it please the court."

What the hell? Mort is walking through the gate into the well of the courtroom. Levin smiles. "Why, Mor—Mr. Goldberg," says Levin, "we haven't seen you in this court in some time."

"Thank you, Your Honor. It's nice to see you." This is a truly touching reunion. I'm waiting for Mort to ask Levin about his grandchildren.

"Your Honor," I interrupt, "may I have a moment with Mr. Goldberg?"

Levin casts a stern glance at me. "You've got one minute, Mr. Daley."

I pull Mort aside. I whisper, "What the hell are you doing? He was just about to rule."

"He was about to rule against you. I think I can help."

"I don't think it's a good idea."

"I know this guy. We go to the same temple. Besides, you got any better ideas?"

I pause. He's probably right. "You think you can pull a rabbit out?"

"Watch me." He turns back to the judge. "Your Honor, I have just been retained as special counsel to Mr. Friedman. I must confess I haven't read the entire file yet."

And I'm reasonably sure you never will.

"Rather than ask you for a continuance," he says, "I have a suggestion as to how the bail issue might be resolved."

Levin looks at me. I look at Joel. Joel looks at his father. "Any objections?" Levin asks.

"Uh, no, Your Honor. I will defer to my colleague, Mr. Goldberg." God help us.

Levin looks interested. "Go on, Mor—I mean, Mr. Goldberg."

"Your Honor," Mort begins, "I understand your concern about bail. The charges are serious."

Skipper is speechless. McNulty stares straight ahead.

"Nevertheless, Your Honor," Mort continues, "I have a creative solution that will ease your concern. I know Your Honor is acquainted with Mr. Friedman's father, Rabbi Neil Friedman, of Temple Beth Sholom."

"Yes," says Levin.

"I would propose, subject to your approval, of course, that bail be set for Mr. Friedman, subject to his agreement to remain at all times in the house of Rabbi Friedman, except when he has to be in court. And we would, of course, expect Your Honor to require a fairly substantial bail."

Levin scowls. He looks at Rabbi Friedman in the gallery. He addresses him directly. "Rabbi, is this acceptable to you?"

"Yes, Your Honor."

Skipper leaps up. "This is highly unusual. The people respect Rabbi Friedman, but it's highly unusual for a defendant to be placed in the custody of his own father. Highly unusual."

You're right, Skipper. It's highly unusual.

Levin ponders. He turns to me. "Is this arrangement acceptable to you, Mr. Daley?"

No. I'd rather let Joel stay with his cellmate the pimp. I glance at Joel. "It's acceptable to us, Your Honor."

"Well, it's highly unusual. On the other hand, this court greatly respects Rabbi Friedman. Bail is set at a million dollars. The defendant will be released to the custody of Rabbi Friedman. He is to remain at Rabbi Friedman's house except to appear in court. He may have visits from his attorneys and immediate family only. That's it. We're adjourned."

Levin pounds his gavel. Joel turns to me. "Am I out?"

"Yeah. We need to post bail. And you have to stay at your dad's house."

"It's better than the place I've stayed the last few nights."

Mort taps me on the shoulder. "So, what did you think of that one?"

"Pretty smooth."

"It helps when the judge is on the board of directors at the temple." Mort walks toward Rabbi Friedman. I hear him say he's willing to have the temple building pledged as collateral for Joel's bond.

I glance at Rosie. She's pleased. As we walk out, she whispers, "Do you think we can find a trial judge who's on the temple board of directors, too?"

15

THE DREAM TEAM

"Hiring Mort Goldberg was brilliant. They should put him in charge."

—NewsCenter 4 legal analyst Morgan Henderson.
Tuesday, January 13.

"It's nice to see the TV stations have been able to rehire their legal analysts from the O.J. trial to give us some helpful suggestions." I'm eating a bagel and talking to Joel as we sit in the heavy wooden chairs in his father's dining room at nine o'clock the next morning. Mort nibbles on a sweet roll. Rosie sips a Diet Coke. I don't know how she can drink soda this early. Pete stands next to Mort. He hates meetings.

I look around the table. It's a tough crowd. Mort is a first-rate prima donna. Rosie runs her own cases. Pete works solo. Rabbi Friedman is used to having everybody listen to him. Joel makes all the important calls on his deals. Not exactly a roomful of team players.

Showtime. "Let's get started," I say. "I'd like to welcome the Dream Team. We have only a week until the preliminary hearing and we have a lot of work to do."

Rosie grins. "Which one are you, Mike? Cochran or

Shapiro? Does that make Skipper Marcia Clark? He'd look good in a dress."

"Enough of that," Rabbi Friedman snaps. We turn toward him. He lowers his voice. "I'd like to thank Mort for his contribution at the arraignment yesterday."

Silence. Mort smiles uncomfortably and waves his unlit cigar. "It was nothing," he says.

All eyes turn toward me. I hand out copies of the first police reports. "I want you to study these. We should have the coroner's report later today." I summarize the evidence. The fingerprints on the gun and the computer keyboard. The taped phone messages. The fight at Harrington's. The argument in Bob's office. The allegations of an affair. Diana's pregnancy.

Rabbi Friedman cringes.

"Our mission is simple," I say. "If we're going to get the charges dropped at the prelim, we have to get a lot of information in a hurry. They have a week to show they have enough evidence to hold Joel over for trial. We have a week to show they don't.

"I want to find out as much as we can about Bob and Diana. We need to find their friends and relatives. We need to talk to the people at S and G. We have to get a copy of Bob's will and look at his investments. He probably had life insurance."

I turn to Mort. "I'd like your help with legal issues, motions and strategy. We should try to get our hands on every piece of evidence before the prelim."

Mort is pleased. "I guess that makes me Alan Dershowitz."

Rabbi Friedman rolls his eyes. "For better or for worse."

Pete looks at me. It's like looking in a mirror. He's a little shorter, stockier than I am, and he has a neatly trimmed mustache. His hair is darker. Otherwise, we could be twins. "Where do you want me to start?" he asks.

"I want you to look at the physical evidence and the forensics. I want you to look for holes in the police report and the coroner's report." It's nice to have an ex-cop on the team. "And I want you to figure out what happened to Vince Russo." I pause. "And, I have something special planned for you. I need you to figure out who was sleeping with whom—and when."

The corners of Pete's mouth turn up slightly. "Sounds like it's right up my alley."

"I want you to look into Bob's personal life. I want you to see what Bob's widow is up to. And there are some other people I'd like you to watch. They're pretty high up in San Francisco society, so you'll have to be discreet. I want you to tail Arthur Patton."

"I like it. What do you want me to look for?"

"The usual. He's in the middle of an ugly divorce. See if he's shtupping anybody. Evidently, he's had some problems keeping his pants on. And he may have sexually harassed Diana Kennedy."

Mort interrupts. "Pete," he says, "if you need some help, I have the name of a couple of PIs that I've used over the years. They're very good."

Pete looks at me. "Mort," I say, "Pete has his own people. He'll be all right."

"Look," Mort says, "I wasn't suggesting that Pete isn't up to it. I was just trying to help."

Before I can answer, Pete stares him down and says, "If I need help, I'll let you know."

Mort shrugs at Rabbi Friedman.

Joel asks, "What can I do?"

"I want you to make a list of everything you saw and everyone who was there."

"I'm on it. I'll have it for you right away."

"One other thing. I want you to get on your laptop and start looking at the corporate filings in every state you think

Vince Russo had business. Maybe we can find him, if he's still alive. Or maybe we can figure out what happened to him."

"Do we need to worry about the attorney-client privilege for Russo?"

It's a legitimate legal point. He's not supposed to divulge the deep dark secrets of his client. The correct legal answer, therefore, is yes. The practical answer, of course, is no. I'll take anything that may help us. "I don't want you to do anything illegal. On the other hand, try to get everything you can. Russo isn't doing you any favors."

"The prelim is before Judge Brown," Mort says. "He's a law school classmate of mine. Kenny and I play cards together at the Concordia Club. It seems to me that it may make sense for me to take a leading role."

Silence. I look around the room. Rabbi Friedman is nodding.

"Mort," I say slowly, "I appreciated your efforts at the arraignment yesterday. But I'm the person most familiar with the evidence. I'll take the lead in the prelim."

Rabbi Friedman frowns. Mort looks at his unlit cigar. "It was just a suggestion."

I glance at Rosie. Then I turn to Mort. "Let's get one thing straight here, Mort. I'll make the final calls on strategy. Do you understand?"

"Yes, I do," he says quietly.

I dart a glance at Rabbi Friedman. I look at Mort. "Listen," I say, "it may make sense for you to argue some of the prehearing motions. Think you're up to it?"

"Sure, Mike. You're the boss."

"Let's get to work," I say.

I'm driving Mort toward downtown on Bush Street in the pouring rain later the same morning. "Do you think we can get this knocked out at the prelim?" he asks.

"It's going to be tough."

He looks at the raindrops hitting my windshield. "So the girl was pregnant."

So much for political correctness. "Yeah."

"You know who the father is?" For all his idiosyncracies, at least he doesn't pull punches.

"Not yet."

"You thinking what I'm thinking?"

"Depends. What are you thinking?"

"If Joel is the father, we're fucked. We'll know in a few weeks. He told the cops he never slept with her. If it turns out he's the father, he lied to us and he lied to the cops. The jury will nail him."

He may be a pleader, but he has good instincts. He cuts right to it.

"Just between us," he continues, "what do you think the chances are that he did it? You know—jealous rage. You've seen it a thousand times."

"NFL, Mort. Not fucking likely. He's just not the type."

"How well do you know him?"

"Very well."

"Well, hypothetically, let's suppose he's not quite the Boy Scout you think he is. You suppose it might be a good idea to see what our new DA has up his sleeve?"

His true colors are coming out. "You can't seriously be thinking about a plea," I say. "It's way too early. We've had the case for just a few days."

"I know how these guys think. New DA. First big case. Doesn't want to fuck up. Doesn't know what he's doing. That's why McNasty's there to hold his hand. If he can get a guilty plea, he's golden. It's instant political capital. He can say he caught the bad guy and saved the city a ton of money in trial costs. In a few weeks, nobody will remember the plea. They'll just remember the case was solved."

You lazy sack of shit. "I respect your instincts, Mort, but

you're way off the mark. I know this guy. He didn't do it. We're going to get this thing knocked out. Or we're going to beat them at trial."

He gives me a knowing grin. "I figured you'd say that. I'm not saying he did it. I'm just saying we should look at all our options. I've been doing this for a long time. There are good times and bad times to talk to the DA. For what it's worth, I think now is a good time."

I can't tell if he's exercising cautious judgment or if he's a tired old man who's lost his nerve. "It's too soon to talk about a plea, Mort," I say again.

"Whatever you say," he replies. "Would it change your thinking if I told you things haven't always been so great between Joel and Naomi?"

Huh? "What are you talking about?"

"You know I'm tight with Joel's dad. Joel and Naomi have had some problems."

"What kind of problems?"

"She had postpartum depression after the kids were born. She's still going through it."

"Their kids are six years old. Nobody has postpartum for six years."

The rain pounds my windshield. "Well, she did. They spent about thirty thousand bucks last year on shrinks. That's one of the reasons Joel wanted to make partner—he needs the money."

I pause to let this sink in. "Rabbi Friedman told you this?"

"Yeah. In fact, a few years ago, he asked me to recommend a doctor for her."

I watch my windshield wipers swish back and forth as I stop at the corner of Bush and Montgomery to let him out. "What are you saying?"

"I wouldn't rule out the possibility that Joel may have had some extramarital relations."

Bullshit. No way. "What makes you think so?"

"It's like President Clinton. Sometimes, a guy's just got to have it. And I'll bet you anything for the last six years she hasn't been giving it to him very often."

The gospel according to the great philosopher, Mort Goldberg.

"What would you suggest?" I snap. I'm trying to remain calm.

"I think we ought to feel out the DA." He opens the door.

"We aren't going to consider a plea until we investigate."

He reaches for his umbrella. "You're the boss. But, if we don't get somebody else to confess by Tuesday, they've got enough to bump this case over for trial."

There's a visitor sitting in my office when I get back at eleven o'clock. "Hi, Mike." Naomi looks embarrassed. "I know I should have made an appointment." She's wearing jeans and a plain white cotton blouse, no makeup. Her eyes look sad.

"You can come see me anytime." I offer her a drink. She asks for a glass of water.

She smiles uncomfortably. "I wanted to talk to you for a few minutes."

"Sure." I don't know why she's here. I figure I'll start slowly. "How are the kids?"

"They're okay, all things considered. It was difficult at school yesterday, but they're more resilient than we think. In some respects, they're more resilient than the grown-ups."

"That's for sure." I look at her closely. Her voice is tentative. "How are you holding up?"

She closes her eyes and slowly opens them. "Fair," she says.

"Understandable." I collect my thoughts. "Naomi, why did you come to see me?"

She looks at her fingernails. "I wanted to see if there's anything I can do to help."

"There is. I need you to take care of the kids. And yourself. And I need you to support Joel. The next few months may not be easy."

"I figured that much already. I'm not sure I'm up to it."

"You are. You're tougher than you think."

"I hope so."

I look directly into the eyes of this decent young woman whose life has been turned upside down through no fault of her own. "Why did you really come here, Naomi?"

Her lips form a tight, thin line across her face. "There are a few things I think you should know." She pauses. "Joel doesn't know I'm here. Do you have to tell him I came to see you?"

"Not if you don't want me to." Actually, if she tells me something that will impact the case, I probably have a legal duty to tell Joel. We'll see. "What is it?"

She folds her hands. "This isn't easy to talk about."

"Take your time."

She takes a drink of water. "We've had some problems the last few years. Things haven't always been so good between us. And when you're the rabbi's son, you don't talk about your problems. You figure everybody at the temple will find out."

"I can relate. My dad was a cop. When other kids got in trouble, it wasn't a big deal. When I got sent home from school, word always seemed to get out that Officer Daley's son got in trouble."

The corners of her mouth turn up almost imperceptibly. "I've had some problems since the kids were born," she says.

"It's tough with little kids. And real tough with twins."

"I've been taking medication for depression, Mike. It started right after the boys were born. And it won't go away."

"A lot of people go through the same thing."

"I know. But I think it bothers Joel." She looks down. "I feel like I've pushed him away."

"The important thing is that you're getting better."

She sighs. "There's been a lot of talk about Joel and Diana. Joel and I don't have any secrets." She's starting to cry. I hand her a tissue. "Joel told me about the incident with Art Patton at Silverado. I don't care what they say. I believe my husband when he tells me he wasn't having an affair with Diana. I came here to tell you that no matter how it looks, and no matter what they say in the papers, my husband wasn't having an affair. I'm sure of it."

I give her a hug. "I believe you." I'm relieved he told her. I wasn't sure he would have.

She buries her head in my shoulder and sobs. A moment later, she lifts her tear-stained face and looks at me. She blurts out emphatically, "My husband isn't a killer, Mike."

"I know."

Later the same afternoon, Rolanda brings in a large manila envelope. It contains police reports and photos and the coroner's report.

I always start with the pictures. They put things into perspective. When you put aside the news reports and the lawyerly posturing, the pictures tell the essential story. Two people are dead. The pictures are about what I'd expect. Bob's partially destroyed head. Diana sitting near the door, eyes open, chest covered with blood. A .38-caliber revolver on Bob's desk.

The coroner's report is succinct. The time of death was somewhere between one and four A.M. Coroners always give themselves at least a three-hour range. Diana was killed by gunshots to her lung and heart. Bob died of a single bullet wound to the head. The wound had the outward appearance of being self-inflicted. Traces of gunpowder were found on his right hand. Powder marks and burns were found on his head at the entrance wound. There was an apparent concussive injury to his head just above the exit wound.

Based on what I've seen so far, Mort's probably right. Unless we get a confession from somebody else by Tuesday, this case is going to trial.

I flip through the police reports. It's all there. The fingerprints. The arguments. The tapes. The alleged threats. I'm about to pick up the phone when the last police report catches my eye. It's signed by Inspector Marcus Banks. It describes an interview with Joel at the Hall of Justice on January 8. It contains no new information, except for the last paragraph, which describes some questions Banks asked Joel. It then says, in capital letters, "SUSPECT CONFESSED TO THE MURDERS OF HOLMES AND KENNEDY."

16

"HOW STUPID DO YOU THINK I AM?"

> "It's an open-and-shut case. We will reveal evidence at the preliminary hearing on Tuesday that will undoubtedly cause Mr. Friedman to change his plea to guilty."
>
> —Skipper Gates. CNN's *Burden of Proof.*
> Wednesday, January 14.

"Of course I didn't confess. For the love of God, Mike, how stupid do you think I am?" I'm at Rabbi Friedman's house at nine the next morning, getting Joel's version of the Marcus Banks interview. I decide to give him the benefit of the doubt and treat his question as a rhetorical one.

"Tell me about your interview with Banks."

He's exasperated. "I already told you. I spent about four hours with Banks and Johnson at the Hall. I told them everything. They were interested in Diana's sex life. I told them I didn't know who she was sleeping with. They seemed to think she was sleeping with me. I straightened them out."

"So, where did Banks get the idea you confessed?"

"He made it up."

"Are you sure?"

"We went over the same stuff about ten times. I told them everything. They said I wasn't a suspect. If I thought I was a suspect, I would have called you. It was about eight at night. I thought we were finished. Johnson left the room for a few minutes. While he was gone, Banks asked me if I did it. I said no. He asked me again. I said no again. He asked me if I was absolutely sure. Finally, I asked him what he wanted me to say. He said he wanted me to say I did it. And I remember exactly what I said. I said, and I quote, the word 'right.' "

"You agreed with him?"

"Of course not. I was being sarcastic. And he knows it."

Joel's his own worst enemy. "He seems to have taken the word 'right' a step farther than you might have intended."

"Then he's full of shit."

"It's still a problem."

He frowns. "There's no way they can use it at trial, is there?"

"We'll get it thrown out before the trial. Did they read you your Miranda rights?"

"No. Nobody read me my rights until I was arrested."

"Good. We'll say you weren't properly Mirandized. We should be able to get it thrown out."

"That's not the point. He's lying. I didn't fucking confess."

"I understand. But it's his word against yours. He's going to testify that you confessed."

The crow's-feet around his eyes become more pronounced. "I'm completely fucked."

He's right. At least for the moment. "We'll try to get it knocked out."

At eleven o'clock the same morning, I'm in my office on the phone. I try my best source first. "Roosevelt," I say, "I got the police reports. Your partner seems to think my client confessed."

Silence at the other end. He clears his throat. "I just got a copy of his report. I didn't know."

I pause for effect. "How is it possible you didn't know? You were there."

"I wasn't there when he confessed," he says.

"Allegedly confessed, Roosevelt. We're going to get it knocked out. For one thing, he didn't confess and Marcus knows it. For another thing, he wasn't Mirandized. If you guys were going to question him, you should have read him his rights. Judge Brown will never let it in."

Silence. "I'll see what I can find out."

"I never would have figured this from you. I don't like being sandbagged."

"I'll see what I can find out," he repeats.

"Skipper, it's Mike Daley." I could leap through the phone.

"What's up?"

"I just got the police reports."

"So?"

"It seems Marcus Banks claims my client confessed."

"Really? Imagine that."

"Don't play games with me."

"What do you want me to say? That Marcus lied?"

"Yeah."

"Well, he didn't."

"Bullshit. We're going to the judge. We're going to get this alleged confession kicked out right away. He'll never let you use it."

"I'll see you at the prelim."

"Mort, I'm faxing the police report I told you about. I need you to prepare a motion to get this thing tossed out. I don't want it to see the light of day. I want it out before the prelim Tuesday."

"I'll take care of it." I can hear a chuckle in his voice. He lives for moments like this. "I talked to the judge's clerk. I told him we want to see the judge. He's available right before the prelim."

Mort may be useful after all.

The phone rings in my office later in the afternoon. "Mr. Daley," a familiar voice sings, "Rita Roberts, NewsCenter 4." I swear the name on her birth certificate is "Rita Roberts, NewsCenter 4."

"I'm a great admirer, Rita."

"Thank you. As you know, I'm covering the Friedman murder case."

I hadn't noticed. "Yes, Rita. I know."

"We've received a tip from a reliable source that Mr. Friedman confessed. Can you confirm this information?"

"Will you tell me who gave you the tip?"

"You know I can't."

"Sure you can. And if you want anything from me, you'll have to tell me who tipped you."

She stops. "I can't do that, Mr. Daley."

I stop to think. If I say there was no confession, I'll sound defensive. If I say no comment, it probably sounds worse. As Mort would say, either way I'm fucked. "For the record, Mr. Friedman did not confess. And if you run a story that suggests that he did, you will be embarrassed and I will bring legal action against your station."

"Come on, Mr. Daley. You don't really plan to sue us, do you?"

She's right, of course. "I know you'll do the right thing so it doesn't come to that."

Late that night, I run my fingers through Rosie's dark hair as she nuzzles my chest. Sex was always the best part of our marriage. We've come a long way since our first date when she said she wouldn't sleep with me until they took off my training wheels. Rosie taught me everything I know about sex. She was a good teacher. Before we started going out, I had dated only younger women. I had one long-term relationship with a woman in my law-school class. She dumped me as soon as she got a job offer from a Wall Street firm. By the time I started seeing Rosie, I had a lot of catching up to do. Nowadays, we have a workable arrangement. We have recreational sex every few weeks. It's not ideal, but it's easier and safer than the personals. Grace is staying at Rosie's mom's house tonight.

She purrs and I kiss the back of her neck. She opens her piercing, dark eyes and looks at me. "So," she says, "do you think he really confessed?"

"It's just like when we were married. Can't we forget about business for just a few minutes and focus on high-quality sex? We're consenting adults, after all."

She laughs. "Sorry, Mike. It's just the way I'm drawn."

I kiss her on the forehead. "That's why I'll always love you. Even if you drive me nuts."

"Are you going to answer my question?"

"Yes, Counselor. I don't think he confessed. Marcus lied or rearranged the facts."

"Good answer. Here's your reward." She kisses me softly on the mouth. As always, she has me eating out of her hand. "Let me ask you another question. After your little talk with Naomi yesterday, how solid do you think their marriage is?"

Interesting question. "Very solid. At least I think so." I pause and smile. "Maybe our marriage wasn't as screwed up as we thought." At least we never cheated on each other.

She kisses me again. "Now for the tough one. Do you think he was sleeping with Diana?"

In this little game, the prizes tend to get better as the questions get harder. I decide it's in my best interests to answer. "I don't think so. He would have told her." She gives me a cynical look and softly bites my left ear. "Then again," I say, "I don't know for sure."

17

THE CORONER AND
THE CRIMINALIST

"You have to be curious to be a coroner. Your patients can't
talk to you."
— SAN FRANCISCO CHIEF MEDICAL EXAMINER RODERICK BECKERT.
SAN FRANCISCO CHRONICLE. THURSDAY, JANUARY 15.

"Thank you for seeing me, Dr. Beckert. I know you're
busy." At eleven o'clock the next morning, I'm meeting with
Dr. Roderick Beckert, chief medical examiner of the city
and county of San Francisco, in his small office on the first
floor of the Hall. A stout sixty-two-year-old with a huge bald
head and black-framed glasses, he is the dean of big-city
coroners. And he knows it. And he'll tell you so. I wouldn't
dream of addressing him other than as Dr. Beckert. Then
again, he'd never call me Mike. He has been chief medical
examiner for almost thirty years. His textbook on autopsy
procedures for victims of violent crimes is a seminal work.
He is very good at what he does.

"Nice to see you again, Mr. Daley," he lies politely.

His neat office smells antiseptic. His bookshelves hold
meticulously arranged texts on anatomy and pathology.
There are carefully framed pictures of his wife, two grown

children and three grandchildren. A model of a skeleton smiles at me from the corner. I've always wondered what coroners talk about at the dinner table.

His glasses are perched on his furrowed brow. His thick lips frown through a brown-gray beard. He wears a paisley tie under his white lab coat. A tweed sports jacket hangs on a wooden coatrack in the corner. "How may I help you, Mr. Daley?" he asks. His voice is the perfect combination of authority and empathy, with a singsong lilt and hint of a New York accent that's particularly effective at trial. I'll bet the anatomy class he teaches at UCSF is terrific.

"Dr. Beckert," I say, "you know I'm representing Joel Friedman."

"Of course, Mr. Daley."

"I was hoping we might go through your autopsy reports on Robert Holmes and Diana Kennedy. Maybe you can help us figure out what happened."

He juts out his lower lip in a mock pout. "Mr. Daley, I already know exactly what happened. It's in my report." He adds, with little enthusiasm, "I'd be happy to discuss it with you." We eye each other. There is no malice in his tone. He knows I'm here to try to find holes in his report. I have a better chance at winning the lottery. "Where would you like to start?" he asks.

"Maybe you can explain how you figured out the time of death."

He flips through his report. It's an act. He's capable of reciting verbatim the contents of his reports from twenty years ago. "In both cases," he says, "I put the time of death between one and four in the morning."

"I've wondered how you figured that out," I say, trying to sound innocent. Actually, I already know. He knows I know. I still want to hear it from him. It's a free preview of his testimony.

"We look at a number of factors," he says. "First, we look

at body temperature, which drops by about one and a half degrees per hour after death. Second, we look at lividity. When you die, your blood pressure goes down to zero and your body begins to discolor. We can calculate the time of death based upon the amount of discoloration. We look at food in the victim's stomach. We see how far the digestive process has gone. We know Mr. Holmes and Ms. Kennedy each ate dinner around ten o'clock. There was undigested food in their stomachs. Mr. Holmes had crab cakes for dinner. Ms. Kennedy ate a little bit of a cheeseburger. Of course, we do a number of other tests."

I try to sound like an earnest high-school student. "And from this evidence, you concluded the time of death was between one and four in the morning?"

"Yes. We always give ourselves a three-hour window."

"Did you find any alcohol in their systems?"

"Yes. Mr. Holmes had a couple of glasses of wine with dinner. Ms. Kennedy had consumed a small amount of liquor late in the evening."

I'll bet he knows the type of salad dressing each of them had with dinner. "Perhaps we could look at the pictures."

"Very well."

We start with Diana. He shows me pictures of her naked body lying on the stainless-steel autopsy table. I've seen hundreds of similar photos. Still, I'm glad I didn't eat a big breakfast.

"Ms. Kennedy," he explains, "died within seconds. The first bullet pierced her right pulmonary artery and the lung parenchyma, causing a hemopneumothorax. In layman's terms, it went through her right lung, causing a collection of blood and air in the space between the lung and the chest wall. The second bullet penetrated the left ventricle of her heart." He nods melodramatically.

He opens a manila envelope and pulls three enlarged pictures of what I presume is Bob's head. He clips them to his bulletin board. He takes out a gold Cross pen and uses it as a pointer. "Entry was in the right parietal, just above the temple. Exit in the left parietal, above his left ear. Slight upward trajectory."

This may help our suicide argument. Bob was right-handed. His analysis is consistent with a right-handed shooter.

"How far was the barrel of the gun from his head when he was shot?" I ask.

"The starburst splitting of the skin indicates it was a contact wound," he replies. "I found powder marks and burns on his head. In other words, the barrel was placed against the head." His delivery is calm and clinical. He could be reciting baseball scores. He gestures toward the picture on the right. "This is the left side of his head, or, if you'll forgive me, what was left of it. The exit wound was quite dramatic."

I'll say. Although I can make out the left ear, the rest of his head above the ear line is virtually unrecognizable. "Did you find evidence of gunpowder on his hands?" When a gun is fired, traces of gunpowder and other chemicals can be found on the shooter's hand. I already know the answer.

"As a matter of fact, we did. We found gunpowder on his right hand and forearm."

This adds to our suicide argument. He looks at the pictures. I stop to think. I decide to probe a little more. "Doctor," I say, "your report indicates there may have been evidence of a concussive wound on his head. How can you tell?"

"There *was* a concussive wound, Mr. Daley," he says emphatically. He moves his glasses down from the top of his head so he can see up close. He points to the area about an inch and a half above Bob's left ear. "Do you see this area right here?" he asks.

"I'm not sure." I'm not playing games. I haven't the slightest idea what he's pointing at.

He zeros in on a spot just above the top edge of the exit wound. It reminds me of the first sonogram pictures of Grace when Rosie was pregnant. They looked like a test pattern to me. The OB could make out a head, a backbone and various organs. Rosie and I stood there and said we could see everything. "I'm sorry. I'm not sure what you're pointing at."

"Look a little closer," he says. "It's a little hard to make out in the pictures."

No kidding.

"Right here," he says, as he gestures again toward a spot near the edge of the exit wound. "It's as clear as night and day to a trained coroner."

I still can't see it. Then again, I'm not a trained coroner.

"It may have been larger," he continues, "but part of it may have been obliterated by the exit wound. What's left is about a quarter of an inch in diameter. There's a small hematoma."

People think lawyers talk in code. Hematoma is doctor-speak for a swelling containing blood. It's hard to make out on the flat pictures. I think I see something, but I'm not sure. "How can you tell it was not just part of the exit wound?" I ask.

He points to a spot on the edge of the exit wound. "The exit wound stops here," he says. "The concussive wound is a separate injury."

"I see. And how was this wound generated?"

"He must have been struck by a hard object."

I look at the pictures again. "Can you figure out the size or the shape of the object, Doctor?"

"No. It was heavy enough to do some damage. There were no traces of paint or wood or metal in the skull. It's not like he was hit by a car."

"Is it possible it may have been an old wound? Maybe he bumped his head a few weeks ago."

"No. It was fresh. It's tough to see it in the picture, but if you had the body in front of you, you'd see the bump was just beginning to form. Of course, the swelling would have stopped as soon as his heart stopped beating. And if he had been hit after he was shot, there would have been no hematoma because there would have been no blood pumped to the wound."

Too bad. "Doctor, can you tell if he was unconscious when he was shot?"

"Probably."

This isn't helping. On the other hand, a big part of their case may turn on his ability to convince the jury that somebody hit Bob on the head. The gunpowder on Bob's hand is evidence he was holding the gun when it was fired. "One last question. Are you sure somebody bopped him on the head?"

He strokes his beard. "In my best medical judgment, the answer is yes."

Sandra Wilson is the best field-evidence technician, or "FET," in the SFPD. She gathers evidence at crime scenes. Now in her late thirties, this articulate black woman may be the ideal prosecution witness—the voice of authority combined with a tone of reason. There will be no Dennis Fung in this case.

I've left Dr. Beckert and climbed the stairs to Sandra's small office on the second floor, which she shares with another criminalist. Her office reflects her meticulous approach. Her pens and paper clips are lined up neatly in front of a small picture of her husband. There's a picture of a toddler on the top of her computer. No pictures on the walls, although her diploma from UCLA is on display. Her short black hair and dark brown skin frame intense eyes. Her sensible clothing isn't accessorized. Her husband is a cop. They aren't rolling in extra cash.

She smiles. "If my boss finds out I'm fraternizing with the enemy," she says, "I'll catch hell."

"I'll never tell." I like her. She's a straight shooter.

"All right," she says, "I've got work to do. What do you need to know?"

"The usual. Got any nice evidence that will exonerate my client?"

She laughs. "Of course. We've been sandbagging you." She takes out a thick manila folder containing crime-scene photos. "As you can see," she says in a matter-of-fact tone, "Holmes was on the floor beneath his desk, Kennedy by the door. They were both pronounced dead at the scene at eight-twenty-two. Gun was on the desk. Your client said he found it on the floor and unloaded it." She studies her notes. "Friedman's fingerprints were on the gun, the spent shells and the unused bullets. Also on the computer keyboard, the door handle, the desk."

"We know he was at the scene."

"There's no doubt about that."

"You got anything to help me prove he didn't fire the gun?"

She hands me a photocopy of a diagram showing exactly where Joel's fingerprints were found on the gun—something she doesn't really have to do. "See for yourself," she says.

I study the diagram. "Did you find Bob's fingerprints on the gun?"

"Several. Just the handle, however."

"What about the trigger?"

"Just an unidentifiable smudged print."

I put the diagram in my pocket. I want Pete's input. "Did you test Joel's hands or clothing for gunpowder residue?"

She pauses. "No, I didn't. He wasn't a suspect at the

scene. By the time he was a suspect, he'd showered and his clothes had been laundered. It would have been too late to get anything."

"Meaning that if you'd done it a couple of days later, it wouldn't have shown anything."

She acknowledges that this is true.

"You know, Sandra," I say, "I'll probably have to use that at the prelim."

"I know. I know. You're just doing your job."

"What can you tell me about the gun?" I ask.

"It's a Smith and Wesson thirty-eight-caliber revolver. Forensics matched the bullets. The blood-splatter analysis indicates that Holmes was sitting in his chair when he was shot."

"What about the keyboard? Skipper thinks Joel typed the suicide E-mail."

"I hope you aren't going to try to come up with some hokey chain-of-custody argument." Defense attorneys frequently argue the cops mishandled or even planted evidence.

"I know better than to try to nail you on chain of custody. I'm curious, though. Did you find Joel's fingerprints on all the alphabetic keys?"

She glances at her notes and frowns. "Yes," she replies.

I make a mental note to see if Bob's E-mail used all twenty-six letters in the alphabet. That seems unlikely. "What about the numeric keys and the function keys?"

"We found your client's fingerprints on all of the numeric keys and three of the function keys."

That's odd. Lawyers use the keyboard to send E-mails and to do some word processing. They rarely touch the numeric or function keys. "Did you find Bob's fingerprints on the keyboard?" I ask.

She frowns again. "No."

That's really odd. "I see. Let's talk about the tapes for a minute."

"The voice mail from Friedman to Holmes was recorded at twelve-thirty. We tested the system. We're sure about the time. We'll call an expert if we have to."

It's probably not worth fighting over the time of the call. "What about the call to Diana?"

"Phone company records indicate the call was initiated at twelve-fifty-one A.M. It lasted one minute and thirty-four seconds. We found the tape in Diana's answering machine."

"You're sure of the timing?"

"Yes. We tested the timing mechanism on the answering machine. It was working. And don't even think about arguing the tapes were tampered with, Mike. The fact is, they weren't."

"You guys aren't doing me any favors."

She looks serious. "This is a high-profile case. Word came from above—no screwups. That's why I'm involved. That's why Rod Beckert did the autopsy. That's why Roosevelt is in charge of the investigation. They put the first team on this one. If Skipper loses this case, it won't be because we screwed up. If you're looking for Mark Fuhrman, he doesn't work here."

Swell. "Sandra, do you have anything else that might be useful?"

"I'll send you copies of the security tapes."

"Any other fingerprints?"

"We found prints from everybody you'd expect—from his partners to his secretary. We found Vince Russo's fingerprints on his desk. We even found one of your fingerprints on his desk, Mike." She grins. "We'll be keeping an eye on you."

I glance at the picture of her son. "Rod Beckert seems to think that somebody smacked Bob on the side of the head with a heavy object. Did you find any blood or hair on anything in his office that could have been used to knock him out? Maybe a book or a stapler or something?"

"No."

That helps our suicide argument. I thank her for her time. She's going to kill us at the trial.

18

"NOBODY'S TALKING"

"Simpson and Gates has no comment concerning Mr. Friedman's case. We have faith in the system and we are confident justice will be served."

—ARTHUR PATTON. *SAN FRANCISCO LEGAL JOURNAL.*
FRIDAY, JANUARY 16.

"Mr. Patton will see you now, Mr. Daley." At nine o'clock the next morning, I'm back in familiar territory—the reception area at Simpson and Gates.

Art Patton's secretary ushers me to his museumlike corner office on forty-six. Like most high-powered civil litigators, there are no files in his office. He has slaves to handle the grunt work. The Louis-the-something furniture contrasts with the heavy oriental rugs. Several modern sculptures adorn his credenza. The walls are covered with photos of Patton with local politicians. He stands to greet me. Chuckles is sitting in one of Patton's overstuffed chairs. He doesn't get up.

Patton's all smiles. "It's good to see you," he lies. He doesn't sit down. If he has his way, this is going to be a short visit.

"I didn't realize you were going to convene an executive committee meeting on my behalf."

Not surprisingly, Patton is going to act as spokesman. "When you called, we thought it would be better to do this together. We're extremely busy." His eyes dart toward Chuckles. "Look," he says, "I know you want to talk about Joel's case. It's a very serious subject. A great tragedy." He nods solemnly. "We have given our statements to the police. We've put Joel on administrative leave and we're going to let the justice system take its course. It's all we can do."

Smooth. And carefully rehearsed, no doubt. I decide to attack quickly. "The police reports said you were in the office that night. I was wondering what time you left."

"If you're suggesting somebody in this room was involved, you're mistaken."

"I'm not suggesting anything. I'm just trying to piece together what happened." He knows I'm lying. On the other hand, he'll appear evasive if he doesn't answer.

"I left at one-thirty. Charles left a little later. We were working on the Estimate. Neither of us saw or heard anything."

It's certainly convenient they can alibi each other. "Thanks. I'm sure your story will be borne out by the security videos." They glance at each other. Let them sweat a little. "I understand from the investigating officers that somebody from the firm said Joel was having an affair with Diana."

"I don't know anything about that. If I did, I'd tell the cops—not you."

"I was hoping you'd confirm *you* made those statements to the police."

"We've given our statements to the police." He starts walking toward the door in an effort to escort me out.

I don't move. "I know you told the cops you thought Joel and Diana were having an affair."

"We have given our statements to the police," he repeats in an even tone.

I decide to try a different angle. "Is it true the firm defaulted on its equipment loans to First Bank?" I want them to think I know more than I really do.

Patton takes the offensive. "The financial health of the firm is excellent. If I were in your shoes, I would be preparing a defense for my client, not harassing us."

"I can subpoena the firm's financial records if you won't answer my questions."

"This meeting is over, Mike."

Things aren't improving later the same morning. First Bank's general counsel, Jeff Tucker, is a tight-assed little man in his mid-thirties who started his career at S&G. He went to work at First Bank two years ago when he didn't make partner. Bob Holmes stabbed him squarely in the middle of the back at the partner election. He's still bitter. He works in a ten-by-ten office with a small window on the third floor of a boxy seventies office building on the south side of Market Street. In the mid-eighties, First Bank was a highflier. By the early nineties, the real-estate market tanked and so did First Bank. Its chairman was indicted for cooking the books and a Japanese conglomerate took over. To cut costs, the bank moved its headquarters from palatial space on the fortieth floor of the Four Embarcadero Center tower to offices formerly occupied by a now-defunct insurance company.

It's a quarter to twelve and Jeff wants to go to lunch. He squints at me through uncomfortable-looking contact lenses. "I don't know anything that would help you," he says.

Not a bad strategy. When in doubt, try to deflect. "I understand S and G is having some financial troubles."

He scratches his balding head. "You know I can't talk about the bank's customers."

"I'm a former S and G partner. If the firm goes belly-up, I may be called upon to cough up money to help cover its debts. As a result, in a very real respect I'm your customer. If you'd prefer, I'd be happy to come back with a subpoena. I'd rather not." A little overbearing, perhaps. But the tough-guy act usually works with people like Jeff.

He performs some sort of mental calculus. "What do you really need to know?"

"I need to know if the firm is in financial trouble."

"The answer is yes."

"Has the firm defaulted on its equipment loans?"

His lips get tighter. "Yes."

"How big were the loans?"

"About twenty million."

"Have you foreclosed?"

"Not yet. My superiors said it would be bad PR to foreclose on the firm right after the tragedy."

"I see."

"So we gave them an extension."

Very unbanklike behavior. "Really? How long?"

"Sixty days. Either they raise the twenty million by the end of February, or we'll foreclose. It'll probably throw the firm into bankruptcy."

Great.

He stands. "I've already told you more than I should have. I'm late for lunch."

At noon, I'm eating a quarter pounder at the McDonald's on Pine Street and talking to Rosie on my cellular. "Were you able to reach Beth Holmes?" I ask.

"Yeah. She isn't saying much. She claims she doesn't

know anything about Bob's finances or investments. She doesn't know anything about his will or his life insurance."

"Great."

"Guess who's the executor of the estate?"

Easy question. "Charles Stern?"

"Yeah. How did you know?"

"Everybody at the firm uses Charles. Dead people feel very comfortable around him."

She laughs. "How did your meetings go with your former partners?"

"Lousy. Nobody's talking. Total stonewall."

"No big surprise. I gotta run."

At one o'clock, I'm admiring the view of the Golden Gate Bridge from the thirty-eighth floor of the Transamerica Pyramid. Jack Frazier, Continental Capital Corporation's mergers-and-acquisitions stud, occupies a corner office that's far too large for a thirty-two-year-old. He's a tall blond with a vacant expression who looks out of place behind his large mahogany desk. It's hard to believe this guy persuaded his corporate masters in Connecticut to pay nine hundred million dollars for Vince Russo's company. From what I gather from Joel, he's one of those young MBAs who got out of school at just the right time. At the next downturn in the economy, he'll be driving a cab.

Before I can sit down, Frazier announces, "Continental Capital Corporation has no comment with respect to the matters surrounding the deaths of Mr. Holmes and Ms. Kennedy."

His ever-present attorney, a sour-looking fiftyish drone named Martin Glass, interrupts him. "Mr. Daley," he says, "we have given our statements to the police. We have nothing further to add at this time." He takes off his thick, frameless glasses and puts them on Frazier's desk. As far as he's concerned, that's the end of the story. It's amazing how everybody clams up when a defense attorney shows up.

Time to play bull in the china shop. "I don't need a lot of your time," I say. "I'm just trying to figure out what happened that night. What time did you guys leave?"

Glass responds. "It's in the police report. I left a few minutes before ten. Jack left around one-forty-five. We went home."

They've compared notes. "Where do you guys live?"

Again, Glass does the talking. "I live in Seacliff. Jack is on Russian Hill."

"I see." I know I can confirm the departure times from the security tapes. So far, so good. Now, let's see if I can get anything good. "How was the deal going?"

They look at each other. "Fine," says Glass.

Good answer. Says nothing. "Was it going to close?"

"Yes," says Glass, nodding. "All the papers were signed."

"What happened the next morning?"

"I got a call from your client. He told me what happened."

I pause. "I understand there was a big breakup fee in this deal."

Before Glass can respond, Frazier says, "Yes there was." I make a mental note that Frazier can be jumpy. If he's really as smart as everyone at CCC seems to think he is, he'd shut his mouth.

"How much?"

"That's confidential," Glass says.

"May I assume it was big enough that you didn't want to pay it?"

Frazier smiles and says, "You never want to pay a breakup fee, Mr. Daley."

Glass interjects, "I don't see what this has to do with your client."

"I'm just trying to figure out what was going on." And to see if your client had motive.

"Mr. Daley," says Glass, "we've told you everything we know. I feel badly. I like Joel Friedman. I hope he didn't do it. Of course, if he did, I'm sure he'll get what he deserves."

At two o'clock, I walk into Assistant City Attorney Ed Ehrlich's windowless office on the fourth floor of a mid-rise fifties office building near the Moscone Convention Center. The city can't be criticized for spending taxpayer funds to lease opulent offices. The owl-eyed Ehrlich looks at home behind his metal desk. There's no artwork on the walls. "I'm due at the redevelopment agency," he says as I walk in. "Can we talk later?"

"Sure. Can I ask you a few quick questions before you go?"

"Make it fast."

"How late were you at the S and G offices that night?"

"I went home around ten."

"Was the deal going to close?"

"As far as I knew. It was approved by CCC's board. Everything depended on Vince Russo."

"Was the city happy with the deal?"

He looks at his blank walls. "For the most part. Some people were worried about funding for our loan. I didn't think it was a big deal."

"When did Dan Morris leave?"

I see distaste in his eyes before he masks it. Seems Ed and the mayor's political fixer may not be the best of friends. "I don't know."

"Why did he stay?"

"To do what he always does—work the room. He wanted to suck up to the CCC people for a while. Guys like that are always playing the angles."

"See anything suspicious that night?"

"No. It was the usual legal bullshit." He looks away. "I gotta go."

At two-thirty, I'm walking up Montgomery Street, talking to Pete on my cellular. "Did you find anything?" I ask.

"As a matter of fact, I did. I did a little checking on Vince Russo. It's correct that he never went back to the Ritz that night. The cop who found his car at the Golden Gate Bridge didn't see anyone. The car was registered to a limited-liability company called Camelot Investments, LLC, which is owned by two trusts in the Bahamas. One is called the International Charitable Trust. The other is the Charitable Trust for Humanity. I'm checking it out."

"Keep looking, Pete."

My day hasn't gotten any better as I sit in Dan Morris's office at three o'clock. Not surprisingly, the political consultant's office is a monument to his favorite person—himself. Two walls are lined with pictures of Dan grinning with local dignitaries whose political fortunes he's orchestrated. Another wall is adorned with framed political posters for his candidates. A paunchy redhead, Morris is known as the Chameleon in San Francisco political circles because he'll represent candidates of every political denomination, as long as they're able to come up with the four hundred thousand dollars he charges to run a campaign. He isn't a nice human being, but his candidates win. Lately, he has been running a Senate campaign for Edward Cross, a Republican, and a congressional campaign for Leslie Sherman, a Democrat.

At three-thirty, I'm still sitting in his office, watching him operate. He's been on the phone since I arrived. In the last fifteen minutes, he's raised about a hundred thousand dollars for Cross and another fifty grand for Sherman. He cups his hand over the phone and mouths the word "Sorry." He holds his thumb and index finger about a quarter of an inch apart, indicating that he'll only be a minute.

Finally, at three-forty, he hangs up. "Raising money is the shits," he says.

"I understand." Don't feel any obligation to apologize to me.

"I hate to do this to you, but I've got to run. I'm due at the mayor's office in ten minutes."

"Can we reschedule for tomorrow?"

He's putting on his coat. "I'll have to call you. I'm flying to L.A. first thing in the morning."

"Can't we talk for just a minute?"

"Can't keep the mayor waiting. I'll call you." He's out the door.

At four-thirty, I walk into Harrington's, an old, dark, wood-paneled pub on Front Street that's now surrounded by high-rise office buildings. I want to get there before the evening rush.

Rick Cinelli is an olive-skinned, dark-haired man with a raspy voice and a reserved manner. He's been tending bar at Harrington's for twenty years. He could run for mayor. I take a seat at the bar and he pours me an Anchor Steam. "Haven't seen you in a while, Mike," he says.

"Been busy, Rick." I sip my beer. "You know I left S and G."

"I heard." He walks down to the end of the bar to attend to a customer, then he comes back. "Helluva thing about Bob and Diana," he says. "I hear you're representing Joel."

"Yeah." I pause. "Actually, that's why I'm here. I understand Joel and Diana were here that night. The cops talked to you."

He nods.

"Mind if I ask you a few questions?"

"Ask away. I've got nothing to hide."

"They say you told the police Joel and Diana had a fight that night."

"They did. One minute they were ordering dinner. The next minute they were arguing. Next thing I knew, she stormed out. It lasted a minute and a half."

"That's it?"

"That's it."

Now, the important part. "Do you happen to know what they were arguing about?"

"Nope." He shrugs. "It was busy. They were sitting in the corner. As long as they pay for their drinks, I leave them alone. That's why I've been here for so long."

It's what I expect him to say. "Could you tell if they were fighting about work?"

"I couldn't tell."

"Did you hear anything in particular?"

He looks across the room. "I heard him say he was going to get her for something. I remember that distinctly. He said it a couple times. 'I'll get you for this.'"

Swell. I pay him for the beer and I thank him. He promises to call me if he hears anything.

"Mr. Kim, may I speak to you for a moment?" I approach Homer Kim, a young Korean custodian, at the employees' entrance to the Bank of America Building at five o'clock. The evening shift is about to start. I introduce myself and hand him a business card. He looks suspicious. "I wonder if I can ask you a few questions."

He looks apprehensive. "Late for work," he says in broken English.

"It'll take just a minute."

He looks perplexed. "Okay."

I explain I'm representing Joel. He recoils. "I understand you spoke to the police."

He's suspicious. He should be.

"Did you tell the police Mr. Friedman and Mr. Holmes had a fight that night?"

His eyes wander. "Yes," he says tentatively. "Mr. Friedman was very angry at Mr. Holmes." He starts to move away.

"Do you know why?"

His eyes dart away. "No."

"What did Mr. Friedman say to Mr. Holmes?"

He shrugs. "Don't know. I walked by the office. Mr. Friedman was yelling at Mr. Holmes."

"Mr. Kim, do you know what they were arguing about?"

"Don't know. Late for work."

"Did you hear any shots?"

"No. Late for work." He pushes his way around me. A good prosecutor will get him to say exactly what he wants.

At six o'clock, I'm in my office with Rosie when Pete calls. I put him on the speaker phone. "You guys get something?" he asks.

"Nothing useful," I reply.

Rosie says, "Me neither."

I ask Pete if he's found anything.

"I had someone watching your friend Arthur Patton last night." I can hear the grin in his voice. "You were right about his divorce. He and his wife separated a couple months ago and he's living in an apartment on Russian Hill. Around eight last night, he went over to pay a condolence call to the Widow Holmes." He pauses. I look at Rosie. "It was a long condolence call. He didn't leave until seven this morning."

If I ever get married again, I swear I'll never cheat as long as Pete's still breathing.

At seven o'clock in the evening on the following Monday, Rosie, Mort and I meet with Joel and his father in Rabbi Friedman's dining room. The preliminary hearing is set for ten o'clock tomorrow, with motions at nine.

Rabbi Friedman is not happy. "So," he says, "are you saying you won't be able to get the charges dropped tomorrow?"

"It looks that way, Rabbi. They've probably got enough to take the case to trial."

Mort nods. "Rabbi," he says calmly, "it doesn't mean they have a strong case. It just means they have enough to get to trial."

Rabbi Friedman doesn't look mollified.

Joel is edgy. "So what do you plan to do tomorrow?" he asks. "Roll over?"

"No," I reply. "We'll challenge their witnesses. We won't make it easy for them. But we won't tip too much of our hand. We don't want to give them anything they can use at the trial."

"You're going to get that so-called confession knocked out, right?"

"Yes. That's the first thing on the agenda. We're going to talk to the judge in chambers before the hearing starts. If he lets the confession in, we'll go straight to the appellate court for a writ. I don't want it to see the light of day."

Rabbi Friedman shakes his head. Joel turns to his father. "They're doing everything they can, Dad. The legal system doesn't work so well sometimes. And it never works very fast."

Thanks, Joel. It's nice when your client defends you. Things usually work better when it's the other way around.

Rosie breaks the silence. "Do you think we should ask for a change in venue? There's been a lot of press coverage. It may be tough to get an unbiased jury."

We've talked about this a couple of times. The defense often asks for a change in venue to a galaxy far, far away, where the potential jurors haven't seen all the press coverage.

Mort chimes in first. "I still think we should stay here," he says. "San Francisco is a liberal town. I'd rather try a murder case here than almost anywhere else in California."

Rosie nods and I add, "I agree. You wouldn't want to try this case in Bakersfield or Orange County. I'd take my chances with a San Francisco jury."

Joel says, "Then, I guess we'll stay here?"

"Yes."

Rosie says, "There's something else we should talk about. Assuming this moves forward, we need to think about trial dates. We'll need to prepare witnesses, get experts, talk to jury consultants. It could take some time." She turns to Joel. "I'm sure you'll want to waive the rule that says they have to start the trial within sixty days."

Mort agrees. "I've never had a case where the defendant didn't waive time."

Joel sets his chin. "I'm not going to waive time."

"Can we talk about this, Joel?" I ask.

"We can talk about it all you want," he replies. "Bottom line, I'm not waiving time. My life has been turned upside down for something I didn't do. My reputation has been destroyed. My wife and kids are going through hell. As much as I like staying here at my parents' house, I want to go home. This case isn't complicated. I didn't do it. I'm not going to give Skipper a year to practice for this trial. I want a trial date as soon as possible. Tell the judge tomorrow I'm not waiving time."

"Joel," I say.

He stops me. "No. I'm the client. What I say goes. I'm not waiving time."

19

THE PRELIMINARY HEARING

"NewsCenter 4 has learned from reliable sources that Joel Mark Friedman has confessed to the murders of two colleagues. Judge Kenneth Brown will preside at the preliminary hearing at ten o'clock today."

—RITA ROBERTS. *NEWSCENTER 4 DAYBREAK.* TUESDAY, JANUARY 20.

"Your Honor," Mort begins, "we have three very serious issues." At nine o'clock in the morning on Tuesday, January 20, Rosie, Mort and I sit in Judge Kenneth Brown's cramped chambers. Skipper and McNulty are with us. Brown's desk is littered with files and law books. There's a picture of him shaking hands with the governor on his credenza.

Judge Brown is late fifties, with a lanky frame, a salt-and-pepper beard and narrow eyes. He's a former prosecutor and political ally of the mayor. He's bucking for an appointment to federal court. At the moment, he's stuck listening to motions and conducting preliminary hearings. Unlike Judge Levin, Brown actually reads the California statutes from time to time and is viewed as an up-and-comer. The scouting report suggests he's never met a prosecutor he didn't like. "What's the problem, Mr. Goldberg?" he asks. He's all business.

This morning's motions will be Mort's show. If he can't convince his poker buddy Judge Brown to exclude the confession, we're in big trouble. It's the closest we will come to having home-field advantage. Mort's actually very good on evidentiary issues. "First," he says, "Inspector Marcus Banks has alleged Mr. Friedman confessed. He didn't. Second, Mr. Friedman wasn't Mirandized when he was questioned. Even if we assume he did, in fact, confess—which he didn't—the confession is inadmissible. Third, somebody from Mr. Gates's office leaked the alleged confession to the press. The potential juror pool has already been tainted. We have no choice but to move for dismissal."

He'll never dismiss the case. Not a chance.

"Your Honor," Skipper begins.

The judge cuts him off. "Mr. Gates, I'll tell you when it's your turn to talk."

Skipper nods submissively. "Yes, Your Honor."

The judge turns back to Mort. "Let's take this one step at a time. I've read your motion. I'm not in a position to determine what was said. For purposes of this hearing, I have to let Inspector Banks testify about what he heard—unless I'm pretty sure he's committing perjury."

Skipper grins.

"But, Your Honor . . ." Mort says.

Brown raises his hand. Mort stops midsentence. "On the other hand," he continues, "your other charges are considerably more serious."

Skipper stops grinning. The judge points his pencil at him. "Mr. Gates, was the defendant properly Mirandized before the interview took place?"

Skipper looks at McNulty. "No, Your Honor," he says. "He wasn't Mirandized because he wasn't a suspect at the time." McNulty nods in agreement.

Brown frowns. "How long was Mr. Friedman questioned?"

Skipper clears his throat. "A couple of hours, Your Honor," he murmurs.

"I'm sorry, Mr. Gates, I didn't hear you."

"A couple of hours, Your Honor." He says it louder this time.

I interrupt. "Actually, the interview took four hours. This issue came up at the very end."

"I see." Brown turns back to Skipper. "Did the defendant volunteer the information or did Inspector Banks ask him if he committed double murder?"

There's a pause. Skipper looks at McNulty. "I believe he responded to a question."

"Mr. Gates," says Brown, "perhaps we should invite Inspector Banks in so he can tell us exactly what happened."

"That's a good idea," Skipper replies.

Judge Brown asks his bailiff to summon Banks, who strolls in confidently a moment later. He's well dressed, in a double-breasted gray suit. His French cuffs are adorned with large gold cuff links. I don't know how he can afford his wardrobe on his salary. He takes the one empty chair.

"Inspector Banks," Brown says, "we understand you interviewed Mr. Friedman."

"Yes, Your Honor."

"And toward the end of the interview, you claim he confessed to committing the murders of Robert Holmes and Diana Kennedy?"

He doesn't hesitate. "Yes, Your Honor. That's right."

"Was the interview taped?"

"Yes, Your Honor."

"Was this alleged confession taped?"

He pauses briefly. "Well, no, Your Honor."

Brown opens his eyes wide. "Why not?"

"My partner, Inspector Johnson, and I had concluded the formal part of the interview. We had turned off the tape recorder."

"And after you turned off the tape recorder, Mr. Friedman confessed?"

"Yes."

Brown taps his pencil on the desk. "What a coincidence. Where was Inspector Johnson when Mr. Friedman allegedly confessed?"

"He was outside the room."

"And why was that?"

"He went to get Mr. Friedman a drink of water."

"So Inspector Johnson didn't hear this alleged confession."

"No he didn't."

"And nobody else heard it?"

"No."

"Your Honor," I say.

He stops me. "It will be your turn in a minute, Mr. Daley. Inspector Banks," he continues, "how long have you been with the department?"

"Thirty years."

"And how many murder suspects have you interviewed in thirty years?"

He thinks. "Hundreds. Maybe thousands, Your Honor."

The judge points a menacing finger toward him. "And you've heard of the Miranda rules?"

He swallows. "Yes, Your Honor."

"Inspector Banks, here's my problem. We understand you didn't give Mr. Friedman his Miranda warnings when you questioned him. Is that correct?"

He glances at Skipper. "Yes, Your Honor. That's correct."

I'm impressed with his truthfulness. He could have lied and said he read Joel his rights. It would have been his word against Joel's.

"And may I ask why not?"

Without hesitation, he says, "He wasn't a suspect at the time of questioning."

"I see." He gestures at Banks with his glasses. "Inspector, did Mr. Friedman volunteer this information, or did he respond to a question?"

"I believe I asked him a question."

"And what was your question?"

Banks looks directly at the judge. "I asked him if he did it."

"You asked him if he did it?"

"Yes, Your Honor."

"But he wasn't a suspect."

"No he wasn't, Your Honor."

"And how did he respond?"

"He responded affirmatively."

"Affirmatively?"

"Yes."

"In other words," Judge Brown says, "he said yes."

"That's correct."

Mort interrupts. "Your Honor," he says, "in point of fact, Mr. Friedman did not say yes. He said the word 'right' in a sarcastic tone. He was being facetious."

Brown turns to Banks. "Is that your recollection of the conversation, Inspector?"

"No, Your Honor. I distinctly asked Mr. Friedman if he did it, and he responded affirmatively."

Nice dance, Marcus. But not good enough. "Your Honor," I interrupt, "Mr. Banks did not answer your question." I turn to Banks. "Isn't it true, Inspector Banks, that in response to your question, Mr. Friedman responded by sarcastically saying the word 'right'?"

"That's not the way I remember it."

McNulty leaps in. "Your Honor," he says, "even if Inspector Banks asked the defendant if he committed the acts in question, he didn't need to be Mirandized because he wasn't a suspect."

Brown is unhappy. "Mr. McNulty," he says, "it seems to me it's a pretty long stretch to suggest Mr. Friedman wasn't a suspect if Mr. Banks was asking if he committed these crimes." He turns to Banks. "If he wasn't a suspect, Inspector, why did you ask him if he did it?"

I'm trying to find an opportunity to continue my argument that Joel didn't really confess at all. I glance at Rosie. She gives me the "shut up" look. Mort keeps his eyes on the judge.

Banks shrugs. "I'm not sure, Your Honor. I guess I just wanted to know."

Judge Brown looks at Skipper. "Mr. Gates, may I assume you have enough evidence to present today without this 'alleged' confession?"

Skipper hesitates. The correct answer, of course, is yes. "Yes, Your Honor," he finally says. "But it really would help me to get this confession in."

"Then Inspector Banks should have followed the Miranda rules," he shoots back. He looks at Banks. "The defendant's motion is granted. The alleged confession is out. I don't want to hear a word about it today at the prelim." He turns to Skipper. "Mr. Gates," he says, "you had better be prepared to move forward without it."

"We are, Your Honor," Skipper replies. He glares at Banks.

Round 1 goes to the good guys.

Mort's expression doesn't change. He's still a warhorse. "Your Honor," he says, "we have another problem. This bogus confession was leaked to the press. I've already received inquiries from several television reporters. In fact, I saw it on the news this morning. The potential-juror pool has been irreparably tainted. I have no choice but to ask that the charges be dropped."

It never hurts to ask. He'll never go for it.

Brown's grin is almost imperceptible. "If that was a motion to have the charges dropped, Mr. Goldberg, it's denied. Nice try, though." Skipper looks pleased. He continues, "I am ordering Mr. Gates to issue a statement saying there was no confession. I will approve its contents. I expect it on my desk by two o'clock."

Skipper is no longer pleased. "I resent the implication that this information was leaked from my office," he says.

Brown looks right through him. "Mr. Gates," he says, "I expect the statement on my desk by two o'clock. If it isn't, I'll hold you in contempt. Do you understand?"

"Yes, Your Honor."

"Good."

"Your Honor," Mort says, "I think Mr. Gates should be sanctioned for this irresponsible leak." The bull is sprinting at full speed through the china shop. I glance at Rosie. The corners of her mouth turn up slightly.

"Your Honor," Skipper implores, "we didn't leak anything to the press."

Mort turns to him. "Oh, and I suppose you think we did?"

Judge Brown taps his pencil. "Children, please. In the spirit of cooperation, I'm not going to sanction anybody right now."

"Your Honor," I say, "I would ask you to issue an order that would prohibit any such leaks in the future."

He glares at Skipper. "I'll do better than that, Mr. Daley. As of this moment, I am issuing a total gag order. I don't want any of you talking to the press. Do you understand?"

We nod in unison.

"Good," he says. "Because if anybody violates the order, I'll put them in jail for contempt. I mean it. Fines don't mean anything to you. I'll put you in jail. For a long time. Understood?"

We nod again. It's like kindergarten. When the bell rings, we get to go to recess. "I'll see you in court," Brown says.

"Nice work, Mort," I say. Joel, Rosie, Mort and I are sitting in a small consultation room just behind Judge Brown's courtroom.

"It's a good result," Mort says. "We didn't get everything, but we got the confession out."

"What does it mean for the prelim?" Joel asks.

"The good news," I say, "is they'll have to show more of their case."

"Can you get the charges dropped?"

Rosie, Mort and I glance at one another. "It doesn't look good," I say. "They don't have to show very much. They've got you at the scene. They've got your fingerprints on the gun and the keyboard. They've got the phone messages. That's probably enough to get this to trial."

"But we can explain all that stuff." He's pleading his case to us.

"I know. But we don't want to telegraph our defense too soon."

"So you're saying we're going to trial."

"Looks like it."

He looks up at the ceiling, and says nothing.

"All rise." Judge Brown enters his small, packed courtroom and takes his place on the bench between the Stars and Stripes and the California state flag. Reporters fill the jury box. There's barely room for a few courthouse groupies. Joel sits at the defense table between Rosie and me. Mort is at the end of the table. Rabbi Friedman and Naomi sit silently in the first row. Joel's mother is home watching the children.

The case is called and Skipper and I state our appearances for the record. Judge Brown reads the charges and says the defendant has entered a plea of not guilty. He reminds us this is a preliminary hearing for the purpose of determining whether there is sufficient evidence to hold the defendant over for trial. Skipper gives a brief opening statement summarizing the evidence. I give an even shorter statement that says, in effect, there are too many gaping holes in the state's case to hold Joel over for trial. Then Judge Brown instructs Skipper to call his first witness.

"Please state your name and occupation for the record," Skipper says.

"Dr. Roderick Beckert. Chief Medical Examiner for the City and County of San Francisco."

"How long have you held that position?"

"Thirty years."

Skipper starts to run Beckert through his credentials. Undergrad at Harvard. Medical degree from Stanford. I interrupt and stipulate to his expertise. Skipper is disappointed. He was just getting to the part where Beckert delivered the tablets at Mount Sinai.

Skipper hands Beckert a copy of his autopsy report. Beckert glances at it briefly. His testimony doesn't take long. He confirms Bob and Diana died from gunshot wounds. Skipper sits down. He's played just enough cards for a prelim. McNulty has coached him well.

"Dr. Beckert," I say, "your report says the wounds to Mr. Holmes may have been self-inflicted."

"Yes it does."

I need to be careful with the next question. "Dr. Beckert, it is possible that the wounds were, in fact, self-inflicted, right?"

"Yes, but . . ."

I interrupt him. "Thanks, Doctor. You've answered my question. I have no further questions."

He looks at the judge. His eyes plead for a chance to explain. Brown tells him to step down.

Sandra Wilson is next. Skipper quickly walks her through her resume. Undergraduate and masters degrees from UCLA. A nine-year veteran of the SFPD. I'll look like an ass if I interrupt her.

She calmly describes the physical evidence. As the sportscasters like to say, we can't stop her—we can only hope to contain her. Skipper takes her through chain-of-custody issues. She leaves no doubt the gun and the other evidence were handled and catalogued in accordance with police procedures. She describes the fingerprints on the gun and the keyboard. She says they're a perfect match for Joel's. She introduces the tape from Diana's answering machine and a recording of Joel's voice mail to Bob. Joel leans over and whispers whether there's anything we can do. I shrug. Skipper sits down. He probably doesn't need to call any other witnesses.

"Ms. Wilson," I say, "did you test the defendant's hands or clothing for gunpowder residue?"

"No."

"Why not?"

"He wasn't a suspect at the scene. By the time he became a suspect several days later, his hands and clothing would have been cleaned and the tests wouldn't have shown anything."

"So you can't prove he fired the gun?"

"His fingerprints were on the gun, Mr. Daley."

"I understand. But you can't show that he fired it."

"That's correct."

"Just one more question. Did you find Joel Friedman's fingerprints on the trigger?"

I'm sure she expected the question. She pauses briefly and says, "There were smudged fingerprints on the trigger, Mr. Daley. We were unable to positively identify them."

"So, you can't affirmatively demonstrate that Mr. Friedman pulled the trigger?"

"We could not identify the fingerprints on the trigger, Mr. Daley," she repeats.

I argue with the judge for a few moments that she's being unresponsive. He finally gets her to admit that the physical evidence does not conclusively show that Joel pulled the trigger.

"No further questions," I say. It's helpful to have an ex-cop like Pete on our side. He notices things.

Roosevelt takes the stand. He confirms Joel admitted he was in the S&G offices the night of the incident. He describes the scene in Bob's office. He provides copies of the phone records showing the call from Joel's office to Diana. His testimony is all factual. And all true. I see McNulty's influence. He figures he doesn't need to show very much to get this case to trial. I can't punch a hole in anything Roosevelt says. I'll save it for the trial. I decide not to cross-examine him.

Skipper trots out a straightforward Rick Cinelli to talk about the fight at Harrington's and an edgy Homer Kim to talk about the argument in Bob's office. On cross, I get each of them to admit that they didn't know what the arguments were about. I get Cinelli to admit Joel and Diana may have been talking about business. I get nothing out of Kim.

I figure Skipper is about to wrap up when he calls Art Patton. The courtroom is silent as the Enormous One walks forcefully to the front of the courtroom.

"Mr. Patton," Skipper says, "were you at the Simpson and Gates firm retreat last October?"

"Yes." His tone is measured.

"And during that retreat, did you have an opportunity to see the defendant and Ms. Kennedy?"

"Yes. I saw them many times."

"I would like to ask you about one particular time. Did you see the defendant and Ms. Kennedy at approximately three A.M. on Saturday, October twenty-fifth?"

"Yes, I did."

"And can you tell us the circumstances of that meeting?"

I'm up. "Objection, Your Honor. I fail to see the relevance."

"I'll allow it," says Judge Brown.

Patton tries to look sincere. "I heard noises from Mr. Friedman's condo. I was concerned, so I knocked on his door. Mr. Friedman answered. I asked him if everything was all right, and he said yes. Then I saw Ms. Kennedy in Mr. Friedman's bed. She didn't appear to have any clothes on."

There are shuffling sounds in the back of the courtroom. I steal a glance at Naomi, who is looking down.

"And what did this lead you to conclude, Mr. Patton?"

"Objection," I say. "Speculative."

"Sustained."

"I'll rephrase," says Skipper. "Did you observe Mr. Friedman and Ms. Kennedy having a physical relationship in his room that night?"

"Objection, relevance."

"Overruled."

Patton tries to look embarrassed. He turns to the judge. "I'm uncomfortable discussing the personal lives of members of the firm."

Bullshit.

Brown says, "I'm going to have to ask you to answer the question, Mr. Patton."

Patton exhales melodramatically. "It appeared that they had been in his bed together."

"No further questions."

Nice move, Skipper. It'll be tough to unring that bell. I glance at Naomi as I stand up. She's still looking down. The rabbi is frowning.

"Mr. Patton," I say, "did Mr. Friedman let you into his room?"

He looks at me through his small, round glasses. "No. I stayed outside."

"I see. And did he open the door all the way?"

"No, he didn't."

"How far did he open the door?"

He stops to think. "Maybe halfway."

"Really. Halfway's about a foot, maybe a foot and a half, right, Mr. Patton?"

"I guess so."

"I'll bet you couldn't see much of Mr. Friedman's room through that twelve inches."

"I could see most of it."

"And how long was the door open?"

"About a minute."

"And what was Mr. Friedman wearing?"

"I don't recall. I think he was wearing a sweatshirt and sweatpants."

"Was the light on?"

He scowls. "No."

"Did you see Mr. Friedman touch Ms. Kennedy?"

"No."

"And was Ms. Kennedy under the covers?"

"Yes. The covers were pulled up over her body."

"I see. Yet you just testified that Ms. Kennedy appeared to be naked."

"Yes. From where I stood, she appeared to be naked."

"But you just said she was under the covers."

"I could still see her."

"But she may have been wearing clothes or pajamas or a sweat suit, right?"

"I suppose that's possible."

"And you were looking through a twelve-inch gap in the door into a dark room?"

"Yes."

Now, the kill. "Mr. Patton, did you actually see Mr. Friedman and Ms. Kennedy in bed together that night?"

"No."

"Did you see them have any physical contact that night?"

Skipper's up. "Asked and answered, Your Honor."

"Overruled."

"No," Patton says, "I cannot confirm that they had any physical contact that night."

So far, so good. Now, we'll see if Skipper is awake over there. "Mr. Patton, isn't it true there was a social gathering at your room that same night?"

"I don't recall."

Skipper, wake up. You should start objecting now. "Mr. Patton, I was there that night. I can provide a copy of the invitation for the party that night." It's nice of Skipper to let me testify. He should be up on his feet screaming. I glance over and McNulty's whispering frantically into his ear.

"Yes, Mr. Daley," Patton says. "There was a party in my room that night."

"Good. And was Ms. Kennedy there?"

"Yes."

"Isn't it a fact, Mr. Patton, that Ms. Kennedy left the party because she was upset?"

"I don't recall."

"Let me refresh your memory. Isn't it true she left the party because she was upset when you demanded that she sleep with you?"

The courtroom roars. Brown pounds his gavel. Rabbi Friedman whispers to Naomi.

"Objection, Your Honor. There's no foundation for this."

Look who woke up.

"Overruled."

Patton is grinning. "I haven't the slightest idea what you're talking about."

"Isn't it true, Mr. Patton, that you followed Ms. Kennedy to her room after she rejected your advances?"

Skipper's up. "Objection, Your Honor. The witness has indicated that he doesn't know anything about this alleged incident if, in fact, it took place."

"Overruled."

"Isn't it true, Mr. Patton, that you attacked Ms. Kennedy in her room, and she went to Mr. Friedman's room for protection? And isn't it true you went down to Mr. Friedman's room so you could tell everyone you saw Ms. Kennedy and Mr. Friedman in bed together if Ms. Kennedy ever accused you of sexual harassment?"

Skipper starts to get red in the face as he screams his objection. Before the judge can rule, Patton stands up and shouts, "That's a lie!"

Judge Brown slams his gavel on the little wooden base. I look at Naomi, who gives me an approving nod. Patton regains his composure and sits down.

Judge Brown looks at me. "The objection is sustained," he says in a measured tone.

"No further questions, Your Honor." If Joel is going on trial, Simpson and Gates is going on trial with him.

After brief closing arguments, Skipper makes his motion to bind Joel over for trial. I move for dismissal. Skipper's motion is granted and mine is denied.

"Mr. Daley," Judge Brown says, "I assume you'll want to move for a change of venue."

"No, Your Honor, we're perfectly happy to stay here in San Francisco."

He's surprised. "May I assume your client will waive time?"

I don't hesitate. "No, Your Honor, my client will not waive time. We want a trial date as soon as possible. We want to go in sixty days—sooner, if we can."

I don't know who looks more dumbfounded—Skipper or the judge. Skipper stands up and says, "Your Honor, we have a very tight schedule at the DA's office. It is highly unusual for a suspect not to waive time in a trial of this complexity. Highly unusual."

"Your Honor," I say, "this is a simple case. My client has a statutory right to a trial in sixty days. We'll take the first trial date you've got. If Mr. Gates insists on proceeding with this unsubstantiated case, we want to clear Mr. Friedman's name right away. Mr. Gates just started at the DA's office. He couldn't have filled his schedule yet." I get a smattering of chuckles from the gallery.

Judge Brown gives me a skeptical look. "Mr. Daley, are you sure about this?"

No, I think my client is out of his mind. "Yes, Your Honor. We won't waive time."

"Very well." He looks at his calendar and confers with his clerk. "I'm setting trial for March sixteenth in superior court before Judge Shirley Chen."

I frown. Brown looks at me. "Is there a problem with that, Mr. Daley?"

"No problem at all." Judge Chen is a newly appointed superior court judge. She's another former prosecutor who will be presiding over her first murder trial. Another lousy draw for us.

"Good. Pretrial motions on March ninth." He pounds his gavel and says, "We're done."

20
MOVIE NIGHT

"We have no intention of discussing a plea bargain."
—SKIPPER GATES. *NEWSCENTER 4 DAYBREAK*.
WEDNESDAY, JANUARY 21.

Lights! Camera! Movie night! We have gathered in Rabbi Friedman's living room at six o'clock the next evening to view the security videotapes from the night of the "incident," as we have taken to calling it. True to her word, Sandra Wilson has provided six hours of grainy footage. Hopefully, we'll be able to use the fast-forward button liberally. All things considered, I'd rather be over at Joel's house watching *The Lion King* video with his kids.

Joel fiddles with the VCR. His father sits in a tall, uncomfortable-looking chair in front of the TV, drinking a Sprite. Rosie and I sit on the sofa, our notepads poised. Mort is in a side chair near the TV. He won't be taking notes. He reminds us he's terribly nearsighted. Joel's mother is watching the kids again, so Naomi has joined us. She sits on the floor in front of the TV, her legs crossed. I haven't talked to her since the hearing yesterday. She seems to be holding up reasonably well. It must be tough on the kids. In a modest concession to whimsy at this otherwise stoic gathering, she's made popcorn.

Pete stands behind the sofa, clutching a clipboard with a printout listing all the people who ran their security cards through the computer scanner to check in or out of the Bank of America Building on the night of December 30. He has a separate list of those who signed in or out by hand. He studies his lists. We're trying to confirm what time everybody came and went. And we're looking for inconsistencies between the tapes and the lists, if there are any.

During the evening hours at the Bank of America Building, pedestrian traffic is funneled toward one exit door in the lobby and toward the escalator to the garage. There are two video cameras in the lobby, one on each side of the guard desk. There's a camera by each of the six elevator banks. There is a service elevator that stops at every floor, but you need a key to use it. There are stairs, of course, but the access doors to the office floors are kept locked. There are cameras by the entrance and exit to the garage. It would be pretty tough to leave the building undetected. So they say.

Pete's interviews with the security guards revealed there are no cameras in the elevators or stairs. Too expensive. Except for a few acts of vandalism, there isn't much crime in elevators. Nobody uses the stairs.

Joel hits the play button. The quality of the black-and-white video is similar to the videos of convenience-store robberies you see on shows like *America's Most Wanted*. The time is stamped in the lower-left corner in block white numbers. The cameras don't move. It feels like we're eavesdropping.

Pete is the master of ceremonies. He's been through this exercise many times. "The tape starts at eight o'clock," he says. "At eight-eleven, you'll see Doris Fontaine leaving the building."

Lo and behold, we see Doris insert her security card into the scanner at the guard desk at exactly 8:11 and fourteen seconds.

Pete gives us an "I told you so" look. "At eight-thirty-seven, Mike leaves."

I see myself leaving the building at 8:37 and eighteen seconds. It strikes me that everyone in a security video looks like a criminal.

Mort chirps, "I presume this means we can rule out Mike as a suspect?"

Rabbi Friedman glares at him, and his smile disappears.

There are no surprises in the first two hours. Most of the people attending Skipper's reception leave by 8:30. The evening word processors show up at 9:00. Skipper and the mayor and their respective entourages leave at 9:15. Everything is just as I'd expect—so far.

At 9:30, the people working on Russo's deal begin to leave for dinner. I take notes. I want to confirm Joel's time line. Jack Frazier and Dan Morris leave at 9:32, followed almost immediately by Bob Holmes and Vince Russo. At 9:48, Joel and Diana leave. Frazier's lawyer, Martin Glass, and Ed Ehrlich, from the city attorney's office, leave at 10:00.

Pete reminds us Frazier and Morris went to Aqua, Holmes and Russo went to Tadich's, and Joel and Diana went to Harrington's. Glass and Ehrlich went home. Pete says he's talked to eyewitnesses and confirmed everybody went where they said they did.

Joel loads the second tape. Not much between 10:00 and 11:15, except for Joel's return at 10:25. At 11:15, the rest of the dinner crowd begins to return. Holmes and Russo check in at 11:16. It's hard to tell, but I think Vince is staggering. At 11:18, Frazier and Morris sign in. Nobody looks refreshed after dinner. The videotapes are consistent with the list provided by the security guards.

It's after nine o'clock when Joel starts the third tape, which should contain everything from midnight to two A.M.—the key times, as far as I'm concerned. Our first surprise is at 12:20. Pete looks at his list in disbelief. "He isn't on the list," he mutters, as we stare at the shadowy figure of Skipper Gates passing the guard desk and walking toward the elevators.

I ask Joel to rewind the tape. The NFL isn't the only place where slow-motion instant replays help. "Look," I say, "he walked past the guard desk, but he doesn't run his card through the scanner. He isn't on the list because the guard let him in."

"He isn't supposed to do that," Pete says.

"Happens all the time," I reply. "I can't tell you how many times I've been waved through after hours. You get to know the guards. They let you in."

Pete shakes his head. He's still a cop at heart. This stuff really bothers him. You should see my mother's house. It's a fortress.

"What the hell was Skipper doing there?" Rosie asks.

"Beats me," I say. "We'll find out." I turn to Pete. "Do you have a checkout time?"

He scans his list. "Nope. As far as the guards were concerned, he was never there."

"Either he left without running his card through the scanner, or he didn't leave that night."

Nobody else comes or goes before one o'clock. We're getting into prime time now, and the rabbi's living room is silent. All eyes concentrate on the black-and-white images on the nineteen-inch Zenith. Nobody is eating Naomi's popcorn.

At 1:10, we see the slender figure of Diana Kennedy hurrying toward the guard desk on her way into the building. She's dressed only in a light sweat suit. At 1:10 and fifteen seconds, she waves to the guard, who lets her in without running her card through the scanner. The building managers will have a fit if they see this tape.

One-fifteen. Skipper saunters past the guard desk. We replay the tape twice. My heart races. Silently, I hope he'll be splattered with blood. He isn't, of course. And even if he was, it would be tough to see on the black-and-white video. He waves to the guard, but doesn't run his security card through the scanner. It confirms Skipper was in the building after Diana returned. I make a note to figure out how long it takes the elevators to get down from the forty-seventh floor to the lobby. Skipper may have been there when Diana died. I'm not ready to accuse him of anything—yet. On the other hand, I want to keep my options open. If nothing else, he has some explaining to do.

At one-thirty, Art Patton lugs his stomach, chins and eyebrows past the guard desk and runs his security card through the scanner. Though there's no sound on the videotape, it's clear Patton harrumphs at the guard. Even in the middle of the night, Art can find a way to be pissed off at somebody he barely knows. Five minutes later, Dan Morris and Jack Frazier walk out together. They seem to be having a friendly conversation. They're an odd couple—the political fixer and the investment banker. I make a mental note to check it out.

Vince Russo waddles out on the heels of Morris and Frazier. He scowls at the guard and walks tentatively toward the escalator to the garage.

Finally, Charles Stern brings up the rear at five minutes after two o'clock, looking, as always, as though he has the weight of the world on his narrow shoulders. He looks even worse in black and white than he does in living color, although there's very little difference.

We quickly fast-forward through the next two hours of videotape. Other than the departures of the S&G night-shift word processors, nobody comes or goes. It's eleven-fifteen when Joel turns off the VCR and Pete turns up the lights.

Naomi brings cold sodas from the kitchen. Mort excuses himself to use the bathroom for the seventh time. He's gone out to the back porch twice for cigar breaks.

"Is that it?" Rabbi Friedman asks Joel.

Joel's rewinding the last tape. "That's it," he replies.

"Before you head home," I say, "let's take a few minutes on these tapes."

Mort was already halfway out the door. Rosie hasn't moved from the sofa.

"Michael," Rabbi Friedman says, "is there anything from these tapes that may help us?"

I look at my notes. "There's a lot that may help us." More importantly, there's nothing terrible in there that could hurt us. "First, we can place everybody at the scene and we know what time everybody left. Everybody was in the S and G offices after Diana returned from her apartment. Even Skipper was there."

"How does that help us?" Rabbi Friedman asks. "It doesn't prove any of them did anything. And it doesn't exonerate Joel."

"Rabbi," Mort interjects, "it's always good to be in a position to argue that there were other people around. It gives us options. It helps to give the jury an opportunity to blame it on somebody else. Especially if somebody else isn't particularly likable."

Joel isn't happy with his explanation. "I thought our defense is going to be suicide," he says.

"It is," I say. "But Rod Beckert is going to testify that Bob was knocked unconscious before he was shot. We'll put on our own expert to rebut his testimony. But we also want to keep our options open—and that means we want to identify as many potential suspects as we can. Tonight, we identified a bunch of people who were in the building at the right time—Vince Russo, Jack Frazier, Dan Morris, Arthur Patton and Charles Stern, by my count."

"Don't forget Skipper," Rosie points out. "He was still there when Diana came back."

"I'm supposed to meet with him first thing tomorrow. I'll ask him what he was doing there at one in the morning. The distinguished district attorney of the city and county of San Francisco will be the first name on our witness list." Under the California rules of criminal procedure, you're required to provide a list of potential witnesses. You can get in trouble if you try to call someone who isn't on the list. You can't get in too much trouble, however, if you put someone on the list and you don't call him or her at trial. Prosecutors and defense attorneys play all sorts of games with their lists. If I thought I could get away with it, I would include every name in the San Francisco phone book on ours.

Mort grins. "I like it," he says.

Rosie is more realistic. "They'll never let him testify."

"I know," Mort replies. "But it'll give them something to think about."

We start to gather our belongings when Joel looks in the Macy's bag in which I brought the tapes. "There's one more tape," he says.

Shit. I'm tired.

Rabbi Friedman wipes his glasses. "It's awfully late," he says. "Can't this wait?"

I look at Joel. "It's your call. I can come back in the morning."

"You're supposed to meet with Skipper in the morning. We'd better look at this tape tonight and see if there's anything else on it."

We return to our seats as Joel pops the tape into the VCR. Pete's puzzled. "The inventory says we've seen all the security tapes," he says.

We leave the lights on. It's getting close to midnight.

The tape starts. It isn't another security tape. First we see a black screen. Then we hear a badly dubbed sound track of familiar music. I realize it's the theme from *L.A. Law*. After about ten seconds, some homemade credits appear. SIMPSON & GATES FIRM RETREAT—S.F. LAW. The music continues as the scene shifts to the lobby of the S&G offices. The picture is grainy. Somebody did a real hatchet job with a hand-held camera. S&G lawyers are videotaped as they walk into the reception area. Bob Holmes mugs. Diana Kennedy smiles. Art Patton scowls. Charles Stern says something that I can't make out.

After a few minutes, the scene shifts to the Silverado Country Club in the Napa Valley. The same S&G lawyers who were shown in their business suits now appear in golf shirts and khaki pants. Some are shown heading toward the golf course. Others are playing tennis. One big, happy family.

"What's the point of all this?" asks Rabbi Friedman.

"This tape was taken at the firm retreat last fall," Joel says. "Why is it here?"

"I can't believe Sandra included this with the evidence tapes by mistake," I say.

Pete looks intently at his lists. He finds a note from Sandra indicating the package includes one miscellaneous evidence tape in addition to the security videos.

After a few more minutes of well-dressed yuppies butchering the tennis courts, the scene shifts to a swimming pool in the outer row of condos in the Silverado complex. I recognize Arthur Patton sitting in a lounge chair.

"The white whale," Rosie says.

"Never mind," I reply.

The theme from *L.A. Law* continues to play as the tape cuts to a dinner party in the main dining room. It looks like a convention for blue blazers. There's a quick shot of a crowded dance floor. I catch a brief glimpse of Diana dancing with Art Patton.

The video cuts to the bar in the main house that overlooks the golf course. The camera pans across the crowded room. I see myself sitting next to Wendy Hogan at a small table in the corner. Bob Holmes and Skipper are sitting at a table near the door. They're surrounded by some of the best wineries in the world and they're drinking martinis. Art Patton is sitting next to Diana at the bar. He's drinking a Manhattan. Two empty glasses sit in front of him.

The cameraman circles to his left and focuses on Diana, who winks at the camera. She staggers toward the door. Patton follows her. She gives him a condescending look and says something to him. They continue toward the door. As she passes the table where Joel is sitting, she arches her eyebrows at the camera, leaps into Joel's lap, cups his face in her hands and forcefully kisses him on the mouth. She turns and waves to the camera and struts out of the room. Patton follows her. The camera pans back to Joel, who smiles sheepishly. He says something that's drowned out by the *L.A. Law* theme song. The tape ends abruptly.

Rabbi Friedman's living room is stone-cold silent. I glance at Joel. His eyes are closed. His face is red. Rabbi Friedman sits quietly, his hands folded in his lap. Rosie stares at the TV screen. Pete looks at his clipboard. Mort looks at his watch. Naomi doesn't take her eyes off Joel.

"Well," I say, "maybe this would be a good time for us to break for tonight."

Joel says in a barely audible whisper, "That's probably a good idea."

I stop at Rosie's on my way home. I sip a Diet Dr Pepper. She eats a carrot.

"How do you think the scene in the bar will play?" she asks.

"Pretty bad."

"The security videos looked pretty good. At least there were a lot of people there when everything happened."

"Yeah."

"You don't seem very convinced."

"The thing at the bar is inflammatory. What are you supposed to think if you're on the jury? We had a decent defense that Joel's a nice, old-fashioned family guy who's being wrongly accused. Now, they'll trot out this cheesy videotape showing a pretty young woman throwing herself at him. It won't be hard to decide he's been sleeping around. Juries don't like liars. And they really don't like people who cheat on their wives."

She takes a bite of a tuna sandwich. "Don't you think you may be overreacting a little bit? It doesn't prove he was sleeping around."

I crunch a potato chip. "Maybe. I just don't like it."

"Maybe we can get it knocked out. You know, that tape was edited a lot."

"We'll try. We'll see what the judge says."

"You think he was sleeping with Diana?"

"I don't think so. But two weeks ago, I would have said no. Now, I'm not so sure." I look into her dark brown eyes. Rosie and I never cheated on each other. Our breakup was the result of fundamental incompatibility, which we took out on each other. "What do you think, Rosita? You've always had good instincts."

"I wouldn't bet Grace's college fund, if we had one." She decides to say something positive. "We got some good stuff from the security tapes. Do you think Skipper was involved?"

"Hard to say. I can't imagine what motive he had. But he's slippery. I just can't tell."

She kisses me on the cheek and puts her plate in the sink. "I guess you'll just have to ask him in the morning."

21

"WHAT THE HELL WERE YOU DOING THERE, SKIPPER?"

"In local news, District Attorney Prentice Gates says he's un-
covered new and compelling evidence in the upcoming
double-murder trial of accused killer Joel Mark Friedman."

—KCBS NEWS RADIO. THURSDAY, JANUARY 22.

It's ten-fifteen the next morning, a Thursday. After making
me cool my heels in his newly redecorated reception area
for fifteen minutes, Skipper grants me an audience. He's
brought his faithful companion, Bill McNulty. To even the
odds, I've brought Mort, who will play the "bad cop." To his
credit, he left his cigars in the car.

"What the hell were you doing there, Skipper?" My
methods lack a certain degree of finesse.

Skipper fondles his seven-hundred-dollar MontBlanc
pen. He looks great today. He has a press conference at
eleven. Turn on the lights.

McNasty has left his jacket in his office. He's wearing a
light blue shirt with a blue polka-dot tie. Two Bic pens sit in
his shirt pocket. It's easy to see how Skipper creamed him in
the election.

Skipper smiles broadly. His blue eyes sparkle. He tilts his

head back and laughs loudly. "I take it you've seen the videotapes we asked Sandra to send over?"

"I trust you wouldn't mind telling us what you were doing in the office that night?"

"It's not a big deal. I had to get some papers for a meeting the next morning."

"That's it?" Mort growls melodramatically.

"That's it," he replies.

Mort snaps, "That's the best you can do? That's a piss-poor story, Skipper."

Skipper ignores him.

I take a deep breath. "I don't suppose you considered the possibility that you should have reported your presence at the firm at one in the morning to the police?"

"I did."

"How come it didn't find its way into any of the police reports?"

"Beats me. Ask them. Picking up my briefcase certainly isn't an event that should make the eleven o'clock news."

He's full of shit. "You charged a man with double murder. You decide who gets prosecuted."

"What do you want?" McNulty asks. "He gave his statement to the police. He didn't see anything. He went to his office on forty-six, picked up his briefcase and left."

Mort leaps in. "Bill," he says in a condescending tone, "the security tapes show that he was there for almost an entire hour. What the hell was he doing? And do you plan to testify on Skipper's behalf at the trial?"

"Don't be ridiculous," McNulty replies. "He was preparing for his meeting the next morning."

Mort glares. In the right setting, he can still be effective. He points a stubby finger at Skipper. "You'd better be ready to testify because you're number one on our witness list. You were there and you're going to have to tell your story. In open court. In front of the jury. For the whole world to hear." He practically spits out the last words.

Skipper and McNulty glance at each other. "Mort," Skipper says deliberately, "go ahead and put me on your witness list. Judge Chen will never let me testify. If she does, I'll say exactly what I just told you. I picked up my briefcase. I didn't see anything. Period. End of story."

"I'm glad you've rehearsed your lines," I say, "because you're going to have to explain to Judge Chen why you shouldn't be called." I turn to McNulty. "I'm surprised at you, Bill," I say in my best kindergarten-teacher tone. "I really thought you knew better."

McNulty rubs his eyes. He really does know better. He's just playing along with his boss.

Skipper is amiable. "I don't think we'll be able to resolve this today."

I glance at Mort. Smoke is coming out of his ears. For ten or fifteen minutes a week, he can still trot out some pretty impressive theatrics when he's in the mood.

"So," Skipper says, "did you like the video from the retreat?" He grins. "Pretty cute scene there when Diana gave Joel that big kiss."

"It was nothing," I reply. "She was drunk and she was showing off."

"Whatever you say."

"Where did you get that video, anyway?"

"One of your former partners came forward. He shot it." I stop to think. "Who?" I ask.

"Hutch was taping that night."

Shit. My former partner Brent "Hutch" Hutchinson is a remarkable package of blond hair, gleaming white teeth and a spectacular line of bullshit. His emotional development came to a screeching halt at a frat party during his sophomore year at USC. After nine years as Art Patton's personal lapdog, he finally sucked his way into the partnership last year. He's not much of a lawyer, but he'd make a terrific TV game-show host. We're hopeful advances in medical science will someday permit his doctors to surgically remove his lips from their permanent position affixed to Art's bottom. Among his other attributes, Hutch thinks he's Cecil B. DeMille. He's always sticking his goddamned video camera in everybody's face. "They should have confiscated his camera," I say.

Skipper is pleased. "I thought the overdubbing of the theme from *L.A. Law* was a nice touch."

Mort growls, "Judge Chen will never let that tape in, Skipper. It's been edited a million times. It doesn't prove anything. It's a piece of shit."

McNulty's jaw tightens as he looks at Mort. "We'll get it in," he says.

Mort blusters, "The hell you will."

McNulty turns to me. "By the way," he says, "we got more video footage last night. We haven't had time to get it copied. If we can get Skipper's VCR to work, we'll show it to you."

Skipper pushes a button behind his desk and the opposite wall opens, revealing a twenty-seven-inch Mitsubishi TV. I bet Skipper is the only DA in California with his own movable wall.

"Impressive," I say. "What's playing today? *Twelve Angry Men?*"

"More film from the firm retreat," Skipper replies. "This one's even better."

Swell. More highlights from Brent Hutchinson's coveted video library.

Skipper dims the lights. I bet there aren't many DAs with a dimmer switch, either.

The annoying music from *L.A. Law* starts. The tape opens with a shot of a swimming pool near the tennis courts at Silverado. Nobody's swimming. The chairs are empty.

The camera pans to the hot tub next to the pool. There are two people in the hot tub—a man and a woman. The theme from *L.A. Law* continues to play. The video is shot from a distance. The camera zooms in on the hot tub. From the rear, I recognize Diana's stylish haircut. She's wearing a string bikini. As the camera focuses in on her, I see the top of her bikini is unfastened.

"I didn't realize Hutch was a Peeping Tom," I say to nobody in particular.

Skipper holds up his hand. He doesn't take his eyes off the screen. McNulty turns my way. I think he's trying to smile at me—an unnatural act for him.

The cameraman moves to his left, staying focused on Diana. As he circles, the camera catches the side of her face. Then he pans back and I realize she's not only in the hot tub with a man—she's embracing him. The photographer moves farther to his left. He focuses on Diana. Then he focuses on the man she's kissing.

It's Joel.

McNulty stops the tape. Skipper turns up the lights. He's triumphant. "You still convinced there was no hanky-panky between Diana and Joel?" he asks.

I don't answer.

"There's one other thing, Mike," he says. "We've decided to ask for special circumstances. We're going to make this a death-penalty case."

Mort's in an expansive mood as we drive toward downtown. He's also happy to get his cigars back. "In every case," he says, "there comes a time when you know whether it's a winner or a loser. Today, I think we came to an important point."

I'm really not in the mood for this right now. "And what point is that, Mort?"

"The point where I'm pretty sure we're completely and totally fucked."

There you have it.

"He has a videotape of you and Diana kissing in the hot tub at Silverado." I'm talking to Joel at Rabbi Friedman's house the same afternoon. It's time to explain the facts of life. Thankfully, his father is officiating at a funeral and his mother is at the grocery store. I add, as calmly as I can, that they've decided to ask for the death penalty.

"Shit," he whispers.

"Did I mention the fact that she'd unfastened her bikini top?"

"No," he says quietly, "you didn't."

"It's put-up time, Joel," I say. "We can't have any more surprises. They're going to blow a hole through our defense if you don't start telling me the truth."

He's not giving. "It was nothing. She got playful in the hot tub. We got a little carried away."

It rings hollow. "If you want to get something off your chest, now's the time. It won't get easier. They're going to use the tape at trial. Tell me the truth. I need to know what was going on."

He looks right at me. "What do you want me to say?" he shouts. "We got carried away. That's it. I admit it. Okay? Diana and I were kissing in the hot tub. Are you happy now?"

"Does Naomi know about this?"

"No."

I pause. "You'd better tell her. It's going to come out. And it's better if she hears it from you."

"I know."

Something's going on. "What is it, Joel?" I ask.

"Naomi said she wants to take the kids down to her mother's in L.A. until the trial is over."

This is not good news. "We need her. It can't look like she's abandoning you." I know how it feels to have a marriage shatter. When Rosie and I split up, the pain in the bottom of my stomach was unbearable for months. I couldn't eat. I couldn't sleep. I blamed myself. She blamed herself. We were both a mess. And we didn't help each other through it. And I wasn't on trial for murder when it happened to me. "Can you talk to her?"

"I'll try," he whispers.

"Good. Now tell me what was really going on between you and Diana."

"Nothing," he says. "Honest to God. Nothing."

He's on the verge of tears. He's begging me to believe him. My gut tells me he's telling the truth. My brain tells me he may be one helluva liar.

22
"I NEED YOUR HELP, DORIS"

"We're delighted with the way the case has progressed so far. We're very confident."
—SKIPPER GATES. NEWSCENTER 4. MONDAY, FEBRUARY 16.

"Jesus, Mikey, you haven't spent a lot of time fixing this place up, have you?" Doris smiles. Three weeks later, on Monday, February 16, at ten in the morning, Doris is getting another look at my office. Nothing much has changed since the last time, except for the boxes of files and evidence for Joel's case.

"I always water your plant."

"Good thing." She gives me a hug. She's tan and more relaxed than I've seen her in a long time. She scrunches her face. "The daily special next door must be kung pao chicken."

She's probably right. "How was your trip?" I ask.

"Great. I love the Bahamas. I've met a lot of people down there over the years. Bob had business with a couple of the bankers. They showed me a good time."

"How's Jenny?"

"Okay." She shrugs. "Last semester. A lot of stress." We exchange small talk. She shows me photos from her trip. After a few minutes, she turns serious. "Mikey, why did you ask me to come down here today?"

I look right at her. "We're getting ready for Joel's trial. Things aren't going so well." I take a deep breath. "I need your help, Doris."

"I figured. It's going to cost you, though."

"How much?"

"At least one, and maybe two, cups of coffee. Maybe even lunch."

"I'll talk to our executive committee. I'll see what I can do."

"If you want to understand Bob," Doris says as she takes a drink of coffee, "you have to go back to his early years at the firm. Things were different. The firm was smaller." She winks. "The legal profession was a lot less complicated." She gets a faraway look in her eyes. Ah, the good old days.

"Anyway," she continues, "they hired Bob right out of Harvard to work with Leland Simpson, as in Simpson and Gates. I was Leland's secretary."

"What was he like?"

"A gentleman, although some people thought he was a greedy old son of a you-know-what."

I never met Leland. According to my sources, he was an elegant man from one of the wealthiest families in the city. Depending on who's telling the story, he may also have been racist, sexist and anti-Semitic.

She continues. "Leland tried to take Bob under his wing, but he wasn't real receptive. He thought he knew everything. He told me on his first day he was going to be running the place within five years. Leland had him pegged. He said we'd have to take him down a rung or two."

"Was Bob married?"

"Yes. His first, to his high-school sweetheart, Sue, who was pregnant with his first son, Robert III. The marriage lasted only a year or two. By the time the baby was born, they were already separated. She left him and went back to Wilkes-Barre. There was a rumor that she ended up in an institution."

If working with Bob was hard, I can only imagine what it must have been like living with him. "Did the divorce have any effect on him?" I ask.

"Not really. He used to say he was going to sleep with every unmarried woman in the Bay Area. There was no such thing as AIDS back then."

It seems he was developing a pattern of behavior he continued for the rest of his life.

"Things weren't going so well for him at the firm," she continues. "To be honest, he was lazy. His career limped along for a few years. At one point, they were going to ask him to leave. Then he married Elizabeth Sutro, whose father was the presiding judge of the San Francisco Superior Court. He started getting introductions into some of the city's tonier circles. Leland decided it might be a good idea to keep him around."

"I guess you don't want to piss off the presiding judge."

"Something like that, Mike."

I find it difficult to picture Bob Holmes in black tie at social functions in Pacific Heights.

She looks at my plant. "Then Bob got involved with Leland's biggest client, Vincent Russo Sr. He was a doctor from Hillsborough who made a lot of money and invested it in real estate. Eventually, he gave up his medical practice altogether to manage his investments full-time. According to Leland, Vince senior predicted every trend in the real-estate business for twenty years. He practically invented the real-estate syndication business. He made a fortune."

"Which his son pissed away," I reply. She knows more about Russo's business than I thought.

"Something like that," she replies.

"So how did Bob get involved with Vince senior?"

She chuckles. "Right place at the right time. Vince senior had two in-house lawyers. Ron Dawson was a decent attorney, but not the brightest star in the galaxy. Joan Russell was really smart and an absolute workhorse. When she got pregnant, she took six months off. Dawson was overwhelmed, so Vince senior asked Leland if he could borrow an attorney until she got back."

"So Leland lent him Bob?"

"That's right. Leland was happy to get Bob out of his hair. Instead of staying for six months, he stayed for three years. He spent his time sucking up to Russo and Dawson. They loved him."

She explains that shortly after Bob returned to the firm, Leland had a heart attack and died. Bob was the only attorney at the firm who had extensive contact with Russo and Dawson.

"Sounds like he had pretty good leverage," I say.

She fingers the small gold chain that holds her glasses. "I'll never forget Leland's funeral. Bob pulled me aside and said he had the firm by the 'short hairs.'" She makes little quotation marks in the air with her hands. "He told me he'd take care of me if I stuck with him. I thought it was disgusting." She scowls. "Anyway, he went out and got a couple of offers from other firms. He told Art if they didn't make him a partner, he'd take Russo's business with him to Pettit and Martin. So they rolled over. Made him a partner two years early. Gave him a big office and his own secretary—me. And pretty much everything else he asked for."

"The monster was born."

"Something like that."

It's noon and we have adjourned to the Chinese restaurant. I munch a spring roll. Doris chews a potsticker. "What happened with Bob and the former Elizabeth Sutro?" I ask.

"Their marriage lasted almost five years. He seemed happy. She was pretty and she had lots of money. They had three kids and bought a big house on Broadway. Servants and everything. The firm was paying him a fortune. They put him on X-Com."

"So he really was running the firm by the time he was thirty-five."

"Yes. But in the early years, he was much more business-like. He instituted financial controls. We opened the overseas offices. Then he started to get on everybody's nerves. The old-timers resented him because he kept insisting they bring in more business. The younger partners resented him, too, because they thought he manipulated the compensation system. Every year, he demanded more money. Every year, they gave in to him. He targeted partners he didn't like. Cut their points. Some got fired."

I'm vaguely familiar with that scenario.

She sips her tea. "Things got nasty during his second divorce," she says. "He actually swore off sex for a short period. It was supposed to be a year, but it only lasted about a week." She arches her eyebrows. "Then he found another girlfriend."

Wife number three was Elizabeth Jorgensen, the weekend anchor on Channel 4. Around the firm, she was known as Elizabeth II. A year later, she dumped Bob and ran off with the weekend weatherman.

It's almost one. The waiter brings us fortune cookies. We're up to wife number four, Elizabeth Ryan, or Elizabeth III, a tenacious litigator with the Anderson firm. She's always been polite to me, but I wouldn't mess with her. "You know Beth used to be married to Art Patton," Doris says.

"I wasn't aware of that."

"Art was not happy when she married Bob."

I'll bet. "Is that when Art began his search for the perfect trophy wife?"

She doesn't dignify the question with an answer. "Bob and Beth were married five years ago," she says. "They had three kids. Of course, he was sleeping around the entire time."

Bob was a busy guy. Give him points for being consistent. Sort of like a dog in perpetual heat, without the charm.

"About two years ago," she says, "Beth told him she'd had enough. She said she'd divorce him and take every penny." She asks the waiter for water. "He was good for about six months."

A new record.

"Then he met Diana. He was infatuated with her."

After almost three hours, we've finally made it to the good stuff.

"Mike," she says quietly, "am I going to have to testify at the trial?"

Damn right you're going to have to testify—if your testimony helps us. "I hope not. If it helps Joel, we may have no other choice. I'll try to keep you out of it if I can, but it may be tough."

She gives me a knowing look. "I figured you'd say that," she says.

"I know you and Bob were close. But I'm running out of time and I'm running out of leads. I need you to tell me what you know. I promise to do my best to keep your part in this as small as I can."

"Okay, Mikey." She takes a deep breath. "Bob and Diana had a torrid affair. He sent her flowers. They met at hotels during the day. They used to sneak off on business trips."

I keep my eyes on her. "How long was this going on?"

"From the time she started until the beginning of this past December. They were at it for a little over a year. That's when Beth found out. Actually, it's a miracle she didn't figure it out sooner. Everyone at the firm knew about it."

Everyone but me, of course.

"I think she put a private eye on his tail. He caught Bob and Diana in bed. Beth told him she was going to file for divorce. I was there the night she confronted him. He begged her for one last chance. He broke it off with Diana."

"And?"

"Obviously, the reconciliation was unsuccessful."

Duh, Mike. She did, in fact, serve him with divorce papers. I ask the waiter for the check. "Doris," I say, "did you know Diana was pregnant?"

Her eyes dart away. "Yes, I knew."

"Do you have any idea who the father might be?"

"I don't know."

"Doris," I say slowly, "do you think it could have been Joel?"

"Come on, Mike. You know Joel. Not a chance."

At two o'clock, we're back in my office. Doris doesn't seem to be getting tired. "What was young Vince Russo like?" I ask.

Her expression turns to genuine disgust. "A pig. A sexist. A self-centered jerk."

"Don't sugarcoat it, Doris. Tell me how you really feel."

She doesn't smile. "He was a wild animal. He treated everyone like dirt. He cheated on his wives. He cheated his business partners. He's lucky he didn't end up in jail."

"Was he friends with Bob?"

"In a manner of speaking. Bob pretended to be friends with any client who paid him a lot of money. Bob hated his guts, but Vince didn't know it."

"Did they socialize?"

"Well," she says, "they went on business trips together to the Far East. If chasing thirteen-year-old virgin barmaids in Thailand falls within your definition of socializing, the answer to your question is yes."

"Do you think he may still be alive?"

"Wouldn't surprise me."

I decide it may be time to change the subject. "Do you know anything about Bob's will?"

She nods uneasily. "I typed it. I'd rather not talk about it. It's private."

"I understand. But it's going to become a matter of public record. It will save me a lot of time if you can tell me a little bit about it."

"What do you need to know?"

"Do you know who the beneficiaries are?"

She pauses. After more than twenty years of guarding Bob's secrets, she's uncomfortable revealing the terms of his most personal document. "A third to Beth, a third to the kids and a third to charity."

Sounds pretty straightforward. "Do you know if Bob was going to change his will?"

She studies me. "Maybe. He asked me to print out a copy of his will the day before he died. If he did make any changes, he didn't ask me to do it."

"Did he have a lot of money?"

"I would think so, but I don't know for sure. He kept his finances private."

No big surprise. "Do you know which charities were named in the will?"

"Actually, it's a charity down in the Bahamas called the

International Charitable Trust. He donated a lot of money to it over the years."

That name keeps popping up. "Do you know what the International Charitable Trust does?"

"I'm not sure."

"Do you know how we can get in touch with them?"

"There's a banker in the Bahamas named Trevor Smith who handles everything. I'll get you his phone number."

I decide it's time to play a hunch. Finding out the story behind the International Charitable Trust is going to the top of Pete's priority list.

23

THE GRIEVING WIDOW

"My husband would have been touched by the great outpouring of love when he died."

—ELIZABETH HOLMES. INTERVIEW ON NEWSCENTER 4.
TUESDAY, FEBRUARY 17.

"I'm terribly sorry about what happened, Beth. I know there isn't much I can say to change things." The next morning, I'm sitting in the Versailles-like living room of the Presidio Terrace mansion Beth Holmes shared with Bob. Although three and a half million bucks doesn't buy as much as it used to in San Francisco, Presidio Terrace is about as tony as it gets. The turn-of-the-century homes are occupied by a U.S. senator and her investment-banker husband, several Fortune 500 CEOs and a smattering of San Francisco aristocracy.

"Thanks," she says unenthusiastically, as she lights a cigarette. "You don't have to lay it on too thick. Everybody knows I served him with divorce papers that night."

It's nice to see she's not overwrought with grief.

She's early forties, with unnaturally bleached-blond hair,

leathery skin from the tanning machine, a slightly altered nose, several minor enhancements to her hips and, if I'm guessing right, breasts. If all of her bodily adjustments slip at the same time, she'll probably look like a rubber band being shot across the room. On the other hand, she's a helluva commercial litigator. She reminds me of her ex-husband, Arthur Patton, without the charm or the chins.

"I know this may be difficult," I say, "but I was hoping you might be able to help us sort out what happened that night."

She smiles knowingly. "I find Skipper's version of the story a lot more convincing than yours."

At least we're starting on an even keel. "I understand you were at Bob's office that night."

"Yes, I was. I wanted to be there when the divorce papers were served. After all the shit he put me through, I wanted to see the look on his face."

"Couldn't you have waited until after the closing?"

She gives me a look of genuine disdain. "You don't get it. I *wanted* to deliver the divorce papers in the middle of his fucking closing, while all his buddies were around. Especially that pimp, Vince Russo, and the little tramp, Diana. Sweet little Princess Diana." She mutters something under her breath that sounds like the word "cunt."

I take a sip of the iced tea from the crystal glass provided by her maid. "I realize it's none of my business, but you know I've got to ask. What happened between you and Bob?"

She takes a long drag on her cigarette. "The same thing that happened with you and Rosie."

I think she may have intended that as a cheap shot. "Was he seeing another woman?"

"For God's sake, Mike, of course. Everybody knew about it. He was shtupping Diana for at least a year. When I found out about it at the beginning of December, I threw him out. He promised he'd make it up to me. Then he hopped right back in the sack again."

"With Diana?"

"Yeah. And with anybody else without a penis. If you think we've had a horny president, you should have seen Bob."

"Why didn't you file divorce papers at the beginning of December?"

"I gave him one last chance. He behaved for a week. Then my PI caught him with another woman. I threw his ass out for good." She stubs out her cigarette forcefully in the crystal ashtray.

"Do you know if he was still seeing Diana at the end of December?"

She lights another cigarette. "Don't know for sure. He was like a fucking rabbit."

"Do you know if he was seeing any other women?"

"I don't know that, either. My PI definitely saw him with little Diana in the beginning of December. And my PI saw him with somebody else after that. We couldn't ID her. It may have been Diana. Maybe a hooker, if my guess is right. He saw them at the Fairmont."

"Would you mind if I talked to your PI?"

"No problem." She turns to a servant who is standing by the door and speaks to her in Spanish. The servant leaves the room for a moment, then reappears and hands me a business card. It says Nick Hanson, Private Investigator. I recognize the name. I put the card in my pocket.

Maybe it's time to change the subject. "We got a copy of Bob's will." A small lie. Actually, all I know about the will is what Doris told me. "It seems you may inherit quite a bit of money from him."

"That's true. It doesn't make up for all the crap, but it's not a bad consolation prize." Interesting choice of words.

She plays nervously with her hair. "Charles Stern is handling everything. He may be as dull as a parking meter, but he's good. A third of the estate goes to me, a third goes to the kids and the rest goes to some charity in the Bahamas. It's going to take a while to sort it out."

"Do you happen to know the name of the charity?"

"It's called the International Charitable Trust."

Hello again. "Do you know anything about it?"

"Nope. Charles might be able to tell you something. Bob gave them a lot of money."

"Did it occur to you that if you split up, he might write you out of his will?"

"Yes."

"And you realize, of course, that his untimely death means your claim to one-third of the estate remains in place."

She stares daggers at me. "Of course." She pushes the phony blond bangs from her eyes. "I don't like the implication. I don't need the money. We can live perfectly well on my draw."

It's true, I'm sure. She must pull down at least four hundred fifty thou a year. Nice piece of change for a woman who's been described from time to time as trailer-park trash from Texas. She may lack a certain amount of finesse, but she's made it on her own in the big boys' world. I decide to try something else. "Was there any life insurance?"

"It's none of your business. But the answer is yes. There's a million-dollar policy for each of his kids and a five-million-dollar policy for me."

At least I know where the money's going. Of course, I'd assume the beneficiary on the five-million-dollar policy would have been changed after the divorce. And she may get nothing if Bob committed suicide. Life-insurance policies contain a clause that says the beneficiary won't be paid if the named insured commits suicide within a couple of years after the policy is issued. "Do you know much about Russo?"

"He's an asshole. And a crook."

"I think we can all agree on that. We're still trying to find out what happened to him. Some people think he and Bob may have had some investments together."

She gives me a condescending look. "Whatever Bob did with Russo was between the two of them. Bob never talked about it with me. And frankly, I didn't want to know. As far as I'm concerned, they were just two horny bastards chasing underage girls in Southeast Asia."

"They really used to do that?"

She nods.

Not much left for discussion there. "Do you still see some people from the firm?"

"Charles Stern has been helpful. Art's been very support-ive. It's nice when your ex still cares."

In many ways. "Do you think Bob was so distraught about the divorce that he decided to kill himself?" I decide I'd better see where she's coming from in case Skipper puts her on the stand.

She tugs at her cigarette and cackles loudly. "Don't be ridiculous, Mike. He was a few hours from a three-million-dollar bonus. That's all he ever cared about. He'd changed wives more times than most people change socks." She throws her head back and laughs again. "No, he wasn't dis-traught about the divorce. Hell, he was probably looking forward to it."

I'm sorry I asked.

"So the answer to your question," she continues, "is no. He wasn't the least bit upset about the divorce or the deal with Russo or anything else. The only thing he was upset about was that his little floozy, Diana, wasn't sleeping with him anymore. He wouldn't have killed himself for it. Not a chance. Not with a three-million-dollar check waiting for him."

She blows a smoke ring toward me. "You don't have to take my word for it. You can talk to his shrink. She's that nutcase up in Marin County with her own radio show. Dr. Kathy Chandler. Give her a call. If you can't get her office, try her on the radio."

"Mrs. Fink," I say, "I know this is difficult, and I appreciate your taking the time to see me." Diana's mother, Ruth Fink, lives by herself in a dark bungalow at Twenty-second and Clement, about a mile from Joel's house. She's a heavyset woman in her late fifties with gray hair and lifeless eyes. The kitchen cabinets are at least sixty years old and look as though they haven't seen a paintbrush in the last forty. There are two pictures of Diana in the living room. Unless someone told you it was the same person, you'd never know. The woman in the first picture weighs at least 250 pounds and has brown hair and a long, crooked nose. The woman in the second picture is the trim, blond, sexy Diana that I knew. Joel was right. It was a rebirth.

"It's been very difficult," she says. "My husband died when Debbie was in her teens."

I'd forgotten that Diana was Debbie until her first year of law school.

"We managed to get by," she continues, "on my salary at the JCC and a few odd jobs that I picked up. We were lucky. We had enough life insurance to take care of most of the basics."

"Did Mr. Fink die young?"

Her eyes turn sad. "He had a heart attack when he was in his late thirties."

"Were you and Debbie close?"

"Yes, until she went to law school at UCLA. She got in with a different crowd. She changed." She glances across the room at Diana's picture. "She became less attentive to her studies. She stopped coming home at the holidays. She became fixated on herself. And making money." She takes a sip of water. "Then she got married to that boy Billy. He was her instructor at the health club. I knew from the start it wouldn't work out. She barely knew him." She shakes her head. "In some respects, I blame myself. I tried to stop her. I'm sure it only pushed her toward him. The marriage lasted less than a year."

For a brief moment I think about Grace and wonder how I'll react when she brings home her first boyfriend. The kid better have an impressive resume.

"Mr. Daley," she says defensively, "I just wanted what was best for my daughter. I wanted her to go to good schools and to get a good education. Is that so terrible?"

"Of course not, Mrs. Fink," I say. "That's what we all want for our kids."

"Toward the end, I hardly knew her. She started dating married men."

"Mrs. Fink," I say gently, "it doesn't always work out just the way you hope. Did she ever mention Joel Friedman?"

She closes her eyes at the mention of Joel's name. "Yes, Mr. Daley. She was very fond of Joel. He was a very popular boy in the neighborhood. I've known Joel and his father for years. I always thought Joel was a good boy. Now, I'm not so sure."

I figure it's best not to push this line of questioning too far. "Did Debbie have many friends?"

"Not really. She kept in contact with some of her friends from law school. The only people she ever mentioned from the office were Bob Holmes and Joel."

I'm beginning to thank her for her time when she interrupts me. "You know, Mr. Daley," she says, "there's one other thing you should be aware of. She had resigned from the Simpson firm. She'd accepted a job with a firm in San Diego."

"Why was she leaving?" I ask.

"She wanted a fresh start. She was pregnant, you know."

"I know." I look out the small window for a moment. "Why San Diego?"

"My sister lives there. I was planning to move down there myself. I thought it might be a good time for a fresh start for all of us. This house has a lot of memories."

"I see." Joel didn't mention that Diana was moving. "Mrs. Fink," I say, "I know this question is going to sound indiscreet."

She stops me. "I know what you're going to ask, Mr. Daley. The answer, I'm afraid, is I don't know who the father is."

"Thank you very much, Mrs. Fink. You've been extraordinarily helpful."

24

"I'D NEVER ASK YOU TO VIOLATE
ANY CONFIDENCES, CHARLES"

"The only things in life that are certain are death, taxes and
the need for tax lawyers."

—CHARLES STERN. CONTINUING LEGAL EDUCATION SEMINAR.

The next morning I'm at the S&G office on a fishing expe-
dition. Charles Stern has promised to give me copies of the
firm's key-man life insurance policies. He's trying to appear
cooperative. I could subpoena the firm's records. He knows
it. It's a shot in the dark. I know S&G carried a life insurance policy on Bob. I'm trying to confirm how big the policy is. More importantly, it's a pretext for me to see if I can
find out anything else about his will and finances.

I'm surprised he's agreed to see me. And I'm really surprised he's agreed to see me alone. Seems like every time I
show up at S&G, I'm greeted by the entire executive committee. I accept his offer of coffee. He buzzes his secretary
and a cappuccino magically appears. There's something to
be said for big-firm amenities.

His functional office on the forty-sixth floor has S&G's
standard-issue executive furniture: large, industrial-strength

rosewood desk, matching credenza, two guest chairs and a bookcase. Most of the power partners have fancy custom-built furniture that they pay for themselves. Not Charles. He's too cheap for anything other than basic inventory. There's a small gray sofa next to the door, which he pilfered when one of my partners was fired a few years ago. The only picture on the wall is a *New Yorker* cartoon of an accountant hovering over a tax return. An antique adding machine sits on a small table beneath the cartoon. He once told me his father is the oldest living person still licensed to practice accounting in the state of New York. The bookcase holds about a dozen black loose-leaf volumes. The gold lettering on the spine proclaims they're called the *CCH Standard Federal Tax Reporter*.

His desk is immaculate. Not a scrap of paper. Not a speck of dust. I've always admired people who have a clean office. I don't know how anybody can possibly work that way. A state-of-the-art laptop sits on a small table next to his desk. It isn't turned on. It's a trophy. It shows he got the firm to buy him the computer. He isn't expected to use it.

He drinks coffee from a mug that bears the S&G logo. He's wearing his gray suit jacket. He straightens his tie and looks at me uncomfortably. "What can I do for you?" he asks. I wonder if he's forgotten his offer.

"I was hoping you had a chance to put together the copies of the firm's insurance policies."

He's relieved. "Yes," he replies. He buzzes his secretary and asks her to bring in a file marked "Insurance Policies." Charlotte Rogers is a middle-aged black woman who's been with Charles for about fifteen years. She's the lucky soul who gets to type all of his memos on billing procedures. She's reasonably pleasant about it. She appears with a large file folder almost as soon as he hangs up.

"Our malpractice policy is in there," he says. "I haven't the slightest idea why you'd want to look at it. I put in a summary of our medical policy. If you want the policy itself, I'll get you a copy."

I couldn't care less about the malpractice and medical policies. "Were you able to track down any life insurance policies?"

He nods. "There's a key-man life insurance policy on every partner. I've enclosed a summary of the policy terms. If you'd like the details, you can talk to our insurance agent."

"Hopefully, that won't be necessary." I'll see what I can get out of the insurance agent later. "How much life insurance do you carry on the partners?" This is, of course, something I should already know. I'm sure it was in a memo Charles sent out to the partners sometime in the last decade or so.

"It depends," he replies.

"On what?"

"On how valuable the partner's practice is to the firm."

"I see." This means they probably had a million-dollar policy on Bob and a five-thousand-dollar policy on me. "How big a policy did you carry on me?"

I get the hint of a grin. The crow's-feet around his eyes crinkle. "The minimum. Twenty-five thousand."

More than I thought. "And the policy on Bob?"

"I think it was about two and a half million dollars."

Not bad. Bob was worth only a hundred times more than I was. I'm sure Bob would have said he was worth more. "Do you have any other policies on the partners?"

"No. We're just starting the process of changing carriers. Brent Hutchinson is in charge of insurance issues."

Perfect. S&G's best bullshitter gets to spend his free time schmoozing with insurance salesmen. I wonder if some sort of harmonic convergence occurs when that much bullshit is jammed into one room. "Maybe I should talk to Hutch," I say.

"I doubt he'll be able to tell you much," he replies. "He was just getting started."

If past history is any indication, Hutch hasn't started at all. I have no doubt he won't be able to tell me much about anything. "I was hoping you might be able to help us figure out Bob's will."

He looks at his watch. "I'll do what I can." He hits the do-not-disturb button on his phone. He probably wishes he'd had a similar button installed on his brain. "I can't say much," he says. "Attorney-client privilege, you know. And I've got a meeting."

So many meetings. So little time. I glance at the picture of the accountant. The resemblance is striking. "I understand. I'd never ask you to violate any confidences, Charles." The game begins. A small grin. For a moment, I think I can see a hint of color in his cheeks. "I understand you're the executor of Bob's will."

He studies his antique adding machine. "I am," he replies. "It'll become a matter of public record as soon as it's submitted to the probate court. We've notified the beneficiaries."

I'm watching him closely. He's being a little too forthcoming. This probably means there's nothing much of any consequence in the will. "I appreciate your honesty, Charles. It's a lot easier to do this informally. I was afraid Art was going to make me get a subpoena just to talk to you."

"He was just being careful. I'd rather tell you what I can. There's no point in turning this into something contentious."

Now I'm sure there's nothing important in the will. "I appreciate that, Charles."

"Besides," he says, "I like to help out my partners whenever I can."

I hadn't noticed this generous side of his personality when he and the other partners voted to fire me. "I under-

stand his estate's divided into three parts. A third goes to
Beth, a third goes to the kids and a third goes to some
charity in Bermuda." I'm trying to set him up. I know the
International Charitable Trust is set up in the Bahamas. I
want to see if he'll correct me. And if he'll talk about it.

"Actually," he says, "the charity is in the Bahamas."

I pretend to make a note on my legal pad. "The
Bahamas," I say slowly. "What's the name of the charity?"

"What difference does it make?" he says, a little too defensively.

"Probably none," I lie. "I'm just trying to complete my
file."

He scowls. "It's called the International Charitable
Trust," he says.

I continue writing. "Does it benefit underprivileged kids
or something?" I ask innocently.

"Something like that. I'm not really sure."

He's a lousy liar. "Is it managed in the Bahamas?"

"Oh yes."

"You wouldn't happen to know who manages it, would
you? I'm sure we could look it up, but it'll save me some
time if you know. I'll bet there's a registry of charitable
trusts."

He looks uncomfortable. "I really don't know very much
about it."

I take it back. He's not just a lousy liar. He's a really
shitty liar. "Actually," I say, trying to sound offhand, "it's
probably not important. I'm sure the money goes to widows
and orphans." I shuffle my papers and look at a blank sheet
on my legal pad. "My investigator got a little information.
Says here the trustee is First Bank Bahamas. A guy named
Trevor Smith. I'll give him a call."

His face returns to its customary pasty color. "I know
Smith," he says. "I've worked with him on some matters. I'd
be happy to give him a call. I'll see what I can find out."

"I don't want to impose on you. I know you're busy. I'll call him."

His eyes always give him away. "It's no problem—really," he says. "Let me save you the trouble. He's a banker in the Bahamas who works with a number of our foreign clients. I'm sure he won't tell you anything more than what I'm about to tell you now."

How magnanimous. Obviously, Mr. Smith has never been subject to my persuasive powers.

"Bob checked it out," he says. "I'm sure everything is completely legal and aboveboard."

I'm convinced. I decide to let him squirm. "Does First Bank get a fee for acting as the trustee?"

"What difference does it make?"

"Probably none. I'm just curious."

"I think they get a fee."

He's digging himself in deeper. "A large fee?"

"I don't know. It's probably based on the amount of assets in the trust."

"I see." I watch his eyes. "And do you know how much that fee might have been last year?"

His eyes dart toward the adding machine again. "I really wouldn't be able to venture a guess."

He's a really really shitty liar. "Are you involved in the administration of the trust?"

He squirms. "Technically, I hold the title of trust protector. It means I'm the administrative agent. It's just a formality. All the management is in the Bahamas. Bob asked me to act as trust protector in case they needed a signature in a hurry."

"Does S and G get a fee for the time you spend assisting with the administration of the trust?"

He tugs at his tie and sips his coffee. It must be cold by now. "No, it doesn't."

I've been watching too many *Columbo* reruns late at

night. "If you're the administrative agent, how come S and G doesn't get a fee?" S&G doesn't do a lot of pro bono work.

"Actually," he says, as he shifts in his chair, "I'm paid a modest fee for my efforts."

"You mean the firm gets a fee, right?"

"No. I get the fee."

"I don't understand. If you're doing this trust administration on behalf of the firm, why doesn't the firm get the fee?"

He takes a gold pen from his drawer and begins to play with it. "I do trust administration on my own time, and not on behalf of the firm. It's a liability issue."

"A liability issue?"

"Yes. This is a law firm. The services I provide to the trust fall into the category of fiduciary activities, which our malpractice policy doesn't cover. We notified our malpractice carrier when I was first asked to serve as trust protector. They wouldn't let me do it unless I agreed to do so in my individual capacity, and not in my capacity as an attorney in the firm."

Sounds like our malpractice carrier wants to insure just the right side of his brain, but not the left. "So you did this at the insistence of our malpractice carrier?"

"I had no other choice." Then he adds, "I had to sign an agreement stating that I would indemnify the firm for any losses it incurs in connection with the activities of the trust." He gives me a "so there" look.

"You must collect a fairly substantial fee for this work—especially if you have to carry your own insurance and bear the risk of indemnifying the firm for any losses."

"In reality, my fee is very modest. I did it as a favor to Bob."

And out of the goodness of your heart. "If you don't mind my asking, Charles, about how much was your fee last year?"

He tenses. "That's none of your business, Mike."

It's the answer I expect. "I understand. What happens to the trust now? Where does the money go now that Bob's dead?"

"I believe it's distributed among various charities in the Bahamas."

Of course. "Charles, do you happen to know what those charities are?"

"I don't recall, Mike." He smiles nervously.

Very persuasive, Chuckles. You're the administrator of a trust in which you don't even know who the beneficiaries are. The fog is getting really thick in here. "Think you could find out for me?"

"Probably. It may take some time."

I'll hear from him the Tuesday after hell freezes over. "Maybe Trevor Smith can get me a list."

"I'll call him for you."

"That won't be necessary." I love to watch him squirm. "Charles," I say, "you know Beth served Bob with divorce papers right before everything happened. Was he going to change his will?"

"Not that I'm aware of," he replies. There's a tentative note to his voice.

"Did you do the estate planning work for Vince Russo?"

He nods. "As a matter of fact, I did."

"Would you mind telling me the names of the beneficiaries of his estate?"

He frowns. "I'm afraid that's confidential, Mike. I realize some people think Vince may have committed suicide. However, until a court declares him legally dead, his estate does not become a matter of public record. As a result, I'm not at liberty to discuss his situation with you."

"I see. You haven't heard from Vince, have you?"

"Nope."

"Well, if you hear from him, I'd appreciate it if you'd let me know."

"I promise."

I glance out the window. "Let me ask you one other thing, Charles. How's the firm doing?"

"Just fine."

He'd never make it as a trial lawyer. "I'm sure the tragedy has taken its toll."

He tries to look solemn. "It has. We've had some difficult times. But nothing insurmountable."

I look at the adding machine. "I saw in the paper you decided to let some people go."

"Yes we did. It wasn't easy."

"Layoffs never are, Charles."

"They weren't layoffs. We do reviews this time of year."

I'm convinced. "I'll let you know if I need anything else, Charles. By the way, could you ask your secretary to give me the phone number for Trevor Smith?"

"He's full of it, Mike," Rosie says. Later the same evening, Rosie, Grace and I are eating at Spanky's, a burger joint in Fairfax, not far from my apartment. It's been Grace's favorite restaurant since she won a free sundae in a coloring contest a couple of years ago.

Rosie's reaction to my report on my discussion with Charles Stern is succinct. "I'll bet he knows everything there is to know about the International Charitable Trust," she says. "He's yanking your you-know-what." Rosie's vocabulary switches from R to PG when Grace is around.

Grace's eyes open wide as she takes a long drink of her milkshake. She wipes her mouth with the back of her hand and says, "What's your 'you-know-what,' Daddy?"

I smile. "Ask your mother."

Rosie looks at her seriously. "I'll explain it later, honey."

I turn back to Rosie. "I called Trevor Smith when I got

back to the office. He has a beautiful British accent." I grab a french fry. "And he wouldn't tell me anything."

"And?"

"He's going to be off the island, as they say, for at least the next four weeks. Meetings in Kuwait."

"Does he have an assistant who can help us?"

"She's going to Kuwait, too."

"What a surprise," says Rosie. "What are you going to do?"

"I'm going to have Pete check it out. He's been looking a little tired lately. I think he may need a vacation."

She grins. "Any place in particular you have in mind?"

"I understand the Bahamas are very nice this time of year."

"When might he be going?"

"I think he might be able to clear his calendar about four weeks from now."

Rosie's pleased.

25

"TERMINATED IN THE ORDINARY COURSE OF THE REVIEW PROCESS . . ."

"We regret the media has characterized our personnel moves as 'layoffs.' While it is contrary to firm policy to discuss individual situations, the attorneys who were asked to leave were terminated in the ordinary course of the review process for performance reasons."

—ARTHUR PATTON. *SAN FRANCISCO LEGAL JOURNAL.*
THURSDAY, FEBRUARY 19.

Wendy Hogan calls the next morning. "I suppose you've heard by now?" she says.

"Heard what?" I ask.

"Come on, Mike."

I haven't a clue. "What is it?"

"There were layoffs at S and G." She pauses. "I got fired."

"Shit."

"They told the papers we were canned for performance reasons. It's all chickenshit. We were laid off because there wasn't enough work and the firm is in financial trouble."

"Everybody knows what's going on at S and G. Nobody will believe their bullshit."

Silence. "How am I supposed to find another job when they said we were fired? We're the lepers of the San Francisco legal community." She pauses. "Andy called last night. He said he's going to go to court to challenge our custody deal."

"He's an asshole. Your attorney should be able to take care of it."

"My attorney's on vacation. He won't be back for two weeks."

I don't say anything.

"Mike," she says, "can you help me with this?"

Except for what I learned when Rosie and I split up, I know nothing about divorce law. "I'll see what I can do. Why don't you come down to my office around noon and we'll talk."

What the hell. It's not like I have to prepare for a murder trial. Besides, I like her.

Wendy and I are eating Chinese takeout in my office at noon. She looks around. "Pretty tight space," she says.

"You get used to it." I nibble on a pork bun. "Sounds like I need to find you a good divorce lawyer," I say.

"I need a job."

She's right. It helps to be employed when you're in a custody fight. Believe me, I know. When Rosie and I split up, I got the bright idea that I was better suited to have custody of Grace. Bad idea. It led to the nastiest fight in my life. Ultimately, at the suggestion of Rosie's mom and mine, I came to my senses and gave in. Then things started to get better.

Wendy's ex-husband may be a horse's ass. At the moment, however, he's an employed horse's ass. "You're good at what you do. You'll find something."

"It's not that easy. I don't have my own clients. Firms aren't hiring tax lawyers." She takes a deep breath. "Could you use some help? Maybe I could work on Joel's case."

I lean back in my chair. I'm buying time. How do I say

this? "We do criminal law around here. You know—we represent crooks."

She twirls her hair with her finger. "And most of my clients are in the real estate business. They're crooks, too. Except for the fact that what they do is technically legal."

Touché. "I'd like to help you. But what I really could use is another experienced criminal defense attorney. Preferably one without Mort Goldberg's ego. It isn't that you aren't good at what you do. It's just that what you do isn't what we do. You wouldn't hire me to do an IPO."

"I can do research. I can interview witnesses."

I frown. This isn't a good idea. I can't afford another attorney.

"I'm in a tight spot," she says. "Maybe there's something else I can bring to the table. I've done tax planning for Bob and Vince. Maybe I can help you with the investigation."

This is intriguing. But it also presents a potential problem. "How much tax planning?"

"A lot."

I pause. "Slow down. For one thing, the judge won't let you testify if you work for me. It confuses the jury."

"I know. I used to work for a superior court judge."

"I remember. There's another thing. The stuff you know is probably protected by the attorney-client privilege."

"Most of what I know is already a matter of public record. Besides, Bob is already dead. In all likelihood, so is Vince." She takes off her glasses. "The privilege died with them. Who's going to complain? Their ghosts?"

Technically, that may not be entirely correct. Just because you die doesn't mean your lawyers can tell the world all your deep, dark secrets. "What about the beneficiaries under their wills?"

"What about them? The beneficiaries under Bob's will have already been notified. Nobody's going to complain. They'll notify the beneficiaries under Vince's will as soon as he's declared legally dead, if that happens. Like I said, who's going to complain?"

Without getting into the finer points of the potential claims of their respective heirs, I have to admit she may have a point.

"I won't tell you anything you couldn't find out yourself from public records," she says. "And you don't have to hire me directly. I could start my own firm and you could retain me as special counsel. My name wouldn't appear on the pleadings. I won't appear in court unless I'm called as a witness. What's wrong with that?"

"Nothing I can think of, I suppose."

She smiles. "You see, we're making progress. As Bob Holmes used to say, good lawyers provide practical solutions to real-world problems."

Right. I've been in practice for a month and a half and I have a real-world problem—another mouth to feed, even if her name doesn't appear on my letterhead. "I can't afford to pay you much."

"I understand. At least I can tell a judge with a straight face I'm building my practice."

"All right. The law offices of Wendy Hogan are hereby retained as special counsel. Don't even think about asking for a retainer. You can help Pete with the investigation."

"Anything you say." She's pleased. "Thanks, Mike."

I finish my moo shu pork. "Let me ask you something. Do you know anything about an entity in the Bahamas called the International Charitable Trust?"

She grins. "What would you like to know? I did the legal work to set it up."

Bingo.

Wendy opens a fortune cookie. "The International Charitable Trust," she begins, "is something of a misnomer. For one thing, it isn't really international. It was formed in the Bahamas by one guy—Bob Holmes. For another thing, it isn't the least bit charitable. Unless, of course, your favorite charity happens to be Bob Holmes. It's a tax dodge. I set up a similar trust in the Bahamas for Vince Russo called the Charitable Trust for Humanity. It isn't charitable, either."

I read my own fortune cookie. It says, "You are about to embark on a great romance." Even the fortune cookies know I'm hard up. "You aren't violating anybody's attorney-client privilege here, are you?"

"What if I was?"

"Nothing. Just asking."

Her eyes sparkle. "Everything I'm about to tell you is a matter of public record. Of course, the public records in the Bahamas are a little trickier to track down."

I grin back. "So what were these two trusts all about?"

"They were set up so Bob and Vince would each have a place to park some money outside of the U.S. in a hard-to-find, safe, tax-free place." She's getting excited. "Bob and Vince hated two things more than anything else in their lives: taxes and alimony. And when you made as much money as they did, and when you got divorced as many times as they did, you paid a lot of taxes and alimony."

I can picture Bob and Vince swapping stories about who paid more to their respective ex-wives. Wendy explains that they wanted to find a place to stash as much money as they could in a tax-free jurisdiction where it would be hard for their ex-wives to find. The Bahamas had everything they needed. Perfect weather. Established financial system. Excellent bank-secrecy laws. So Bob and Vince each formed a trust. First Bank Bahamas was the trustee. Trevor Smith handled all the arrangements. It's a standard tax scam. She says Smith is very smooth.

I take a gulp of water. "Actually, I spoke with him yesterday," I say. "You're right. He's very polished."

"And very slippery. Trying to get a straight answer from him is like trying to hold a gallon of water in your bare hands. They did all their investing through the trusts."

I'm pleased. She may be telling me a little more than what I would have been able to find out from the public records in the Bahamas. "Who dreamed this up?"

"Who do you think?"

"You?"

"I had a little help from Chuckles."

It fits. "So it's Chuckles who set up this elaborate charade."

She says in a businesslike tone, "It's all perfectly legal, Mike."

"So it is." In this case, the word "legal" is spelled S-L-E-A-Z-Y.

She confirms that Chuckles holds the title of trust protector, and First Bank is the trustee. "First Bank won't do anything without instructions from Chuckles," she says. "He gets a fee for his trouble. He got permission from X-Com to manage the offshore trusts on his own time. The firm decided it didn't want to have the fiduciary liability for managing somebody else's money."

"How big is his fee?"

"I bet he gets at least half a million bucks a year just from Bob's trust."

Jesus. "What does he have to do to earn his fee?"

"Not much."

"What does it take to get money out of one of the trusts?"

"A signature from Chuckles, or, in the case of Bob's trust, a signature from Bob. Or, in the case of Vince's trust, a signature from Vince."

"So Vince could take money out on his own?"

"Sure. All he needs is a fax machine. He's moved money in and out of the trust all the time."

"So if Russo is alive, he could get money out just by faxing instructions to First Bank?"

"That's right. Except, of course, for the fact that Russo appears to be terminally dead."

"So it would seem." Unless he's still alive.

"Who gets the income from the trusts while Bob and Vince are alive?"

"It's distributed among a group of people who are called income beneficiaries."

"Do you know who they are?"

"Nope. It's a secret. The names of the income beneficiaries are listed in separate, confidential documents. Chuckles never let me see them."

"What happens to the trusts when Vince and Bob die?"

"The assets are sold and the proceeds are distributed to a different group of people called the remaindermen." She pauses. "Before you ask, I don't know the names of the remaindermen, either. It was the best-kept secret in the Western Hemisphere."

That figures. "What happens to the fees paid to Chuckles when they die?"

"They stop." She thinks for a moment. "He can't prevent the trusts from liquidating. But he can probably slow down the process for years. If he does, he can collect his fees for a few more years."

Chuckles wouldn't have had any incentive to kill Bob if his death triggered the liquidation of his trust. "Do you know if Bob was planning any changes in his trust?"

"I think so. A few weeks before he died, he asked me to prepare a list of the steps to amend his trust. He didn't tell me what he had in mind, but I suspect he was considering the possibility of changing the income beneficiaries and the remaindermen."

"That would make sense if Beth was an income beneficiary or a remainderman."

"Could be. He was also talking about changing the deal with Chuckles. He always complained that Chuckles made too much money in admin fees."

Interesting. "What about his will? Was Bob making any changes there?"

"I know he talked to Chuckles about it."

This is showing some promise. "Did he ever get around to amending his will or his trust?"

"Not that I know of. My guess is he died before anything could happen."

So close. Still, if we can figure out who gets the money from Bob's trust, we may be able to figure out who had motive to kill Bob. Unless, of course, he killed himself.

Later the same afternoon, Joel, Mort, Rosie, Pete and I meet in Rabbi Friedman's dining room. I've brought Wendy. "I'd like to introduce you to the final member of our team," I say. "Wendy Hogan is taking a permanent leave of absence from S and G."

Wendy smiles uncomfortably. "That's Mike's way of saying I've been downsized, and I need something to help me pay the bills."

"Welcome to the Dream Team, young lady," Mort says. "I'm Mort Goldberg."

"I've heard a lot about you."

"It's all true," he replies.

I explain that she isn't going to be of record on the case and she's not going to be employed by our firm. "For now," I say, "she'll be a consultant. Just like you, Mort."

He gives me a sideways look.

"Wendy is familiar with Bob's will and his investments," I say. "I've asked her to work with Pete to help figure out how Bob's money gets divided up."

Wendy smiles at Pete. "Hi," she says to him. "I think I

may be able to enlighten you about the International Charitable Trust."

Pete says, "Sounds good to me," but he's uncomfortable. He likes to work alone.

"Wendy," I say, "I have another special task for you. You're a tax lawyer. You're good at money. I want you to figure out everything about the firm's finances and Bob's finances. I have a hunch we'll find some answers. Moreover, you'll get to see why you'd never want to be a partner at a firm like S and G."

"I'll get right on it," she says. "Mort, maybe you can help me subpoena some of the firm's financial records?"

Mort beams. "I'd love to, honey."

I'm going to have to remind him not to call her "honey."

"You sure you know what you're doing with Wendy?" Rosie asks as we stand on her back porch the same evening.

"Yeah. She's real smart." I pause. "I'd like to help her out. She's a good lawyer."

"She's a tax lawyer, Mike." She says it in the condescending tone that trial lawyers reserve for transactional attorneys.

"I know. But she's tenacious. I think she'll help."

She smiles. "You like her, don't you?"

I smile back. "Is it that obvious?" I've had a crush on Wendy for five years.

"Yes." She adds, "And she's pretty."

"That, too." I drink my beer. "You aren't jealous, are you?"

She shrugs. "Don't let it color your judgment. Keep it professional. You're running a law practice, not a counseling center."

She's right, of course. "I wouldn't have brought her in if I didn't think she could help us."

Her eyes glow in the moonlight. "I'm going to remember you said that. And she'd better keep her hands off my sex slave."

"Syc-o-phant n. One who attempts to win favor or advance himself by flattering persons of influence; a servile self-seeker; a toady."

—*World Dictionary of the English Language.*

The next morning, I'm back at the S&G offices. Anyone who believes substance will ultimately triumph over style hasn't met Brent Hutchinson. His entire career is an ongoing charade of teeth, blond hair and good looks. So far, he's been wildly successful. His office overlooking Alcatraz Island and the Marin Headlands is furnished with an antique roll-top desk and two antique chairs. A small oriental rug graces the middle of his floor. He has his own collection of Currier and Ives lithographs. A picture of his cheerleader wife, Barbi, smiles at him from his spotless desk. Life is good in Hutchworld.

"So, big guy," he says, "how's the new firm working out?" To Hutch, everyone is a "big guy."

"So far, so good. I seem to have stumbled onto a big murder case."

"I know. Cool."

Someday, a team of graduate students will do a dissertation on Hutch called "The Mind of the Sycophant." It will take up many volumes. "Hutch, I came to ask you for your help."

"Anything. I always try to help out my friends."

I wasn't aware that we were friends. "I understand from Charles Stern that you've been appointed the czar of the firm's insurance policies."

He throws his head back like Burt Lancaster. "Insurance czar. I like that." He laughs too loudly. "It's true. I'm the chairman of our risk-management committee. I get to deal with all our insurance issues." He winks. "It's real exciting, Mike."

I wink back. "I'll bet." The potential exposure for malpractice claims at a firm like S&G is hundreds of millions of dollars. Why they've put a moron like Hutch at the head of the professional liability team is beyond my comprehension. "I'm trying to sort out all of the life insurance policies on Bob. I don't expect to find anything very interesting, but I thought I should talk to you. Does the firm carry any key-man insurance on the partners?" It's the first rule of cross-examination—never ask a question unless you know the answer.

"As a matter of fact, we do. You know, there was a memo on this sent out to the partners toward the end of last year."

"I must have missed it." Or tossed it.

"Well," he says, "we carry life insurance on all the partners. On guys like us, we don't carry much. I think the minimum's about twenty-five thousand. We carry a lot more on the heavy hitters like Bob and Art." He gives me the Cheshire cat grin.

"How much?" I ask.

"In a couple of cases, over a million bucks."

"Do you know how much you're carrying on Bob?"

The grin disappears. "You know, Mike, now that you

don't work here anymore, I'm really not supposed to talk about this stuff with you."

"But I'm still on the line for the firm's debts that were incurred while I was a partner. If you're going to collect a big piece of change on the key-man insurance, I have the right to know about it." I'm amiable when I add, "If you'd prefer, I can come back with a subpoena." You pretentious little jerk.

His phony smile returns. "Let's not get excited. We're carrying two and a half million dollars on Bob."

Good. It confirms what Chuckles told me. "Thanks, Hutch." That wasn't so hard, now, was it? "Charles said you're looking into changing the firm's carrier."

"That's true. We got some of the first policies in place right before the end of the year."

Really? I got the impression from Charles that Hutch was just starting the process. "Did the firm take out any additional life insurance on the partners?"

"Yes. We were trying to bump up the policy levels for some of the more junior people. I know I got bumped up from twenty-five thousand to a half a million."

That's because you're worth so much. "Was the policy on Bob bumped up?"

"I don't recall. I can find out."

"Actually, Hutch, if you'd give me the name of the insurance agent, I can give him a call."

"It's no problem, Mike. I can find out." Affability reigns.

"I don't want to take any more of your valuable time, Hutch. Really, it's no big deal."

He concedes. "His name is Perry Guilford. I'll have my secretary get you the number."

"Hutch," I say a few minutes later, "Skipper was kind

enough to show me some of your cinematographic work from the firm retreat last year."

He's pleased with himself. "I thought it turned out pretty well."

Right. "You know, there was some pretty inflammatory stuff in there."

There's a pause. "You know how it gets at the retreat."

"Yes, I do." It doesn't mean you have to stick your god-damned camera in everybody's face. "Hutch, the judge asked me whether there's an unedited version of the tape. You know—without all the music from *L.A. Law.* Any chance you saved the original?"

He's unhappy. He probably thinks I'm trying to compro-mise his artistic integrity. "I don't have the original. We used it to make the overdubbed version. Our methods are pretty rudimentary."

I'll say. The special-effects wizards at Industrial Light and Magic won't be real worried. "Did you give Skipper everything you had?"

His eyes get large. "Yeah."

"What else was on the tape?"

"Nothing much. I really don't remember." He isn't look-ing at me.

Bullshit. "Who else saw the tapes?"

"Chuckles and Art."

What a surprise. "Did they tell you to destroy part of the tape?"

"No," he says.

He's lying. "What else was on the tape, Hutch?"

"I don't remember."

"We can do this the easy way or the hard way. Now, tell me what was on the tapes."

No way. He purses his full lips. "I don't remember, big guy."

Sure.

27

DR. KATHY CHANDLER

"If you'd like to speak to Dr. Kathy Chandler, call 1-800-GET-HELP."

—KTLK TALK RADIO. FRIDAY, FEBRUARY 20.

Dr. Kathy Chandler fancies herself the Bay Area's very own Dr. Frasier Crane. Of course, Dr. Frasier Crane has an imaginary degree from Harvard. Dr. Kathy Chandler, on the other hand, has an honorary doctorate in family counseling from Southwestern Texas City College and an honorary degree from the Great Pacific School of Broadcasting. More importantly, Dr. Frasier Crane only talks to imaginary patients. Dr. Kathy Chandler, unfortunately, talks to real people. Every weeknight from seven until ten, she dispenses bubblegum psychology on the live one, KTLK Talk Radio.

I must confess that her show is mildly entertaining. I listen to it sometimes on my way home from work. I think I'll appreciate it more if and when I get the lobotomy I keep promising myself.

Like many radio talk-show hosts, she's always known as Dr. Kathy Chandler. She's never simply Dr. Chandler—or,

God forbid, Dr. Kathy. And she always refers to herself on the air in the third person, kind of like ballplayers and politicians do. "Dr. Kathy Chandler says to break up with your boyfriend," or "Dr. Kathy Chandler says your husband's no good," or "Dr. Kathy Chandler says your sex life could be a lot better." Makes you want to puke.

At three-thirty the same afternoon, I make the pilgrimage across the Golden Gate Bridge to the picture-postcard town of Mill Valley, where Dr. Kathy Chandler maintains her office in a turn-of-the-century building across the town square from the old train depot, which has long since been turned into a trendy bookstore and cafe. When I called to make an appointment, Dr. Kathy Chandler's receptionist told me she wasn't taking new patients. When I explained I was a lawyer representing Joel Friedman, I was put on hold for only a moment before the sickly-sweet voice of Dr. Kathy Chandler found its way onto the phone and promised me an appointment. Ah, the smell of free publicity.

Dr. Kathy Chandler's second-floor office is decorated in earth tones, with gray-beige furniture, light-wood end tables and two large ferns. Her receptionist looks as if she's been through at least a dozen twelve-step programs. There are self-help magazines on the end tables and a large poster of Dr. Kathy Chandler on the wall, along with the KTLK radio logo. As I stare at it, I realize it's the same poster that appears on the side of Muni buses in the city. Dr. Kathy Chandler's office is considerably different from the office of the shrink Rosie and I went to see in our abortive attempts at marriage counseling. Chuck was a terrific guy, but I sort of lost faith in him when I found out he was a fifty-five-year-old bachelor. Somehow, I figured no matter what he'd read in all the textbooks, he couldn't quite relate. He tried very hard to get us to see what he kept calling the big picture. He never realized he was dealing with little-picture people.

The receptionist gives me a warm smile, and I take a seat

between a suntanned woman with bleached hair who is hiding behind a pair of dark sunglasses, and a man I recognize as a local television personality. Dr. Kathy Chandler's clientele is pretty well-heeled.

At exactly four o'clock, the door opens and I'm granted entry into the inner sanctum. The receptionist shows me into a tastefully furnished room with more muted tones and ferns. Quiet music surrounds me. One of those tacky miniature artificial waterfalls cascades behind Dr. Kathy Chandler's desk. In all fairness, the whole thing is very soothing.

I feel like Dorothy waiting for the grand entrance of the Wizard. The door opens. I expect to hear trumpets. I'm not prepared for what I see. The posters on the buses and in the reception area don't begin to do her justice. Dr. Kathy Chandler is about six feet tall and Cindy Crawford beautiful. I'm beginning to see why Bob Holmes paid her a fortune to spend forty-five minutes a week with her. "I'm Dr. Kathy Chandler," she purrs. Her tone is soothing. She pushes her long blond hair out of her striking blue eyes.

"I'm Michael Daley. I represent Joel Friedman."

"I know." The voice is pure caviar. She sounds better in person than she does on the radio.

"Dr. Chandler," I say, "I understand Bob Holmes was a patient of yours."

"Yes he was, Mr. Daley." She licks her lips. "It's a terrible tragedy."

"Yes it is." Composure. "Dr. Chandler, how long had you been treating Mr. Holmes?"

"Not for very long. Probably about three months."

"I see. And how was his treatment going?"

She pouts. "Mr. Daley," she says, "you're a lawyer. You know I'm not permitted to talk about my patients. It's privileged." She blinks her big blue eyes and gives me a look that says she'd love to help me, but the big bad lawyers won't let her.

"I understand your concern," I reply, "but the privilege ends when a patient dies." This isn't exactly true, but she isn't exactly a lawyer. "And it would be very helpful for us to understand the nature and extent of your treatment of Mr. Holmes."

The kittenlike facade disappears. The claws come out. "Mr. Daley," she says in a businesslike tone, her voice dropping at least half an octave, "it has always been my policy not to discuss the treatment of my patients with other people."

This is an interesting argument from a woman who gives free advice on the radio every night.

"Dr. Chandler," I say, "I'd rather just ask you a few questions. If you insist, I'd be more than happy to come back with a subpoena." And then you'll really have a lot to talk about from seven to ten tonight.

The kitten reappears and the voice goes back up. "Very well. Ask your questions. If I don't want to answer, I'll tell you so. And if I need to get my lawyer involved, I will. Believe me, I will."

I believe you, Dr. Kathy Chandler. "Dr. Chandler, what were you treating Mr. Holmes for?"

"A lot of things. But mostly, he had relationship issues. He'd been divorced several times."

No shit. "And he was about to get divorced again."

"So I understand," she says. "I was working with Mr. Holmes on creating a foundation for solid relationships—and to try to temper his enthusiasm for extramarital activities."

"I see. And were you aware that he was having an affair with Diana Kennedy?"

"Oh, yes. That's really where his treatment started. He

and Ms. Kennedy had been seeing each other for about a year. When Mrs. Holmes found out at the beginning of December, she asked Mr. Holmes to leave. About the same time, Ms. Kennedy broke up with Mr. Holmes. He was quite upset."

"Did he try to reconcile with his wife?"

"Yes. The reconciliation was unsuccessful. He began seeing someone in late December. I assumed he had rekindled his relationship with Ms. Kennedy, but it may have been somebody new. He was terribly conflicted about it. He missed his last couple of appointments."

I decide to probe a little deeper. "Was Mr. Holmes depressed the last time you saw him?"

"In the clinical sense, no. He was quite distraught, but he wasn't clinically depressed."

"Was he upset about the breakup with his wife?"

"Yes. But not terribly upset. He seemed to have expected it."

"I see. And was he upset about the breakup with Ms. Kennedy?"

She smiles. "Oh, yes, Mr. Daley. He was terribly upset about it."

"And are you aware of any attempts to reconcile with Ms. Kennedy?"

"Not that I'm aware of, Mr. Daley. But it's possible."

"Do you think it's possible Mr. Holmes attempted to reconcile with Ms. Kennedy and she rejected him?"

She pauses. "If you were my lawyer, you'd instruct me not to answer a hypothetical question."

"That's true. On the other hand, we have reason to believe that he did, in fact, attempt to reconcile with Ms. Kennedy. And we know, for a fact, that she was not agreeable to such a reconciliation because she had decided to leave the firm."

She looks surprised. "I didn't realize that," she says.

Put-up or shut-up time. "What this is leading to is the question of whether you think Bob Holmes was so distraught about his pending divorce and his breakup with Diana Kennedy that he may have committed suicide. In your professional judgment, did you see any signs that he was suicidal?"

She laughs. "Mr. Daley, I'd been seeing Mr. Holmes for only about three months. He was an unhappy man with some serious relationship issues. We were just beginning to work on those issues. But, in answer to your question, it is inconceivable to me that he was suicidal. He didn't display any of the tendencies or signs. And if I'm called upon in court to testify, I'll say just that."

It's more or less what I expect. I'll see you on the radio, Dr. Kathy Chandler. You're of no help to our defense.

28

"DID YOU COME TO GLOAT?"

"We are confident we will be able to work out a deal with our creditors that will allow us to continue our practice without interruption as we proceed through the bankruptcy process. We will continue to provide the highest-quality legal services to our clients during this difficult period."

—ARTHUR PATTON. *SAN FRANCISCO CHRONICLE*. MONDAY, MARCH 2.

"Jeff Tucker, please," I tell the person at First Bank who answers my call on the morning of Monday, March 2. I'm studying the article in the *Chronicle* detailing the bankruptcy filing of my former law firm. I figure it might be a good time to get reacquainted with the bank's general counsel. As Jeff promised me a few weeks ago, the bank has foreclosed on S&G's equipment loans right on schedule.

"Who's calling, please?"

"Michael Daley."

My first reaction to the article could be summed up by the words "Nyahh nyahh nyahh—you went bankrupt, and I got my capital back!" I realize this may not be the most mature reaction to the impending meltdown of my professional home for the better part of the last five years. Then again . . .

"Jeff Tucker speaking."

"It's Mike Daley."

"Hi, Mike." He pauses. "You saw the note in the paper about the S and G bankruptcy filing?"

"Indeed I did. Couldn't miss it."

"I don't take any pleasure in any of this, Mike," he lies.

"Me neither." Heh heh heh. I'd give everything I own to see the look on Art Patton's face right now. "Jeff, do you happen to know if the loans were recourse or nonrecourse?" If the loans were "recourse," the bank can try to collect from the partners and perhaps the former partners of the firm. If the loans were "nonrecourse," the bank can seek repayment only from the assets of the firm, but not from the assets of the individual partners and former partners. I learned this from Joel. It's all I know about commercial law: recourse—bad; nonrecourse—good.

"They're all recourse loans. Fully guaranteed by each of the partners."

Shit.

"And," he adds gratuitously, "since you were a partner at the time the loans were taken down, and at the time of the default, you're still on the hook." I can hear the smirk in his voice.

"Wait a minute," I say. "I left on December thirty-first. How do you figure I was still a partner at the time of default?"

"That's when the loans were due. You were still a partner. Ipso facto, you're still on the hook."

I hate lawyers who talk Latin. "But you extended the due date. I wasn't a partner when the extended due date came up."

"It wasn't an extension. We simply decided not to foreclose until the sixty-day grace period ended yesterday. Our foreclosure guys looked into it. All the S and G partners who were at the firm on December thirty-first are still on the hook. That includes you."

And you're an asshole. I'm sorry we didn't fire you sooner, you little shit.

"Look," he says in a condescending tone, "the fact is, the bank doesn't want to spend a lot of time and money suing the partners individually. If you're like most of your partners, all your money is going for alimony and fancy cars."

He's right about that—except in my case, there's no fancy car.

"I'm sure we'll end up cutting some sort of a deal with the firm," he says. "We'll probably take the firm's receivables and sell off some assets. We'll sue the partners individually as a last resort."

Somehow, I don't get a warm and fuzzy feeling from this conversation. Maybe I'll ask Wendy about one of those sleazy tax shelters in the Bahamas to hide some of my assets.

At eleven o'clock the same morning, the reception area of Simpson and Gates looks considerably different. Only one receptionist is working the phone console. The double doors are closed. There are no fresh flowers. The Currier and Ives lithographs are gone. If I'm guessing correctly, the artwork at the First Bank headquarters has improved dramatically since yesterday.

Art Patton's secretary escorts me to his office. The long hallways look barren without the high-priced artwork. The plants are gone, too. His door is closed when we arrive. She knocks and opens the door. I'm somewhat surprised he's agreed to see me. Then again, it gives him a golden opportunity to yell at me if he wants to. I suspect he'd rather do it in the privacy of his own office, rather than in open court. Art is standing behind his antique desk, bellowing into his telephone. Something about the repossession of the computers and phones. He motions toward a dark brown leather chair. I admire the view of the Golden Gate Bridge as he castigates some poor collection attorney.

He slams the phone down. He looks like a bulldog shaking himself after he's had a bath. "So," he snaps, "what the hell do you want? Did you come to gloat?"

As a matter of fact, I did. "Art," I lie, "I take no pleasure in this. I think it's unfortunate." I look solemn. I decide to lay it on thick. "Some good people are going to lose their jobs."

It seems to disarm him slightly, at least for a moment. His chins jiggle. "The bankruptcy filing was just a precaution," he growls. "We'll still be here when the dust settles."

I'm not sure if he's trying to convince me or himself. "I hope you're right. I'm on the line for the equipment loans along with the rest of you. I have a vested interest in resolving this, too."

He doesn't seem mollified. "So," he grumbles, "besides making your little speech about firm finances, why the hell did you come here to see me?"

"I wanted to talk to you about Joel's case."

"We've been through this. We've told the police everything we know. If we find out anything new, I'll call you." He picks up his telephone.

"There are some things I'd like to talk to you about informally. If you're going to be a shit, I'll get a subpoena."

He hangs up the phone. "What things?"

"It's a little ticklish."

He looks right at me. "You aren't going to start up again about that nonsense about a sexual-harassment claim, are you? It's all bullshit. I have a good mind to file a lawsuit for slander against you for the stuff you brought up at the prelim." The best defense is a good offense.

"This isn't easy for me, either," I say, "but, if you won't cooperate, I'll have no choice." I let my words trail off and look away from him.

"What is it?" he asks.

"First, two people are prepared to testify you were propositioning Diana at the retreat, and she rejected your advances." I watch him closely. He doesn't flinch. "One person said you touched Diana in the bar and she stormed out. Another person said you asked her to go to bed with you at your party. When she refused, you followed her back to her room and . . . well . . . we aren't sure what happened."

He turns red. The pit bull comes out. "That's a crock of bullshit. Who the hell do you think you are coming here and making these wild accusations? What the fuck is wrong with you, anyway?"

I try to keep the tone measured. "I take it that means you deny those accusations?"

"Damn right, I do."

"And you're prepared to testify to that effect in court, if necessary?"

"Of course."

I nod. "Good. I'm glad we've eliminated any misunderstanding on that subject." I fold my hands. "Is it true that you and Beth Holmes have a social relationship?"

"I should throw you out of my office right now." He starts to pick up the phone again.

"Art," I say, "let me show you something." I take out a picture of him entering Beth's house.

"That doesn't mean anything," he blusters.

"I understand. But here's a picture of you leaving Beth's house the next morning. My investigator is prepared to testify that you spent the night."

The beady little eyes flare. "You little shit. You had me followed? Are you trying to blackmail me?" He grits his teeth. "Beth and I have had a social relationship for some time. It's one of the reasons for my divorce. My wife knows all about it."

"I see. Did you know Bob was going to write Beth out of his will just before he died?"

"Wouldn't surprise me. So what? She doesn't need the money. If you want to get up in court and tell the jury that Beth and I were sleeping together, so be it. It proves we were having an affair. She's my ex-wife. We still have feelings for each other. It doesn't have anything to do with your client's case."

Unfortunately, he may be right about that. "Let me ask you about something else. Didn't you and Bob invest in a restaurant together?"

"Yes, we did. Le Bon Vivant in Palo Alto."

"How was the restaurant doing?"

"Great. Except in the restaurant business, you can be doing great, but it doesn't mean you're making any money."

"I see." I'm surprised he admitted it.

"We were thinking about closing the place down. I've lost all the money I intend to lose on that damn thing."

"I don't suppose you had a key-man policy on Bob for the restaurant?" It's a shot in the dark.

"No, we didn't."

"Thanks for your time, Art."

When I return to the office that night, I find Wendy is sitting at a table in the hallway, studying copies of life insurance policies. "You can sit in my office, you know," I say.

"I like it better out here. Your office smells like chow mein."

I'm sure it does. "Find anything we can use?" I ask.

"Nothing yet. Bob's life insurance policies named Beth and the kids as beneficiaries."

"We knew that. Keep looking."

"I will." She takes off her glasses. She's very pretty when she wants to be.

"Are you okay?" I ask.

"I guess so."

"Andy?"

"Yeah. We have a custody hearing a week from Tuesday. Will you come with me?"

I put my hand on her shoulder. "Sure."

She pulls back. "Thanks, Mike."

A moment later, I sit down in my office and dial a familiar number. "Pete," I say, "do you have any plans for the weekend?"

"You got Warriors tickets?" he asks hopefully. "The Lakers are in town."

"Nah. I've got something better. I need your help. How would you feel about doing a little pro bono work?"

Silence. "For whom?" he asks cautiously.

"Wendy."

Long pause. "Sure," he says reluctantly.

"Thanks."

29

"WE'RE MISSING SOMETHING. I'M SURE OF IT"

"Pretrial motions are set for Monday, March 9. Except for Mort Goldberg, it seems the entire defense team is sound asleep."

—NEWSCENTER 4 LEGAL ANALYST MORGAN HENDERSON.
TUESDAY, MARCH 3.

We're having an all-hands meeting of the Dream Team in Rosie's office at nine the next morning. We have a pretrial hearing on Monday and it's time to add things up. We sit around the small conference table. Rosie drinks a Diet Coke and looks at our preliminary witness list. Wendy nurses a cup of coffee and studies her notes. Pete is going through an inventory of the evidence. Mort plays with an unlit cigar.

"Mort," I begin, "did you finish our motions to keep the Silverado videotapes out?"

"Yeah. We filed our papers on Thursday." He drums his fingers on the tabletop. "It's going to be a close call. The tapes have been heavily edited. We have a decent argument the potential inflammatory effect outweighs the probative value. I wouldn't bet a box of cigars we'll win."

Rosie agrees. "Even if she doesn't let them use the tapes,

they can always call Brent Hutchinson to testify that he saw Diana and Joel kissing in the hot tub."

"There's nothing we can do about that," Mort replies.

I turn to Wendy. "Did you find out anything more about Bob's finances?"

"Not much," she says. "He and Art Patton owned a restaurant in Palo Alto called Le Bon Vivant. It's been open for about four years. There are no financial records available to the public."

"According to Art," I say, "it's losing money."

"You may be right," she says. "We haven't found any suspicious liens."

"Keep looking." I turn to Rosie. "Any surprises on their witness list?" I ask.

"Not really," she says. "They're loading up their list just the way we are. They've put you and Wendy down as witnesses just to tweak us."

"We'll be able to get around that," I say. "We included Skipper and McNulty on ours, right?"

"Of course. Turnabout is fair play. Judge Chen will never let them testify."

"I know. But it'll give us an opportunity to show the judge that Skipper was there that night."

Mort is pleased. "That discussion should be a lot of fun," he says.

"Who else is on their list?" I ask.

"The people you'd expect. Roosevelt. Marcus Banks. Rod Beckert. Sandra Wilson. Art Patton and Charles Stern." Rosie flips through her notes. "Brent Hutchinson. Beth Holmes."

"Not surprising," I say. "A little testimony from the grieving widow to soften up the jury."

Rosie nods. "Dan Morris, Jack Frazier, Rick Cinelli and Homer Kim."

"Any surprises?"

"Your good friend Dr. Kathy Chandler is on their list, too."

Wendy asks, "Why are they calling her?"

"She was Bob's therapist," I reply. "She'll probably testify that Bob wasn't suicidal."

"Is she a real doctor?" she asks.

"Depends on your definition of the word 'real,'" I reply sarcastically. "She has an honorary doctorate from a mail-order college in Texas."

I turn back to Rosie. "Did you include all the S and G partners on our witness list?"

"Yeah. Just like you asked."

"Good. And did you send out subpoenas to each of them?"

"Oh, yes," she says, smiling. "We served them yesterday."

"Let me guess. They were not particularly well received by some of my former partners?"

Her eyes gleam. "You could say that, Mike. I let Wendy have the pleasure of serving Art Patton, Charles Stern and Brent Hutchinson."

Wendy is triumphant. "Makes you want to become a litigator," she says.

"Great," I say. "I bet Skipper is getting a few friendly phone calls from his former partners." Lawyers hate to get subpoenas. And we really hate to testify.

"Mike," Wendy says, "I took the liberty of asking Rita Roberts and the NewsCenter 4 team to come with me to the S and G office when I served the subpoenas." She bats her eyes innocently. "I hope that was okay."

"Absolutely," I say. "The public has a right to know. By the way," I ask, "did you find out anything more about the International Charitable Trust?"

"Trevor Smith is still in Kuwait." She grins at me. "I talked to his secretary. I've done a lot of work with them over the years, so I've gotten to know her very well. Her name is Felicity Smoot."

"You're kidding," Mort says.

"No, I'm not. I told her I was following up on the trust so we could close the file."

"What did she say?" I ask.

"Not much. Chuckles asked them to prepare a final inventory of trust assets, so they can begin liquidation. For now, the trust assets are frozen."

"I see. Have you been able to pin down how much his fee is?"

"Not yet. His deal isn't stated in the trust instrument. He has a separate administration contract that I haven't seen. I asked Felicity to send me a copy. We'll see if she does."

Not bad. "Did you have any luck figuring out who the income beneficiaries and the remaindermen of the trust are?"

"Nope. Felicity didn't know. I didn't want to push her too hard. I thought it might make her nervous."

"That was smart," I say. "You never want to make a banker nervous." I tap my pencil on my legal pad. "I'm surprised she talked to you. I'll bet Chuckles told her not to talk to anybody who doesn't work for S and G."

She gives me a conspiratorial grin. "Maybe I didn't exactly tell her I'd left the firm."

Wendy may have the makings of a fine criminal defense attorney. "When do you think you'll hear back from her?"

"Probably not until Smith gets back."

Swell. We'll be halfway through the trial by then. "See if you can find out when he's coming back. I want you and Pete to be there."

"An all-expenses-paid trip to the Bahamas? Cool."

"Think of it as a working vacation." I turn to Pete. "What have you found, Mr. Gumshoe?" Pete doesn't like being called Mr. Gumshoe. He doesn't joke around when it comes to business. Actually, he doesn't joke around about much of anything.

"I ran an asset search on the company custodian, Homer Kim. Seems his bank account recently became twenty thousand dollars fatter. Nice chunk of change for a man who makes only twenty-six thousand dollars a year."

That's a surprise.

"You think somebody paid him off to testify?" Mort asks.

"I can't tell for sure," Pete says. "On the other hand, he doesn't look like the kind of guy who gets twenty-thousand-dollar checks in the mail from Publisher's Clearing House. When we ran the search on his bank accounts, we saw one big deposit come in. It went out the next day. We don't know where the money came from or where it went. He's had some gambling problems."

"Stay with him, Pete," I say.

"There's something else," he says. "You remember Beth Holmes said her private eye caught Bob with another woman at the Fairmont in December?"

We remember. The infamous mystery woman.

"Well," he continues, "I talked to her private eye. You know she hired Nick Hanson?"

I do. Mort and Rosie don't. They burst into laughter. "Nick the Dick!" Mort shouts. "She hired Nick the Dick?"

Wendy's bewildered. "I give up," she says. "Who the hell is 'Nick the Dick'?"

Mort, Rosie and I glance at one another. Mort grins at Wendy. "Honey," he says, "Nick Hanson is a legend. Maybe you're too young. He was the lead investigator for a defense lawyer named Nunzio Della Ventura. Nunzio wasn't the best lawyer in town, but he was one of the most flamboyant. He had a storefront office on Columbus Avenue in North Beach for fifty years. The prosecutors hated him. Nunzio was quite a character. So's Nick."

"You have to see him to believe him," Pete says.

"That's right," says Mort. "He may be all of five feet tall. Always dresses impeccably. Quite the man about town. Always has a fresh flower in his lapel. You'd look at him and you'd be inclined to underestimate him. And you'd be making the biggest mistake of your life. He's the most tenacious private eye I've ever met. He's in his eighties. Still a pistol. Still lives in North Beach. Still working every day."

"He's written several mystery novels based on cases he's worked on," I add. "One was made into a movie. I think Danny DeVito played him."

"I'll look for him next time I'm at the bookstore," Wendy says. "So, what did Nick the Dick find out about Bob?" she asks.

"Just what you would have thought. Nick saw Bob with a woman in a room at the Fairmont in late December. He couldn't ID her. He was in the building across the street. The drapes were partially closed and the lights were dim. By the time Nick got to the hotel, she was gone. He took some pictures. He promised to let me see them."

"Will he testify?" I ask.

"Of course. This is a high-profile case."

Rosie looks puzzled. "How does that help us?"

"If it wasn't Diana, it undercuts Skipper's argument that Joel acted in a jealous rage," I reply.

"On the other hand," she points out, "if it wasn't Diana, it may undercut our suicide argument. If Bob already had another girlfriend, he couldn't have been too distraught about his breakup with Diana. In that case, it doesn't seem logical that he would have killed himself." As always, Rosie sees the situation with great clarity.

"Unless," I say, "the mystery woman was just a rebound for Bob and she blew him off, too. Who knows? Maybe she was a hooker."

Rosie is skeptical. "Seems like a stretch to me," she says. It begs the obvious question. "Pete, can you talk to the staff at the Fairmont to see if you can get an ID on the woman?"

"I'm already working on it," he says.

"Good." I look at my notes. "We're missing something. I'm sure of it." I turn to Pete. "Any leads on Vince Russo?"

He winks. "Maybe. You remember his car was found at the Vista Point at the north end of the Golden Gate Bridge? His overcoat washed up at Fort Baker yesterday. He wasn't wearing it."

"Do you think he might still be alive?"

"It's possible," he says. "I talked to the cab companies in Marin County. Marin Taxi had a pickup at the Vista Point at about three A.M. on December thirty-first. The dispatcher and the driver both confirmed the fare was taken to the international terminal at San Francisco International. The driver said the passenger was a heavyset male in his thirties or forties, who paid cash."

"Did you show the driver a picture of Russo?"

"Yeah. He wasn't sure."

"You think it was Vince?"

"You bet your ass I do."

Pete usually has very good instincts about these issues. Rosie hits the nail on the head when she says, "Sounds like we may have to bring a key witness back from the dead."

30

"YOU CAN'T CROSS-EXAMINE A VIDEOTAPE"

"Judge Shirley Chen will hold a pretrial conference at ten o'clock today to discuss scheduling and evidentiary issues. The trial will start in one week."

—*NEWSCENTER 4 DAYBREAK*. MONDAY, MARCH 9.

March 9 is a day for the lawyers to argue about evidentiary issues, legal motions and scheduling. We'll also get our first taste of Judge Shirley Chen. The tenor of the trial will be set by the decisions she makes today. Rosie, Mort and I park in the pay lot next to the Hall and lug our heavy trial briefcases through the daily El Niño downpour. Skipper's Lincoln is parked illegally in front of the main entrance to the Hall. The minicams are out in force. Rita Roberts stands under a large umbrella with the NewsCenter 4 logo. The wind is howling at thirty-five miles per hour, but her hair doesn't move. I shrug when she asks for a comment. We push our way into the building, shake our umbrellas and walk through the metal detectors. It would be bad form to be late.

Judge Shirley Chen is in her mid-forties, although she looks younger. She began her career at S&G twenty years ago. It seems as if every judge in California started at S&G.

She moved to the San Francisco District Attorney's Office three years later. I tried two cases against her when I was a PD. I won one and I lost one. She was an ambitious prosecutor. She'll bring the same tenacity to the bench.

Her chambers are sterile. Her law-school diploma hangs on the wall, but her books and files are still in boxes. I'm reminded she's single as I notice there are no pictures of a spouse or children. There's a plaque on her wall from the San Francisco Women's Bar Association. There's a gavel from her alma mater, the Hastings College of Law in San Francisco, which indicates that she was named distinguished alumna three years ago. There's a small picture of her with the California attorney general.

Skipper and McNulty arrive a few minutes after we do. Everybody is decked out in their Sunday best. Skipper's navy blue pinstripe looks as if it was delivered earlier this morning from Wilkes Bashford. McNulty is wearing charcoal gray. We can't compete on clothing. Besides, the rain has taken the starch out of our best going-to-court clothes. Skipper plays with his MontBlanc pen. McNulty sits quietly.

"Let's get started," Judge Chen says. "You're not the only people on my schedule today."

We nod in unison. No chitchat.

"First," she says, "let's talk about scheduling." She looks at me. "May I assume, Mr. Daley, that your client hasn't reconsidered his position concerning the timing of his trial?"

"That's correct, Your Honor. My client doesn't intend to waive time. We're ready." Or as ready as we're going to be.

She isn't happy. "Very well," she says. "We're scheduled to start one week from today, on March sixteenth." She looks at Skipper. "Mr. Gates, how many trial days would you estimate for the prosecution's case?"

He turns to McNulty. "One moment, Your Honor," he says. He and McNulty whisper to each other. Skipper turns back to the judge. "I don't think it will take us very long, Your Honor. If Mr. Daley is reasonable, we won't need a lot of time qualifying our witnesses as experts."

She holds up her hand and asks impatiently, "How many trial days, Mr. Gates?"

"No more than ten, Your Honor," he says. "And perhaps substantially fewer," he adds quickly. "We think jury selection may take longer than our case."

"You may be right about that, Mr. Gates." She turns to me. "What do you estimate for the defense, Mr. Daley?"

This is tricky. With a little luck, we won't have to present a lengthy defense. On the other hand, we may be here for weeks if they trot out a slew of experts. "No more than a week, Your Honor," I say. Then I add, gratuitously, "Maybe less."

She seems pleased. "Very well, then. We'll begin jury selection one week from today."

"Your Honor," I say, "we did present several motions on evidentiary issues."

"I was just getting to that, Mr. Daley." She glances at Mort's papers. She says she'll give us some leeway in the jury-selection process, called voir dire. She asks us for draft questionnaires to be given to the potential jurors. McNulty and Rosie have agreed on most of the major points. She reiterates Judge Brown's gag order with respect to the media.

"Your Honor," I say, "there are some matters regarding the prosecution's witness list."

She cuts me off and wags her right index finger at me. "Let's keep this very simple," she says slowly. "Nobody in this room is going to be a witness at this trial. Period."

Skipper and I glance at each other. Skipper smiles.

"Your Honor," I say, "we have a very significant issue here."

She looks at me skeptically. "Come on, Mr. Daley. You

know I'm not going to let any of you testify at the trial. Let's not waste our time."

Skipper's grin gets wider.

"Your Honor," I say, "have you seen the security videos?"

"Your Honor," Skipper interjects.

She stops him. "I'll tell you when it's your turn to talk, Mr. Gates."

"But, Your Honor . . ."

She cuts him off again. "Mr. Gates, the rules here are simple. I get to tell you when it's your turn to talk. I get to interrupt you. You don't get to interrupt me. Are we clear on that?"

I like it. An early show of control.

Skipper nods submissively. "Yes, Your Honor."

"Good." She turns back to me. "I haven't seen the security videos, Mr. Daley."

"Your Honor," I implore, "Mr. Gates was there that night. He was in the building. We can put the tapes on right now, if you'd like."

She shakes her head. "I know he was there. The police reports said there was a reception for him at the office."

"No," I say. "He came back later that night. Much later. He was in the building at one o'clock when Diana came back. He was there when Bob and Diana died."

Skipper shakes his head contemptuously. "Mr. Daley was there too, Your Honor. I'll withdraw his name from our list in the interests of justice."

"For God's sake, Skipper," I say, "I left at eight-thirty that night. You know it. I didn't come back at one in the morning at exactly the time you claim Bob and Diana died."

He turns to Judge Chen. "Your Honor," he says, "I resent Mr. Daley's implication."

"Your Honor," I reply, "he's brought charges against my

client for the murder of two people. I can prove he entered the building around the same time Diana Kennedy did. He has to be a witness, Your Honor. I need him. Frankly, I don't understand why he wasn't considered a suspect at the time."

A little over the top, but so be it. At least she's interested now.

"Mr. Daley," she begins.

I decide to break the cardinal rule and interrupt her. "Judge Chen," I implore, "he came back at twelve-thirty in the morning. He was there at the time he claims Bob and Diana were killed. It's right there in the security tapes." I'm pushing myself up on the arms of my chair.

She looks troubled. She turns to Skipper. "Is this true, Mr. Gates?"

"Yes, Your Honor," he replies. "I was in the office for a few minutes around one o'clock to pick up my briefcase. I didn't see or hear anything. My office wasn't even on the same floor as Bob's."

"He was there for almost an hour," I say. "It was a lot longer than just a few minutes."

She stares silently at her diploma. "This isn't good," she says slowly, her jaws clenched. "This is a mess. The district attorney could be a witness." She looks at Skipper. "And you actually plan to try this case yourself, right?"

"Absolutely, Your Honor."

"If this doesn't beat everything," she mutters. She looks at me. "Do you really think you're going to need his testimony?"

I don't hesitate. "Absolutely, Your Honor."

She turns back to Skipper. "And I don't suppose you'd agree to let Mr. McNulty handle this case?"

"No, Your Honor," he says quietly. "It's too close to the trial."

"And I don't suppose you'd be willing to testify about what you saw that night?"

"For obvious reasons, Your Honor, you know I would prefer not to. You know it confuses the jury if a lawyer is both an advocate and a witness."

"And what, if anything, did you see that night, Mr. Gates?"

He looks right at her. "Your Honor, I went to my office on the forty-sixth floor, picked up my briefcase and left. That's it." He pauses. "And if you want me to testify to that effect, I guess I'm prepared to do so. Everybody is going to look very silly if we proceed in that manner, however."

He's right about that.

She gets a faraway look. "I'm going to take this under advisement," she says. "I'll give you my decision by the end of the week." She looks at Skipper. "Mr. Gates," she says, "I'd suggest that you think very carefully about your testimony, in case I rule in favor of Mr. Daley." Then she turns to me. "Mr. Daley, I'd suggest you think long and hard about whether you want to call the district attorney of the city and county of San Francisco as a witness."

We nod in unison.

"Finally," she says, "we need to address the motion to quash the presentation of two videotape recordings of certain activities at the Simpson and Gates firm retreat in October of last year."

"Yes, Your Honor," I say. "We believe those videotapes are highly inflammatory and should not be shown to the jury."

Skipper begins to interrupt me and she holds up her hand. "Not yet, Mr. Gates," she says. "It'll be your turn in a minute." She turns back to me.

"Actually, Your Honor," I say, "I'd like to let my colleague, Professor Goldberg, make our presentation on this

matter." We've rehearsed this. I want Mort to play the part
of the gray-haired sage on legal and evidentiary issues. Although I'd never say it out loud, the truth is that I trust him
to speak for only a few minutes a day. I pause for effect, and
add, "You know Mr. Goldberg was an adjunct professor of
criminal procedure and evidence at Hastings."

She gives me a knowing look. "I'm familiar with his
credentials. I was a student of his. It's my turn to see if he's
prepared for class." She turns to Mort. "What do you have
to say, Professor?"

He smiles at her. "Your Honor," he says, "may it please
the court." His diction is a little slurred. The words "Your
Honor" come out as a single word, which sounds like
"yawner." "We have a potentially serious evidentiary matter
concerning two videotapes from the Simpson and Gates
firm retreat last fall."

She stops him. "Mr. Goldberg," she says, "I've read your
motion and looked at the tapes. You don't need to describe
the tapes to me and you don't need to summarize your
motion. Let's cut straight to the chase. If you don't have
anything new to tell me, I'll rule based on your papers."

"Very well, Your Honor." He acts as if he was expecting
this. Give him credit. He doesn't fluster. "The prosecution
would like to introduce into evidence a highly edited videotape of activities at the Simpson and Gates retreat last fall. In
addition, all of the original sound in the tapes was edited out
and replaced by the theme music from a popular television
show. In all likelihood, the events in the tapes will be taken
out of context. And it's all but certain that the events in the
tapes will have an inflammatory and highly prejudicial effect on the jury."

Nice work, Mort. Concise. Direct. And you didn't use
the words "kissing," "hot tub," "sex" or "affair."

She gives him a skeptical look. "Mr. Goldberg," she says,

"isn't it true that the tapes really do, in fact, speak for themselves?"

Like all good lawyers, Mort pretends he's agreeing with her, while he's actually disagreeing. It's patronizing, but it works. "In general, Your Honor," he says, "that's true. What better evidence could there be than a videotape? On the other hand, when the videotape has been tampered with, as this one has, or there is a substantial likelihood that it could be taken out of context, it could be unfairly damaging evidence."

She isn't convinced. "Mr. Goldberg, these videotapes show a man and a woman kissing. Coincidentally, the man is the defendant and the woman is the victim. Doesn't that speak for itself? They were kissing. Nothing more. Nothing less. A jury can figure out what was happening."

Mort takes off his glasses to gesture. "Let's face it. The people who serve on juries are only human. They see news stories about politicians having affairs and doing indiscreet things. They think it's the truth if they see it on TV. If they're like most of us, they'll jump to the conclusion that something was going on. It isn't a great news flash that Mr. Gates is going to claim our client was having an affair with Ms. Kennedy. He has no evidence except for these tapes. And if he shows these heavily edited tapes out of context, it will have an enormously prejudicial effect on the jury."

She looks at Skipper. "What do you have to say about this, Mr. Gates?"

"Your Honor," he says, "Mr. Goldberg is blowing this issue entirely out of proportion. We believe the videotapes do, in fact, speak for themselves. The jury will be free to draw whatever inferences it chooses. That's what juries are supposed to do—figure out what happened. The tapes are the best evidence of what happened. It isn't our fault the defendant and Ms. Kennedy were caught on tape kissing. It would be irresponsible to ignore it. We acknowledge that a part of our case will be to demonstrate that Mr. Friedman and Ms. Kennedy were having an affair. We believe the breakup of the affair led Mr. Friedman to murder two people. The tape speaks for itself. It is what it is."

It is what it is. It's actually a very effective legal argument.

She turns back to Mort. "Your Honor," he argues, "the problem, quite simply, is that you can't cross-examine a videotape. If Mr. Gates thinks he can demonstrate that Mr. Friedman and Ms. Kennedy were having an affair, let him bring forth witnesses at trial. Let us have an opportunity to cross-examine them."

She seems to be absorbing this thoughtfully. I watch Mort carefully. He's staying true to his word and keeping the discourse on a professional, if not scholarly, level. He can still play law professor when he wants to.

Skipper and Mort volley back and forth for another ten minutes. Finally, Judge Chen says she's heard enough. "Gentlemen," she says, "I've come to my decision. I find Mr. Goldberg's argument slightly more persuasive." She turns to Skipper. "Mr. Gates," she says, "if you want to introduce evidence of these tawdry events at the trial, you'll have to do so through witnesses who can be cross-examined by the defense." She's ruling in our favor, but sending a message. He can't use the tapes, but he can call witnesses who will testify about their contents. "For example," she continues, "I see no reason why Mr. Gates couldn't call as a witness the individual who was operating the camera."

There's nothing we can do to prevent Skipper from calling Brent Hutchinson to testify that he saw Joel and Diana kissing—even if it was through the lens of his video camera. Of course, there's nothing to prevent us from going after him on cross.

Skipper attempts to plead his case one more time. "But, Your Honor," he begins.

She holds up her hand. "I've ruled, Mr. Gates." She starts to stand.

"Your Honor," I say, "there's one other thing. Mr. Gates has requested that this trial be televised. For obvious reasons, we're against it. We saw what happened at the Simpson trial."

Skipper is mortified. He's expecting free TV time. "Your Honor," he says, "I realize there was some fallout from the Simpson trial. However, the public has a right to observe the criminal process at work. We should televise this trial to win back the faith of the American people in the justice system."

And crown thy good with brotherhood, from sea to shining sea. I want to throw up.

"Your Honor," I say, "I'm only thinking of the interests of my client and the interests of justice. I don't want my client tried in the media. Mr. Gates's leaks have already contributed to a potentially irreversible tainting of the juror pool."

If you don't have a better argument, always try invoking the interests of justice.

She looks troubled. "I knew this was going to come up," she says. "I have mixed feelings. In my judgment, it is possible to televise a trial without turning it into a circus. Nevertheless, I'm inclined to agree with Mr. Daley."

"But Your Honor," Skipper says.

"I've ruled, Mr. Gates. I'll see you next week to begin jury selection. We're done."

This round goes to the good guys, but not by much.

Skipper and McNulty stop us outside the courtroom. "Nice work on your motions, Mort," Skipper says.

Mort waves him away. "It's all part of the process," he replies.

Skipper stares at Mort. "You know," he says, "we'll get all the stuff from the tapes into evidence at the trial. There's no doubt. We were planning to call Brent Hutchinson anyway."

"At least we'll be able to cross-examine him," I say. "Hutch can be a little jumpy. He hasn't spent a lot of time in court the last few years."

He laughs. "All the more reason for us to spend a little extra time in preparation."

Mort turns to McNulty. "You guys have any more evidence you'd like to share with us? I'm sure you aren't planning any surprises at trial."

"Nothing yet," McNulty says. "You've seen everything we've seen."

"Did the results of the paternity test come in?" I ask.

"Not yet," Skipper replies. "You aren't nervous, are you, Mike?"

"Nope."

"Good. I'm sure your guy was telling you the truth when he said he wasn't the father."

"Me too."

"It's a good result," Mort says to me as we're pulling out of the parking lot. "At least we got the goddamned videotapes out."

"Nice work," I say. "Let's go back to the office and call Joel with the good news." I pause. "What do you think that was all about in the hallway? You think they know something?"

He takes out a cigar. "Probably," he says.

31

"WHAT ELSE CAN YOU TELL ME, ROOSEVELT?"

"We have been asked to prepare papers to have Mr. Russo declared legally dead."

—CHARLES STERN. *SAN FRANCISCO LEGAL JOURNAL.*
TUESDAY, MARCH 10.

Tuesday, March 10. We get to take a break from our trial preparation to attend to an equally depressing matter: Wendy's custody hearing. Her ex-husband, Andy, has filed papers to revise their custody agreement. Wendy and I wait outside divorce court at ten o'clock in the morning. We're joined by her divorce attorney, Jerry Mills, a quiet, rational man in his mid-fifties with a gray mustache. Wendy is nervous. I don't blame her. I haven't been in this corridor in five years. It brings back some unpleasant memories. It was in this very corridor that I gave up on my lamebrained idea that I was better suited to have custody of Grace. I'll never forget the look of relief on Rosie's face. It was the only time during our divorce that she allowed herself to cry.

A moment later, we are joined by Wendy's ex, Andy Schneider, a high-strung advertising executive in his late thirties with slicked-back hair, who is dressed in a flashy double-breasted suit and a loud designer tie. He is accompanied by his attorney, a fiftyish asshole named Craig Sherman, who bears an uncanny resemblance to a rattlesnake.

In my experience, divorce attorneys come in two species. Most of them are rational people like Jerry, who act more as counselors than adversaries. Some have a knack for defusing tense situations. The really good ones steer their clients toward counseling and sometimes salvage marriages. Then there are people like Sherman, who relish the role of barracuda. He represents only men. He actually has a picture of a shark on his business cards. If you're going to war with your ex-wife, he's your guy.

Sherman says, "You guys don't think the judge is actually going to believe this crap that Wendy has her own law firm, do you? We're going to call in child-custody services to review this case."

Nice guy.

Mills looks at him. "We have an agreement, Craig. It's been approved by the court. It isn't going to change."

Sherman cracks his knuckles. "Sure, Jerry," he says. "I've had this judge modify custody orders for a lot less than this."

And you wonder why people hate lawyers. In reality, he's probably bluffing. In California, custody orders can be modified only if there is a significant change in circumstance. A change in one spouse's economic situation generally isn't enough.

Wendy glares at Andy. "You're an asshole," she says quietly. "You aren't fit to take care of a hamster, let alone a six-year-old."

He tugs at his tie. "At least I've got a job."

I get between them and glance at my watch. "It's time for court," I say calmly. Andy winks. Wendy moves closer to Mills.

We turn toward the heavy double doors to the courtroom

when Pete walks up, soaking wet. "Sorry I'm late," he says. "I got hung up."

Sherman looks at him. "I didn't realize we were going to have a family reunion."

"Craig," Pete says, "can I see you and Andy in private for a moment?"

Sherman throws up his hands. "What the hell is this all about?"

"Thirty seconds," Pete says. "That's all I need."

"Humor him," Andy says confidently.

Pete, Andy and Sherman walk down the hall about thirty feet. Pete takes out a manila envelope from under his jacket and hands it to Andy. They huddle. They argue. Sherman gesticulates wildly. Pete remains stone-faced. A moment later, the arrogance leaves Andy's face.

Wendy turns to me. "What's this all about?" she asks.

"Beats me."

Five minutes later, Pete, Andy and Sherman return. Sherman looks at Wendy, then he turns to Mills. "Jerry," he says, "we've decided not to pursue any changes in the custody deal. We're going to drop our motion." He looks at me and wags a menacing finger. "You and your brother are both assholes." He and Andy walk down the hall toward the elevators.

I turn to Pete, who arches his eyebrows. Wendy walks over and gives him a hug. He hugs her back uncomfortably. "I don't know what you gave them, Pete," she says, "but it worked."

Pete gives us a wicked grin and pulls out a stack of snapshots. "Sorry I didn't get here sooner," he says. "I took these last night and it took a little longer to get them developed than I thought."

He starts flipping through the pictures, the way little kids flip through baseball cards. "Here's Andy's executive assistant, Karen." It's a picture of an attractive woman going into a large house in Pacific Heights. "Here's Andy going into the house. Here's Andy taking off his clothes. Here's Karen taking off her clothes." He says, "The next few pictures are a little tough to see." He shuffles through them quickly. "Here they are rolling around on the floor."

Wendy is smiling. "We get the idea, Pete," she says.

Pete glances at me. "You know," he says, "it seems Karen is married to Andy's boss."

"I was not aware of that," I say.

"I'd say we're holding Andy's career right here in the palm of my hand," Pete says.

Jerry Mills is admiring. He asks Pete for a business card. "You guys play in a different league," he says.

Thursday, March 12. Four days before the start of jury selection. We've spent the last week interviewing witnesses, rehearsing my opening and working on jury-selection strategy. The clock is ticking—and we don't have anything that will give us an acquittal.

The process of preparing for trial is far more of an art than a science. You spend a lot of time honing your presentation. While the law professors and commentators like to talk about the pursuit of justice, when you cut to the chase, it's all theater. In our MTV world, you can't just inform the jury; you have to entertain them and, if possible, dazzle them with special effects.

Unlike real theater, a trial attorney has to perform all the important roles: producer, director, lead actor, costume designer, special effects supervisor, production accountant and, perhaps most importantly, food provider. We have created an impromptu "war room" in the narrow hallway just outside my office. Exhibit binders, easels, enlarged pictures, diagrams and charts are everywhere. It will take a minor miracle just to put everything in order for presentation at the trial. My biggest worry is that our stuff will get soaked as we lug it from the parking lot to the courtroom.

Rosie, Mort and I spend the day with our jury consultant, Barbara Childs, who is considered an up-and-comer in a growing field. I've worked with her on a couple of cases. She's a little full of herself, but you have to be in her line of work. I take her suggestions with a grain of salt. We don't have the time or the resources to do a full mock trial.

At three in the afternoon, I walk past Wendy, who is poring over some S&G financial records at a table just outside Rosie's office. "Find anything we can use?" I ask.

"Nothing yet." She looks at me. "Where are you going? I would think you might have a few things to do today."

"I thought I'd take the afternoon off," I reply. "You know—conserve my strength for trial."

"Really, Mike. Where are you off to?"

"I'm going to take one more run at Roosevelt. Maybe he's found something that'll help."

I meet Roosevelt in the back of a cop bar not far from the Hall. The cops and detectives respect each other's private space here. The place is run by a heavyset man named Phil Agnos. It's sort of a cross between a saloon and a halfway house for Greek immigrants. Phil is the only person permitted to handle the money. Every three weeks or so, there's a new, large young man with a toothpick in his mouth standing at the grill. Since the only English words he ever knows are "cheeseburger" and "double," your culinary options are somewhat limited. I opt for a single cheeseburger today.

Roosevelt is sitting in the back room, nursing a cup of coffee and reading the paper. A picture of Joe DiMaggio hangs on the wall behind him. He stands to greet me when I walk in. "I was just reading about you in the paper," he says.

"What are they saying now?"

"The usual. You're spending all your time on a hopeless disinformation campaign in a feeble attempt to find some technicality to get your client off. Typical stuff for a defense attorney."

"I knew they'd get my number sooner or later." I take a bite of my cheeseburger. "Have you guys found anything else?"

He sips his coffee and wipes his mouth with a paper napkin. "Nothing I haven't told you already. Skipper has poor Bill McNulty living with two jury consultants. One of them told me Skipper has practiced his opening in front of two different mock juries."

"How are the test audiences playing?"

"Pretty well. For all his faults, the man has charisma."

Indeed. Believe me, I know. "What else can you tell me, Roosevelt? Anything else I can use?"

"Not a thing, Mike. You're doing everything you're supposed to be doing. Once you got the confession knocked out, it turned into a circumstantial case. It isn't an easy one."

For either side.

He wipes his glasses and gazes at the Yankee Clipper. "Why don't you ask for more time? Your client isn't rotting in jail at the Hall. Why the hell are you rushing to trial?"

"He won't listen to reason on that particular subject."

"So I gather."

"Any new leads on Vince Russo?"

"Nope. His story went cold at the Golden Gate Bridge."

"Pete thinks a cab driver may have picked him up and driven him to the airport," I tell him.

"That's more than we've found."

Great. Just great.

Mort calls me at the office at five o'clock the same afternoon. "I got a fax from the judge," he says.

"And?"

"She ruled we can't call Skipper as a witness at the trial."

"No big surprise there, Mort."

"Nope. I was surprised she didn't rule against us on the spot."

Four days until trial. On Monday, we start playing for keeps.

32

OPENING CEREMONIES

"We are extremely confident."
—MICHAEL DALEY. NEWSCENTER 4. MONDAY, MARCH 16.

"I'm scared to death, Rosie," I say. "I haven't been this nervous in a long time." We're driving toward Rabbi Friedman's house in a light rain on the morning of Monday, March 16. El Niño's giving us a small respite today, but the gray skies further dampen my mood.

"First-day jitters," she replies. "You're like a baseball pitcher. After you make it through the first inning, you'll be fine." We pull into Rabbi Friedman's driveway. She gives me a peck on the cheek. "Go get 'em," she says. "Once the trial starts, there's no looking back."

The rabbi meets us at the door. He looks grim. Per my instructions, Joel and his dad are dressed in dark business suits, with white shirts and subdued ties. Joel's mom and

Naomi are wearing conservative clothes, no jewelry and a minimal amount of makeup.

I gather everyone in the dining room. "I know we've gone over this," I say, "but I want to remind you one more time that trials are theater. It sounds paranoid, but you have to assume everything you say and do will be scrutinized by the jury. I want you to act normal, but be careful. An inappropriate gesture could have greater impact than you'd think."

They listen attentively. "Michael," says Rabbi Friedman, "are we allowed to show any emotion?"

Tough call. Generally, histrionics don't play well in the courtroom. They tend to distract the jury and irritate the judge. "It won't hurt to shake your head every once in a while. I don't want you to draw unnecessary attention to yourselves. I want to keep the jury focused. And I don't want the judge to think we're trying to disrupt her courtroom. She's very businesslike."

Rosie looks at her watch. "Time to go," she says.

Joel and Naomi hold hands in the back of Rosie's car as we drive to the Hall. I can only imagine what's going through their minds. As Rosie makes a left onto Bryant, I turn around and face them. He's stoic, almost serene. She's tugging her hair. "It's going to be all right," I say.

Joel is silent. Naomi says quietly, "I know."

We pull into the pay lot next to McDonald's. Joel's parents take the spot next to us a moment later. They huddle under a large black umbrella while Rosie and I pull our trial cases out of the trunk.

Even though it's now raining steadily, reporters from all the local stations are waiting for us on the front steps of the Hall. The nerdy guy from CNN is here. The arrogant woman from Court TV who's been calling me an idiot for the last six weeks has left the comfort of her studio to insult me in person. A dozen police officers form a human barricade for us. The cameras and reporters follow us. It starts to rain harder. We're pelted with questions and rain as we push our way to the doors.

"Mr. Daley, is it true you're discussing a plea bargain?"

"Mr. Daley, is your client going to take the stand?"

"Mr. Daley, is it true you're going to have a surprise witness?"

"Mr. Daley? Mr. Daley? Mr. Daley?"

As we reach the door, I turn back and face the nearest camera. Channel 7 will get the best footage tonight. Two dozen microphones are held up to my face. "Ladies and gentlemen," I say, "we are extremely confident Mr. Friedman will be fully exonerated of these outrageous charges." I turn and walk into the building. Reporters continue shouting questions to my back.

Mort is waiting for us inside. We make our way through the metal detectors and up the elevators. Police mill around. Security is tight. As I turn to open the heavy wooden doors to Judge Chen's courtroom, I see Skipper's smiling countenance as he strides forcefully toward us, reporters nipping at his heels. If he's nervous, he isn't showing it. It's sound-bite time. I can't hear what he's saying, but I'm sure he's extolling the strength of his case and his faith in the criminal justice system. I catch his eye. It's opening day. Let's play the National Anthem and start the game.

The small, windowless courtroom is packed. The roar is deafening. The hot, heavy air smells of mildew. Umbrellas and raincoats are strewn about. McNulty and two law clerks lug in four trial bags. Skipper and McNulty take their places at the prosecution table near the jury box. Joel sits between Rosie and me at the defense table and Mort sits at the end. Mort has his game face on. He sits quietly, looking forward intently. His eyes are moving constantly. He's looking for any nuance or advantage.

The gallery is full. Naomi and her in-laws are in the first row, directly behind us. Diana's mother sits right behind Skipper. The courtroom artists have their sketch pads poised. Reporters and onlookers crowd into the remaining seats.

Judge Chen's bailiff is an older black woman named Harriet Hill. At precisely ten o'clock, she instructs us to stand. The judge hurries to her tall leather chair on the bench and nods to Skipper, and then to me. Her hair is pulled back tightly. She calls for order. The courtroom becomes silent. "Any last-minute issues?" she asks.

"No, Your Honor," Skipper and I say almost in unison.

"Good." She's trying to set a businesslike tone. "Let's get started."

To the great chagrin of the media, we will spend the first few days, and perhaps weeks, of the trial picking a jury. Like most trial lawyers, I believe cases are won or lost during jury selection. Unfortunately, picking a jury is the most important and least scientific part of the entire enterprise. Jury consultants get paid hundreds of thousands of dollars to identify personality traits and biases gleaned from juror questionnaires that may not have been answered honestly. Some jury consultants claim they can help you pick a sympathetic jury just by watching the body language of the potential jurors. At the end of the day, you go with hunches and gut instincts as much as demographics.

Picking a jury is more difficult than it used to be. In June of 1991, California voters passed Proposition 115, which gave judges, rather than the prosecutors and defense attorneys, the authority to question prospective jurors during the voir dire. Before Prop. 115, jury selection in a capital case could take months. With the judges asking the questions, the process tends to go much more quickly. Lawyers can still give the judge a list of questions we want asked—which the judge is free to ignore. Although Judge Chen has promised to give us some leeway, she reminds us that she'll be asking the questions.

Skipper has hired one of the jury consultants from the Simpson trial, who's appeared on CNN from time to time. My jury consultant, Barbara Childs, has been on Ted Koppel's show. I suspect the battle of the consultants will end up about even.

The best thing about jury selection is that it tends to bore the media to tears. The judge asks the same questions of a large group of people for days on end. Occasionally, the lawyers get to stand up and make a speech to try to have a juror excused. After a few preliminaries, Judge Chen tells Harriet Hill to bring in the first panel of potential jurors.

Thursday, March 19. Three days later, we're still at it. The first-day media blitz has died down. Although the local TV stations are still sending reporters to monitor the proceedings, we've been relegated to the third page of the *Chronicle* and the fourth story in the local news broadcasts. We get a little more play on CNN every night. Everybody will be back once we've picked the jury.

We must select twelve jurors and six alternates. So far, we've managed to select nine jurors. I'm having a tougher time than Skipper. He's looking for people who hate lawyers. That includes about 99 percent of the population. Skipper wants people who have had a bad experience with the legal system, who might take out their hostility on Joel. I'm trying to avoid anybody who's ever been arrested, divorced or sued. That doesn't leave much. I like his odds better.

According to my consultant, I should try to fill the jury with women, because they're more open-minded. On the other hand, they tend to turn quickly in cases where a woman is a victim, especially if the accused is a man. So much for statistics.

By three o'clock on Thursday, we've picked our twelve jurors and six alternates. Judge Chen has kept the process moving. We've finished sooner than I would have predicted.

The jury is a mixed bag. Eight women and four men. Two of the women are Asian, one black. One man is Asian, another Hispanic. Seven are married and three have been divorced. Two are lawyers. The black woman is a supervisor for the phone company. I have a hunch she'll be one of the leaders. I tried to get her excused because she was divorced. Judge Chen ruled against me. There are two homemakers, a retired Muni bus driver, a data-entry clerk, a hotel clerk and an accountant. How they'll react is anybody's guess.

After the last juror is seated, Judge Chen looks at her watch and turns to Skipper. "I trust you'll be ready to begin your opening statement tomorrow?"

"Absolutely, Your Honor."

Back at the office the same evening, Barbara Childs congratulates me for picking a terrific jury. Her words ring hollow. What else would she say? After she leaves, I get a more realistic view from Rosie and Mort.

"Could be worse," Mort says.

Rosie agrees with him. "We've done the best we could," she says. "It's a crapshoot."

She's right. All the studies and all the empirical research go straight out the window when you're in a courtroom picking a jury. It's a feeling you never get used to. Your client's life is in the hands of twelve strangers. You never know if you've picked twelve Mother Teresas or twelve Jack the Rippers.

"Which ones did you like the best?" I ask.

Mort clutches his cigar. "You should get a pretty good shake from the two lawyers. I think the accountant will be okay." He shrugs. "Tough to tell with the rest of them."

Rosie adds, "I think the Asian women and the Hispanic man will be conscientious."

"Anybody you didn't like?"

They look at each other. "I wasn't happy with the phone company supervisor," Rosie replies. "She looks like she has a chip on her shoulder."

Mort puts his cigar in his mouth. "I wasn't crazy about her, either," he says.

At eleven-thirty that night, I'm at home watching the legal analysts on CNN dissect our jury. As always, the panel of eight "experts" sits in two rows of bleacher seats on one side of the studio, fielding questions from the strident woman with the bad hair and the wormy guy with the bad glasses. Their program looks like a pregame show for a football game. You know you've made the big time when your trial has its own graphics and theme song. The voice of James Earl Jones intones that we're watching coverage of "Special Circumstances: The Law Firm Murder Trial."

After voting 6–2 in favor of Skipper's jury-selection acumen, the people in the bleachers turn to the TV monitor in the middle of the studio and begin a heated discussion with a jury consultant from the Menendez case, who seems to have a television studio in her home. The camera pans back. It looks very odd to see the two hosts and the eight panelists talking to the woman's head.

"Mr. Gates clearly got the better of the jury-selection process," says the disembodied head. "Asians are good prosecution jurors. They like order. On the other hand, the Hispanic man has probably had trouble with the law. I'm sure he'll be sympathetic to the defense."

It's frightening to observe how these people think. She should know better. It was revealed in the voir dire that the Hispanic man is a senior vice president at Chevron and lives in the most expensive corner of the ritzy Seacliff neighborhood. He's a big contributor to the Republican party.

"The black woman," she continues, "will almost certainly favor the defense. I'm sure she's had friends or relatives hassled by the cops. She's probably going to give the defendant a pretty fair shake."

I'm not so sure. The woman's husband is a cop. If the disembodied head had been paying attention during the voir dire, she would have known this.

The female host interrupts her. "Don't you think the jurors will be predisposed against Mr. Friedman because he's a lawyer?"

The consultant smiles. "Absolutely. That's the big wild card. Most people think lawyers get away with murder every day." Raucous laughter. They take another vote before they go to commercial. This time it's unanimous. The jury is clearly going to be on Skipper's side.

I flip to CNBC. Marcia Clark is lecturing on the strength of Skipper's case. I turn off the TV and run through my opening statement one more time.

———

Friday morning arrives with a driving rainstorm. The mini-cams are lined up on Bryant and umbrellas blanket the front steps of the Hall. We push our way through the crowd and march up to the courtroom. Reporters surround Skipper outside the door. We have barely enough time to take off our raincoats when Harriet Hill instructs us to rise. Judge Chen walks briskly to her chair. She asks Harriet Hill to bring in the jury. She greets them warmly and says they'll have the privilege of hearing opening statements today. Without another word, she turns to Skipper. "You may begin your opening statement, Mr. Gates."

He stands and buttons the jacket of his navy suit. He walks slowly but forcefully to the lectern, and places a stack of notecards just below the small light. He doesn't look at them. The courtroom is silent. It's like the moment at the symphony when the conductor raises his baton. He nods to the judge and turns to the jury. He scans their faces. "May it please the court," he begins, "my name is Prentice Gates. I am the district attorney for the city and county of San Francisco. We are here today to address a serious matter. A matter of life and death."

The jurors shift uncomfortably. The phone company supervisor's eyes meet Skipper's. Judge Chen watches intently. I focus on the jury. Joel swallows.

Skipper leaves the lectern and walks slowly toward the jury. They size each other up. He takes his gold pen from his breast pocket and points toward enlarged color photos of Bob and Diana, which sit on an easel placed in front of the jury box. "We are here today because of these two people. Robert Holmes and Diana Kennedy. I knew both of them. They were colleagues of mine. They were my friends."

I could stand up now and object because he's supposed to stick to the facts in his opening. On the other hand, it's considered bad form to interrupt. I stay quiet.

"We are here today because of that man sitting over

there." He points at Joel. "We will show you evidence that the defendant knowingly and willfully, with malice afore-thought, killed Diana Kennedy and Robert Holmes."

McNulty has coached him well. Skipper is always going to refer to Joel as "the defendant." It's easier for the jury to convict a nameless "defendant." I remind myself to refer to Joel by name.

Skipper spends twenty minutes expressing his outrage and disappointment that a member of the legal profession and his former colleague would have taken the lives of two respected attorneys. Joel stares straight ahead. Skipper holds up his right index finger melodramatically and says, "I want you to remember these two pictures. Bob Holmes and Diana Kennedy can't speak for themselves. We can't undo the pain suffered by their families. But we can bring their killer to justice. We have to speak for them."

I stand slowly. "Excuse me, Your Honor," I say. "Would you please remind Mr. Gates that opening statements should stick to the evidence? There will be time at the end for closing arguments."

She looks at Skipper. "Mr. Gates," she says, "please keep to the facts."

"Yes, Your Honor," he replies. He turns back to the jury. "Ladies and gentlemen," he continues, "we're going to show you incontrovertible evidence that places the defendant at the scene of the crime." He goes on to describe the physical evidence for about forty minutes. The jurors sit quietly. He's finding his rhythm. "In addition," he says, "we will present evidence that the defendant was having an affair with Diana Kennedy." Murmuring in the back of the court-room. I glance at Naomi. Our eyes meet. "When the rela-tionship soured and the defendant found out that Ms. Kennedy was romantically involved with Mr. Holmes, he became enraged.

"The defendant was also angry at Mr. Holmes because

the defendant was passed up for election to the partnership at the Simpson and Gates law firm." He clears his throat. "Imagine. He killed another human being because he didn't make partner." Rabbi Friedman looks down. Joel remains stoic.

"Finally," Skipper says, "I realize there are many people who aren't particularly enamored of members of the legal profession." A couple of jurors nod. "But," he continues, "I want to make something clear to you. The legal profession is not on trial here. The defendant is. It's my job to show you enough evidence to give you the tools that you need to convict. I will give you those tools.

"You'll be hearing today from Mr. Daley, who is the defendant's attorney. It's his job to try to confuse you. It's his job to try to put doubts in your mind. I'm saying this not as an indictment or criticism of Mr. Daley. It's just the way our system works."

That's not entirely true. He is, in fact, saying it as an indictment and a criticism of me.

"I ask you to use your common sense." He points to the pictures of Bob and Diana. "Above all, I want you to keep these pictures in mind. I need your help to find justice for Bob and Diana."

He makes eye contact with each of them. He walks past the easel and looks at the pictures of Bob and Diana. He unbuttons his jacket and sits down.

Judge Chen turns to me. "Mr. Daley, will you be making an opening statement today?" We have the option of deferring our opening statement until after the prosecution has completed its case. If I wait, I can tailor my opening to address issues raised in Skipper's case. On the other hand, it may be several weeks before the jury hears me say anything of substance. We've agreed that if Skipper opens strong, I'll make our opening today. I glance at Rosie and Mort. They both nod.

"Your Honor," I say, "we'll be giving our opening statement today."

I stand up and button my jacket. I walk toward them and look each one in the eye, one at a time. I move almost to the edge of the jury box. I like to start close to them. In a quiet, conversational tone, I begin by saying, "My name is Michael Daley. I represent Joel Friedman, who has been unjustly accused of a terrible crime he didn't commit."

Skipper could leap up right now and demand that I stick to the evidence. Fortunately, McNulty's told him to stay in his chair. I'm going to take advantage of it while I can.

"Joel Friedman is an honest, hardworking man with a wonderful wife and two young children. His life has been turned upside down because he happened to be at the office doing his job on the night two people died. Imagine what it must be like when the police come to your house and arrest you in front of your wife, your parents and your children for two murders you didn't commit. What do you tell your wife? What do you tell your parents?" I pause. "What do you tell your kids?

"That's why we're here. Mr. Gates is absolutely right that this is a very serious matter. It isn't the slightest exaggeration to say it is a matter of life and death. I need your help. I need you to sort out what happened. I need you to sift through the evidence so we can figure out the truth—together. In our system, Mr. Gates is required to prove his case beyond a reasonable doubt. That's a tough standard." I pause. "After you hear the evidence you're going to come to a simple conclusion. He can't do it."

I get the hint of agreement from the accountant.

"You'll hear Joel was in the office that night. You'll find out he phoned Diana Kennedy and asked her to return to the office. You'll hear he left an angry voice-mail message for Bob Holmes. All of these things are true." I describe the fingerprints on the gun. I argue that they got there when

Joel unloaded the gun. I claim they can't prove he pulled the trigger.

"Mr. Gates is going to introduce circumstantial evidence to show that Joel Friedman and Diana Kennedy were having an affair. He's going to claim that she broke up with him and initiated a romantic relationship with Mr. Holmes. There was, in fact, no such affair between Joel Friedman and Diana Kennedy. It didn't happen."

I spend thirty minutes trying to cast doubt on every piece of evidence, liberally using the words "shaky," "contrived" and "convoluted." I think the jury is with me. I glance at Rosie, who blinks twice. It's my signal to wrap up. "Ladies and gentlemen," I say, "I realize Mr. Gates has suggested to you that my job is to obfuscate and confuse you. Let's be realistic. We all saw the Simpson trial. We all know that there are lawyers who will do just about anything to get their client off." I move closer to them. "I want you to understand something. I'm not that kind of lawyer. I will not lie to you. I will not attempt to confuse you. And I will not, under any circumstances, try to mislead you."

Actually, I'd try to obfuscate and confuse them in a New York minute if I thought it would help get Joel off. "I need you to keep an open mind and review the evidence. I know there's a lot of animosity directed toward lawyers. I would ask you not to take out your feelings toward the legal profession against Joel Friedman. You don't have to look very far to find cases where justice isn't served. In this trial, I would ask you to help me try to make the system work the way it's supposed to. When we're done, I know you will agree that Joel Friedman is not guilty of these terrible crimes."

I sit down. The judge says we'll break for the weekend.

At nine o'clock the same evening, Rosie and I are watching CNN. The panel of experts in the bleachers has proclaimed

Skipper the hands-down winner of opening statements. "Daley should have waited until after the prosecution's case to give his opening," says the woman with the bad hair.

"Nah," says the head of the disembodied woman on the TV screen. "Gates has too much charisma. At least Daley got to the jury before the horse was out of the barn."

The prosecutor from Texas who always wears a Stetson hat in a hot TV studio sides with Skipper. "They should have tried for a plea bargain," he drawls.

We flip to CNBC. "If I were in Daley's shoes," says Marcia Clark, "I'd be begging the prosecution for a deal."

Thanks, Marcia. Rosie shuts the TV off. "Was it that bad?" I ask her.

"You held your own. The prosecution gets to play its good cards first."

I hope she's right. It doesn't make me feel any better.

33

LAYING THE FOUNDATION

"The most important thing prosecutors learned from the Simpson trial is to keep your case short and sweet."

—NEWSCENTER 4 LEGAL ANALYST MORGAN HENDERSON.
MONDAY, MARCH 23.

The sun makes a cameo appearance for a few minutes on Monday morning. By the time we reach the Hall, it's raining again. We push our way past the ever-present TV cameras.

We take our seats at the defense table. Joel asks, "Who do you think they'll call first?"

The conventional wisdom is that prosecutors build their case one piece at a time. They have to prove the defendant was there. They have to prove he had opportunity. They have to show he had contact with the murder weapon. And they have to show motive. Piece by piece. Block by block. If all the blocks don't fit, the defendant walks. It's that simple.

"They'll probably start with the first officer on the scene and work their way through the physical evidence," I reply. "It lays the foundation for their entire case."

Harriet Hill calls for order and instructs us to rise. Judge

Chen takes her seat on the bench and pounds her gavel. She looks at Skipper. "Are you ready to call your first witness?"

"Yes, Your Honor."

Harriet Hill brings in the jury.

Skipper straightens his tie. "The people call Officer Paul Chinn."

It's not a bad place to start. He was the first officer at the scene.

The young police officer's uniform is freshly pressed. He walks to the front of the courtroom and is sworn in. His demeanor is stoic. Cops are trained to stay calm. Some are better at it than others. My dad used to hate going to court.

"Officer Chinn," Skipper begins, "were you the first officer to arrive at the Simpson and Gates offices on the morning of December thirty-first?"

"Yes, sir," he says a little too quickly. "I arrived at eight-twelve A.M. I responded to a nine-one-one dispatch." His delivery is a little wooden but the tone is straightforward. Juries pay close attention to the early witnesses. Then they start to get bored. Chinn says he was met by Chuckles in the lobby. In response to Chinn's preliminary questions, Chuckles said nobody was in danger. Then he escorted Chinn to Bob's office, where Joel was waiting outside.

Skipper nods to McNulty, who places an enlarged diagram of Bob's office on the easel in front of the jury. Skipper has Chinn identify it as a diagram of the crime scene. Skipper turns to Judge Chen and requests that the diagram be introduced as an exhibit.

She looks at me. "No objection, Your Honor," I say. I'm glad they've decided to use a diagram instead of the crime-scene photos. I'm sure these will come later.

"Officer Chinn," he continues, "would you mind showing us where the bodies were found?"

Chinn leaves the stand and walks to the diagram. He

uses a Bic pen to point to the places on the floor where the bodies were found. Skipper walks him through a brief tour of the scene. Then Skipper picks up a revolver wrapped in clear plastic from the evidence cart. "Officer," he says, "do you recognize this?"

"Yes. It's the weapon I found on the desk of Mr. Holmes."

At least he didn't call it the murder weapon.

Next Skipper has him identify the three spent shell casings and the three unused bullets that were sitting on the desk when he arrived. "Where did you find the casings and the bullets?"

"On the desk."

"Did that seem odd to you?"

"Yes. I would have thought the bullets would have been in the gun."

"Do you know how the bullets got on the desk?"

I'm up. "Objection. Calls for speculation. Officer Chinn has no personal knowledge of how the bullets made their way to the desk." It's good to get your first objection out of the way.

"Sustained."

Skipper says, "I'll rephrase. Did the defendant explain to you how the casings and the bullets found their way to the desk?"

Chinn responds, "The defendant said he unloaded the gun after he found the bodies. He directed me to the casings and the bullets." His tone is measured.

Skipper scowls. Not the answer he wanted. "Did you see the defendant unload the gun?"

"No."

Skipper glances at the jury. "Was the defendant acting suspiciously?"

"Objection. The question goes to the defendant's state of

mind." Well, not exactly, but I'm going to try to break up Skipper's rhythm while I can.

"Your Honor," Skipper says, "I'm not asking Officer Chinn to read the defendant's mind. I'm simply asking for his observations of the defendant's behavior immediately following the incident."

"Overruled."

Chinn looks at Joel. "The defendant was agitated and extremely upset."

Skipper is pleased. "And did you have any basis to conclude that the defendant may have had any involvement in the deaths of Mr. Holmes and Ms. Kennedy other than as a witness?"

"Objection. Speculative."

"Sustained."

I'm going to take my shots while I can. Skipper is going to get the hang of this sooner or later.

Skipper strokes his chin. "Officer, after you found the bodies, the murder weapon, the bullets and shells, what did you do?"

"Objection. There's no foundation for the characterization of the gun as the 'murder' weapon."

"Sustained." She turns to the jury and says, "The jury will disregard the characterization of the revolver as the 'murder' weapon."

Sure they will. Skipper rephrases the question, leaving out the word "murder."

Officer Chinn says he followed standard procedure; he secured the scene and called for reinforcements. He describes the arrival of the police and the paramedics, followed by the technicians from the coroner's office, the police photographers and the homicide inspectors.

"No further questions, Your Honor."

Not a bad direct exam for a guy who's never done it

before. And not a bad performance by a young cop who's
batting leadoff in his first big case.

"Officer Chinn," I say calmly, as I stand, "you've told us you
found the revolver, the spent shells and the unused bullets
on the desk of Mr. Holmes."

"That's correct."

"And you've testified Mr. Friedman told you he unloaded the gun."

"Yes."

"Did he tell you why he unloaded the gun?"

"He said he did it to protect the safety of the other members of the firm."

"I see. That's an admirable goal, isn't it?"

"Objection. Speculative."

"Sustained."

I've made my point. "Officer, did you have any reason to
disbelieve Mr. Friedman when he told you he had disarmed
the revolver?"

Chinn looks helplessly at Skipper. "No," he replies.

"Did you see any evidence on his hands or clothing that
suggested he fired the gun?"

"It would have been very difficult to see any such evidence with the naked eye, Mr. Daley."

"I understand. But did you see any such evidence?"

"No, sir." It's generally a good sign when the witness
starts calling you "sir."

"And did you collect any samples of tissue or clothing
from Mr. Friedman to obtain evidence that he did, in fact,
fire the gun?"

He scratches his cheek. "No, sir."

"So you have no personal knowledge as to whether he
fired the gun?"

Skipper stands. "Asked and answered, Your Honor."

"Sustained. Move along, Mr. Daley." I was wondering how long she'd let me go.

"Officer, you testified that you secured the scene."

"That's right."

"So nobody could have left the Simpson and Gates suite once you arrived, correct?"

"That's true."

"You secured the elevators?"

"Yes."

"And the stairs?"

"Yes."

I give him an inquisitive look. "You were the only officer at the scene when you arrived, right?"

His eyes dart toward Skipper. "Yes."

"And you were able to secure six elevators and two internal stairways all by yourself?"

He looks perplexed. "Other officers arrived right away. We secured the scene as soon as possible."

"What about the freight elevator?"

"We secured it."

"When?"

He purses his lips. "When the other officers arrived."

"So, Officer, it is possible that any number of people could have fled the scene on the elevators or the stairs or the freight elevator before additional officers arrived, isn't it?"

"Objection. Speculative."

"Overruled."

Officer Chinn looks troubled. "I suppose that's possible."

So far, so good. "Officer, you testified Mr. Friedman was agitated and upset when you arrived."

"That's correct."

"How long have you been on the force?"

He looks away. He seems to be adding it up in his head. "Three and a half years."

"How many times have you been the first officer at the scene of an alleged homicide?"

"This was the second time."

"How many dead bodies have you seen in three and a half years?"

"Objection," Skipper says. "I fail to see any relevance."

Judge Chen looks impatient. "Overruled."

"I've seen three dead bodies," Chinn replies.

I get right in front of him. "Officer Chinn, in your experience, when you arrive at the scene of the homicide, isn't it usually the case that the people are upset?"

"Yes."

"And isn't it true that the people who are most upset are often the people who found the body?"

"Yes, sir."

"Wouldn't it be fair to say that Mr. Friedman's reaction was not unusual in the circumstances?"

Skipper should object. I'm shamelessly asking him to speculate. "That's fair," Chinn says.

Gotcha. "One last thing. When you arrived, you were met by Mr. Stern, who told you nobody was in danger."

"That's correct."

"Officer," I say, "you arrived within minutes after Mr. Stern discovered the bodies. How did he know there wasn't a killer on the loose in the Simpson and Gates office?"

Chinn looks at Skipper and then at McNulty. "I guess he assumed nobody was in danger because he found the murder weapon on the desk of Mr. Holmes."

"Move to strike the word 'murder' from Officer Chinn's testimony."

"Sustained. The jury will disregard the characterization of the weapon as the 'murder' weapon."

"Officer Chinn," I continue, "isn't it possible that Mr. Stern knew that nobody was in danger because he knew Mr. Holmes had committed suicide?"

"Objection. Speculative."

"Sustained."

"Isn't it possible Mr. Stern knew that nobody was in danger because he knew who the real killer was? And the real killer may have even been him?"

Murmurs in the back of the courtroom.

"Objection. Speculative."

Judge Chen pounds her gavel. "The objection is sustained." She points her gavel toward the gallery. "If there are any other disruptions, I will clear this courtroom."

"I have no further questions of this witness, Your Honor," I say.

"You took him apart," Joel says as we take a short break after Chinn's testimony. We're in the consultation room behind Judge Chen's courtroom.

"He's a kid, Joel. He's just a table-setter."

"Still," he says, "you made him contradict his story. That's good."

I get a more realistic view from Mort. "Nice cross," he says. "The jury seems to like you."

"We have a long way to go," Rosie observes.

After the brief recess, Skipper calls Sandra Wilson. She spends the next hour describing how she meticulously gathered every shred of evidence in Bob's office and Diana's apartment. Skipper is doing it by the book. He's confirming to the jury that there are no chain-of-custody issues. He's introducing all the evidence he'll need later in the trial. She describes how she handled and catalogued the revolver, the spent shells and the unused bullets. She confirms the revolver was registered to Bob. She identifies the keyboard. I interrupt periodically. Realistically, I'm not going to win any battles with Sandra on the stand. Pete and I looked at every piece of evidence. There's no point in making an ass of myself while she's testifying. It will only piss off the phone company supervisor.

I ask a few perfunctory questions on cross. I want to get her off the stand as fast as I can.

After lunch, Skipper raises the stakes. Marcus Banks looks ready for battle as he strides confidently to the front of the courtroom. After he's sworn in, Skipper picks up a neatly labeled cassette tape from the evidence cart. "Inspector," he says, "do you recognize this?"

Banks nods solemnly. "Yes. It's a recording of a message left on Diana Kennedy's answering machine at approximately twelve-fifty-one A.M. on December thirty-first."

"And could you describe the contents of the message?"

"Objection, Your Honor. Hearsay."

"Overruled." I'm not surprised. I know she's going to let them introduce the tapes into evidence. We've fought this battle and lost.

"The message was from the defendant. He asked Ms. Kennedy to return to the office."

Nice response. Straightforward. Noninflammatory. I can see McNulty's influence. They're going to build their case carefully. They don't need theatrics—yet.

"Inspector, did the defendant sound agitated or upset in the message?"

"Objection. Asks for Mr. Friedman's state of mind."

"Sustained."

Skipper introduces the tape into evidence. He asks the judge for permission to play it to the jury. Judge Chen gives me an inquisitive glance.

"Your Honor," I say, "the defense renews its objection to having this tape entered into evidence." She won't go for it.

I'm stating it for the record so we can challenge her decision on appeal. She knows it.

"We've been over this before, Mr. Daley. Your motion is denied."

"The defense therefore requests that Your Honor instruct the jury to consider the fact that this tape is being played in the absence of context."

Skipper says, "Your Honor, we believe the tape speaks for itself."

Judge Chen looks at the jurors. "Ladies and gentlemen," she says, "you are about to hear a recording of a conversation between Mr. Friedman and Ms. Kennedy. You should consider the fact that you have not been given information concerning the context in which this recording was made."

Skipper hands the cassette to McNulty, who puts it into the tape player. The courtroom becomes silent. The jurors all focus on the tape player. The heated voices of Joel and Diana resonate in the courtroom. Joel closes his eyes. Naomi's lips form a tight line across her face.

The tape ends. Skipper turns back to Banks. "Were you able to identify the voices?"

"Objection. Inspector Banks has not been qualified as a voice-recognition expert."

"Overruled."

"The male voice was that of the defendant," Banks says. "The female voice was that of the victim, Ms. Kennedy."

They go through a similar exercise for the voice-mail message from Joel to Bob. "Inspector Banks," Skipper says, "do you believe Mr. Friedman was angry enough at the time these tapes were made to kill two people?"

I'm up like a shot. "Objection, Your Honor. Speculative. State of mind."

"Sustained. The jury will disregard the last question."

Oh, sure. Skipper smiles. "No further questions," he says.

———

I stand up right away. "Inspector Banks," I say, "you weren't present when these telephone conversations were recorded, were you?"

"Of course not."

"So you don't really know why Mr. Friedman called Ms. Kennedy, do you?"

He looks indignant. "It's obvious. He was angry at her."

I deserved that. "Inspector, are you aware that Ms. Kennedy and Mr. Friedman were working on a very large transaction?"

"Yes."

"And they were under a lot of pressure to close that transaction the next morning and that millions of dollars were riding on the successful closing?"

"Objection. Leading."

"Overruled." It's okay to lead on cross. McNulty whispers to Skipper.

"Isn't it possible Mr. Friedman called Ms. Kennedy because he needed help on the deal?"

"I don't think so."

"But it's possible, right?"

"I don't think so," he repeats.

He isn't going to budge. "Inspector, let's talk about Mr. Friedman's voice-mail message to Mr. Holmes. Are you aware that Mr. Friedman was told that he wasn't going to make partner that night?"

"Yes."

"And do you believe that Mr. Friedman was upset about that?"

"Yes."

"If you'd worked for eight years to try to make partner, you'd probably have been upset, too."

He shrugs.

"But you've interpreted Mr. Friedman's voice-mail message to Mr. Holmes as a threat."

"Yes. I think it's obvious."

"Let me ask you this, Inspector. Have you ever worked in a law firm?"

"No."

"But you've spent a lot of time around lawyers, right?"

He smiles sardonically. "More than I'd care to," he says.

"And you know a little bit about how lawyers think, right?"

"Objection, Your Honor. Can we get to the point?"

"Sustained." Judge Chen rotates her hands like a basketball referee making a traveling call. "Speed it up, Mr. Daley."

"Inspector, lawyers sometimes say things just for effect, or just to make a point, right?"

"Right. Kind of like right now, right, Mr. Daley?"

Touché. "As a matter of fact, yes. Lawyers sometimes take exaggerated positions just as a negotiating tactic, don't they, Inspector?"

"That's true."

"And isn't it possible, Inspector, that Mr. Friedman's voice-mail message to Mr. Holmes was, in fact, lawyerly posturing?"

"Not the way I heard it."

"But, it's possible, isn't it, Inspector?"

"I don't think so."

"Come on, Inspector. Be reasonable."

Skipper stands up and objects in a measured tone. "Your Honor, Inspector Banks has answered Mr. Daley's question."

The hell he has.

"Sustained."

I've gone as far as I can. "No further questions."

———

Joel isn't happy about my cross-exam of Banks. We're in the consultation room during the break. "Jesus, Mike," he says, "couldn't you have nailed Banks?"

Mort sticks up for me. "Banks wasn't going to move an inch. Mike got him to look like a stubborn jerk. It's the best we could do."

Thanks, Mort.

Joel scowls. "Maybe Mort should take a few witnesses."

Mort looks pleased. I turn back to Joel. "The prosecutor always looks good at the beginning," I say. "We have to chip away at their case a little at a time."

He tosses a crumpled paper cup into the trash and doesn't respond.

34

"I AM THE CHIEF MEDICAL EXAMINER FOR THE CITY AND COUNTY OF SAN FRANCISCO"

"Dr. Beckert has testified at hundreds of murder trials. His testimony will undoubtedly be very damaging to the defendant's case."

—NEWSCENTER 4 LEGAL ANALYST MORGAN HENDERSON.
MONDAY, MARCH 23.

At three o'clock the same afternoon, Skipper stands and says in a clear voice, "The people call Dr. Roderick Beckert."

Beckert nods to the judge as he walks confidently to the front of the courtroom. The college-professor tweed jacket that was hanging on the coatrack in his office has been replaced with a charcoal-gray business suit and a burgundy tie. He's the living embodiment of the voice of authority.

Skipper stands at the lectern. He doesn't want to crowd Beckert. "Would you please state your name and occupation for the record?"

"Dr. Roderick Beckert." The hint of a smile. He closes his eyes and slowly reopens them. "I am the chief medical examiner for the city and county of San Francisco." He nods, as if to reassure himself that he is, in fact, who he says he is. "I've held the position for twenty-seven years."

Skipper begins to run Beckert through his credentials. I stop him almost immediately and stipulate to his expertise. There's no point in giving Skipper twenty minutes of free time to wave Beckert's diplomas in front of the jury.

"Dr. Beckert," Skipper says, "did you perform autopsies on the bodies of Robert Holmes and Diana Kennedy on January first of this year?"

"Yes."

"And would you be kind enough to describe the results of those autopsies?"

He smiles politely and turns slightly toward the jury. "Of course, Mr. Gates." He says Bob and Diana died of gunshot wounds, his to the head, hers to the chest. Time of death between one and four A.M. He explains that Diana was two months pregnant and that the unborn fetus also died. His tone is conversational, yet forceful. I let him drone on for a few minutes about body temperature, lividity and discoloration before I interrupt him and stipulate that we'll agree to his determination on the range he has established for the time of death. The jury already believes him. It's not to our advantage to let him build empathy.

On cue, McNulty trots out a poster-size version of one of the photos Beckert showed me in his office. We tried to keep it out. "Doctor," Skipper says, "what is this a picture of?"

"It's the left side of the head of the victim, Robert Holmes."

"Doctor, would you please describe the gunshot wound that killed Mr. Holmes?"

"Of course. Entry through the right parietal, just above the right temple. It severed the cerebral cortex and pierced the mesencephalon, or midbrain, before exiting through the left parietal lobe and the left parietal bone of the skull, just above the left ear." In other words, Beckert explains that the gun was placed against Bob's right temple and shot laterally through his head, causing instantaneous death as the bullet passed through the midbrain structure.

The courtroom is completely silent.

"Doctor, would you mind pointing out to the jury the exit wound that you just described?"

"Of course." Beckert climbs down off the witness stand and walks to the easel holding the picture. He takes out his pen and points at the area just behind Bob's left ear.

"Dr. Beckert," Skipper continues, "was there another wound to the head?"

"Yes, Mr. Gates." Beckert points toward the area above Bob's left ear, just above the edge of the exit wound. "Right here, on the parietal bone, there's a small hematoma, or concussive injury."

"Objection," I say. "I'm afraid we can't tell what Dr. Beckert is pointing at."

Judge Chen says, "I'm afraid that I can't either. Doctor, I'm going to have to ask you to mark the wound more precisely."

"Of course, Your Honor." He pulls a felt-tip marker from his pocket and he draws a circle on the picture. "Right here, Your Honor."

Judge Chen nods. "Thank you, Dr. Beckert."

Skipper studies the picture. "Doctor," he says, "would you mind describing the concussive wound in greater detail?"

"Yes. Mr. Holmes suffered a blow to the head, which caused a hematoma, or bump, to the parietal bone of his skull. Based upon the swelling and the freshness of the wound, I believe he was knocked unconscious shortly before he died. It's similar to a blow suffered by a football player in a helmet-to-helmet collision."

"Is it possible he was killed by the concussive blow?"

"It's unlikely. There was trauma to the skull, but not enough to kill a healthy male."

"Why would somebody go to all the trouble of knocking him out before they shot him?"

"Objection. Speculative. Dr. Beckert is a pathologist, not a clairvoyant."

"Sustained."

"I'll rephrase. Doctor, do you have a theory as to why someone would have knocked Mr. Holmes unconscious and then shot him moments later?"

"Objection. Still speculative."

"Sustained."

"Doctor, does it appear to you that the killer was attempting to make this look like a suicide?"

"Objection."

"Sustained." Judge Chen glares as Skipper. "That's enough, Mr. Gates."

"No further questions, Your Honor."

I don't wait. "Dr. Beckert, can you show me this alleged concussive wound one more time?"

He walks to the easel and points toward the circle he drew a moment ago. "Right here."

"And you're one hundred percent sure that mark you just showed me was caused by someone taking a heavy object and hitting Mr. Holmes?"

"Yes. One hundred percent sure."

"And it is not possible the wound was caused by the bullet that obliterated much of his head?"

"In my best medical judgment, no."

"Doctor, did you find any evidence of the object that you claim was used to strike Mr. Holmes?"

"I'm not sure I understand."

"Well, Doctor, if Mr. Holmes was hit with a piece of wood or a piece of metal, you may have found fragments of wood or metal or perhaps paint in the wound. Did you find any such evidence?"

"No," he says.

"Why not?"

"Excuse me?"

"How is it possible that somebody hit Mr. Holmes hard enough to knock him unconscious, yet you found no evidence of the object?"

"Objection. Speculative."

"Overruled."

Beckert shakes his head. "He must have been hit with an object that didn't leave any traces."

"I see." I pause. "Doctor, you will recall that the body was found on the floor."

"That's correct."

"Is it possible the concussive wound was caused by Mr. Holmes hitting his head on his desk as he slumped to the floor?"

He furrows his brow. "No, Mr. Daley."

"Why not?" I'm taking a bit of a chance here.

"Mr. Holmes died instantly. The hematoma was fairly well developed. If he'd hit his head on his desk after he'd been shot, there would have been no bump on his head." He explains that bumps are formed by blood rushing to the injured area. When you die, your heart stops beating and your body is therefore incapable of pumping enough blood to create a bump. "Mr. Daley," he says, "you can hit a cadaver as many times as you'd like, but you can't generate a bump on its head. As a result, I concluded that Mr. Holmes was very much alive when he was struck on the head."

I'm sorry I asked. I pick up a copy of his autopsy report from the evidence cart. "Doctor, do you recognize this report?"

"Yes. It's my autopsy report on Mr. Holmes."

"Right." I hand it to him. "You dictate these reports as you conduct your autopsy, right?"

"Yes."

"Doctor, could you please turn to page fourteen."

He puts on his glasses. He flips through the report. "I've found it, Mr. Daley."

"Doctor, would you please confirm that page fourteen describes the concussive wound."

He studies it quickly. "Yes, it does, Mr. Daley."

"And would you be kind enough to read the portion of the report that I highlighted?"

"Of course. 'Approximately three centimeters from the top of the exit wound, there appears to be a small concussive wound on the parietal bone of the skull. The wound appears relatively fresh.'"

"And those were your exact words, Doctor?"

He looks serious. "Yes, Mr. Daley. Those were my exact words as I dictated them."

"At the time you dictated your notes, were you looking at Mr. Holmes's head?"

Skipper stands, then sits down. He probably could object, but he can't figure out a reason.

"Of course I was looking at his head," Beckert replies with a hint of irritation in his voice.

"Well, Doctor, when you were looking at Mr. Holmes's head, you described what 'appears' to be a 'small concussive wound' that is 'relatively' fresh. Yet, a moment ago, you testified that you were one hundred percent sure that it was, in fact, a concussive wound and it was most certainly fresh. How did your tentative observation turn into such an absolute conclusion?"

He pouts. "Mr. Daley," he says, "I've been a medical examiner for thirty-three years. You read my preliminary observations. I examined the wound more closely during my more detailed autopsy procedures. The size and depth of the concussive wound led me to conclude, unequivocally, that Mr. Holmes was struck on the head."

I glance at the jury. "How much time elapsed between the day you performed the autopsy and the day you issued your final report?"

"About a week."

"And how many times did you look at the body again during that week?"

"I didn't."

"You didn't? Yet, during the course of a week, your view on the concussive wound seems to have changed."

"After reviewing the evidence, I became certain that there was, in fact, a concussive wound."

"And it certainly helps the prosecution's case if there's such a wound, right?"

Skipper and McNulty both stand. "Objection," Skipper shouts. "Move to strike."

"Sustained."

I turn back to Beckert. "Could you please read the portion of your report that I've highlighted on page nineteen?"

" 'Chemical residue was found on victim's right hand.' "

"What sort of chemical residue?"

He stops. "Gunpowder," he says slowly.

Judge Chen's eyes open wide.

I try to look perplexed. "Gunpowder? There was gunpowder residue on his right hand?"

"Yes."

"How did it get there?"

Skipper pops up. "Objection, Your Honor. Speculative."

"Sustained."

"I'll rephrase." I turn back to Beckert. "Isn't it true that when a gun is fired, it emits chemicals, including gunpowder, traces of which can be found on the hands of the party who fired the gun?"

"Objection. Dr. Beckert isn't an expert on firearms or chemical substances."

"Your Honor," I implore, "Dr. Beckert wrote the seminal textbook on forensic science. Surely he's capable of answering such a basic question."

"Overruled."

Beckert pushes his glasses to the top of his head. "Yes, Mr. Daley. When someone fires a gun, it is possible to find traces of gunpowder and other chemicals on his hand."

"Gunpowder traces are one of the first things the police test for on the hands of a person charged with a shooting, right?"

"Yes."

"So, Doctor," I say, "the gunpowder traces on the right hand of Mr. Holmes suggest that it is possible that Mr. Holmes fired the gun that killed him."

"Objection. Speculative."

"Overruled."

"Yes," he says grudgingly. "It's possible. However . . ."

"In fact, Doctor, the gunpowder traces on the right hand of Mr. Holmes almost certainly indicate he did, in fact, fire the gun."

"Objection, Your Honor. Speculative."

"Sustained."

"No further questions, Your Honor."

Skipper leaps up for redirect. "Doctor, in your best medical judgment, was Mr. Holmes unconscious when he was killed?"

"Yes."

"And how do you account for the gunpowder traces on his right hand?"

"Objection. Speculative."

"Overruled."

He nods as if he expected the question. "I believe Mr. Holmes was knocked unconscious by a blow to the side of his head. I believe someone placed the gun in his right hand and caused Mr. Holmes to pull the trigger. It was a clumsy attempt to fake a suicide."

"Thank you, Doctor. No further questions."

I jump up for one more crack at him. I search for my best tone of incredulity. "So, Doctor, it's your testimony that you think somebody sneaked up behind Bob Holmes, whacked him on the head, and while he was unconscious, put a revolver in his hand and caused him to use the same hand to shoot himself. Is that about it?"

He nods. "Yes, Mr. Daley," he says in an even tone. "That's about it."

"You realize that nobody in their right mind would believe such a preposterous scenario."

Skipper's up. "Objection," he screams.

"Sustained," Judge Chen snaps. "Mr. Daley, I don't want to see any more grandstanding in my courtroom. Do you understand?"

I try to sound contrite. "Yes, Your Honor. No further questions."

35

BUILDING BLOCKS

"Prosecutors build their cases one block at a time."
—CNN's *BURDEN OF PROOF*. TUESDAY, MARCH 24.

It's the next morning. "Please state your name and occupation for the record," Skipper says.

"Edward O'Malley. Ballistics technician, SFPD."

Ed O'Malley is a forty-seven-year-old civilian scientist who is the department's ballistics guru. He works in a hermetically sealed area in the basement of the Hall. The police refer to guys like Ed as white coats. He can determine with statistical precision whether a bullet was discharged from a particular weapon. His demeanor is studious. His tiny, rimless glasses perch on a large nose above a tidy gray mustache. His role in this play will be relatively short.

Skipper runs him through his resume, then picks up the plastic-wrapped revolver from the evidence cart and holds it up as if it's the Super Bowl trophy. "Mr. O'Malley," he says, "do you recognize this revolver?"

"Yes." He pauses. "That's the murder weapon."

I'm up right away. "Objection. There's no foundation for Mr. O'Malley's characterization of this revolver as the 'murder' weapon."

"Sustained." Judge Chen sighs. We're starting early today. "The jury will disregard the characterization of the weapon." She turns to Skipper. "Try it again, Mr. Gates."

Skipper leads O'Malley through a detailed description of the revolver. He concludes that it was the weapon that fired the fatal shots. Skipper sits down.

There isn't an iota of doubt in my mind that the bullets were fired from this gun. Of course, this doesn't stop me from trying to plant a few seeds of doubt in the mind of the phone company supervisor. "Mr. O'Malley," I say as I stand up, "how long have you been a ballistics expert with the department?"

"Fourteen years."

"Ever been suspended?"

Skipper leaps up. "Objection, Your Honor. Relevance."

"Your Honor," I say, "Mr. Gates called this witness as an expert. His record is highly relevant."

"Overruled."

O'Malley glances at the clock. "I was suspended for a week eleven years ago."

"No further questions." The jury doesn't have to know he was suspended when he pled no contest to a DUI charge. One could make a credible argument that it was wholly unrelated to his credentials as a ballistics expert. Skipper doesn't seem to know about it. If he did, he might try to rehabilitate O'Malley on redirect. On the other hand, he might not. The jury may not like the idea that his ballistics expert was picked up for drunk driving. O'Malley glares at Mort, who has brought his integrity into question for the second time. Mort found out about O'Malley's suspension when he was defending a case about five years ago. His client walked in that case. I hope we get the same result.

———

"My name is Sergeant Kathleen Jacobsen. I'm an evidence technician with the SFPD. I've been with the force for twenty-two years."

Skipper stands at the lectern. "Do you have a particular area of expertise?"

"Yes. Fingerprints and other chemical and physical evidence."

Kathleen Jacobsen is a tall, gray-haired woman in her late fifties with a professional demeanor and a commanding aura. One of the first lesbians to work her way up the ranks, she's become a nationally known figure on evidentiary matters. Skipper begins to walk her ever so slowly through her impressive resume: undergrad at USC, master's from UC Berkeley. I stipulate to her expertise. She confirms she was the lead evidence technician in the investigation.

Skipper strolls to the evidence cart, picks up the revolver and parades it in front of the jury. "Are you familiar with this weapon?" he asks.

"Yes. It fired the shots that killed the victims, Mr. Holmes and Ms. Kennedy." Her authoritative tone is a prosecutor's dream.

Skipper is pleased. She's delivered her lines on cue. "Did you find any fingerprints on this weapon?"

"Yes. The defendant's." Her delivery is precise.

They go through the same exercise for the computer keyboard. She confirms that Joel's fingerprints were found on it, too. Skipper signals to McNulty, who turns on a projector. The suicide E-mail appears on the screen. "Sergeant, could you please describe the message displayed on the screen?"

"It's an E-mail message generated from Mr. Holmes's computer at one-twenty on the morning of December thirty-first."

Skipper asks her to read the message out loud. When she

finishes, he says, "Does that appear to be a suicide message to you, Sergeant?"

"Objection. Sergeant Jacobsen is an expert on evidence, not suicide."

"Overruled."

"I believe it was intended to look like a suicide message. However, it was obvious the message was a fake. We found the defendant's fingerprints on the computer keyboard. We believe the defendant typed the message."

"And why would he do that?"

"Objection. Speculative."

"Sustained."

"Wouldn't he have done so to make it appear that Mr. Holmes had committed suicide?"

"Objection. Leading."

"Sustained."

"No further questions, Your Honor." He's made his point. McNulty turns off the projector.

I approach her cautiously. "Sergeant, who was the registered owner of this gun?"

"The victim, Robert Holmes."

"So Mr. Holmes had a loaded gun in his office on the night he died."

Jacobsen agrees. "It would seem that Mr. Holmes had a loaded gun in his office that night."

"Sergeant," I say, "did you find any fingerprints on the weapon besides Mr. Friedman's?"

"Yes. We found smudged fingerprints belonging to the victim, Robert Holmes."

"On what part of the weapon did you find his fingerprints?"

"On the handle."

"And could you please show us where you found the fingerprints of Mr. Friedman?"

"I'd have to review my report." I introduce her report

into evidence. I hand it to her and she studies it. She explains she found Joel's right thumb and right middle finger, ring finger and pinky on the handle. His right index finger was on the cylinder.

I hand her the plastic-wrapped revolver. "Sergeant," I say, "isn't it a fact that you didn't find any of Mr. Friedman's fingerprints on the trigger?"

She looks at Skipper. Then she looks back at me. "We found smudged fingerprints on the trigger, Mr. Daley."

"I understand. But, isn't it true that you could not positively identify any of Mr. Friedman's fingerprints on the trigger?"

"That's correct."

That helps. "And isn't it possible that the fingerprints of Mr. Friedman's that were found on this weapon were generated while Mr. Friedman was unloading the weapon, just the way he described it to Officer Chinn?"

Skipper stands up, but doesn't say anything. If he objects, he undercuts her testimony. She's supposed to be *his* expert. She looks hopelessly at Skipper. "It's possible," she says quietly.

I pause to let her answer sink in. "And isn't it true that while you may have fingerprint evidence that Mr. Friedman touched this revolver, you have no hard evidence that he actually fired it?"

"Objection, Your Honor." Skipper's trying to stop the bleeding. "Argumentative."

"Overruled."

She looks right at me. "That's true. I can say to an absolute certainty that Mr. Friedman held this revolver. I can't say to an absolute certainty that he pulled the trigger."

I take the computer keyboard from the evidence cart and ask her to identify it. "Would you please tell us which keys had Mr. Friedman's fingerprints?" I ask.

"All of the alphabetic keys."

I take a half step back. "*All* of them?"

"Yes."

"What about the numeric keys and the function keys?"

"We found his fingerprints on all of the numeric keys and three of the function keys."

I signal to Rosie. She turns on an overhead projector. The suicide E-mail flashes up on the screen. "Sergeant," I say, "you and Mr. Gates contend this message was actually typed by Mr. Friedman."

"That's correct. The defendant's fingerprints were found on the keyboard."

"I understand." I pause. "Did you find the fingerprints of Mr. Holmes on this keyboard?"

She looks at McNulty. He shrugs. "No, we didn't."

"Isn't it odd you didn't find Mr. Holmes's fingerprints on his own keyboard?"

"Objection, Your Honor. Speculative."

"Sustained."

"I'll rephrase. Sergeant, based on your experience as a fingerprint expert, wouldn't you expect to find Mr. Holmes's fingerprints on his own computer keyboard?"

She frowns. "Probably, although we think he may not have been a secretor." She pauses. "In other words, Mr. Holmes didn't sweat profusely enough to give off a lot of fingerprints."

Sure. "But you've said you didn't find any at all."

"Objection. Asked and answered."

"Sustained."

I've made my point. "You've said you found Mr. Friedman's fingerprints on *all* of the alphabetic keys. Did you stop to determine whether the E-mail used all of the letters of the alphabet?"

"No."

"May I ask why not?"

She looks straight ahead for a moment. "We were looking for his fingerprints. We didn't attempt to analyze the contents of the E-mail message."

"Would it surprise you to find out that the E-mail didn't use all of the letters of the alphabet?"

She looks at Skipper. "It wouldn't surprise me."

"In fact, Sergeant, if you read the E-mail carefully, you'll find that it does not contain the letters J, K, Q, X or Z, or any punctuation marks other than periods, and no numbers at all. Yet you found Mr. Friedman's fingerprints on all of the alphabetic keys."

"Yes, we did."

"How do you account for that?"

"Perhaps he typed the message several times, or made corrections or erased."

I move closer. "The fact is, you don't know. The fact is, you can't explain it. Isn't that right?"

"Objection. Argumentative."

"Overruled."

"Yes, Mr. Daley. We can't explain why his fingerprints were found on all the alphabetic keys."

Now we'll see if Skipper's awake over there. "Isn't it possible, Sergeant, that the reason his fingerprints were found on all the alphabetic keys is that somebody switched his keyboard with that of Mr. Holmes?"

"Objection, Your Honor. Speculative."

Judge Chen looks at me. "Unless you're prepared to bring evidence concerning this allegation, the objection is sustained."

"Withdrawn." We'll get back to this subject when it's our turn. "No further questions."

Judge Chen looks at Skipper. "Redirect?"

"Yes, Your Honor." Skipper picks up the wrapped revolver and hands it to Jacobsen. "Sergeant," he says, "could you please show us once again where you found Mr. Friedman's fingerprints?"

She picks up the revolver and points to various spots where fingerprints were found.

"Would you please grip the gun in the manner that would have generated these fingerprints?"

"Objection, Your Honor. There's no foundation for this."

"Your Honor," Skipper says, "Mr. Daley asked Sergeant Jacobsen to describe the locations of the defendant's fingerprints. I'm just amplifying her answer."

"Overruled."

Shit.

She picks up the revolver in her right hand. She grips it in her palm with her right thumb, middle finger, ring finger and pinky. Her right index finger rests on the cylinder.

"Sergeant," Skipper says, "without moving your thumb or other fingers, would you please move your index finger down to the trigger?"

She holds up the gun so that the jury can see it. She easily moves her index finger from the cylinder to the trigger.

"What would you conclude from this demonstration?" Skipper asks.

"Objection. Speculative."

"Overruled."

Jacobsen nods knowingly at the jury. "I would conclude that the defendant could have created the fingerprints I've described while pulling the trigger of this weapon."

"No further questions."

I'm back in her face. "It's still your testimony that you could not find identifiable fingerprints of Mr. Friedman on the trigger, right?"

"Yes. The fingerprints on the trigger were smudged and unidentifiable."

"So, you can't prove he pulled the trigger."

"Objection. Asked and answered."

"Sustained."

"No further questions."

"The people call Richard Cinelli." The bartender walks forcefully through the courtroom and is sworn in. He takes his seat on the witness stand. He pulls the microphone toward him. He's used to talking to people. Before he's said a word, he's already connected with the jury. Skipper walks him through the preliminaries. He was at work on the night of the thirtieth. He confirms that Joel and Diana came in about nine-forty-five. It was crowded. They ordered drinks and dinner.

"Around ten o'clock, Mr. Friedman and Ms. Kennedy had a disagreement," Cinelli says.

"Would it be more accurate to call it an argument?" Skipper asks.

Cinelli shrugs. "I'd call it a disagreement."

"But it could have been described as an argument."

"Perhaps it might have been an argument," he says without raising his voice. "She threw a glass of water in his face and she left."

"Was she upset?"

He raises his eyebrows. "Obviously."

"Did you hear anything they said?"

"Not much. I'm a bartender. I get paid to be discreet."

"But you did hear something, right?"

"Yes. Mr. Friedman told Ms. Kennedy that he'd get her for something. Those were his exact words. 'I'll get you for this.'"

"So he threatened her, right?"

"Objection, Your Honor. Speculative."

"Sustained."

"No further questions, Your Honor."

I walk toward Cinelli. "Do you know what they were arguing about?"

"No."

"And you know that they were attorneys, right?"

"Yes."

"And you knew they were working on a big deal together?"

"Objection. Foundation."

"Overruled."

"That's what I understand."

"Is it possible Mr. Friedman and Ms. Kennedy may have been arguing about work?"

Skipper stands. "Objection. Speculative."

"Overruled. The witness will answer." Give her credit. She's treating us equally.

"Yes, Mr. Daley. That's entirely possible."

"No further questions."

"My name is Homer Kim. I'm a custodian at the Bank of America Building." Homer Kim sits nervously in the witness chair late in the afternoon. He's uncomfortable in a new, ill-fitting suit.

"Mr. Kim," Skipper says, "you were at work at the Bank of America Building on the night of December thirtieth of last year, right?"

"Yes." His pronunciation is pretty good, but his tone is tentative.

Skipper gets Kim to explain that he walked by the office of Robert Holmes at approximately twelve-thirty in the morning. "Was there someone in the office with Mr. Holmes?" Skipper asks.

"Yes. Mr. Friedman." He points at Joel. It's a wooden gesture that's been rehearsed. "Mr. Holmes and Mr. Friedman were having an argument."

"Was it a loud argument?"

"Yes. Very loud. Mr. Friedman was very angry at Mr. Holmes. Very angry." His eyes dart.

"Did you hear Mr. Friedman say anything to Mr. Holmes?"

"Objection. Hearsay."

Skipper explains he isn't trying to prove the truth of what was said.

"Overruled."

Kim gulps water from a paper cup. "Mr. Friedman said to Mr. Holmes, 'I'll get you for this.'" He gestures with his right index finger for emphasis.

Skipper looks solemn. "Did it sound like Mr. Friedman was threatening Mr. Holmes?"

"Objection. Calls for Mr. Kim to make a determination of Mr. Friedman's state of mind."

"Sustained."

"No further questions."

I'm in his face in an instant. "Mr. Kim, how long have you observed Mr. Friedman?"

He looks perplexed. "A couple years."

"And have you ever heard him raise his voice?"

He looks at Skipper, who shakes his head. "No," he answers.

"Mr. Kim, do you know what they were arguing about?"

He hesitates slightly. "No." He sounds tentative again.

"Is it possible they may have been arguing about work?"

"Objection. Speculative."

"Overruled."

"I don't know," Kim says. He glances at Skipper for help. Skipper closes his eyes.

"It's possible, right?"

Out of the corner of my eye, I see Skipper nod.

"Yes, it's possible."

"Mr. Kim, you've had some problems over the years with your finances, haven't you?"

Skipper's up immediately. "Objection. Mr. Kim's financial situation is irrelevant."

"Your Honor," I say, "Mr. Kim's financial situation is very relevant to this discussion."

Judge Chen looks troubled. "I'll give you a little leeway, Mr. Daley."

"Mr. Kim," I continue, "isn't it true you've had some significant debts over the last few years?"

He looks desperately at Skipper, then says, "Yes." He's starting to turn red.

"And isn't it true that you filed for personal bankruptcy last year?"

"Yes."

"And isn't it true that you've lost some substantial amounts of money gambling?"

His shoulders slump. He hesitates. "I don't recall."

"You're under oath, Mr. Kim. I'd be happy to introduce the bankruptcy court filings into evidence." I turn to the judge. "Your Honor, would you please instruct the witness to answer."

"Mr. Kim," she says, "I'm going to have to ask you to answer Mr. Daley's question."

He shrugs. "Yes. I have lost some money gambling."

"Mr. Kim, isn't it a fact that you received a check in the amount of twenty thousand dollars shortly before you agreed to testify in this case?"

He shakes his head forcefully. "No."

I walk back to the defense table. Rosie hands me a note. "Isn't it true, Mr. Kim, that twenty thousand dollars was deposited into your account at Bank of America on February twentieth of this year?"

"No."

"Mr. Kim," I say, "you're under oath. We can subpoena your bank records."

He looks at Skipper. "Yes. I received a bonus."

"And would you mind telling us who promised you the bonus?"

He looks around the room wildly. "Mr. Arthur Patton."

"Mr. Patton? The managing partner of the Simpson and Gates firm?"

"Yes."

"And why did Mr. Patton promise you twenty thousand dollars?"

"He wanted to be sure I was available to testify at this trial. He said he wanted to bring Mr. Holmes's killer to justice." Suddenly, his hesitant English is more fluent.

"Mr. Kim, let me ask you again. There was no argument between Mr. Holmes and Mr. Friedman, was there? You were paid to say there was, but there really wasn't."

"No. I mean, yes. There really was an argument. Mr. Friedman was very very angry."

"No further questions, Your Honor."

36

MY FORMER PARTNERS

"It is unfortunate we must testify in the murder trial of one of
our colleagues."

—ARTHUR PATTON. NEWSCENTER 4. WEDNESDAY, MARCH 25.

At six-thirty the following morning, I'm watching the early
news on Channel 4. Every day at this time, Morgan Henderson, a self-absorbed former federal prosecutor who now
works for a big downtown firm, reports on the trial and gives
a preview of today's attractions. "Today should be very interesting," he drones. "District Attorney Gates is going to call
several of his former partners to testify against Mr.
Friedman. Things should liven up quite a bit."

I'm surprised he isn't giving odds.

"My name is Charles Stern. I have been a partner at
Simpson and Gates for twenty-seven years." Chuckles looks
stiff as he takes the stand at ten-fifteen.

Skipper's primed. He gets to put on *his* guys now. No
more idiot cops who can't get a legitimate confession. No

more arrogant medical examiners and uppity lesbian evidence technicians who won't give him exactly the answers he wants to hear. The Skipper Network is on the air.

He slowly walks Chuckles through his resume. Chuckles gives clipped answers directly to Skipper. He never turns his eyes even slightly toward the jury. He confirms he was at the office the night of the incident. He says he was preparing for a partners' meeting the next morning. He doesn't go into detail on the ceremonial reading of the Estimate.

"Mr. Stern," Skipper says, "did you attend a meeting with the firm's associates that evening?"

"Yes." The crow's-feet around his narrow eyes become more pronounced. "We had convened a meeting to discuss certain issues involving associate compensation and the partnership track."

To me, the "royal we" doesn't fit Chuckles very well. The jury may have other ideas, however.

"Was the defendant there?"

He glances at Joel. "Yes."

"And could you tell us what happened?"

"We announced that we were extending the track to partnership by one year. The vote on Mr. Friedman was going to be postponed. Mr. Friedman became very angry. He was upset that my partner, Mr. Holmes, had not told him about our decision. He expressed his displeasure and stormed out."

"Did you see the defendant later that night?"

"Yes. He came to my office. He said he was going to read Mr. Holmes the riot act."

"Did his tone sound threatening?"

"Objection. State of mind."

"Sustained."

"Did the defendant appear very upset to you?"

"Objection. State of mind."

"Overruled."

Chuckles fingers his reading glasses. "Yes. He appeared very upset to me."

"Upset enough to kill two people?"

"Objection, Your Honor," I shout.

"Sustained," she says loudly. She glares at Skipper. "The jury will disregard the last question."

Skipper looks contrite and turns back to Chuckles. "Mr. Stern, you and the defendant found the bodies of Mr. Holmes and Ms. Kennedy the following morning, did you not?"

"Yes." Stern describes how he and Joel found the bodies. He says that he called 911 and went back to the partners' meeting.

Skipper picks up the revolver from the evidence cart. "Mr. Stern, do you recognize this gun?"

"Yes. It belonged to Bob. We found it on the floor."

Skipper bobs his head melodramatically. "Did you touch this revolver at any time that morning?"

"No."

"Did you see the defendant touch this revolver at any time?"

"No."

Joel leans over and whispers, "He's lying."

"Did you see the defendant unload the gun?" Skipper asks.

"No."

"Mr. Stern, is it possible that the defendant unloaded the gun while you weren't watching?"

"It's highly unlikely. We went to the partners' meeting together. We returned to Bob's office together. We were both there until the first officer arrived. If he unloaded the gun, I didn't see it."

"No further questions, Your Honor."

I'm up right away. "Mr. Stern," I say, "you said you were with Mr. Friedman the entire time before the police arrived."

"Yes."

"Mr. Stern, Officer Chinn testified that you met him in the lobby."

He shifts in his chair. "That's true," he says slowly.

"And Mr. Friedman wasn't with you when you met Office Chinn, was he?"

He takes a drink of water and clears his throat. "No."

"So you weren't with Mr. Friedman the entire time before the police arrived, were you?"

He looks at the clock. "I guess not."

"And it's possible Mr. Friedman may have unloaded the weapon while you were meeting with Officer Chinn, isn't it?"

"Objection. Speculative."

"Overruled."

Chuckles shakes his head. "I was with Officer Chinn in the lobby for only a few moments. I don't see how Mr. Friedman could have unloaded the gun so quickly."

I look at the revolver. "Mr. Stern, you were in the military service, weren't you?"

"Objection. Relevance."

"Your Honor, Mr. Stern has expressed an opinion as to how fast this particular weapon could have been unloaded. His background and experience with weapons is relevant."

"Overruled."

Chuckles pinches the bridge of his nose. "I was in the Marines."

"And you're familiar with firearms, aren't you? In fact, you've shot this weapon, haven't you?"

He adjusts the microphone. "Yes. Mr. Holmes and I went to the range from time to time."

"And you've unloaded this weapon at the range, haven't you?"

He scratches the back of his head. "Yes."

"How long did it take you to unload it?" I emphasize the word "you" as I say it.

"A few seconds."

"And it took you more than a few seconds to meet with Officer Chinn, didn't it?"

"Yes," he says grudgingly.

"Mr. Stern, you knew Mr. Holmes kept this revolver at his desk, didn't you?"

"Yes," he replies. "For self-protection, I might add."

Of course. "And he kept it loaded, didn't he?"

Heavy sigh. "Yes, he did."

"No further questions."

During the recess, I ask Joel when he unloaded the gun.

"Right after we walked in," he replies. "He saw me do it. He's lying."

"Did anybody else see you?"

"No. We were the only people there."

"Why would he lie?"

"I have no idea. Maybe he has something to hide."

"The people call Arthur Patton," Skipper announces forcefully later that morning.

Patton lugs his chins through the courtroom. He smiles at the jury as he's sworn in. He says he's the managing partner at S&G. He confirms he was there on the fatal night.

"Did you have occasion to see the defendant late that evening?" Skipper asks.

"Yes." The avuncular Art has joined us today. His tone is sincere, meant to charm. "I saw him in the hall around twelve-thirty in the morning. He was walking into Bob's office."

"Could you describe his demeanor?"

"He was very upset." He describes his brief conversation with Joel. He looks toward the jury and scowls. "That's when he started shouting at Bob."

"Do you know what he was shouting about?"

"I believe he was expressing his unhappiness about the fact that Bob hadn't told him that the vote for his election to the partnership had been deferred." He pauses. "And I believe they were arguing about Ms. Kennedy. I heard her name mentioned several times."

"Mr. Patton, were you at the firm retreat at the Silverado Country Club last October?"

"Yes."

"And did you have an opportunity to see Mr. Friedman at about three o'clock in the morning on Saturday, October twenty-fifth?"

"Yes. He was in his condominium."

"Why did you have occasion to see him in the middle of the night?"

"There was a loud noise coming from his room. I wanted to make sure he was all right."

Skipper hides a smirk. "Was he alone?"

"No. There was somebody else in his room."

"And who was in his room at three o'clock in the morning?"

"Diana Kennedy."

"No further questions."

"Mr. Patton," I begin a few minutes later, "what time did you go home on the morning of December thirty-first?"

"Objection. Relevance."

"Overruled."

"Around one-thirty in the morning," he replies.

"And you heard a discussion between Mr. Holmes and Mr. Friedman?"

"It was an argument. It lasted a few minutes. I heard most of it."

"Was the door to Mr. Holmes's office open or closed?"

He looks up toward the American flag. "Closed."

"You stood outside the closed door and eavesdropped on their conversation?"

He takes a drink of water and chews on the ice. "I wanted to help my partner. Mr. Friedman was quite upset."

Sure. "Of course, for all you know, they could have been arguing about work."

"I don't think so," he says with disdain.

"But you aren't sure."

He looks right at me. "I'm sure," he says with authority.

"Let's talk about the incident at Silverado."

His eyes brighten. Skipper looks eager.

"Mr. Patton," I say, "there was a party earlier that evening in your room, wasn't there?"

Skipper's no longer happy. "Yes," Art says curtly.

"And Ms. Kennedy was at that party, wasn't she?"

"Yes." His eyes dart. He looks over my left shoulder.

"Isn't it true, Mr. Patton, that you accosted Ms. Kennedy at the party?"

He tries to look indignant. "Absolutely not."

"Isn't it true that you followed her to her room and attacked her?"

He sits up taller in his chair. "I did not."

He sounds just like my daughter. "Isn't it true she went to Mr. Friedman for protection?"

He squints through his tiny spectacles. He points a menacing finger at me. "That's a lie."

"We'll see about that, Mr. Patton. No further questions."

A few minutes later, Skipper calls another old friend. Brent Hutchinson slithers to the front of the courtroom, a smarmy grin plastered on his pretty face. His golden hair glows. Whenever I see him, I want to punch his lights out.

"Mr. Hutchinson," Skipper says, "we've known each other for some time, haven't we?"

"We were partners at Simpson and Gates. I still work there." He looks like a cocker spaniel who wants to be petted.

"Mr. Hutchinson, you have a nickname around the firm, don't you?"

"Most people call me Hutch."

He sounds like Forrest Gump. Makes me sick.

"Would you mind if I call you Hutch today?"

"Sure." His grin widens. All this male bonding turns my stomach.

"Now, Hutch, you attended the firm retreat at Silverado in October of last year, didn't you?"

His eyes light up. "Yes. We have our retreat there every year. It's a great time."

"I know. Could you tell us a little bit about what happens at these retreats?"

"Objection. Relevance." This love-fest has to stop. Hutch is actually very likable on the stand—if you're into handsome airheads.

"Overruled."

"We have attorney meetings and social events. We play some golf and tennis."

"Did you attend a social gathering in the cocktail lounge at the main house at Silverado at approximately nine o'clock in the evening of Friday, October twenty-fourth?"

"Yes."

"And were Diana Kennedy and the defendant also there?"

"Yes."

"Would you mind describing what happened as Ms. Kennedy was leaving the party?"

He turns toward the jury and shows them his most sincere expression. "Joel was sitting at a table near the door. Diana was at the bar. She walked toward the door. As she passed Joel, she stopped, leaned over and kissed him." He smiles. Good Hutch.

I look at Naomi. She stares at the floor. Joel doesn't move.

"Did she kiss the defendant on the mouth?"

"Yes."

"Did she kiss him hard?"

"Objection. The witness has no personal knowledge of the intensity of the kiss."

"Overruled."

"It looked pretty hard to me," Hutch says.

A few snickers from the gallery. Judge Chen pounds her gavel.

"Hutch," Skipper says, "did the kiss appear to you to be a romantic one?"

"Objection, Your Honor. Speculative."

"Sustained."

Skipper gives the jury a conspiratorial wink. "Did it appear to you that the defendant was enjoying himself when she kissed him?"

"Objection. State of mind."

"Your Honor," Skipper says, "I'm not asking Mr. Hutchinson to make a determination as to whether he thought Mr. Friedman actually enjoyed the kiss. I'm simply asking him to describe it."

"Nice try, Mr. Gates," she snaps. "The objection is sustained. Move on."

"Hutch, did you also see the defendant and Ms. Kennedy in a hot tub the next day?"

"Yes."

"And would you mind telling us what they were doing?"

"They were kissing."

Skipper turns toward the jury, his eyes wide. "They were kissing again? Could you describe how Ms. Kennedy was dressed?"

"She was wearing a bikini, but the top was unfastened."

Murmurs in the back of the courtroom. Judge Chen slams her gavel.

"Hutch," Skipper says, "was it a hard kiss?"

"Yes."

"And did it appear to you that the defendant was, for lack of a better term, kissing her back?"

"Absolutely."

"And how long did this go on?"

"About a minute. Then I thought it would be best if I moved on."

How sensitive.

"I see." He looks at the jury, then back at Hutch. "Did you see Ms. Kennedy and the defendant together at any other time during the retreat?"

"Later that evening, I saw them sitting in the same hot tub. I'm pretty sure they were both naked. However, it was dark and I was on my way back to my room. This time, I didn't stop."

"No further questions."

"Mr. Hutchinson," I begin, "we've known each other for a long time, too, haven't we?"

"Yes." His teeth gleam when he smiles. "We used to be partners, too."

"And you have another nickname around the firm, don't you?"

The smile disappears. "I'm not sure what you're talking about, Mr. Daley."

"Well, most people call you Hutch. But some people call you something else, don't they?"

He looks around the courtroom. "Yes."

"And what's your other nickname, Mr. Hutchinson?"

"The Party Guy," he says quietly.

I make my voice go up a half octave. "The Party Guy?" I grin. "Could you please tell us why they call you the Party Guy?"

He smiles sheepishly. "I guess it's because I like to party, Mr. Daley."

"Were you partying the night you saw Ms. Kennedy kiss Mr. Friedman at the bar?"

"I guess you could say that."

"And did you have a glass of wine or two that night?"

"Probably."

"How many glasses of wine?"

"Several."

"More than two?"

"Probably."

"More than three?"

"Maybe."

"Enough so that you wouldn't have gotten behind the wheel of a car that night?"

"Yeah."

"So, when you saw Ms. Kennedy kiss Mr. Friedman, you may have been intoxicated."

"I don't think so."

"You had at least four glasses of wine. Your memory of that night may be a little cloudy."

"Maybe."

"Now, let's talk about the incident on Saturday afternoon where you saw Ms. Kennedy and Mr. Friedman in the hot tub. Could you tell us where the hot tub was located?"

"Near one of the pools at Silverado."

"And you just happened to be walking by the pool?"

"Yes."

"And you walked right by the hot tub and you saw Ms. Kennedy kissing Mr. Friedman?"

"Not exactly. I was walking down a path that leads to the golf course."

"How far was the path from the pool?"

"I'm not sure."

"Ballpark figure, Mr. Hutchinson. Fifty feet? A hundred feet? The length of a football field?"

He darts a glance at Skipper. "Maybe the length of a football field."

"Really? From a hundred yards, you were able to see Mr. Friedman and Ms. Kennedy kissing?"

"Yes."

"And you're sure the top of Ms. Kennedy's bikini had been unfastened?"

"Yes. I'm sure."

"You must have really good eyes, Mr. Hutchinson."

"Objection. Move to strike."

"The jury will ignore Mr. Daley's remark."

I leave it at that. "I don't suppose you were standing in the same place when you saw them in the hot tub later that night."

"As a matter of fact, I was standing in almost the same place."

"I see. So, late at night, from a hundred yards away, you were able to identify Mr. Friedman and Ms. Kennedy in the hot tub. You were also able to determine that they were kissing. And you were able to determine that they were naked. Is that about it?"

"Yes."

"Did they get out of the hot tub?"

"No."

"Were the jets on?"

"I think so."

"Weren't there bubbles in the hot tub?"

He's starting to look a little older now. I can see the lines on his forehead. "Probably."

I look at the jury. "If it was night and they didn't get out and the jets were on and there were bubbles in the hot tub, how in the world were you able to determine that they were both naked?"

He takes a deep breath. "I saw them. I could tell."

It's his story, and he's sticking to it. "Mr. Hutchinson," I say, "you realize that what you've just told us is utterly preposterous, don't you?"

"Objection."

"Sustained."

I look directly at Hutch. "No further questions. Next he'll say he saw them in a hot tub while he was flying over Silverado in a hot-air balloon." I get a few chuckles.

Judge Chen pounds her gavel. "Enough. The jury will disregard Mr. Daley's last remark."

At eight o'clock the same night, I'm at my mom's house meeting with Pete. Mom's having one of her not-so-good nights. We sit at the dining-room table. She clears Pete's plate and says to me, "You didn't finish all your carrots, Tommy. No dessert until you do."

"I will, Mama. Right away."

She walks into the kitchen. Pete shrugs. "She'll be back in a few minutes. Sometimes she spends a little while in the fifties. Then she comes back."

"It's getting worse, isn't it?"

"Yeah."

"Look, Pete, if we need to get you some help . . ."

"Not yet." He coughs. "Not yet." He takes a drink of water. "How did things go at court today?"

"Not great."

He cuts himself a piece of French bread. "So I gather."

I finish my carrots. "Have you found anything else on Russo?"

"The trail goes cold at the international terminal at SFO. One person said she thought he might have gone to Hong Kong, but nobody on the flight crew recognized his picture. If he's flying on a fake passport, it's going to be tough to find him."

"Shit."

"We may not be the only people looking for him. He had some coinvestors from Saudi on a few deals. They aren't real happy that he disappeared. They're looking for him, too. We haven't found anything else, though."

"What about the banker in the Bahamas?"

"Still in Kuwait. Longer than expected—he won't be back for another couple of weeks. Wendy and I are going to pay him a visit as soon as he is."

"Good." I pause. "Has Wendy been helpful?"

"Yeah. She's great." He looks at the picture of my dead brother Tommy in his Cal football uniform, frozen in time at the age of twenty. Pete and Tommy look almost identical, except Tommy was taller and Pete has a mustache. "Mike, is she, well, seeing anybody?"

Unlike Rosie, who is all too familiar with my crush on Wendy, Pete doesn't have a clue. Let's just say it never came up in conversation. I'd like to tell him he's out of luck and that I have dibs. Instead, I say, "I don't think so."

"Do you think she'd have any interest?"

"I'm not sure. She's been divorced a couple of times."

His eyes dart.

"Then again," I say, "you'll never know if you don't ask." I decide to change the subject. "Did you get anything from Nick Hanson on the mystery woman at the Fairmont?"

"He hasn't been able to ID her. The people at the Fairmont couldn't, either."

We keep coming up empty. "Did Nick think it was Diana?"

"He was pretty sure it wasn't. The woman had longer hair. Nick's real good on details like that. He thought it might have been a hooker."

"Does he have any ideas?"

"Just one. But he said it was just a wag."

"A wag?"

"Yeah. W-A-G. Wild-ass guess. Guess who was making an appearance at the Fairmont that night?"

"The mayor?"

"Get serious. Somebody more famous."

"Come on, Pete, I'm tired."

"Dr. Kathy Chandler."

I sit back in my chair. "You don't really think? No. It couldn't."

He smiles. "We shouldn't jump to any conclusions. I did some checking on Dr. Kathy. She's very single. She's had a little trouble with long-term relationships. She fits the description."

"But is there any real evidence she was with Bob that night?"

"Nope. Like I said. It's just Nick's wild-ass guess."

At the moment, Nick the Dick's wild-ass guess is the only lead we have.

37

"AND WAS YOUR MARRIAGE A HAPPY ONE?"

"In what promises to be an emotional moment, the widow of Robert Holmes will take the stand today."

—NEWSCENTER 4 LEGAL ANALYST MORGAN HENDERSON.
THURSDAY, MARCH 26.

The next morning is a Thursday. Skipper calls Beth Holmes to the stand. In lieu of her customary gray business suit, she's wearing a light blue dress with a tiny gold chain and a small brooch. Today, she'll be playing the role of grieving widow instead of legal barracuda. "My name is Elizabeth Barnes Holmes," she says after she's sworn in. "Robert Holmes was my husband."

Skipper has set up the pictures of Bob and Diana in front of the jury. It's contrived, but he's going to play to their heartstrings today.

"How long were you and Bob married?" Using his first name is a nice touch.

"Five and a half years." Skipper has her describe how she and Bob met, the children, the vacations to the Italian Riviera and the mansion in Presidio Terrace. The idyllic power marriage between power partners at power law firms. She doesn't mention her divorce from Art Patton.

Skipper turns serious. "And was your marriage a happy one, Mrs. Holmes?"

She gets a faraway look in her eyes. "Yes. At least until recently."

Skipper nods thoughtfully. "And then what happened, Mrs. Holmes?"

"He became distant. I began to suspect he was seeing another woman."

"Was he?" he asks gently.

"Yes. He was having an affair with Diana Kennedy."

Murmurs in the back of the courtroom.

Skipper moves closer to her. "How did you find out about the affair, Mrs. Holmes?"

"I hired a private investigator. He found them in bed together in early December." She holds her head high. "I confronted Bob. I told him he had to break off the affair, or I'd leave him."

"What happened?"

"He broke up with her." She doesn't hide her disdain. "A few weeks later, my private eye found them together again. I decided to end our marriage. I was there when he was served on December thirtieth."

"Mrs. Holmes, was your husband upset when he was served with the divorce papers?"

"Objection. State of mind."

"Overruled."

"He took it pretty well. He'd been divorced several times."

"Do you think he was so upset that he may have been driven to suicide?"

"Objection. Speculative."

"Overruled."

"No. He took it in stride. I think he was relieved when I filed the papers."

I glance at Diana's mother in the gallery. She closes her eyes.

Skipper cringes only slightly. "No further questions."

"Mrs. Holmes," I say, "what time was your husband served with divorce papers?"

"About five-thirty in the evening."

"And who was present when he was served?"

"A bunch of people. They were all in the main conference room at Simpson and Gates."

"What was your husband doing when he was served?"

She scowls. "I believe he was on the telephone."

"Wasn't he sitting in a room with his client and a group of attorneys? And weren't they in negotiations on a significant business transaction?"

"Yes."

"Isn't it a fact that he barely looked up when you and your process server walked in because he was in heated negotiations on a multimillion-dollar deal?"

"I was barely able to get his attention."

"So, it's not really surprising that he didn't react when he saw you, is it?"

"He knew what was going on."

I take a step back. "Did he look at the papers your process server handed him?"

"Yes."

"For how long?"

"Briefly."

"You mean he may have glanced at them."

"He knew what the papers were."

"The fact is, Mrs. Holmes, your husband had very little

reaction to the papers because he was concentrating on his deal and he expected you to file the papers. Isn't that true?"

Skipper leaps up. "Objection. Argumentative."

"Sustained. Move along, Mr. Daley."

"Mrs. Holmes, did your husband carry any life insurance?"

"Objection. Relevance."

"Overruled."

She says Bob carried a five-million-dollar policy naming herself as beneficiary, and a million-dollar policy for each of the kids.

"Have you received the proceeds from the policies yet?"

"No. The insurance company is working on the claim. They're very slow."

I'll bet. I'm sure the insurance company is hoping it's a suicide. Then they won't have to pay anything. "Did it occur to you that your husband might change the beneficiaries if you were divorced?"

"Objection. Speculative."

"Overruled."

"Of course, Mr. Daley. I fully expected it." She gives me her "big-firm evil litigator" look. "And if you're suggesting I had some incentive to see my husband dead, you're out of your mind."

Out of the corner of my eye, I see the phone company supervisor nod. I've gone a little too far. I have to remember that she's the grieving widow. "Mrs. Holmes," I say, "do you know the names of the beneficiaries of your husband's will?"

"I get a third, the children get a third and the balance goes to a charity in the Bahamas."

"Did it occur to you that he may have decided to change his will after you got divorced?"

"Of course, Mr. Daley." Then she adds, gratuitously, "I don't need the money, you know."

"One last item. You said your investigator found your husband and Ms. Kennedy together in late December."

"That's correct."

"Where did that incident occur?"

"At a room in the tower of the Fairmont Hotel."

"I see. And how did your investigator find out about it?"

"He was viewing the room from a building across the street."

"Did your investigator positively identify Diana Kennedy in the room with your husband?"

"He told me he thought it was Diana. He said the woman looked like Diana."

"But he wasn't sure."

"He was sure it wasn't me."

"I understand. But isn't it true, Mrs. Holmes, that he wasn't able to positively identify the woman in the room with Mr. Holmes that night?"

"That may be true."

"And it's possible that it wasn't Ms. Kennedy."

"Yeah. It's possible. What difference does it make, Mr. Daley?"

Thanks, Beth. "I'm sorry to make you relive these difficult times, Mrs. Holmes," I say. She's given me what I need. "No further questions."

38

"HOW LONG HAVE YOU BEEN A PRACTICING THERAPIST?"

"KTLK's very own Dr. Kathy Chandler will be testifying to-day at the murder trial of Joel Mark Friedman. Dr. Kathy Chandler will be able to tell you all about it in her regular time slot at seven tonight."

—KTLK TALK RADIO. THURSDAY, MARCH 26. 11:45 A.M.

We're standing just outside the courtroom at one o'clock when Dr. Kathy Chandler and her entourage arrive. She has just finished an impromptu press conference in the corridor. She is surrounded by cameras and microphones as she and her handlers inch their way down the hall. She towers over most of the reporters. Her long blond hair flows. She stops and faces the assembled media horde. She brushes her hand against her hair and flashes the smile that graces Muni buses all over town.

"Dr. Chandler, what are you going to talk about today?"

"Dr. Chandler, do you think Robert Holmes killed him-self?"

"Dr. Chandler, was Mr. Holmes having an affair with Diana Kennedy?"

"Dr. Chandler? Dr. Chandler? Dr. Chandler?"

"I'm sorry, fellows," she purrs. "I don't want to be late for court. I don't want the judge to get mad at me." Big smile. "I'll talk to you again after I'm done." She walks into the courtroom.

Skipper walks Dr. Kathy Chandler through her credentials, such as they are. I interrupt frequently. After the ordeal is concluded, Skipper says, "How long did you know Robert Holmes?"

She smiles. "I began treating him in September. I was his therapist for about three months."

"And what were you treating him for, Doctor?"

"You know," she coos, "I usually don't talk about my patients' problems." She bats her eyes.

Skipper smiles like Robert Young in *Father Knows Best*. "I know. But your testimony is very important. If you're uncomfortable answering a question, let me know, and we'll talk it over with Judge Chen."

Who will be more than happy to lock you up for contempt. Then you'll have the honor of being the first person to initiate a radio broadcast from the new jail at the Hall. Judge Chen looks at Dr. Kathy. "Doctor," she says sternly, "let me simplify this for you. If there's a question I think you shouldn't have to answer, I'll tell you so. For now, unless I instruct you otherwise, I expect you to answer Mr. Gates's questions. Are we clear on that?"

The kitten disappears. "Yes, Your Honor," she replies in a businesslike tone.

"Good." Judge Chen nods to Skipper. "Please continue, Mr. Gates."

"Dr. Chandler, why did Mr. Holmes first come to see you?"

"He was having relationship problems."

"What kind of relationship problems?"

I'd give everything I own to hear her say, "He was having trouble keeping his zipper zipped."

"With his wife. Mr. and Mrs. Holmes were very angry."

"Why were they angry with each other?"

"They were angry because Mr. Holmes was seeing another woman."

"Oh dear," Skipper says quietly. "Do you know who the woman was?"

She exhales loudly. "Diana Kennedy."

"Doctor, was Mr. Holmes still seeing Ms. Kennedy at the time they were murdered?"

"Objection. Move to strike the use of the term 'murdered.'"

"Sustained." The judge glares at Skipper. "The jury will disregard the term 'murdered.' Try it again, Mr. Gates."

"Do you know if Mr. Holmes was seeing Ms. Kennedy on December thirtieth of last year?"

"I don't think so. He was pretty sure Mrs. Holmes was going to serve him with divorce papers. He broke up with Ms. Kennedy. He said he was seeing somebody new toward the end of last year. He was very uncomfortable talking about it."

I lean over to Joel and whisper, "Know anything about this?"

He shakes his head.

Skipper's thinking the same thing when he asks, "Did he mention the name of the woman?"

"No. It may have been Ms. Kennedy. It may have been somebody else. And, to be honest, he may have been making the whole thing up. Sometimes, you couldn't tell with Mr. Holmes."

Skipper nods understandingly. "Doctor," he says, "based upon your observations of Mr. Holmes in the final weeks of his life, did he appear distraught to you?"

"Objection. State of mind."

"She was his therapist," Skipper says. "I'm asking for her professional observations."

Judge Chen scowls. "I'll allow the witness to answer."

"No," she replies. "He didn't appear distraught. In fact, he appeared relaxed the last few times I saw him. I think he was relieved that he'd resolved his issues with Mrs. Holmes."

Oh, bullshit.

Skipper moves closer to Dr. Kathy. "Did he appear emotionally disturbed?"

"Good heavens, no."

"Depressed?"

"No."

"Unhappy?"

"No."

Enough. "Objection. We can spend all afternoon trying to identify every range of emotion not exhibited by Mr. Holmes."

"Sustained. Let's move on, Mr. Gates."

He doesn't flinch. "One final question. Did he appear at any time to you to be suicidal?"

"Absolutely not," she purrs. She smiles demurely at the jury.

"No further questions."

"Dr. Chandler," I begin, "I'd like to ask you a few more questions about your credentials. You got your degree from Southwestern Texas City College, right?"

"Yes."

"Is that an accredited school?"

"It depends on what you mean by the term 'accredited.' "

"I mean it in the conventional sense. You know—schools like Stanford, Cal, UCLA—they're accredited. Was Southwestern Texas City College accredited?"

"Not exactly."

"And your doctorate in family counseling is from the same institution, right?"

"That's correct."

"Did you actually attend classes there?"

She pauses. "Yes."

"But most of the courses were offered by correspondence, weren't they?"

"Yes," she acknowledges.

She probably could have gotten any title she wanted if she paid them enough money. "And you got a master's from the Great Pacific School of Broadcasting?"

"Yes."

"Not exactly Harvard and Yale, are they, Doctor?"

"Objection. Argumentative."

"Sustained."

I shift direction. "Dr. Chandler, how long have you been a practicing therapist?"

"Seventeen years."

"I see. And how many years have you been doing your radio show?"

"Fourteen years."

"And you've got one of the top-rated programs in your time slot, don't you?"

She smiles proudly. "Yes, I do. It takes a lot of people to make the program a success."

I interrupt her. "I'm sure that's true. I'll bet your radio show takes up a lot of your time, doesn't it?"

"Yes, it does. It's a very demanding job."

"How many hours are you on the air every day?"

"Three. From seven o'clock until ten."

"You must have a very busy schedule."

Skipper stands. "Your Honor, I fail to see the relevance of all this."

"Mr. Daley," says Judge Chen, "get to the point."

"I will, Your Honor." I turn back to the good doctor. "Do you handle a full caseload?"

"Yes. I wouldn't be comfortable giving advice over the radio if I didn't maintain a private practice."

"I see. And how many patients do you see in a typical day?"

"Two or three."

"That's all?"

"Yes."

"That's what you consider a full practice? That's ten or fifteen patients a week. If each of them gets an hour of your time, that's only one or two days' work."

"As I said, Mr. Daley, my radio show takes a lot of time."

"And you also write self-help books, don't you, Doctor?"

"Yes."

"Does that take much time?"

She smiles. "Well, my publisher gives me a lot of help with those."

"Somebody helps you write your self-help books?"

"Yes."

She fails to see the irony. "Is it fair to say that you spend a lot less time seeing patients than most of your colleagues?"

She sits up. "Most of them don't have a radio show."

I look at Rosie. She shakes her head almost imperceptibly. I'm having a great time tweaking Dr. Kathy Chandler. Unfortunately, the jury doesn't seem to care. "Doctor," I say, "have you ever had a personal relationship with one of your patients?"

The facade disappears. Her eyes bore in on mine. "No," she says. "That would be unethical."

"Doctor," I say, "isn't it a fact that your license was suspended several years ago because you had a sexual relationship with one of your patients?"

The claws come out. She answers slowly. "It is true that my license was suspended. It is not true, however, that I had a sexual relationship with one of my patients. A very sad and lonely man made some wild accusations. They were never proven."

"You arrived at a settlement with the patient, didn't you, Dr. Chandler?"

"That's confidential."

I turn to Judge Chen. "Your Honor, I must ask you to instruct the witness to answer."

Judge Chen nods. "Answer the question, Dr. Chandler."

She strokes her bangs. "We settled the matter out of court." She glares at me. "Any other questions, Mr. Daley?"

"Your Honor," I say, "would you please remind the witness that the attorneys are supposed to ask the questions?"

Judge Chen looks at Dr. Kathy. "Mr. Daley is correct, Dr. Chandler." She turns back to me. "So, Mr. Daley, any other questions for Dr. Chandler?"

"Yes." I look straight at Dr. Kathy. "Isn't it true that your ex-husband was one of your patients?"

Her tiny nose twitches. "Yes," she hisses. "He was one of my patients."

"So it wasn't exactly true when you said you've never had a personal relationship with a patient."

She's angry. "He was no longer a patient when we began our personal relationship."

Of course. I allow myself a brief smile. "Just one more question, Doctor." I look at the jury, then I turn back to her. "Were you having an affair with Robert Holmes, Dr. Chandler?"

Skipper screams his objection before he can pull himself to his feet. "Your Honor," he says, "this is utterly irrelevant and insulting to Dr. Chandler."

"Your Honor," I say, "we believe Dr. Chandler was having a sexual relationship with Mr. Holmes. It would clearly color her credibility. I would ask you to instruct her to answer."

Judge Chen studies her bench book. She bites her lower lip. "Dr. Chandler," she says, "I'm afraid I'm going to have to ask you to respond."

"The answer is no. I was not having an affair with Mr. Holmes."

I decide to go for broke. "Dr. Chandler, we have evidence you and Mr. Holmes were having a sexual relationship in a room at the Fairmont in December of last year. Do you deny it?"

"Objection. There's no foundation for any of this."

"Your Honor, we're prepared to bring forth the private investigator hired by Mrs. Holmes. It would save us an extraordinary amount of time if Dr. Chandler simply answers my question."

Judge Chen turns to Dr. Kathy. "I'm going to ask you to answer, Dr. Chandler."

Her eyes are on fire. "No, Mr. Daley," she says evenly. "I wasn't with Mr. Holmes."

"No further questions."

"What was that all about?" Joel's father is incredulous as we sit in the consultation room during the afternoon recess. "How does it help to attack Bob's widow? How does it help to attack his therapist? What were you thinking?"

"Rabbi," I say, "they put those two witnesses on the stand to demonstrate that Bob was a happy guy who didn't kill himself. They're undercutting our suicide argument. And they're doing a good job of it. That's why we have to go after them. We have to show that Beth Holmes is lying to protect her husband's reputation. And we have to show that Dr. Kathy Chandler is nothing more than a bubblegum-spewing radio jockey. That's what this is all about. And if you don't like the way I'm trying the case, you can get Joel another lawyer."

Mort interjects, "Everybody. Shut up. Right now. We don't have time for this. We have to keep our eye on the ball here. Maybe it wasn't the greatest cross in the history of the legal profession. But we have to keep at it. They put on witnesses for a purpose—to put together enough of a case to get a conviction. We're here to get in the way of that. We can't stop now because we're afraid we're going to hurt somebody's feelings."

Rosie holds up her hand. "Could you please be quiet for a moment," she says in a measured tone. "We aren't going to be able to deliver a knockout punch on every witness. We have to stay focused."

Joel stands up. "May I say something here? Seeing as how it's my ass on the line, I'd appreciate it if you'd keep your petty squabbles to yourselves. If you guys fuck up, I'm going to jail. So I don't want to hear anything else about who's doing a good job or a bad job on cross-exam. I don't want to hear you argue about strategy. I'm not interested in blaming anybody. We've just wasted prep time so you all could yell at each other. Now, I don't want to see this again. Let's get our heads screwed back on and get back in there and do our jobs."

Rabbi Friedman scowls. I look away. I hate it when the client is right.

39

"WE WERE WORKING ON A VERY BIG DEAL"

"Of course everybody wanted the Russo deal to close. It was good for the city."

—THE MAYOR OF SAN FRANCISCO. THURSDAY, MARCH 26.

Jack Frazier, the pride of Continental Capital Corporation, looks like he's ready for a board meeting when he takes the stand at three o'clock the same afternoon. He's wearing the standard investment-banker uniform. His shirt is so heavily starched, it could walk across the courtroom by itself.

Skipper is wearing a subdued gray pinstripe today, with huge gold cuff links. "Would you mind telling us why you were present at the Simpson and Gates office on the night of December thirtieth?"

Frazier gazes past Skipper's left shoulder. "We were working on a very big deal. My company was going to purchase the assets of a conglomerate called Russo International." He explains the deal for a few minutes. "The closing was scheduled for the following morning," he says.

"Was the deal going to close on schedule?"

"As far as I knew, yes. All the papers had been signed. Everything was ready."

Skipper clears his throat. "Why didn't it close?"

Frazier looks serious. "With the tragic deaths of Mr. Holmes and Ms. Kennedy, there was no way we could proceed."

"Did you see Mr. Holmes that night?"

"Yes."

"Did he appear to be in a good mood?"

"Yes. He was looking forward to the closing."

"Did you see any signs that he may have been distraught or stressed out?"

"Objection. State of mind."

"Sustained."

"I'll rephrase. Did Mr. Holmes appear to you to be distraught that evening?"

"No. Nothing out of the ordinary."

"No further questions, Your Honor."

I walk slowly toward Frazier. "There were problems with the deal, weren't there, Mr. Frazier?"

"There are always problems with big transactions." He glances toward the jury.

"Fair enough. But this deal had more than its share, didn't it?"

"Not really."

"Isn't it true there was substantial doubt about whether your company would approve this deal?"

"No. The deal was approved." Frazier looks at his lawyer, Martin Glass, who's in the gallery today.

"Isn't it true your board of directors had an emergency meeting that night to discuss whether they should pull the plug?"

"It's true that they met. It's not true that they wanted to pull the plug."

Right. "Isn't it true your board would have voted against the deal if you hadn't been able to negotiate a forty-million-dollar reduction in the purchase price at the last minute?"

"It's true that I was able to negotiate a reduction in the purchase price. I have no idea whether the board would have approved the deal without the reduction. I wasn't at the board meeting."

I have no idea why he's resisting. I'm just trying to show that Bob may have been stressed out. Frazier seems to be trying to justify the deal to his superiors at headquarters. "Isn't it true," I ask, "that the seller in the transaction, Mr. Vince Russo, was undecided about whether he would close the deal? And isn't it true that even though all the papers were signed, Mr. Russo told everyone he wouldn't make up his mind until morning?"

Skipper pops up. "Objection, Your Honor. Argumentative."

They're trying to avoid mention of Russo's name. "Your Honor," I say, "Mr. Russo was a key player in this transaction. Mr. Frazier has testified that the deal was proceeding according to plan. However, the evidence will suggest that Mr. Russo didn't want to close."

Judge Chen thinks for a moment, then says, "I'll allow it."

I glance at Bill McNulty. He's frowning. He realizes this is a significant ruling. It opens the door for me to blame everything on Russo.

I turn back to Frazier. "Isn't it true that Mr. Russo was waffling on whether he would proceed?"

Frazier looks toward Glass again. "I firmly believe he intended to close the deal."

I get right in front of him. "What time did Mr. Russo leave that night?"

"I don't know."

"Could you tell us what time Mr. Russo showed up the next morning for the closing?"

"He didn't show up." He pauses. "He seems to have disappeared."

"Did he ever call you?"

"No."

"Leave a message?"

"No."

"Try to get in touch with you?"

"Objection," says Skipper. "We get the idea."

"Sustained. Move along, Mr. Daley."

"What time did you leave the building that night, Mr. Frazier?"

"About one thirty-five."

"And was Mr. Russo still in the building when you left?"

"As far as I know."

"When was the last time you saw him?"

"Around one o'clock. He was with Mr. Holmes."

"What were they doing?"

"They were talking."

"About what?"

"Objection, Your Honor. Hearsay."

"Your Honor, I'm not trying to establish precisely what was said or the truth of what was said. I'm simply asking Mr. Frazier to report on the subject that was being discussed."

"Overruled."

"They were talking about the deal."

"Is it possible Mr. Russo told Mr. Holmes that Mr. Russo did not intend to close the deal?"

"Objection. Speculative."

"Overruled."

Frazier holds up his hands. "It's possible. I just don't know."

"And was that the last time you saw Mr. Russo?"

"Yes."

I take a deep breath. "Isn't it possible, Mr. Frazier, that Mr. Holmes may have become distraught and killed himself if Mr. Russo told him that he didn't want to close the deal?"

Judge Chen looks at Skipper, who should object. I've just asked a highly speculative question.

"It was just a business deal," Frazier says. "It may have been a big deal, but it wasn't worth committing suicide for."

Good point. "Isn't it possible that Mr. Russo's disappearance can be explained by the fact that he killed Mr. Holmes and Ms. Kennedy, and that he fled after he committed these terrible acts?"

"Objection," Skipper shrieks. "Highly speculative."

Look who woke up.

"Sustained."

I turn back to Frazier. "Isn't it true that you really didn't want the deal to close?"

He looks incredulous. "Of course not."

"Isn't it true you figured out that you couldn't make the profit margins on the deal that you had originally anticipated?"

"No." He's indignant.

"Isn't it true, Mr. Frazier, that if you killed the deal, you would have had to pay Mr. Russo a fifty-million-dollar breakup fee?"

"Objection. Relevance."

"Overruled."

"Your Honor," Frazier implores, "the terms of the deal are confidential."

She looks right through him. "Mr. Frazier," she says, "a moment ago you were trying to impress us with the enormous size of this deal. You can't have it both ways. Answer the question."

His jaws tighten. Another promising corporate career is heading for the Dumpster. "The breakup fee was fifty million dollars," he says. The suits in Stamford just got a severe case of indigestion.

I glance at the jury. "Just so everybody understands this, Mr. Frazier, if you pulled the plug on the deal, your company would have had to pay Mr. Russo fifty million dollars. Is that correct?"

His shoulders slump. "Yes."

"And if Mr. Russo pulled the plug, you wouldn't have owed him a penny, right?"

"Right."

"And you wouldn't have had to buy a company you really didn't want."

"We wanted the company, Mr. Daley."

"Right. You could have saved your company a fifty-million-dollar breakup fee and you could have avoided buying a company you really didn't want if you could have found a way to get Vince Russo to kill the deal. Isn't that about it, Mr. Frazier?"

Skipper's up. "Objection. I don't believe there was a question there."

He's right. There wasn't.

"Sustained."

"No further questions."

Ed Ehrlich from the city attorney's office is next. "Mr. Ehrlich," Skipper says, "you were representing the city of San Francisco in connection with the Russo deal, weren't you?"

He looks nervously through his thick glasses. "Yes," he replies. A member of the board of supervisors is here to make sure he doesn't screw up.

"And the city had agreed to provide financing for the deal, right?"

"Yes." Good answer. Keep it short. Stick to the facts.

"When did you leave the Simpson offices that night?"

"Around ten o'clock."

"And did you expect the deal to close?"

"Yes. All the papers were signed."

"And, as far as you knew, everything was on schedule to close?"

"Yes."

Skipper gets Ehrlich to say that Bob was in a good mood that night and was looking forward to the closing. Then he sits down.

"Mr. Ehrlich," I say, "the mayor had some serious issues with this deal, didn't he?"

"There were some concerns about our ability to obtain sufficient funds to finance the deal."

"How serious?"

"Not serious," he says slowly.

"Yet you were prepared to move forward."

"Yes."

"And you believe Mr. Russo and Mr. Holmes were prepared to move forward?"

"Yes."

"And you were aware that Mr. Russo had serious reservations about proceeding with the deal?"

"I knew he had some issues."

"Isn't it true, Mr. Ehrlich, that the mayor had instructed you to do everything in your power to terminate the deal?"

He looks at the mayor's henchman from the board of supervisors. "No."

"Isn't it true that the mayor determined that the city didn't have sufficient funds to conclude the deal on the original terms?"

"There were cash-flow issues. But we wanted to close the deal and keep the jobs in the city."

I may have him cornered. "Mr. Ehrlich, where was the

city going to get the money to conclude the financing of the deal?"

"From sources within the San Francisco banking community."

"What was the interest rate?"

"Prime plus four."

"And what rate were you charging the buyer?"

"Prime plus one."

"So the spread was three percent?"

"Right."

"And how big was the loan?"

"A hundred million dollars."

"I see. The spread at three percent is three million dollars a year, right?"

"That's right."

"And how many jobs would you have saved for the city?"

"About three thousand."

"By my math, that's about a thousand dollars a job."

He nods. "I guess you could look at it that way."

"And you're sure this was okay with the mayor?"

Skipper's up. "Asked and answered, Your Honor."

"Sustained."

"And it's your testimony that throughout all of this, Bob Holmes was in a great mood."

Ehrlich takes off his glasses and rubs his eyes. "He did not appear upset to me."

Add the city to the list of parties that look like idiots. "No further questions."

The parade continues a few minutes later when Dan Morris takes the stand and smiles confidently. "I was present that evening," he replies to Skipper's first question. "The mayor asked me to assist with the closing. He wanted to be sure it got done. A lot was riding on it."

"What time did you leave the office, Mr. Morris?"

"Around one-thirty-five." Skipper gets him to say that Russo and Holmes were ready to close the deal. According to Morris, everybody was in a great mood.

"Did you have any indications from Mr. Holmes or Mr. Russo that they would not proceed with the closing?"

"None."

"No further questions."

I stand. "Mr. Morris, isn't it true that the city couldn't afford the deal?"

He shrugs. "I'm not sure I understand the question."

"Isn't it true that the city didn't have enough money to fund the deal? And isn't it true that the mayor sent you and Mr. Ehrlich to the Simpson and Gates offices to try to torpedo it?"

"That's ridiculous. It was a good deal for both parties."

"If it was such a good deal for Vince Russo, why did he disappear?"

"Objection. Argumentative. Speculative. Foundation."

"Sustained."

"Did Mr. Russo appear agitated to you that night, Mr. Morris?"

He's smug. "He always appeared agitated."

"Do you have any idea why Bob Holmes committed suicide?"

"Objection," Skipper says. "Move to strike the suggestion that Mr. Holmes committed suicide."

"Sustained."

"I'll rephrase." I look him right in the eye. "Come on, Mr. Morris. Level with us. Two people are dead and another person disappeared. Why did it happen? Why were so many people unhappy about this deal?"

"Objection. Speculative."

"Sustained."

"Certainly, you must have a theory, Mr. Morris?"

"Objection. Speculative."

"Sustained."

There's nothing else I can do. I've planted the seed with the jury. "No further questions."

40

"I'VE BEEN A HOMICIDE INSPECTOR FOR THIRTY-SEVEN YEARS"

"They've finished the preliminaries. Gates is going to bring in his cleanup hitter, Inspector Roosevelt Johnson."

— NEWSCENTER 4 LEGAL ANALYST MORGAN HENDERSON.
FRIDAY, MARCH 27.

The next morning is Friday, and Skipper goes to his strength. Roosevelt looks directly at Skipper. "My name is Roosevelt Johnson. I've been a homicide inspector for thirty-seven years."

Joel tenses. Naomi scowls. Rosie eyes Roosevelt. Mort studies the jury.

"Inspector Johnson," Skipper begins, "could you tell us what time you arrived at the Simpson and Gates offices on the morning of December thirty-first of last year?"

"Eight-thirty-seven." His tone is authoritative. The court-room is silent.

"Would you please describe what you found at the scene?"

Skipper's approach is textbook. You lob open-ended questions to strong witnesses like Roosevelt. This will allow him to tell his story the way he's rehearsed it. I'm going to have to try to figure out ways to break up his flow.

Roosevelt clears his throat. He turns slightly toward the jury. He's not just going to tell his story. He's going to tell his story to *them*. "The office was in a state of chaos and shock. Word had spread throughout the firm of the homicides."

I stand and interrupt. I try to sound respectful. "Your Honor, there's no foundation for Mr. Johnson's characterization of the events that day as 'homicides.' We must move to strike."

She turns to Roosevelt. "Inspector, please limit your testimony to factual matters. We'll determine whether the deaths of Mr. Holmes and Ms. Kennedy should be characterized as homicides."

"Yes, Your Honor," Roosevelt says.

She tells the jury to disregard his characterization of the deaths as homicides. She looks at me with a pained expression, as if to say, "Are you happy now?"

"Inspector," Skipper continues, "you were telling us what happened when you arrived."

He describes his interviews with the police on the scene and his discussions with the paramedics and the technicians from the coroner's office. He confirms that Bob and Diana were pronounced dead at 8:22. He describes the all-hands meeting in the reception area. After twenty minutes, he concludes by saying, "We knew this was an important case. We wanted to make sure we got everything right."

"Inspector Johnson," Skipper says, "what happened next in your investigation?"

"We interviewed witnesses and gathered evidence." He says the police obtained statements from everyone who was present that night. They talked to building security and impounded the security videos.

"Did you interview the defendant?"

He takes off his glasses. "Yes. He confirmed he was at the office that night."

"Was he a suspect on December thirty-first?"

"No. Originally, we thought this case was a murder-suicide. It wasn't until later that we began to focus more closely on the defendant." He never mentions Joel by name.

"Inspector, when did you first begin to suspect the defendant may have been involved?"

Roosevelt says they became suspicious of Joel when they received the coroner's report and began to examine the physical evidence.

Skipper picks up the cue. He signals to McNulty. "This would probably be a good time to turn to the physical evidence."

Rosie whispers in my ear, "We're going to take a pounding for a while." She's right.

Skipper picks up the gun and hands it to Roosevelt. "Do you recognize this weapon?"

"Yes. It's the weapon that fired the bullets that killed the victims, Robert Holmes and Diana Kennedy."

Time moves slowly for the next two hours. Skipper has Roosevelt describe every piece of physical evidence in detail. Ten minutes on ballistics. Fifteen minutes on fingerprints. Fifteen minutes on the message on Diana's answering machine. Ten minutes on the voice-mail message to Bob. Ten minutes on the fingerprints on the computer keyboard. I object frequently, ferociously and, for the most part, futilely. We have a fundamental problem with the physical evidence. It all points toward Joel.

At eleven o'clock, they're still going strong. Skipper's on today. Roosevelt and the jury seem like old friends. Rita Roberts sits quietly in the gallery. Rabbi Friedman stares straight ahead. Naomi is stoic. At eleven-forty-five, Skipper asks Roosevelt to summarize his views on the physical evidence.

"We concluded the defendant fired the shots that killed the victims. In a clumsy attempt to cover up his crime, he typed a bogus suicide message on Mr. Holmes's computer."

Judge Chen looks at her watch and says, "This is a good time to break for lunch."

Joel ignores his sandwich. "We're getting killed, Mike," he says. We're sitting in the cramped consultation room behind Judge Chen's courtroom. Mort eats a corned beef sandwich. Rosie drinks a Diet Coke. I hold a can of Diet Dr Pepper. There won't be much fine dining until the trial is over.

Mort takes a fatherly tone. "You take some lumps when the prosecution presents its case."

I add, "We haven't had a chance to cross-examine Roosevelt yet."

Joel is unconvinced. Without a word, he puts his uneaten sandwich into the white paper bag and drops it into the wastebasket.

The afternoon session doesn't start any better. "Inspector Johnson," Skipper begins, "this morning, we spent a great deal of time discussing *how* Robert Holmes and Diana Kennedy were killed. We talked about the murder weapon. We listened to incriminating tapes. The defendant's fingerprints were found on a computer keyboard that was used to type a bogus suicide message."

Enough. "Objection. Mr. Gates is making his closing argument a little early."

"Sustained. Mr. Gates, do you think you can find a question to ask Inspector Johnson?"

"Yes, Your Honor." He continues to lecture. "This afternoon," he says to nobody in particular, "we need to discuss *why* the defendant killed Mr. Holmes and Ms. Kennedy."

I interrupt again. "Your Honor," I say sarcastically, "is there a question in there somewhere?"

"Let's get to it, Mr. Gates," she says sharply.

"Yes, Your Honor." Then he turns back to Roosevelt. "Inspector Johnson, do you have any reason to believe the defendant was angry at Mr. Holmes and Ms. Kennedy?"

"Yes."

"Angry enough to kill them?"

I'm up. "Objection. Inspector Johnson isn't a mind reader."

"Sustained." She points her gavel at Skipper. "Please, Mr. Gates."

He's undaunted. "Do you have any reason to believe the defendant was angry at Mr. Holmes?"

"Yes." Skipper leads Roosevelt through a description of Joel's anger at Bob about the partnership decision.

"Why would he have been upset at Mr. Holmes?" Skipper asks.

"Mr. Holmes was his mentor. Mr. Holmes had been assigned the task of telling the defendant he wasn't going to make partner. Apparently, he did not do so."

"That led to the agitated voice-mail message to Mr. Holmes?"

"Objection. Speculative."

"Sustained."

"I'll rephrase. Do you believe the defendant's voice-mail message to Mr. Holmes related to the fact that Mr. Holmes failed to inform the defendant that he wasn't going to make partner?"

"Objection. Speculative."

"Overruled."

"Yes," Roosevelt says. "I believe the defendant's voice-mail message related to the fact that Mr. Holmes failed to tell him he wasn't going to make partner."

Joel leans over and whispers, "Can't you object to this? You think I'd kill somebody because I didn't make partner?"

I signal him to be quiet. I whisper, "The jury's watching us."

Next, Skipper takes Roosevelt through the evidence that suggested that Joel may have been having an affair with Diana. "Inspector," Skipper says, "are you aware of any reason why the defendant may have been angry with Ms. Kennedy?"

"Yes. The defendant told us Ms. Kennedy did not complete a set of escrow instructions for the Russo deal. He stated that he was upset because he had to complete the task himself."

Skipper gives him a puzzled look. "Isn't it odd that the defendant would kill Mr. Holmes because he didn't make partner, and Ms. Kennedy because she failed to complete a legal document?"

"Objection. Speculative."

"Sustained."

"Inspector, are you aware of any other reasons why the defendant may have been upset with Mr. Holmes and Ms. Kennedy?"

"We believe the defendant was having a romantic relationship with Ms. Kennedy, which she terminated in order to rekindle an earlier romance with Mr. Holmes."

"Move to strike. Foundation."

"Overruled."

Joel looks straight ahead. I look back to the gallery. Rabbi Friedman is rocking back and forth in his chair. Naomi is staring directly into the back of Joel's head. Ruth Fink rubs her forehead.

Skipper is pleased. After a week of forensics, guns, fingerprints, autopsy reports, computer keyboards and tape recordings, we've finally got some really juicy stuff for the jury. "Inspector, I want to be sure I'm clear on this. Are you saying that Ms. Kennedy, for lack of a better term, dumped the defendant in order to resume a romantic relationship with Mr. Holmes?"

"Objection. Foundation."

"Overruled."

"Yes."

"Is it your belief that he killed Mr. Holmes in a jealous rage after Ms. Kennedy dumped him?"

"Objection. Speculative. State of mind. Foundation." The kitchen sink.

"Sustained." Judge Chen gives Skipper a sharp look. "Let's stick to the facts, Mr. Gates."

He barely blinks. He's getting to all the sordid goodies now. "Inspector, let's take this one step at a time. What evidence do you have that Mr. Holmes and Ms. Kennedy were romantically involved?"

"Mrs. Holmes's private investigator confirmed that he had discovered that Mr. Holmes and Ms. Kennedy were having a romantic relationship." He testifies that Beth stated she had found out about the affair in early December and told Bob she would file divorce papers if he didn't break it off. He terminated his relationship with Diana at that time.

"Yet on December thirtieth, Mrs. Holmes served divorce papers on her husband."

"Yes. The private investigator observed Mr. Holmes having a rendezvous at the Fairmont with a woman other than Mrs. Holmes."

"Was the private investigator able to identify the woman?"

"He wasn't absolutely sure. He said the woman may have been Diana Kennedy. That led to the filing of the divorce papers by Mrs. Holmes."

Skipper glances at the clock at the back of the courtroom. "You also determined that the defendant was having a romantic relationship with Ms. Kennedy, did you not?" I glance at Ruth Fink.

"Objection. Foundation."

"Overruled."

"Yes. We interviewed several partners at the Simpson and Gates firm who attended the firm retreat at Silverado last fall." He confirms Hutch's accounts of the hot-tub incidents. He reiterates Patton's story about finding Diana in Joel's room at three in the morning.

Naomi looks at the floor. This is going to be the bloodiest cross-examination I've ever done.

Skipper asks, "Inspector, if the defendant and Ms. Kennedy were romantically involved, why would the defendant kill her?"

"Objection. Speculative."

"Sustained."

"Inspector, do you have a theory as to why the defendant would have killed Ms. Kennedy?"

"Objection. Speculative."

Judge Chen glances at her bench book. "Overruled."

Roosevelt takes off his glasses. "We believe Ms. Kennedy was the woman in the hotel room with Mr. Holmes. We believe she told the defendant that she had resumed her relationship with Mr. Holmes. And we believe she told the defendant that she no longer wanted to see him."

"Objection. Move to strike. There's no foundation for any of this."

"Overruled."

"So, Inspector, you believe that the defendant was so upset about the end of his relationship with Ms. Kennedy that he killed Ms. Kennedy and Mr. Holmes in a jealous rage?"

"Yes."

Joel starts to stand up. I grab his arm and pull him back into his seat. "Stay calm," I whisper.

Skipper spends the rest of the afternoon lobbing softball questions to Roosevelt, who keeps pounding out winners. He describes his interviews with Rick Cinelli and Homer Kim. I object frequently and, for the most part, inconsequentially. Skipper stretches out Roosevelt's testimony until four-thirty.

Judge Chen looks at her watch and says, "I think we should break here until Monday."

It's a bonanza for Skipper. The jury has all weekend to mull over Roosevelt's testimony.

Judge Chen looks at me. "I trust you're prepared to begin cross-examination on Monday?"

"Absolutely, Your Honor."

She pounds her gavel.

41

"THE CROSS-EXAMINATION OF A LIFETIME"

"After Inspector Johnson's devastating testimony on Friday, Michael Daley better be at the top of his game today."

—NEWSCENTER 4 LEGAL ANALYST MORGAN HENDERSON.

MONDAY, MARCH 30.

We spend the weekend preparing for my cross-examination of Roosevelt. Mort keeps pounding on the idea that we have to give the jury a reason to think somebody else did it. Our best bet is Vince Russo. As Mort leaves on Sunday night, he summarizes our defense succinctly. "When all else fails," he says, "blame it on the dead guy."

Monday morning arrives too soon. I'm watching Morgan Henderson give his daily sermon on Channel 4 at six-forty-five. "You know," he says, "it might be a good idea to let Mort Goldberg handle Johnson's cross. Goldberg's an old war-horse. He has more capacity for all-out war than Daley does."

Thanks, Morgan.

The former talk-show host who now fancies himself a

serious newsman furrows his brow under his blond, blow-dried hair. "Who do you think's winning, Morgan?"

"The prosecution has scored a lot of points, but they haven't delivered a knockout blow."

"Any predictions?" the anchorman asks.

"It's looking pretty good for the prosecution," Henderson says. "I wouldn't want to be wearing Michael Daley's shoes today."

Frankly, neither would I.

The reporters swarm around me today when we get to the Hall because they know I'll have a major speaking role. I remind them I'm not permitted to talk about the case. That doesn't stop them. I utter the usual platitudes about my faith in the justice system. I can't ignore them. On the other hand, I don't want to say anything that may get me in trouble. The judge watches the news, too.

The routine in court is familiar to us all. Joel takes his seat between Rosie and me. Mort sits at the end of the table. Harriet Hill asks us to rise. The judge takes her seat. The jury is brought in. Roosevelt is called back to the stand. The judge reminds him he's under oath. Then she turns to me and says, "It's your turn for cross-examination, Mr. Daley."

I walk to the lectern. "Good morning, Inspector." I turn to the judge. "May I approach the witness?" I want to appear respectful. She nods. I walk toward Roosevelt. As of this moment, the battle is now fully engaged. "Inspector," I say, "I'd like to go over a few of the items you discussed on Friday in a little more detail."

Our eyes lock. "Of course, Mr. Daley."

I pick up the revolver from the evidence cart. I go over to

the jury box and slowly hold it in front of them. Then I walk back to Roosevelt. "Inspector," I say, "you have identified this revolver as the weapon that fired the bullets that killed Mr. Holmes and Ms. Kennedy, did you not?"

"Yes."

I hand it to him. "And you've testified that Joel Friedman's fingerprints were found on the revolver, right?" I'm trying to elicit one-word answers.

"Yes."

"When you arrived, Officer Chinn told you Mr. Friedman had informed him that he had picked up the revolver and disarmed it when he found the bodies, right?"

He pauses. "That's true."

"So it's possible Mr. Friedman may have gotten his fingerprints on the revolver when he picked it up and disarmed it, isn't it?"

"Objection. Speculative."

"Overruled."

Roosevelt looks at Skipper and shakes his head. "Yes. It's possible," he says.

One small victory for the good guys. I hold out my hand and he gives me the revolver. "Inspector, you've studied the lab reports on this gun, haven't you?"

"Yes."

I hand it back to him. "Would you mind showing us exactly where Mr. Friedman's fingerprints were found on this revolver?"

He asks to see the lab report. Rosie hands it to me, and I turn it over to him. She's marked Sandra Wilson's diagram of the location of the fingerprints on the revolver. I direct him to the correct page. He puts his glasses on the top of his head. I turn to Rosie, who turns on the overhead projector. The diagram appears on a screen I've placed in the front of the courtroom. "Inspector," I say, pointing toward the screen, "is this the diagram that you're looking at?"

"Yes."

"Would you please show us where Mr. Friedman's fingerprints were found on the revolver?"

He holds up the revolver and fumbles with it. He goes through the same exercise that Kathleen Jacobsen, the evidence technician, went through last week. He explains that fingerprints from Joel's thumb, middle finger, ring finger and pinky were found on the handle. He says the fingerprint from Joel's index finger was on the cylinder. He shows the jury how Joel was holding the gun.

"Inspector," I say, "could you please show us how Mr. Friedman would have fired the revolver with his hand in that position?"

"He couldn't, Mr. Daley. His finger wasn't on the trigger."

"Thank you, Inspector."

"But, Mr. Daley . . ."

"You've answered my question, Inspector." I nod to the jury. "Just so we're clear about it, isn't it a fact that you didn't find Mr. Friedman's fingerprints on the trigger?"

"We found smudged, unidentifiable fingerprints on the trigger, Mr. Daley."

"I understand. But you couldn't identify Mr. Friedman's fingerprints on the trigger, could you?"

"That's true."

"So, it's fair to say that you have no evidence to demonstrate that Mr. Friedman pulled the trigger. Isn't that true?"

"We have no identifiable fingerprints of Mr. Friedman on the trigger. That's all."

I'm not going to wage a war of semantics. Juries hate it. "Isn't it a fact, Inspector, that the locations of Mr. Friedman's fingerprints were consistent with the act of unloading the revolver?"

"Objection. Foundation."

"Overruled. Inspector Johnson is capable of giving an opinion on whether the fingerprints are consistent with the act of unloading the gun."

"Mr. Daley," Roosevelt says, "I believe that Mr. Friedman left a smudged fingerprint on the trigger of this revolver when he fired it. On the other hand, his fingerprints were in a position that might have been consistent with the act of unloading it."

Good answer. "Thank you, Inspector. You're also aware that when a gun is fired, it emits a cloud of gas and particles of gunpowder fly into the air."

"Yes, Mr. Daley, that's correct."

I ask him whether any such traces were found on Joel's hands or clothing.

The room is silent. He confirms Kathleen Jacobsen's testimony that they didn't test Joel's hands or clothing. "By the time he became a suspect, he had showered several times and his clothes had been laundered or cleaned. As a result, we would not have found traces of gunpowder or other chemical substances."

"So you decided not to do the tests because you thought you wouldn't find anything."

"Objection. Asked and answered."

"Sustained."

I've made my point. For good measure, I add, "And you can't show that Mr. Friedman ever touched the trigger of the revolver."

"Objection."

"Overruled."

"That's true," he says quietly.

We hammer at each other for the rest of the morning and into the afternoon. I challenge the handling of the evidence and the phone messages. We argue about the fingerprints on the keyboard. At three o'clock I glance at Rosie, who tugs on her left ear. "Inspector," I say, "did you ever seriously consider any other suspects?"

"Yes. We ruled them out very quickly. Not enough evidence."

"For example, Inspector, did you ever consider Vince Russo as a potential suspect?"

"For a brief time, yes. But we ruled him out."

"But you knew, of course, that Mr. Russo had been at the Simpson and Gates offices that night, and that he was very upset about the deal that he was supposed to close the next day."

"Yes."

"He was so upset that he drove to the Golden Gate Bridge and has not been seen since."

"We're aware of the circumstances, Mr. Daley."

"He may even have jumped off the bridge."

"We don't know that, Mr. Daley."

"Yet you didn't consider him a serious suspect?"

"Objection. Argumentative."

"Sustained."

I'm blowing smoke. "Is it possible he fled because he killed two people?"

"Objection. Speculative."

"Sustained."

"You would at least acknowledge Mr. Russo had a substantial motive to commit this terrible crime, wouldn't you, Inspector?"

"No."

"Come on, Inspector. Mr. Russo was very unhappy about this deal. By killing Mr. Holmes and Ms. Kennedy, he had an opportunity to disrupt the deal and flee the country."

"Mr. Daley, we have no evidence to that effect."

"You haven't found his body, have you, Inspector?"

"No."

"And it's possible, isn't it, that he may have faked his suicide and fled the country?"

Skipper's up. "Objection. This is all hopelessly speculative."

It certainly is.

"Sustained."

"Inspector, there was evidence confirming that Mr. Russo was in Mr. Holmes's office that night, wasn't there?"

Roosevelt eyes me slowly. "Yes, Mr. Daley. We found his fingerprints on the desk of Mr. Holmes. However, we have no way of knowing what time he was in Mr. Holmes's office, and we did not find a single shred of evidence that suggests that he was involved. His fingerprints were not on the weapon. His fingerprints were not found anywhere near the bodies of Mr. Holmes or Ms. Kennedy. As a result, we ruled him out as a suspect."

Sure. "Inspector," I say, "you were able to determine who was present in the building that night by reviewing the security tapes, right?"

"Yes."

"And you were able to rule out several individuals as suspects because the security tapes indicated that they left the building, right?"

"That's correct."

Now, for some serious smoke and mirrors. "Inspector, are you aware that it is possible to get into the building without passing by the security desk in the lobby? In fact, it is possible to enter the building by the stairways or the freight elevator, isn't it, Inspector?"

"The stairways and the freight elevators are kept locked," he says.

"I understand. But it is theoretically possible for someone to have entered and exited the building via the stairways or the freight elevator without passing by the security desk, isn't it?"

"Objection. Relevance."

"Overruled."

"Yes, it's theoretically possible," Roosevelt says. "However, you would need a key to access those areas."

"I know. But if somebody had a key, or a stairway door was propped open, it is possible somebody could have gotten upstairs and entered and exited the Simpson suite without passing by the guard desk, right?"

"That's true."

"And it's true that there are no security cameras on the stairways or the freight elevator, right?"

"That's also true."

"So somebody could have entered the building, gone up the stairs or the freight elevator, killed Mr. Holmes and Ms. Kennedy, and left the same way, without ever being detected, right, Inspector?"

"Objection. Speculative."

"Overruled."

"Yes, Mr. Daley," Roosevelt says. "That's theoretically possible."

I glance at Rosie, who nods. We have one more item on today's agenda. "Inspector," I say, "we've heard a lot of talk about the personal lives of Joel Friedman and Diana Kennedy."

"We certainly have," he agrees.

"You've testified that you believe Joel and Diana were having an affair, which she terminated."

"That's correct."

"And you base your conclusion on the testimony of Mr. Patton and Mr. Hutchinson?"

"Yes."

"You realize Mr. Patton did not say he actually saw Joel and Diana in bed together."

"That's true."

"And you realize Mr. Patton saw Joel and Diana in the same room together immediately after he attempted to attack her?" A bit of a stretch, but I decide to go for it.

"Objection."

"Overruled."

Roosevelt looks right into my eyes. "We questioned Mr. Patton at length. We have no reason to doubt the veracity of his testimony."

"Mr. Hutchinson claims he saw them in a bar and in a hot tub. Yet Mr. Hutchinson admitted that he was intoxicated at the time. Surely, you must have doubted Mr. Hutchinson's testimony?"

"We had no reason to question the truthfulness of Mr. Hutchinson's testimony, either."

Great.

"Inspector," I say, "Mr. Hutchinson said he thought he saw them in a hot tub from a distance of about a hundred yards away. He could have been mistaken. It was dark that night. He'd had a lot to drink. Other than the highly tentative testimony of Messrs. Patton and Hutchinson, you really don't have any evidence that Joel Friedman and Diana Kennedy were having an affair, do you?"

Skipper leaps up. "Objection, Your Honor. Speculative. Leading. Asked and answered."

All of the above.

"Sustained."

"No further questions." I return to my seat. The courtroom is silent.

Judge Chen turns to Skipper. "Mr. Gates, I think we'll call it a day."

She pounds her gavel.

———

Joel, Rosie, Mort and I sit in the consultation room behind the courtroom. I'm beyond exhausted. "Mike," Mort says, "that was nice work on cross today."

"Thanks. Coming from a pro like you, it means a lot to me." A small lie.

Rosie's always a step ahead. "We'll move for dismissal tomorrow."

Joel perks up. "Do you think they'll really dismiss the case?"

Mort gestures with his cigar. "Maybe. Mike got Johnson to admit they have no hard proof that you fired the gun. He made a lot of points on motive. That's always been the weakest part of their case. They've never been able to prove conclusively that you and Diana were having an affair."

"That's because we weren't," he replies.

Mort adds, "I've seen cases tossed for a lot less."

Joel smiles briefly. "I'm not going to get my hopes up too high," he says.

"We'll see tomorrow," I say.

Roosevelt is waiting for me by my car. "Nice work today," he says.

I toss my trial bag into the trunk. "Thanks, Roosevelt. I'm sorry if I beat you up in there a little today. Nothing personal."

He glances at the cars roaring by on the 101 freeway. "I hear they've found something. I don't know what it is. You're going to find out tonight and it's going to come down tomorrow."

I pause. "You think he's innocent, don't you, Roosevelt?"

"There's a lot of evidence that points in his direction. There are a lot of holes in the case, too." He motions toward the Hall and shrugs. "But it's not up to me. The guy on the third floor is making the decisions."

I watch a police car drive by on Bryant. He's silent as a uniformed cop walks by us.

"I've got to run," he says. "It'll be my ass if anybody sees me talking to you." He turns and walks away.

"Thanks, Roosevelt," I call out to his back.

42

THE FACTS OF LIFE

"District Attorney Prentice Gates says he'll call only one more witness tomorrow. Court watchers expect Friedman's defense attorneys to move for dismissal."

—KCBS NEWS RADIO. MONDAY, MARCH 30. 6:00 P.M.

Rosie's secretary, Rolanda, hands me a large manila envelope when I return to the office at six o'clock the same evening. Theoretically, she's supposed to be working just for Rosie. During the trial, she's been helping me out, too. "Thanks for sticking around," I say.

"You did a nice job on cross, today. Even the bitchy woman on CNN said so."

Small consolation. "Thanks."

I tear open the envelope and pull out a thick stack of paper. "Skipper didn't call, did he?"

"No. But McNulty did. Said it was important. He left his pager number."

"Thanks." I rifle through the pages.

"What is it, Mike?"

I give her page 5 of the report. "Read this," I say.

Her eyes get bigger. " 'The blood and DNA tests conclusively prove that Joel Friedman was the father of Diana Kennedy's unborn child.' " She stares at the report. "Shit," she whispers.

"Yeah." I think Rolanda's going to go to law school after she finishes at City College. "I'll call McNulty. Could you see if you can get Mort and Pete to come down here? Rosie's on her way."

"I'll be here as long as you need me tonight. You okay, Mike?"

Just great. We've built our defense on the fundamental proposition that my client wasn't sleeping with the victim and therefore had no motive to kill her. I've probably created enough doubts in the minds of the jurors to get an acquittal. And now I realize he was probably lying all along. "I'll be okay. It may be a long night."

"Bill McNulty speaking." Even on a cheap cellular phone, his delivery is crisp.

"It's Mike Daley." My voice is hoarse as I cradle the phone in my shoulder.

"You get the lab results?"

"Yeah."

"We're going to introduce it into evidence tomorrow."

"I'm going to ask the judge for some time to study it and have our own experts look at it."

"She won't go for it. You pushed for the early trial date. You're going to have to live with it."

"If she doesn't give us some extra time, we'll appeal."

"We'll take our chances."

I would, if I were in your shoes. "It doesn't change anything, Bill. You guys still can't prove your case beyond a reasonable doubt. You still can't show he pulled the trigger."

"We'll take our chances."

Asshole.

———

Pete arrives first. He walks in with authority, dressed in blue jeans and a black leather bomber jacket. He glances at the report. "Looks like we've got a problem," he says.

"You got that right. You know any good DNA guys?"

"Not really."

"I'll ask Mort." I rub my eyes. "We had them. We were going to move for a dismissal."

"They said on the radio your cross on Johnson was really good."

It was. "Anything new on the search for the elusive Vince Russo?"

"Nothing. We've drilled a bunch of dry wells. They're supposed to be looking for him at border crossings. Fat chance."

Rosie is already here when Mort walks in. He's heard. "So," he says, "turns out our client was the father after all."

"Seems that way, Mort," I reply. I show him a copy of the paternity test in the report.

"You realize, of course, we're completely and totally fucked."

Rosie snaps, "That's helpful. Got any other suggestions, Mort?" She may as well have added, "you asshole."

"Easy, Rosie," Mort says. "I'm not ready to throw in the towel just yet. We've still got some cards to play."

"He's right," I say. "When in doubt, go back to the evidence. Point one: If we can put on a good enough expert to rebut Rod Beckert, we can argue it was a suicide. We could win the case right there."

Mort smiles. "Now you're starting to think like a lawyer again."

"Our expert better be good in court," I reply.

"He's the best. Full professor at UCSF. And he's my brother-in-law, for God's sake. If he fucks up, he's going to have to listen to me piss on him at the Passover seder for the next twenty years." He turns serious. "Wait till you see him in court. He's beaten Beckert. He can do it again."

Rosie's quiet. She's thinking.

"Point two," I say. "Even if the jury decides it wasn't suicide, they still can't show Joel fired the gun. Maybe he handled it, but they can't prove he fired it. Reasonable doubt right there."

"Another perfectly legitimate argument," Mort agrees.

Rosie still isn't biting.

"Point three. They've got a problem with the computer keyboard. Joel's fingerprints are all over it. But Bob's aren't. It doesn't make sense. If Joel was going to try to fake a suicide, why would he get his fingerprints all over Bob's keyboard?

"Point four. The paternity test will prove Joel and Diana had an affair. They're going to argue he killed her because she broke it off to get back together with Bob. If we can show that Bob and Diana weren't together at the end of the year, it blows a big hole through their motive."

Rosie shrugs. "It's tough to prove a negative, Mike."

"I know. But we've got to try." I look at Pete. "Are you thinking what I'm thinking?"

"The mystery woman at the Fairmont?"

"Exactly. If we can prove she wasn't Diana, we've got a pretty good argument that Bob and Diana never got back together. It might be a good time for you to have a talk with Nick the Dick."

"He'll testify," Pete says. "He has another book coming out this fall. It's free publicity."

I stop to think for a minute. "The one thing we haven't considered is the possibility that Joel isn't the father. We could argue the test results were flawed. How reliable are these tests, anyway?"

Silence. Rosie finally says, "Ninety-nine percent."

Mort adds, "It probably means we're ninety-nine percent fucked. On the other hand, I know a guy at UC who's good. I can get him to confirm the test results. It'll take a little time, though."

"You guys got any better ideas?" I ask.

Mort says, "You forgot point five."

"Point five?"

"Yeah. If everything else fails, we'll use the S-O-D-D-I defense."

"SODDI?" Pete asks.

"Some Other Dude Did It. We need to try to pin it on somebody else. Give the jury a choice."

He's right. It may be our best shot. "Vince Russo's perfect," I say. "He's dead. He can't defend himself. If he didn't do it, why did he jump off the Golden Gate Bridge? Art Patton's a great candidate, too. For one thing, he's a first-rate asshole. For another thing, he's been sleeping with the Widow Holmes. And he put the moves on Diana. We don't have to prove anything. We just have to suggest it to the jury in a plausible manner to give them something to let them reach reasonable doubt. Hell, we should try to find a way to work in the fact that Skipper was there that night."

"You're stretching, Mike," Rosie says.

Mort tells her, "You'll see, Rosie. It works."

She isn't convinced. I've always trusted her instincts.

Mort rubs his fingers around a cigar. "Well," he says, "what should we do first?"

"Rosie, I need you to prepare papers to get things delayed until we can find our own expert and do our own tests. Mort, I want you to call your guy at UC. Pete, I want you and Wendy to go to the Bahamas right away and see what you can dig up before Trevor Smith gets back. Before you leave, I want you to set up a meeting for me with Nick Hanson. And I need you to pound on a few more witnesses to see if we can nail Art Patton. And anything you can get on the whereabouts of Vince Russo would be greatly appreciated."

"What are you going to do tonight?" Rosie asks me.

"I guess it's time for me to have a little talk with our client about the facts of life."

"We need to talk." I meet Joel at the front door of his father's house at nine-thirty that evening. I try for my best subdued tone. He seems to be in a pretty good mood. Then I remember that the last time we spoke, we were suggesting that we may be able to get the case dismissed tomorrow.

"Whatever you need, Mike." He smiles. "Great job on cross today."

"Thanks." My eyes dart. "Your mom or dad around?"

"No. They're at an Israel Bond dinner."

Relief. "Good." We walk into the living room and sit down. The TV is tuned to CNN. "Something's come up. It's serious."

His smile vanishes. His eyes bore in on mine. I look right back into his. "I thought things went pretty well today." He finds the remote and turns off the set.

"They've gotten the test results back on Diana's baby."

The color leaves his face. "And?"

"I think you know."

He takes his glasses off and rubs his eyes. "It's me, isn't it?" he whispers.

"Yeah."

He folds his hands and looks out the window for a moment. In my family, such news would have been met by at least twenty minutes of world-class histrionics, followed by another half hour of assignment of blame. When you're the rabbi's son, you aren't allowed such luxuries.

We sit in silence. "Are they sure?" he finally asks.

"Ninety-nine percent."

He rubs his index finger across his lips. "I was afraid of that."

"Did you know?"

"I wasn't sure." He scratches his head. "Diana said it was possible."

"I see." But I really don't.

"What am I going to tell Naomi?" he says to nobody in particular.

"You might start with the truth," I reply. I realize my tone is harsh as I say it.

He swallows hard. "You don't understand," he says through gritted teeth. "You just don't fucking understand." He stands up and walks toward the kitchen. I follow him. He pulls a glass from a cabinet and fills it with water. He leans against the refrigerator and I lean against the counter. We're barely five feet apart. There's a look of desperation in his eyes.

"Then explain it to me," I say. "If you want me to defend you, I have to understand."

"You can't."

"Maybe not. But I can try."

He blinks back tears. "You don't know what it's like being the rabbi's son, Mike. You live in a fishbowl. Everything gets blown out of proportion. If you get sent home from school, you aren't just another little kid getting in trouble. You're the rabbi's son getting in trouble. If you aren't dressed perfectly for services, it's viewed as a poor reflection on the rabbi and on the entire Jewish community. People notice." He looks away. It's hard to believe he's the same guy who was working on a billion-dollar deal a few weeks ago.

I don't say anything.

"Naomi is more fragile than she lets on," he says. "She's been on antidepressants. I didn't mean to sleep with Diana, Mike. It just sort of happened. And it only happened once. It was stupid. And I have to live with it."

"Joel," I say, "for the moment, you have to remember you're a defendant in a murder trial. You can't dwell on the fact that the Jewish community may find out about your relationship with Diana. You have to tell Naomi and your parents tonight. They're going to introduce the lab report in open court tomorrow. I may not be able to stop them."

"I'm completely fucked," he says. The stress overwhelms him. He dissolves into tears. He knocks his glass of water off the counter. I put my arm around his shoulder. The sobs are long and loud. "What am I going to tell her?" he repeats several times.

For a guy who thinks he has all the answers, I'm speechless.

I hear the front door open behind me. I hear Mrs. Friedman's voice. "Anybody home?"

Rabbi Friedman says, "Joel, are you still up?"

I see that Joel has miraculously regained his composure. His parents find us in the kitchen. We stand in silence for a moment.

"What is it?" Joel's mother asks.

Joel looks at me. Then he turns to them. "Something's come up. We need to talk."

"How did he react?" Rosie asks later that night. We're watching the news in her living room.

"Not well," I reply. "He broke down. He's humiliated. His marriage is falling apart."

She closes her eyes. She and I were down the same path not so long ago. "Did he tell Naomi?"

"They were talking when I left. They were both crying. She wasn't as angry as I thought she'd be. I don't think she has the energy to be angry. She looked so sad."

"And his parents?"

"He told them, too."

"How did they take it?"

"Stoic. It's the way they are."

"Shit."

"Do you think I should have stayed there, Rosie?"

"Probably not. You have to deal with some things in private."

"Would you do me a favor?" I ask. "Would you stop by Naomi's on your way in tomorrow? I think she's going to need some support. It might be better if it comes from you."

"Sure."

"Thanks."

She turns off the TV. "What are you going to do in court tomorrow?"

Beats me. "We have two choices. We can ask for a continuance and get Mort's expert to challenge the validity of the paternity test."

"Medical science isn't perfect."

"Paternity testing is pretty close. I'm sure he's the father."

"What's the other choice?"

"We stipulate that Joel is the father. We get to the truth quickly without a lot of hysterics."

"Why would we do that?"

"To avoid pissing off the jury with three weeks of expert testimony on the unreliability of paternity tests that we know are accurate."

"Tough choice. What does Joel want to do?"

"He wants to stipulate. He's ready to come clean."

"You think he's lied about anything else?"

"I don't think so." I don't add that I'm not sure.

"Let's talk in the morning with Joel."

I'm still lying awake at one o'clock in the morning when my phone rings. "Mike, it's Naomi." Her voice breaks. She's been crying.

"Hi."

"Mike," she says slowly, "I just don't know what to do."

"You don't have to decide tonight."

"I know. I just can't believe he'd lie to me."

I have no response. "Maybe we should talk about it in the morning, Naomi."

She tries to catch her breath. "I can't go to court tomorrow. It will be too humiliating."

I pause. "I understand."

"No, you really don't," she replies sharply. "You really don't."

"I know things will be tough for you. But it would help us if the jury sees you there."

"I don't know if I can."

"Let's talk about it in the morning. We'll stop by on our way in."

Five minutes later, the phone rings again. "It's Rabbi Friedman." He clears his throat. "This isn't good news."

"No, it isn't."

"How reliable are these tests, Michael?"

"Very."

"What would you suggest?"

I pause. "We're going to ask for more time to let our expert review the evidence. The judge may not give it to us.

At the very least, we'll find another expert and blow some smoke at the jury." I regret saying it as soon as I've said it.

"You mean you think we should lie?"

"No. It's my job to get the jury to reasonable doubt. If I have to trot out an expert for three weeks of testimony, that's what I'll do."

He clears his throat. "This is very difficult."

"Maybe we should talk about it in the morning."

43

"THE PROSECUTION RESTS"

"District Attorney Prentice Gates is expected to call his final witness today."

—KCBS NEWS RADIO. TUESDAY, MARCH 31. 7:40 A.M.

It's pouring when I reach Rabbi Friedman's house at seven-thirty the next morning. Joel and his parents are ready to go. Nobody says a word about last night.

"Michael," Rabbi Friedman says, "we don't want to be late for court."

"Rabbi, may I have a word with Joel in private?"

"Of course."

I pull Joel into the kitchen. "You okay?"

"As okay as I'm going to be."

"What about your parents?"

"They're pissed off."

"And?"

"They're still my parents. They're embarrassed and they'll probably kill me after the trial is over. Until then, they're going to play out their roles."

This helps. "What about Naomi?"

"That's tougher. She said she didn't want to go to court this morning. She may take the kids down to her mother's in Southern California until the trial's over."

"One step at a time."

We gather our umbrellas and raincoats. As Rabbi Friedman opens the heavy front door, I see Naomi and Rosie walking up the steps under a large umbrella. Even though it's dark out and it's raining, Naomi is wearing sunglasses.

"What are you all looking at?" Naomi snaps. "It's time to go to court."

Joel tries to give her a hug, but she pulls away. "We have a lot to talk about when the trial's over," she says to him.

Rosie repeats firmly, "It's time to go to court." I give her hand a quick squeeze as we walk down the steps toward our cars.

"Your Honor," I say, "the prosecution has just provided some new and potentially inflammatory evidence. We need some time to review it." We're sitting in Judge Chen's chambers. I asked for a meeting as soon as we got to court and before the jury was brought in.

Judge Chen isn't in a particularly gregarious mood this morning. She gives Skipper a sharp look and demands, "What's this all about, Mr. Gates? It's a little late to bring in new evidence."

He smiles confidently. He hands her a copy of the lab report. "Your Honor," he says, "we just got this. We would have introduced it sooner if we'd had it, but the defendant insisted on an early trial date." He clears his throat, but he's still grinning. "The defendant was the father of Diana Kennedy's unborn baby."

Silence. She puts on her reading glasses and studies the report.

"Your Honor," I begin.

She holds up her hand. "Let me look at this, Mr. Daley."

Rosie remains silent. Mort studies the judge. Skipper and McNulty exchange satisfied looks. I'm waiting for the high fives to start.

After what seems like an eternity, she puts down the report. "This is serious," she says. "These tests are very reliable."

Skipper agrees vigorously. "Very reliable, Your Honor. Close to one hundred percent."

"Thank you, Mr. Gates."

"Your Honor," I say, "we just got the report last night. We haven't had an opportunity to review it with our expert. And we certainly haven't had an opportunity to conduct an independent test."

"That could take weeks," Skipper protests. "If they wanted to verify the results, they should have made the request months ago. They pushed for the early trial date. We're ready to conclude our case. We can't wait six weeks while their experts redo the paternity test. It isn't fair. We'll lose the jury. They're going to come back with the same results, anyway."

The judge looks at me. "Mr. Daley, you really should have made your request sooner."

She's right. I've made a significant blunder. I believed my client when he told me he didn't have an affair with Diana Kennedy. "In the interests of fundamental fairness, Your Honor," I say, "we would request that you give us at least a few weeks to examine the report and consult with our expert." When all else fails, I try fundamental fairness.

She shakes her head. "I'm not going to put this jury on ice for a month."

"Judge Chen," I say, "I won't ask for a few weeks. But you have to give us a couple of days."

"I don't have to give you anything."

"I know. But all I'm asking for is just a few days."

She turns to Skipper, who's whispering to McNulty. "Mr. Gates," she says, "it's Tuesday. I was planning on a couple of short trial days this week so I can attend to some other business. Would you object if we recess until Monday so the defense can review the lab report?"

"Your Honor," he replies, "I think we should proceed. I see no purpose for this delay."

"Mr. Gates," she says, "it looks like the rain may stop for a while this afternoon. Why don't you and Mr. McNulty go out and hit some golf balls?"

Skipper gets the message. "When you put it that way, Your Honor, I guess we might be in a position to adjourn until Monday."

"We're done," she says. Skipper and McNulty dart out the door. As I'm packing my trial case, she says to me quietly, "He lied to you about Diana, didn't he?"

I swallow. "Yeah."

"There isn't much I can do about it, you know."

"I know."

"Mike," she says, "I know you'll be tempted to try to get me to declare a mistrial so you can start over and retool your case."

I'm silent.

She looks right at me. "I won't let it happen. Don't push my buttons on this one, understood?"

"Understood."

"Good. I'll see you Monday."

We spend the rest of the week trying to fill some of the holes in our case. On Thursday, Mort's DNA expert from UCSF confirms what we all expected. The paternity tests were conducted by a reputable lab. Unless we can demonstrate that there were some shenanigans, it's virtually certain that Joel was the father. Pete and Wendy leave for the Bahamas on Friday.

I have one bright spot on Friday. I take Nick Hanson out for lunch at Moose's, an upscale eatery on Washington Square in North Beach. At eighty-something, he's still a character. He assures me that he'd be delighted to testify, as long as we agree to pay him for his time at his standard hourly rate.

I spend all day Saturday and most of Sunday working with our medical expert, Dr. Robert Goldstein, on his testimony to rebut Rod Beckert. At seven o'clock Sunday night, Rosie, Mort and I regroup in our office. Joel has agreed to stipulate that he's the father. I phone Skipper with the news. He's pleased. Within fifteen minutes, McNulty faxes a draft stipulation to us. We agree on the language.

Mort inspects a fine Cuban cigar. "It's the best we can do. We'll get the issue off the table as quickly as we can."

I'm not so sure.

Rosie and I drive home on Sunday night. As we head north-bound on the Golden Gate Bridge, I turn to her and say, "How did you get Naomi to come to court the other day?"

"She's tougher than you think. I told her she and Joel have big issues to work out, but that it would help Joel if she waited until after the trial."

Rosie is one smart cookie. "You think they'll be able to hold it together after all this is over?"

"Tough to predict. They're going to have to make some changes." She looks out the window and tugs at her hair.

I've learned there are times when I shouldn't ask too many questions. We drive in silence.

On Monday morning, Judge Chen is pleased when we inform her in chambers that we've agreed to stipulate about the paternity test. We've just saved a couple of weeks of trial time. She has Skipper read our stipulation to the jury as soon as they're brought in. Although there are a few raised eyebrows among the jurors, there isn't much reaction. They're getting tired.

"Mr. Gates," Judge Chen says, "do you have anything further at this time?"

"No, Your Honor." He turns toward the jury. "The prosecution rests."

"Very well." She looks at the jury. "The prosecution has completed its presentation. We're going to take a short break while the attorneys discuss some legal issues." She nods to Harriet Hill, who leads the jury out. "Mr. Daley," she says, "I presume you'd like to make a motion at this time."

"Yes, Your Honor. The defense moves that all charges be dropped." The motion is routine. The defense always moves for dismissal at the end of the prosecution's case.

"On what grounds?"

"As a matter of law, the prosecution has failed to prove its case beyond a reasonable doubt."

Skipper stands. "Objection."

"Sit down, Mr. Gates." She turns to me. "Mr. Daley, your motion is denied. The defense should be prepared to call its first witness tomorrow morning."

44

THE BRAIN TRUST

"After two weeks of damaging testimony from the prosecution's witnesses, Friedman's attorneys will begin their defense. I hope they have a few rabbits in their hats."

—NEWSCENTER 4 LEGAL ANALYST MORGAN HENDERSON.
MONDAY, APRIL 6.

"Have you heard anything from Pete and Wendy?" Joel asks. We're meeting in Rabbi Friedman's dining room at two o'clock the same afternoon. Joel looks intense. Rabbi Friedman is in a contemplative mood. Mort fingers a cigar. Rosie is drinking iced tea.

"The banker isn't back in town yet, but Wendy was able to sweet-talk his secretary into giving her copies of some of the correspondence in the file. She's faxing it to us tonight."

Joel scratches his head. "So, who goes first?"

"We'll start with our medical expert, Dr. Goldstein."

Rabbi Friedman glances at Mort. "He's good," Mort says.

"I worked with him on his testimony over the weekend," I say. "If he can persuade the jury it was a suicide, we can all go home."

"And if he can't?" Joel asks.

"We'll attack the physical evidence. If we have to, we'll show the jury that Russo and Patton had a lot more motive and opportunity than you did. If things get really tight, we'll put some of my former partners on the stand and try to deflect the blame over to them."

"What about me?" Joel asks.

"What about you?"

"When do I go on?"

"We'll see how it goes. If things are going well, you don't."

"I want to testify, Mike." He pauses. "I need to testify."

Over my dead body. "We'll decide when the time comes."

We conclude our discussion after an hour or so and I begin to gather my notes. Rosie starts to put on her coat. Mort clears his throat. "There's something I'd like to bring up," he says.

"What is it, Mort? Did we forget something?"

He takes a drink of water. He chews the ice. He looks at Rabbi Friedman and then he turns to Joel. "No," he says, "we didn't forget anything. I wanted to discuss something."

Joel's eyes narrow. Rosie looks puzzled.

Mort glances around the table. "I wanted to discuss this privately with Joel, but it doesn't appear that I'll have an opportunity to do so. So, let me explain the situation to all of you."

Rosie's expression turns to a severe scowl. "What situation, Mort?" she asks.

"After we got the results of the paternity test, I decided to talk to the DA."

What? I lean across the table and say firmly, "You didn't have the authority, Mort."

He holds up his hand. "Hear me out," he says. "In light of the test results, I thought it would be in Joel's best interests to feel out the DA about a possible deal." He looks at Joel. "I think we need to explore all of our options."

My heart races. It's all I can do not to leap out of my seat and grab him. Rosie's eyes are on fire. She doesn't say anything, but her eyes say, "Light up this asshole."

I struggle to keep my tone measured. "Why didn't you tell me you were going to the DA?"

He doesn't flinch. "Because I knew you wouldn't agree to it."

"That's not true. We would have discussed it. We would have consulted with Joel. Then we would have made a decision."

He shrugs. "I doubt it."

"Bullshit," I reply. "You should have told us," I shout.

"Look," he says, "I talked man-to-man with Skipper. He thinks his case is shaky enough that he'd be willing to let Joel plead to voluntary manslaughter. He'll say it was heat of passion. It takes the death penalty off the table. And he's willing to recommend a fairly lenient sentence."

I look at Joel. Joel glares at his father. They both turn to me. Joel breaks the silence. "Seeing as how I'm on trial, maybe you guys would be interested in my opinion."

Mort interrupts him. "Look, Joel. I know how it sounds. But I was doing it for your own good. I think you should consider all your options."

"You think I'm guilty, you asshole." Joel's father looks away.

"I didn't say that," Mort replies. "I just thought it was important to know your options."

"How could you possibly think I might agree to a plea bargain?"

"Look at their case. You're an admitted adulterer. You're an admitted liar. How big a leap is it for the jury?"

"You're right," Joel says sharply. "I am an adulterer. I'm not proud of it. I lied about it. I'm not proud of that either.

But I am not a murderer. I did not kill two people. If the jury wants to convict me for something I didn't do, so be it. But I'll be goddamned if I'm going to admit to something I didn't do. Period." He stares Mort down. Then he glares at his father.

"Give it some thought," Mort says.

"I've given it all the thought that it deserves, Mort," he replies. "No deal."

Mort nods. "Okay," he says. "I understand." He reaches for his briefcase.

"There's one other thing," Joel says. He looks directly at Mort. "Your assistance on this case is no longer required. You're fired."

Mort glances at Rabbi Friedman, who closes his eyes. Mort turns to Joel. "I thought you might have that reaction." He picks up his briefcase. "Good luck, Joel. No hard feelings." He hesitates for a moment, then says, "I can show myself out."

After the door shuts, I turn to Joel. "You okay about this?"

"Yeah," he answers quietly. "I'm fine."

Rosie and I sit in her office later the same evening to talk about strategy. The hallway is lined with binders, charts and exhibits. It looks like the backstage area of a theater. "Well, Rosita," I say, "it's just you and me again."

"Just like old times," she says. "You ready?"

"You bet. We've got them right where we want them."

She grins. "You've never been at a loss for self-confidence."

"I just hope we don't have any more surprises." I pause. "And I sure wish Pete would find that goddamned Vince Russo."

45

OUR TURN

"Friedman Defense Begins Today."
>   —*San Francisco Legal Journal.* TUESDAY, APRIL 7.

I knock on Rosie's door at seven the next morning. "Come in for a minute," she says. "You won't believe this." She opens the door. Grace is eating a bowl of Froot Loops at the kitchen table. She's happy to see me. I say hi to Rosie's mom, who has been logging overtime with Grace as the trial has continued. Being a trial lawyer isn't a nine-to-five job. I remind myself that we'll have to do something nice for her after the trial is over.

Rosie leads me into the living room. The TV is tuned to Channel 4. Morgan Henderson is delivering his daily sermon. "The defense will begin its case today," he intones.

"So what?" I say to Rosie.

"Just a sec," she says. She turns up the volume.

"As we reported earlier this morning," Henderson continues, "last night Professor Morton Goldberg resigned from the defense team. His office said his departure was the result of 'philosophical differences.' "

"Philosophical differences my ass," I say.

"Just wait," Rosie says.

Henderson smiles at the morning anchorwoman. She bats her eyelashes. "Susan," he says, "Mr. Friedman's loss is our gain. I'm pleased to introduce the newest member of our legal team here at NewsCenter 4." His grin widens. "We are joined by Professor Morton Goldberg, who will be providing commentary on the trial for the duration."

"For the love of Jesus Christ," I say.

Rosie grins. "Unbelievable."

The camera shifts to a beaming Mort, who is in a separate studio, fiddling with a small earphone. "Is that you, Morgan?" he stammers. "What did you say?"

Henderson looks down at his monitor. "Uh, Professor Goldberg will join us in a moment."

The picture stays on Henderson, but Mort's voice is heard. "I'm ready, Morgan."

They're going to have to decide who's going to play Laurel and who's going to play Hardy.

"Mort," Henderson says, "what are your thoughts on the beginning of the defense's case?"

The camera shifts to Mort. The bright lights reflect off his huge glasses. "You know, Morgan, I want to remind our viewers that I've just terminated my association with the defense team for philosophical reasons. I have to be careful not to divulge any client confidences."

I rub my temple. "Can you believe this?" Rosie says.

"At this point, I'll believe anything."

Henderson looks serious and asks, "Without divulging any confidences, how do you feel about the defense's case, Mort?"

"The defense has a lot of ground to cover, Morgan. But

Michael Daley is a very good lawyer. I'm sure justice will prevail."

How insightful. "Turn it off," I say. "Just turn the damned thing off. I can't stand it."

Grace looks at me. In between bites of cereal, she says, "Are you okay, Daddy?"

Oops. "Yeah, sweetie. Everything's fine." Daddy has a slight case of indigestion.

It's overcast, but not raining, when we reach the throng of reporters at the Hall.

"*Mr. Daley, are you going to consider a plea bargain?*"

"*Mr. Daley, is it true Mr. Goldberg was fired?*"

"*Mr. Daley, does Mr. Friedman's affair change your defense?*"

"*Mr. Daley? Mr. Daley? Mr. Daley?*"

I feel like screaming, "Shut the fuck up, you assholes." Naturally, I simply look composed as Rosie and I push our way past them and meet Joel and his parents just inside the doors.

"Naomi is in the bathroom," Joel says. "She said she'd meet us upstairs."

Rabbi Friedman glances at me. "Looks like it's up to you, Michael."

"We'll just keep going, Rabbi."

We go upstairs and take our seats. Skipper says blandly, "I understand we have a change in the lineup today."

"Yeah. We decided to trim some of the fat."

He grins.

Joel leans over and whispers, "You ready?"

I don't have time to think of all the things I would have done differently. With hindsight, I would have deferred our opening statement until now. I might have had a chance to undo some of the damage. "You bet," I reply. "Now we get to tell our side of the story."

Before the jury is called in, Judge Chen turns to me and says, "I understand there's been a change in the team at the defense table."

"Yes, Your Honor," I reply. "Mr. Goldberg won't be with us for the remainder of the trial."

Out of the corner of my eye, I see McNulty whisper to Skipper. Judge Chen nods. "Very well," she says. "Let's proceed." She instructs Harriet Hill to bring in the jury. I didn't expect her to stop the trial just because Mort's gone. He hasn't said a word to the jury, anyway.

"Please call your first witness, Mr. Daley."

"The defense calls Dr. Robert Goldstein."

Mort's brother-in-law, Bob Goldstein, is a professor at UCSF Medical Center. His physical appearance might be described as the anti-Mort. He's in his late sixties, with a full head of gleaming silver hair and dazzling blue eyes. He glides his six-foot-four-inch frame across the courtroom with the grace of a senior squash champion. His double-breasted light gray suit matches his hair. A tasteful white kerchief sits in his breast pocket. He looks like he'd be right at home in a boardroom or a country club. The Rolex and gold cuff links suggest he's very successful and probably very rich. Pound for pound, he can hold his own with Skipper in the charisma derby.

He's sworn in and takes his place on the witness stand. He casually adjusts the microphone. He knows his way around a courtroom and he knows how to work an audience. From what I gather, he and Mort don't get along very well. Mort says he isn't the kind of doctor you'd call if you're sick. On the other hand, he *is* the kind of doctor you'd call if you need someone to testify.

He states his name for the record. He smiles knowingly at the jury. On someone else, it would appear condescending. "I'm a full professor in the departments of Pathology and Trauma Surgery at UCSF Medical School."

I begin taking him through his impressive credentials. We get through his undergraduate degree at Stanford and his medical degree from Johns Hopkins when Skipper interrupts us. "We'll stipulate to Dr. Goldstein's expertise," he says.

Goldstein smiles. The two lawyers on the jury seem to nod to each other. I hand him copies of Beckert's autopsy reports. "Dr. Goldstein," I say, "are you familiar with the autopsy reports prepared by Dr. Roderick Beckert with respect to Mr. Robert Holmes and Ms. Diana Kennedy?"

"Yes. I have reviewed both reports very carefully."

Skipper starts to stand, then he sits down. He's a little jumpy today.

"Would you be kind enough to tell us whether you agree with Dr. Beckert's conclusions?"

"Objection. There's no foundation for this."

"Your Honor," I say, "Mr. Gates just stipulated on the record that Dr. Goldstein is, in fact, an expert. He did not object when I asked Dr. Goldstein whether he had reviewed the reports. Certainly, he can't object when I ask Dr. Goldstein for his opinion as to the validity of the conclusions in the reports. Why else would I call him to the stand?"

Judge Chen isn't buying into this completely. "I'll overrule the objection for now. But Dr. Goldstein better be prepared to explain his conclusions."

"He will." I turn back to Goldstein. "You were going to tell us your views on the autopsy reports."

"I have reviewed both reports. I have known and worked with Rod Beckert for many years. We are colleagues on the

UCSF faculty in the Department of Pathology. I respect him."

You also have more titles than he does, Bob, but don't lay it on too thick just yet.

"In the case of the autopsy of Ms. Kennedy," he continues, "I think Rod got it absolutely right. She never had a chance." He explains in both medical and layman's terms that she died of gunshot wounds to her lung and heart.

"And the autopsy report on Mr. Holmes?"

He looks at the jury and grimaces. "That's where I have a problem with Dr. Beckert's conclusions. There's no doubt Mr. Holmes died from massive trauma from a gunshot wound to his head. However, I have very serious doubts about Rod's conclusion that Mr. Holmes was knocked unconscious prior to the shootings. In fact, I would go so far as to say that I believe Rod was wrong."

I glance at the jury. They seem to like him so far. I'll have to ask Rosie when we're done.

"Would you mind explaining your conclusions, Doctor?" I'm taking a chance. It may be better to lead him with short, precise questions. On the other hand, at our rehearsal—I mean our trial preparation—he was able to explain some very complicated concepts in terms that I could understand.

"Of course," he says. He looks at Rosie. "I wonder if we could look at the autopsy photos."

Rosie sets up the easel and puts an enlarged picture of the left side of Bob's head in front of the jury. Dr. Goldstein turns to the judge and asks whether he can stand by the picture so he can point out certain items. He speaks to her in a tone that suggests they're old friends. She agrees.

He buttons his suit jacket as he walks toward the easel. He takes a thin gold pen out of his pocket. "Ladies and gentlemen," he says to the jury, "we're looking at an autopsy photograph of the left side of the head of Mr. Holmes. For your reference, here's the outer edge of the skull." He makes a sweeping circular motion with the pen. The jurors look at the photo. Goldstein studies the jurors one by one. As I instructed him, he looks at the phone company supervisor at the end of the second row and points to her. "Madam, can you see all right?"

She says, "Yes."

"And can everybody hear me? I hate using microphones."

They nod in unison. Mort was right. This guy is smoother than good scotch.

He turns to the photo and draws an imaginary circle around the exit wound just above Bob's left ear. "This area here is called the parietal bone. As you're all aware," he says, "here's where the bullet came out. We call it the exit wound. Although we don't have a picture of it here, the entrance wound was, as you know, in the right parietal bone, just above the right temple." He's striking a perfect balance between knowledgeable and folksy. The accountant is looking receptive. "Everybody with me so far?"

They all nod again. Skipper stands. "Your Honor," he says, "would you please instruct Dr. Goldstein not to ask questions of members of the jury. This isn't his anatomy class at UC."

Judge Chen looks annoyed. "If that was an objection," she says, "I'll have to sustain it." She turns to Goldstein and says gently, "Please answer the questions Mr. Daley asks you, Dr. Goldstein. Please don't ask the jury any questions."

"Yes, Your Honor."

I say, "Dr. Goldstein, you were describing the exit wound."

"Yes." He looks at the photo. He describes the wound in detailed medicalese for the next five minutes. Then he interprets in language Grace could understand. "As you can plainly see," he concludes, "the trauma to the head was massive."

"Were you able to make a determination about the accuracy of Dr. Beckert's conclusion that the wound may not have been self-inflicted?"

"Objection, Your Honor. He's leading the witness."

No, I'm not. I give the judge a puzzled look. "Your Honor," I say, "that wasn't a leading question." Skipper is trying to break Goldstein's rhythm.

"You're right, Mr. Daley. Overruled."

Goldstein says, "In my judgment, Rod was wrong. I believe the wound was self-inflicted."

Murmurs in the back of the courtroom. This shouldn't be a news flash to anybody. Did they think my medical expert was going to agree with Beckert? Judge Chen pounds her gavel. I ask Goldstein to explain his conclusion.

"I am certain Mr. Holmes fired the gun." He says that gunpowder residue was found on Bob's right hand. "There's no other way he could have gotten gunpowder on his hand, unless, of course, he happened to fire another gun the same day." This brings mild chuckles from the gallery.

"Isn't it possible that someone may have placed the gun in his hand while he was unconscious and caused him to fire it? Wouldn't that generate the same chemical residue on his hand?" I'm trying to mitigate Skipper's argument that somebody knocked Bob unconscious, placed the gun in his hand and caused him to pull the trigger, making it look like a suicide.

"Yes. But that assumes that Mr. Holmes was unconscious at the time the gun was fired."

"Was there any evidence that Mr. Holmes was unconscious at the time the gun was fired?"

"No." He pauses. "I have all the respect in the world for

Rod Beckert. I've known him for many years. But this time around, I think he's just flat wrong."

I pretend to study the picture of Bob's head. I'm actually glancing at the jury. I was hoping I'd get a little more than the halfhearted reactions I'm seeing. "Could you please explain why you believe Dr. Beckert's conclusion was wrong?"

"Certainly, Mr. Daley." He explains that the report indicated that Holmes wasn't under the influence of drugs, and the amount of alcohol in his system was so small he couldn't have been prosecuted for a DUI charge. As a result, he ruled out the possibility that he was rendered unconscious by the use of any chemical substance.

He turns back to the photo. "Consequently," he says, "it seems the only way Mr. Holmes would have been rendered unconscious would have been through a blow to his head." He points to a spot just above the top of the exit wound. "This is the area where Dr. Beckert claims there was a major concussive wound. In fact, the blow to the skull, if there indeed was such a blow, wasn't nearly as traumatic as Dr. Beckert says. It certainly wasn't enough to render him unconscious."

I try to look skeptical. "How can you be sure, Dr. Goldstein?"

"For one thing, it's small. It's less than a quarter of an inch in diameter. It's not as though somebody hit him with a hammer. There was no significant contusion. More importantly, Dr. Beckert took X rays of Mr. Holmes's head. There was no skull fracture. It was probably caused when the head banged against the desk immediately after he shot himself." He pauses. "Let me put it this way. If he was a football player and he sustained such an injury, he wouldn't have left the game. Based on my best medical judgment, it is my opinion that he fired the gun and that he took his own life."

"Dr. Goldstein," I say, "you understand that Dr. Beckert concluded that the injury could not have been sustained after the shooting because the hematoma, or bump, could not have formed after the shooting."

He smiles. "In general, that's true. A hematoma cannot form once the heart stops beating because it cannot pump blood to the injured area. However, in circumstances such as this where there is a wound to the head, the heart may continue to beat for seconds or even minutes after the shooting. As a result, it is likely that the hematoma was caused when Mr. Holmes bumped his head on the desk after he'd shot himself."

"No further questions, Your Honor."

Skipper's up like a shot. "Dr. Goldstein," he says, "you didn't examine the body, did you?"

"No."

"And you didn't have an opportunity to question Dr. Beckert, did you?"

"No."

"And isn't it likely that Dr. Beckert's exam was more comprehensive than yours?"

Watch out, Bob. I've warned him to deflect hypothetical questions.

"Of course, Mr. Gates. Dr. Beckert had the body in front of him when he performed the autopsy. I've been working off photos and X rays."

"Well, Dr. Goldstein, wouldn't it seem to make more sense in this context to rely on Dr. Beckert's description of the wounds than yours?"

"Objection. Speculative."

"Sustained."

"I'll rephrase. Don't you think Dr. Beckert's descriptions of the wounds would be more reliable than yours given the fact that he was observing the body as he performed the autopsy?"

"Objection. Still speculative."

"Sustained."

Surely he's going to do more than just ask Goldstein to agree with Beckert. On the other hand, if he gets into hand-to-hand combat, Goldstein will probably hold his ground. If I were in Skipper's shoes, I wouldn't push too hard. The jury understands Goldstein is our hired gun.

They joust for another twenty minutes. They argue about the blow to the head. Goldstein doesn't give an inch. "Dr. Goldstein," Skipper finally says, "are you being paid to testify today?"

"Yes I am."

"And how much are you being paid?"

Goldstein looks at me. This is a standard question. If Skipper can't shake him, at least he can try to show that we've bought his medical opinion, which, of course, we have. Unfortunately, we're paying him a lot of money.

"Four hundred fifty dollars an hour." Then he adds, sarcastically, "Plus two dollars to ride the streetcar each way." A smattering of laughter breaks out in the back of the courtroom.

"And how many hours have you spent on this case?"

"Counting today, about fifty."

Skipper looks at the jury and nods melodramatically. "So, they were able to buy your medical opinion for about twenty-five thousand dollars?"

"Objection. Argumentative."

"Sustained."

Skipper pouts briefly. "No further questions, Your Honor."

As Goldstein steps down, Joel whispers, "That went pretty well, didn't it?"

I nod. Thanks, Mort. I hope you get good ratings tonight.

Our next witness is Dr. Greta Hudson, a dignified black woman who is a professor at USC. She used to be one of the top evidence technicians in the FBI crime lab. She's written several texts on evidentiary issues. We decided to go out of town for our expert on guns and fingerprints to make it tougher on Skipper's team to learn much about her. In all honesty, we picked a black woman because we thought she'd play well to the jury.

After she states her name for the record, I ask her if she's a medical doctor.

"No," she replies. "I'm a Ph.D. in the field of criminology. My area of expertise is forensics and, in particular, the gathering and analysis of physical evidence. I've written extensively on the subject of fingerprints. I'm also an expert on certain types of firearms, including revolvers."

Just the way we rehearsed it. We spend a few minutes going over her credentials before Skipper stipulates to her expertise.

In response to my question concerning Bob's position when he was shot, she explains that the trajectory of the bullet and the blood-splatter patterns on Bob's desk indicate that he was sitting at a ninety-degree angle to his desk, with his left side closest to the desk. He slumped to the floor, possibly banging the left side of his head against his desk.

"Dr. Hudson," I say, "were you able to make a determination as to whether Mr. Holmes or Ms. Kennedy was shot first?" I want to show Bob died last. If he died first, it doesn't look like a suicide.

"Yes," she replies. She explains that the tattooing at the entrance wound indicates that the barrel of the gun was placed against Bob's head. In such circumstances, a vacuum is created when the gun is fired, which sucks a minute amount of blood into the barrel of the gun. "If the last shot fired from the gun was the shot that killed Mr. Holmes," she says, "there would be traces of his blood in the barrel of the gun. Of course, if the gun was fired again to kill Ms. Kennedy, the traces of blood in the barrel would have been cleared out and no traces of his blood would have been found."

"Were any traces of Mr. Holmes's blood found in the barrel?" I ask.

"Yes," she replies. "As a result, I concluded that the last shot fired from this weapon was the shot that killed Mr. Holmes."

Good answer. I take the revolver from the evidence cart and hand it to her. "Dr. Hudson," I say, "have you reviewed the police reports and the lab reports concerning this weapon?"

"Yes."

"In particular, did you have an opportunity to review the fingerprint analysis prepared by the crime lab?"

"Yes, I did."

I signal to Rosie. She puts an enlarged diagram showing all sides of the revolver on the easel in front of the jury. I ask Dr. Hudson to give the jury a summary of the fingerprint report.

Skipper objects. "Your Honor, the report on this weapon has already been entered into evidence. Surely we don't need Dr. Hudson to restate the entire report."

Actually, I want her to do just that—and to put our spin on it. "Your Honor," I say, "the prosecution has had its turn. If Mr. Gates has a problem with Dr. Hudson's analysis, he can take it up on cross-examination."

"Overruled."

I restate my question. Dr. Hudson looks at the jury. She asks Judge Chen for permission to leave the witness box so she can point out various items. Then she uses her pointer to show exactly where Joel's fingerprints were found, carefully noting that only unidentifiable, smudged fingerprints were found on the trigger of the gun.

I hand her the gun, which is still wrapped in clear plastic. "Dr. Hudson," I say, "would you mind showing us exactly how you believe Mr. Friedman gripped this weapon in order to generate the fingerprints that you've described?"

"Objection. Speculative."

"Overruled."

Hudson holds the handle with her thumb, middle, ring and pinky, carefully avoiding contact with her index finger. She holds it up for the jury to see. "There," she says. "That's as close as I can get."

"What about your index finger?"

She carefully places her right index finger on the cylinder of the gun and holds it up again. "The index finger was on the cylinder."

"Could you explain why Mr. Friedman's index finger may have been on the cylinder?"

"Objection. Speculative."

"Sustained."

"I'll rephrase. Dr. Hudson, how do you open this revolver to unload it?"

"You press against the cylinder with your finger."

"And Mr. Friedman's right index fingerprint was found on the cylinder, was it not?"

"Yes."

"And if he was unloading the weapon, it would have been very likely that he would have gotten his fingerprint on the cylinder, right?"

"Objection. He's leading the witness."

"Overruled."

"Yes, Mr. Daley. Mr. Friedman's fingerprint was in a place that is consistent with the act of loading or unloading this weapon."

Good. "One final question, Dr. Hudson. Were any identifiable fingerprints found on the trigger of the gun?"

"No. There were unidentifiable smudged fingerprints on the trigger."

"So, in your opinion, is there any conclusive evidence that Mr. Friedman fired this weapon?"

"No."

"No further questions."

Skipper tries in vain for the next hour to trip her up. He's in a tough spot. He can't simply ask her if she thinks it's possible that Joel fired the gun. For one thing, she'll say there's no evidence that he did. For another, she can say anything's possible. Neither will help him. He tries to get her to admit that Joel could have left smudged fingerprints on the trigger when he shot the gun. She says there's no evidence to prove it. She holds her ground. Finally, he takes the same approach he took with Dr. Goldstein and asks her how much she's being paid for her testimony. This time, the bill is only fifteen thousand. Skipper sits down in frustration.

46

"YOU'RE THE HEAD COMPUTER GUY, RIGHT?"

"Daley's presentation has been a little wooden so far."
—NEWSCENTER 4 LEGAL ANALYST MORTON GOLDBERG.
TUESDAY, APRIL 7. NOON.

"How many more witnesses, Mr. Daley?" Judge Chen asks when we return from lunch.

Jesus, we've just started. "Two for sure, maybe three or four."

Skipper perks up.

"The defense calls Eric Ross," I say.

Whispering in the gallery. "Who's he?" Skipper looks at McNulty. They pore over our witness list. Ross has been head of information systems at S&G for five years. He's the head computer dweeb. Skipper never spoke to him. He probably never figured out how to turn on his computer.

Ross is sworn in. He's early thirties and uncommunicative. His eyes dart through thick wire-rimmed glasses. He's wearing his only suit for the first time in years. Somebody should inform him that wide lapels are out. His mustache twitches. He doesn't make eye contact.

"Mr. Ross, we've known each other for a while, right?"

"Objection. Relevance." Skipper is buying time.

"Overruled."

"We knew each other when you were at our firm," Ross says.

"Right. And could you please tell everyone what your job is at the firm?"

"Yes. I'm the head of information systems." His delivery is stiff.

"Right. The head of information systems. In layman's terms, what does that mean?"

"I'm in charge of firm-wide information and technology systems."

I nod melodramatically. "Firm-wide information and technology systems." I stroke my chin. "For those of us who are technologically challenged, that means you're the head computer guy, right?"

He's annoyed. How dare I not respect his two years of computer classes at Diablo Valley Junior College. I'm treating him like he's a TV repairman. "Yeah, I guess you could say that," he replies.

"As the head computer guy, are you in charge of keeping track of all the firm's computer stuff?"

He looks at the judge. "Computer stuff?"

"Yeah, you know—the hardware, the software—the computer stuff."

"Yeah." His irritation is showing. Just the reaction I want.

"Actually, I'm most concerned about the hardware. You know—the machines."

He hasn't the foggiest idea where I'm going. "Mr. Ross," I continue, "as the head computer guy, you're in charge of keeping track of all the equipment, right?"

"Yeah. That's right."

"And Simpson and Gates is a big firm, so you've got a big job, right?"

Skipper rises slowly. "Your Honor," he says sarcastically, "we're happy to stipulate that S and G is a large firm and Mr. Ross has a lot of computers to keep track of. What's the point?"

The judge says, "Overruled. I presume this is leading somewhere, Mr. Daley?"

"Yes, Your Honor. Mr. Ross, how many computers do you keep track of at S and G?"

"Firm-wide?"

"Yes. Firm-wide."

"You want an exact number?" he asks incredulously.

"Ballpark's fine."

He sits up a little taller. "I'd say about eighteen hundred."

"Eighteen hundred. Wow. That's a lot of computers, isn't it?"

Skipper stands. "Your Honor, please?"

She glares at me. "Mr. Daley."

"Yes, Your Honor." I just want to play with him for another question or two. "Now, of the eighteen hundred computers, how many of them have keyboards?"

"Keyboards?" He looks at me like I'm out of my mind.

"Yes, Mr. Ross. Those nifty detachable keyboards."

"All of them, of course." He may as well have added the words "you moron." "You can't use them without keyboards," he adds.

"That's what I figured. You're in charge of keeping track of the keyboards?"

I get the "you moron" look again. "Of course," he says.

"Okay. Now, do you keep a list of all the keyboards?"

"Basically, they're all the same. Some are a little newer than others."

"I understand. But do you make a list of all the people who have keyboards?"

He looks indignant. "As a matter of fact, I do. When a

new person comes to the firm, they're issued a computer and a keyboard."

"And do you keep a list of those computers and keyboards?"

"Yes." Then he pauses. "But . . ." He stops.

"Yes, Mr. Ross? Did you want to add something?"

He winces and takes a deep breath. "Well, sometimes people switch keyboards without telling me. Some of our keyboards are pretty old. The action is better on the new keyboards. They're faster."

Imagine. People taking each other's keyboards. What's the world coming to? "Is it a problem when people switch keyboards?" It's probably a felony in some jurisdictions.

"Not really. It just makes it more difficult to keep track of everything."

"I see. How often do you update the list?"

"Whenever a new keyboard is issued."

"And do you take an inventory of all the keyboards from time to time?"

"Once a year. We don't always get around to it. Sometimes we're too busy."

Too busy to count keyboards? Hard to believe. "When did you take the last inventory?"

"We just finished right before the end of the last year."

"That's great, Mr. Ross." I signal to Rosie, who hands me a thirty-page computer printout. I give copies to Skipper and Judge Chen. "Your Honor, the defense would like to have this keyboard inventory entered into evidence. This list was provided to Mr. Gates before the beginning of the trial." Along with eighteen boxes of Simpson and Gates records that we subpoenaed, but never had any intention of using.

Skipper and McNulty look at it. It's nothing more than a list of names and serial numbers.

Judge Chen turns to Skipper. "Any objection?"

Skipper looks at McNulty and shrugs. "I don't think so."

"Good," I say, as I hand the list to Ross. "Can you please tell us what this printout is?"

He tenses. "It's the inventory we took in December. How did you get a copy?"

Laughter in the courtroom. Judge Chen admonishes him not to ask questions.

"We have our ways," I say. It's nice to know all the time Wendy spent poring over mountains of S&G records was not in vain. "Can you tell us what's described in this list?"

"The first column has the serial number for each of our keyboards. The second column shows the first initial and last name of the employee to whom each keyboard is issued." It's in alphabetical order.

"Including attorneys?"

"Including attorneys."

"Can you please look at the serial number of the keyboard opposite the name JFRIEDMAN?"

"Sure."

"And would you please confirm that JFRIEDMAN refers to the defendant, Joel Friedman?"

"Yes. He's the only Friedman in the firm."

I'm sure he is. "Would you please read the serial number opposite his name?"

He studies it. "It's 7-1-4-5-8-1-1-2-6-3."

I walk over to a large flip chart that I've set up just for this little exercise. "Would you mind reading that number again?"

"Sure." He repeats it, and I write it in big block numbers on the flip chart.

I pause for a moment. I walk over to the evidence cart and pick up the keyboard found in Bob's office. It's wrapped in clear plastic. I walk back to Ross and hand it to him. "Mr. Ross," I say, "can you see through the plastic?"

"Yes."

"Good." I walk back to my flip chart. "Can you read the serial number on the back?"

"7-1-4-5-8-1-1-2-6-3."

I write each of the numbers on the flip chart directly below the identical numbers that are already there. The grandstand play seems to be working. I pause to look at the two rows of identical numbers on the flip chart. "Mr. Ross," I say, "are you aware that the keyboard you are holding was taken from the office of Robert Holmes on December thirty-first?"

Skipper's up. "Objection. The witness has no basis to answer that question."

"Mr. Daley," Judge Chen says, "perhaps you could rephrase?"

"Sure." I turn back to Ross. "Mr. Ross," I say, "would it surprise you to find out that the keyboard you're holding was found in the office of Mr. Holmes on December thirty-first?"

He looks helplessly at Skipper. "Uh, no, I didn't know that. I mean, yes, it would surprise me."

"Yet the keyboard you're holding is inventoried as the one belonging to Joel Friedman."

"Uh. Yes it is." His mustache twitches furiously.

"Well, how can you account for the fact that Mr. Friedman's keyboard was sitting in Mr. Holmes's office on the morning of December thirty-first?"

"Objection. Speculative."

"Sustained."

"I'll rephrase. Do you have any idea how Mr. Friedman's keyboard got into Mr. Holmes's office, Mr. Ross?" I realize I'm smiling.

"No, I don't."

"You didn't move it, did you?"

"No, sir. I didn't."

"Well it probably didn't get up and walk next door, now did it, Mr. Ross?"

"Objection."

"Sustained."

"No further questions."

Skipper confers with McNulty and approaches Ross. He hands Ross the inventory. "Mr. Ross," he says, "what is the date in the upper right-hand corner of the printout?"

"December first of last year."

"I see. Does that mean the inventory was conducted on December first of last year?"

"Not exactly. It means the inventory was completed on December first. It usually takes us a few days to check the serial numbers. And we have people in our other offices who do it there."

"I see. And was this inventory updated after December first?"

"No, sir. We have too many other important things to keep us busy."

I'll bet you do.

I see where Skipper's going. "So, Mr. Ross, this inventory means that on December first, the keyboard in your hands was sitting on Mr. Friedman's desk, right?"

"Right."

"And it could have been moved from Mr. Friedman's desk to Mr. Holmes's desk at any time after December first, right?"

I decide to slow down the train a little. "Objection. Speculative."

"Sustained."

"I'll rephrase. Do you have any way to account for the whereabouts of this keyboard after December first?"

"No, sir."

"No further questions."

I ask for a brief recess.

Joel, Rosie and I caucus in the consultation room. I look at Joel. "We may have a problem. There's a thirty-day window when the keyboard could have been moved from your office to Bob's."

Rosie says, "I say we go with what we've got, Mike. The jury probably already figures there's been some monkey business because Joel's keyboard ended up in Bob's office."

She's right. "I say we leave it where it is. The jury knows it was moved."

Joel looks troubled.

"I think we stop now," I say.

We return to the courtroom. I tell Judge Chen we will have no more questions for Ross.

"I'm inclined to adjourn for the day," she says. "How many more witnesses do you have?"

"Two or three. We should have the case in the hands of the jury by the end of the week."

I look over to Skipper. I'm hoping he'll spend all night preparing to cross-examine Joel.

Pete calls from the Bahamas that night. "They're expecting a storm in the morning," he says.

"Great. You and Wendy have any luck tracking down Trevor Smith?"

"He's back the day after tomorrow. See if you can stall until then."

Swell. "Time's getting short."

"I know."

47

NICK THE DICK

"A good dick can't be afraid to wear out a little shoe leather."
—PRIVATE INVESTIGATOR NICHOLAS HANSON.
SAN FRANCISCO CHRONICLE. WEDNESDAY, APRIL 8.

The next morning, at precisely nine-fifteen, I stand up and say in a clear voice, "Your Honor, the defense calls Nicholas Hanson."

The doors in the back of the courtroom open. Nick the Dick—all four feet ten of him—comes strutting down the center aisle. He's wearing a dark gray double-breasted Wilkes Bashford pinstripe with a burgundy tie. A matching kerchief sits in his breast pocket. A small red rose adorns his lapel. His three-thousand-dollar toupee has been carefully groomed. He nods to the press. He looks like the president walking down the center aisle in the House of Representatives just before the State of the Union speech.

The secret weapon just arrived.

The courtroom breaks out in a combination of laughter and chaos. Judge Chen bangs her gavel. I hear McNulty mutter, "For the love of God."

Joel leans over and whispers, "Is this for real?"

"The fun's about to start," I tell him. "I wish we were on Court TV."

Nick stops in front of the bench and acknowledges Judge Chen, like they're old friends. "Hello there, Your Honor," he says. "It's been a long time."

A very long time, indeed. They've never met.

She can't help herself and she smiles. "Hello, Mr. Hanson. I believe you're familiar with our procedures."

"Indeed I am, Your Honor." When Harriet Hill asks him if he swears to tell the truth, he replies, "Indeed I do." He climbs into the witness box and casually adjusts the microphone. He pours himself a glass of water and beams at the jury.

I've been waiting for this moment for weeks. I stand at the lectern. I let him bask in the spotlight. "Good morning, Mr. Hanson."

"Good morning, Mr. Daley," he replies cheerfully. He told me he'll be eighty-three on his next birthday. I should look so good.

"Would you please state your occupation for the record?"

"Yeah. I'm a private eye."

"How long have you been a private investigator, Mr. Hanson?"

He closes one eye and looks up, as if he's running an imaginary calculator in his head. "I've been doing this since I was seventeen." He nods. "I guess that means I've been doing this for almost sixty-six years."

"And you've been working in San Francisco the entire time?"

"Born and raised in the heart of North Beach. I played a little ball with the DiMaggio boys when we were kids." The accountant looks impressed. If Joe DiMaggio was the Yankee Clipper, maybe Nick was the San Francisco Dinghy.

"Mr. Hanson, did Elizabeth Holmes retain your services in the fall of last year?"

"Yeah." He talks out of the corner of his mouth, like Sean Connery.

"For what reason?"

"She wanted me to put a tail on her husband. She thought he was sleeping around."

Just the tone I was hoping for. Polished. Professional. Dignified.

"Were you able to determine whether Mr. Holmes was in fact having an extramarital affair?"

He turns to the jury. "Oh yeah." He nods for emphasis. "He was."

"And how were you able to make this determination?"

"How do you think? I followed him all over town."

The jurors are eating this up. "And you found him with another woman?"

"Indeed I did."

"Where was that?"

"In the woman's apartment at the Golden Gateway Commons."

"I see. And when was that?"

"On December first of last year."

Skipper stands up. He's seen enough. "Your Honor, I must object to this entire line of questioning. What possible relevance does this have to this case?"

"Your Honor," I say, "Mr. Hanson was retained to investigate the possibility that Mr. Holmes was having an affair. He has critical information concerning his social life in December of last year. The prosecution has suggested that Mr. Friedman acted in a jealous rage because Mr. Holmes had rekindled his relationship with Ms. Kennedy. As we're about to show you, Mr. Holmes had terminated his relationship with Ms. Kennedy in early December. By the end of

December, there was nothing for Mr. Friedman to be jealous about."

"Overruled."

Skipper is sorry he said anything. "Mr. Hanson," I continue, "are you sure he was having a sexual relationship with this woman?"

He reaches into his pocket. "I can show you some pictures, if you'd like."

Skipper leaps up. "Your Honor," he shouts.

Judge Chen turns to Nick. "That won't be necessary, Mr. Hanson."

He pouts. "I understand, Your Honor."

"Mr. Hanson," I continue, "were you able to identify the woman?"

He juts out his lower lip and nods at the jury. "Oh yes. It was Diana Kennedy."

"So, on December first, you saw Mr. Holmes and Ms. Kennedy engaging in sex at Ms. Kennedy's apartment?"

"Yeah." He shrugs. I don't expect him to blush.

"And you reported this to Mrs. Holmes?"

"Indeed I did."

"And what did she do?"

"She paid me."

Judge Chen beats back a smile.

"Didn't she also confront her husband with pictures you provided?" I ask.

"Yeah." He frowns. "I think she laid it on him pretty thick."

I'll bet she did. "And did Mrs. Holmes ask you to do anything else?"

"Yeah. She wanted to be sure he stayed on the wagon, if you know what I mean." He winks.

"I take it you mean that she wanted you to keep Mr. Holmes under surveillance to be sure that he didn't continue his relationship with Ms. Kennedy?"

"Yeah. Or anybody else, for that matter." He grins. "Except for Mrs. Holmes, of course."

"Of course. Mr. Hanson, did you continue to observe Mr. Holmes?"

"Yeah."

"Did he 'stay on the wagon,' as you've so eloquently put it?"

"Your Honor," Skipper says.

"Sit down, Mr. Gates," she replies.

Nick shakes his head. "No, Mr. Daley," he says. "Sadly, Mr. Holmes fell off the wagon."

More grins in the gallery. I can see how this guy writes mysteries in his spare time. "Oh, dear," I deadpan. "When exactly did he fall off the wagon, Mr. Hanson?"

"On December twenty-eighth."

"Would you mind telling us what happened?"

"Sure." He clears his throat. "Mrs. Holmes told me Mr. Holmes was going to attend a dinner at the Fairmont. On a couple of occasions, he'd met Ms. Kennedy there. He had a favorite room in the tower where they used to go for, uh, recreational purposes." He glances at the judge. "When I heard he was going to be at the Fairmont, I got a room across the street at the Mark Hopkins. It had a direct view into the room where Mr. Holmes liked to hang out. I ordered room service, set up my telescope and telephoto camera, and waited. At eleven-forty-five, he came back to the room with a woman. It was hard to tell what was going on because it was dark."

"But you could see that Mr. Holmes was in the room with a woman."

"Oh yeah."

"And you're sure the woman was not Mrs. Holmes?"

"I'm sure about that. I was talking to Mrs. Holmes on my cellular phone the entire time. She wasn't very happy about it."

"What were Mr. Holmes and the woman doing in the hotel room?"

He looks at the judge. "Am I allowed to say this in court, Your Honor?" he asks innocently.

"Please be discreet," she says. "But you must be truthful, of course."

"Of course, Your Honor." He shrugs and looks at me. "For lack of a better term, Mr. Daley, Mr. Holmes and the woman were engaging in oral sex."

I stand at the lectern. I try not to move a muscle until the roar dies down. Judge Chen pounds her gavel. Skipper shouts his objections. I look at the jurors. They're all smiling.

Judge Chen points her gavel at me and says, "Mr. Daley, you've made your point. Can we move along, please?"

"Yes, Your Honor." I turn back to Nick. "Mr. Hanson, were you able to identify the woman in the room with Mr. Holmes?"

"No. Like I said, it was pretty dark. She left quickly. I ran across the street to try to identify her, but by the time I got up the elevators, she had already left."

Somehow, I have trouble imagining Nick running anywhere. "Can you describe the woman?"

"Yes. Young. Slender. Long hair."

"Long hair?"

"Yes. I'm sure."

"Mr. Hanson, you're aware that Diana Kennedy had short hair, aren't you?"

"Indeed I am."

"So, what did you conclude?"

"I concluded the woman in the room was not Diana Kennedy."

I glance at Rosie. "Mr. Hanson, did Mrs. Holmes ask you to follow Mr. Holmes during the entire month of December last year?"

"Yeah. I was on him like a glove."

"And from December first through December twenty-eighth, did you ever see Mr. Holmes and Ms. Kennedy together, other than at work?"

"No."

"Did you take any nights off during that period?"

"No. For what Mrs. Holmes was paying me, I would have stayed up for six months straight."

"And you never saw Mr. Holmes and Ms. Kennedy together?"

"Objection, Your Honor," Skipper says wearily. "Asked and answered."

"Sustained."

"No further questions."

Skipper's cross-examination ends quickly. First, he questions Nick's eyesight. It's twenty-fifteen. He questions how Nick could have been able to determine that Bob and the woman were having oral sex in a dark room. Nick replies that he has a very powerful telephoto lens and offers to describe their every move in intimate detail. Skipper decides not to pursue it. He questions Nick's stamina. He suggests that an eighty-two-year-old man may not be able to stay up all night watching Bob Holmes for an entire month. This irritates the retired bus driver on the jury. Nick explains that he and his three sons and four grandsons work in shifts. Unbeknownst to Bob Holmes, there was a set of Hanson eyes on him virtually every waking moment in the month of December. Another set of Hanson eyes chased Diana Kennedy. Skipper sits down. He knows the jury is entranced with this diminutive PI. After five minutes, Nick marches triumphantly down the center aisle and out of the courtroom. As soon as he's out the door, Judge Chen turns to me and says, "This might be a good time for a short break."

Rosie and Joel are all smiles in the consultation room. "Cherish the moment," Rosie says. "You may never get a chance to examine him again."

Joel shakes his head. "I wouldn't have believed it if I hadn't seen it with my own eyes."

"We've got some good momentum now," I say. "Let's keep pushing."

48

"TOEING THE PARTY LINE"

"Defense attorney Michael Daley is expected to call several witnesses who were at the Simpson and Gates offices on the night two attorneys died."

—NEWSCENTER 4 LEGAL ANALYST MORTON GOLDBERG.
WEDNESDAY, APRIL 8.

Jeff Tucker slithers to the stand after lunch. I stand right in front of him. "You used to work at the Simpson and Gates firm, didn't you, Mr. Tucker?"

"Yes. Currently, I am general counsel of First Bank."

"I see. And was your bank involved in the sale of Russo International that was supposed to close on December thirty-first?"

"Yes. We were one of Mr. Russo's lenders."

"Were you going to have a continuing relationship with Mr. Russo's company?"

"No. Our loans were being paid off. We were delighted with the result."

"Mr. Tucker, you visited with Mr. Russo at Simpson and Gates in the early evening of December thirtieth, didn't you?"

"Yes. My superiors asked me to check on the deal. I had no reason to believe it wasn't going to close."

"Did Mr. Russo appear upset to you?"

This prompts a grin. "Mr. Russo always appeared upset to me. He was particularly nervous that night."

"Was he happy about the deal?"

"No. He wanted to keep his company. He thought he could manage it back to profitability."

"So, Mr. Russo didn't really want to close the deal."

"I didn't say that."

"Let's not argue about semantics, Mr. Tucker. Isn't it fair to say that Mr. Russo was unhappy about selling his father's company and that you had doubts as to whether the deal would close?"

"That's fair."

That pretty much covers it. "Mr. Tucker, did you talk to Mr. Holmes about the deal that night?"

"Briefly. He was very agitated. He said he couldn't predict what Vince Russo would do."

"It's possible that Russo pulled the plug before he disappeared, isn't it?"

"Yes."

"And it's even possible Russo killed Bob Holmes and Diana Kennedy, isn't it?"

"Objection. Speculative. No foundation."

"Sustained."

"No further questions." I've made my point.

The parade continues throughout the afternoon. Ed Ehrlich swears that the deal was going to close. He assures us the city was 100 percent behind the deal.

Dan Morris is even more reassuring than Ehrlich. And far more polished. Morris tells us he was certain that the deal was going to close. "The only way it wouldn't have closed," he says, "was if Vince Russo changed his mind."

"Is it possible that he did so?"

"Anything's possible, Mr. Daley."

That's as far as I get before Judge Chen sustains Skipper's objection.

The afternoon concludes with testimony from Jack Frazier, who agrees with everyone who preceded him that Russo was going to close the deal, come hell or high water.

"Mr. Frazier," I say, "isn't it true that you negotiated a forty-million-dollar reduction in the purchase price at the last minute?"

"Yes."

"And wasn't Mr. Russo quite upset about it?"

Frazier looks at his attorney, Martin Glass, who is sitting in the gallery. "Yes," he replies. "He was quite upset. At one point, he stormed out of the conference room. He made quite a scene. He interrupted a cocktail party for Mr. Gates." He nods sheepishly at Skipper, whose face is impassive.

"So it's possible Mr. Russo may have been so upset he decided to terminate the deal?"

He shakes his head. "I'm not sure. I mean, I guess so. But the fact is, I really don't know. He seemed ready to close the last time I saw him."

"And when was that?"

"Around one o'clock."

"And what time did you leave?"

"Around one-thirty-five. Mr. Morris and I left together. We were talking about business."

"Where did you and Mr. Morris go?"

"We went home."

There's nothing more that I can do. "No further questions, Your Honor."

———

Joel is beside himself in the consultation room at the end of the day. The trial is nearing its conclusion and he is wearing down. "I thought the idea was to make them believe it was a suicide," he says. "If that doesn't work, I thought we were going to blame Russo. Why are you fucking around?"

I'm exhausted. My patience is short. "All we can do with these witnesses is to ask them to speculate about what happened that night. The other side has the right to object. We have to do everything indirectly. We can't just ask them if they think Bob committed suicide. We have to give them a bunch of reasons why Bob would have been suicidal. I think we've shown the jury that Bob had a lot on his mind: a divorce, a deal that was going to implode, a girlfriend who was leaving him and a bonus that he wasn't going to get. That's as far as we can go."

Rosie interjects in a calmer tone, "We have the same problem with Russo. Nobody saw him do anything. His fingerprints weren't on the gun. There's no evidence connecting him to the scene. All we can do is show he had opportunity and perhaps a lot of motive. That may be enough to get us to reasonable doubt and get an acquittal."

Joel slumps back into his chair. He stares at the gray steel table. He chews on his lower lip. "That's really all we're trying to do at this point, isn't it? We're trying to punch holes in their case to generate enough doubt in enough members of the jury to get me off."

He's hit the nail right on the head.

"I want to testify," he says emphatically. "I want to set the record straight once and for all."

Rosie and I look at each other. "Let's see how things go in the next few days," I say gently. "We don't have to make a decision until we've finished with the other witnesses."

———

Rosie and I sit in her office at eight o'clock the same evening. She's finishing her cashew chicken. I'm drinking a Diet Dr Pepper. I'm just not hungry these days.

"You think Joel is starting to crack?" she asks.

"Maybe. Yeah. Probably." Time for a reality check. "You think we've got enough for reasonable doubt?"

She ponders for a moment. "Hard to say. If you're on the jury, you're looking at a guy who's an admitted adulterer who's lied about his relationship with the victim. They've heard enough to conclude she dumped him. They know he was really pissed off at Bob. They may even decide that Bob stole his girlfriend. His fingerprints were all over the murder weapon and the keyboard. He left a threatening voice mail for Bob and he made a threatening phone call to Diana. He had a fight with her at Harrington's. He may have even lured her in. All we've shown so far is that they couldn't positively identify his fingerprint on the trigger. And that his keyboard somehow walked from his office to Bob's."

"But our experts were good," I say. "They made a decent case for the suicide theory."

"Our experts were expensive hired guns who were paid to say what we wanted them to say. The jury knows that. They'll discount their testimony."

She's right, of course.

The phone rings. Rosie puts Wendy on the speaker. "It's pouring in Nassau," she says.

"Have you been able to talk to Trevor Smith yet?"

"Not yet. Delayed again. He won't be back until Sunday. We'll be waiting for him." She pauses. "Have you put Chuckles on the stand yet?"

"Not yet. Why?"

"I was looking through the correspondence I got from Smith's secretary. And I went down to the office of public records. I'm going to fax some stuff to you."

We talk for a few minutes and I hang up. I stand and put on my jacket.

"You going home?" Rosie asks.

"Not yet."

"Where are you going?"

"To play a hunch."

49

"IT JUST GOES TO SHOW WHAT
A LITTLE PLANNING CAN DO"

"The Guilford Insurance Agency. Life. Health. Peace of
Mind."

—BROCHURE FOR THE GUILFORD INSURANCE AGENCY.

My hunch pays off. At nine o'clock the same evening, I'm
paying a visit to the darkened offices of Perry Guilford,
S&G's insurance agent. His office is in a high-rise building
on Market near Van Ness, a few blocks from City Hall. Most
of the tenants in this building are state and local government agencies. The Guilford Insurance Agency occupies
half of the third floor. The walk from the Civic Center
underground parking garage through the homeless encamp-
ment on the Civic Center Plaza was treacherous. The streets
are mean in this part of town, especially after dark.
Guilford's reception area has lots of brochures on variable
annuities. They promise life, health and peace of mind.

"Mr. Guilford, I'm Mike Daley."

Guilford and I are the only people here. "Please, Mr.
Daley," he rasps, "it's Perry." Incandescent smile. His age
and waistline are right around fifty-five years and inches,

respectively. His jowls measure right up there with Art Patton's, who is, coincidentally, his former brother-in-law from Guilford's first marriage about twenty years ago. His toupee is flattering in a pathetic sort of way.

"Fair enough, Perry. It's Mike." His cuff links are in the shape of gold cigars. His jowls jiggle. His red suspenders shake. "I appreciate your taking the time to see me. I know it's late."

He laughs. "I'm sorry I've been hard to get hold of. I have a lot of evening appointments. Make yourself at home. Brent Hutchinson said you'd be calling. Anything I can do to help a member of the firm. Anything." He pats his ample gut and takes a gulp of Coke Classic. My arteries are beginning to harden just looking at this guy.

"Actually, Perry, I left the firm at the end of last year. I've started my own shop. I was hoping you could help me get my insurance situation squared away."

He's pleased. Fresh meat. "Great, Mike. That's just great. Anything I can do to help you. You know I handle all the insurance for S and G. It's my biggest account. I handle a couple of the other big law firms in town, too. I'm sure I can take care of you."

"That's great, Perry. Let me tell you what I have in mind." We spend forty-five minutes discussing my insurance needs. I tell him I've purchased malpractice insurance through the state bar and ask him if he can get a better deal. I tell him about Grace and he describes various whole life policies. I haven't a clue what he's talking about. I figure if I let him talk, he may wear himself out.

At the one-hour mark, he's starting to slow down. We're already on our third diagram. Insurance agents can't sell anything without drawing pictures. The last one looks like a basketball court, with a half-court line and two free-throw lines. I'm lost when we start on variable annuities.

An hour and fifteen minutes into this torture, I ask him

to prepare a written estimate of everything we've talked about. After he reminds me for the sixth time that he isn't in insurance just for the money, I decide it's time to see if I can get any useful information. "Helluva thing over at the Simpson firm, eh, Perry?"

"Unbelievable, Mike. Helluva thing. Were you there that night?"

"Yeah. Helluva thing."

"You know, they'd really be in the soup if they hadn't planned ahead." He shuffles his papers. "It's a good thing they had life insurance on Bob Holmes."

"It just goes to show what a little planning can do, right Perry?"

"You bet. That's why you need to plan now, Mike. You want to take good care of little Mary if anything ever happens to you."

"Actually, my daughter's name is Grace."

He doesn't miss a beat. "That's right. Grace. Five years old."

Close enough. "Did you handle all of Bob's life insurance?"

"Yeah. And between us girls, it's a damn good thing I did. I talked him into buying some extra coverage. Didn't cost much. Got his wife a five-million term policy, and each of the kids got a million. They're set for life." He frowns melodramatically. "I was talking to Art about it. Helluva thing."

"Yeah. And it was a damn good thing you got the firm to take down those key-man life insurance policies. Hell, without those, they'd really be in the soup."

"No shit. Art was telling me you guys were going to get a big fat fee for Vince Russo's deal. Now, he says you guys may not get anything. Helluva thing."

"Looks that way, Perry. Maybe I should take down some more life insurance. How much was the firm carrying on Bob?"

He smiles. "They were carrying two and a half million until December. Lucky for them, I talked them into taking down a big term policy on some of the heavy hitters right before all the excitement. The policy on Bob went effective only a couple weeks before the end of the year. Art knew about it."

Hello? "Yeah, Perry. Sure is a good thing they got that big policy in place when they did. Do you recall how much the policy was for?"

He laughs. "Hell, you should know. It was a big, fucking deal, Mike. The damn thing's worth twenty fucking million. Biggest fucking policy I've ever sold. Art says it's going to save his ass."

Twenty fucking million dollars? Jesus. "Perry, another client of mine was asking about key-man insurance. Do you have a copy of the key-man policy on Bob?"

"If my secretary were here, I'd be able to pull it up for you. I'm lost without her."

"Maybe you can messenger it to me in the morning? The client's in sort of a hurry."

Big smile. "Sure, Mike. First thing."

I give him my business card. "Perry, how soon can you get those quotes to me?"

"End of the week sound all right?"

"Sounds great to me."

"There was a twenty-million-dollar life insurance policy on Bob?" Rosie asks. There's something wildly erotic about talking life insurance with a naked woman. I've stopped by her house for a meeting on the way home a little after midnight. Grace is asleep. Dave Brubeck's on the stereo. She rubs my back with her long, thin hands.

"Yeah. Twenty million bucks. It all goes to the firm." I

turn over and kiss her ear. "Does any of this strike you as a little odd?"

"How's that?"

"I'm not sure. Something just doesn't feel right."

She runs her fingers through my hair. "Maybe this will feel better," she says.

50

"EXACTLY WHAT DOES THE ADMINISTRATIVE PARTNER DO?"

"Friedman Defense Grasping at Straws."
—*SAN FRANCISCO LEGAL JOURNAL.* THURSDAY, APRIL 9.

The next morning, Chuckles sits uncomfortably on the witness stand, gulping water. "Exactly what does the administrative partner do at a large law firm?" I ask.

He gives me a sour look. "The administrative partner handles all aspects of day-to-day operations." He gestures with his reading glasses. "Finances. Personnel. Facilities. Computers."

"Sort of the glue that holds the firm together as an institution?"

He almost smiles. "Why, yes."

"And how many years have you served as administrative partner?"

"Eleven," he says proudly. He sits up. "I sit on the executive committee, too."

I glance at the accountant, who nods with admiration.

"Could you please tell us about the current financial situation at the firm?"

"Objection," Skipper sings out. "Relevance."

"Overruled."

"Your Honor," Chuckles pleads, "this information is highly confidential."

She glares at him. "I don't expect you to reveal the details of how much money each of your partners makes. Answer the question."

"We have filed for bankruptcy protection," he acknowledges. "We are in the process of reorganizing our finances and negotiating with our creditors." He arches an eyebrow, as if to say, "Are you happy, now?"

"Thank you, Mr. Stern," I say. I leave out, "You condescending ass." I look at Rosie, who gives me the "cheap shot" scowl. I add, "I'm sure it hasn't been easy." I pause. "Mr. Stern, you were at the Simpson and Gates offices on the night of December thirtieth, weren't you?"

"Yes."

"What time did you go home that night?"

"About two in the morning."

"And when was the last time you saw Mr. Holmes?"

"About twelve-thirty."

"After twelve-thirty, did you see Mr. Friedman together with Mr. Holmes or Ms. Kennedy?"

"No."

I bore in. "Did you see anyone else there that night?" Let's see who he's willing to implicate.

He pauses and looks at the clock. Then he rattles off the names of Vince Russo, Art Patton, Ed Ehrlich, Dan Morris, Jack Frazier and Martin Glass. "Of course," he says, "I don't believe any of them had anything to do with the tragedy."

Of course not. "Anybody else?"

He purses his lips. "Not that I can think of."

"Mr. Stern," I say, "you didn't perhaps see Mr. Gates at the office that night, did you?"

His eyes dart toward Skipper. "Why, yes. We had a reception for him. It was his last day at the firm." I see the accountant frown.

"But did you see him later that evening? After the reception had ended?"

He looks helplessly at Skipper. "I saw Mr. Gates at about one o'clock in the morning. He was in our suite for a few minutes."

I walk over to the evidence cart and pick up a copy of Bob's will. "Mr. Stern," I say as I hand it to him, "do you recognize this document?"

"Yes. It's the will of Mr. Holmes. I prepared it. It is a matter of public record."

"Mr. Stern, would you mind turning to page thirty-four?"

He puts on the reading glasses. He flips to the correct page.

"Would you mind telling us the names of the beneficiaries of the will?"

He glares at me over the top of the reading glasses. "I'll have to refresh my memory."

Bullshit. You can recite all eighty-nine pages by heart. "Take your time, Mr. Stern."

He pores over the entire will, pausing briefly to lick his index finger to turn the pages. Finally, he says a third went to Beth, a third to the kids and a third to the International Charitable Trust. He takes off his reading glasses and puts them back into his pocket.

"Mr. Stern, you're aware Mr. Holmes was served with divorce papers on December thirtieth."

"Yes."

"Did Mr. Holmes ever ask you to prepare an amendment to this will to change the beneficiaries?"

His eyes dart momentarily. "No," he says.

Rosie hands me three copies of a document. I hand one to Skipper, one to the judge and one to Stern. "Your Honor," I say, "we'd like to introduce this document into evidence."

"Any objections, Mr. Gates?"

He's trying to speed-read. "I don't think so, Your Honor."

I turn back to Stern. "Do you recognize this document, Mr. Stern?"

He studies it. "Yes." He takes a drink of water. "It's a draft of an amendment to the will."

"Really?" I'm trying for biting sarcasm. "And did you prepare this amendment?"

"No. One of my associates prepared it."

"And did she do so at your instruction?"

"Yes."

"And which associate was it that prepared this document?"

"I believe it was Ms. Wendy Hogan."

"I see." You'd never believe what may turn up in somebody's files when she leaves the firm. "And could you please tell us what this amendment purports to change in the will of Mr. Holmes?"

His shoulders slump. "It was intended to change the beneficiaries of the will."

"Really?" I scowl melodramatically. "When was this amendment prepared, Mr. Stern?"

"In December of last year, I believe."

"Why do you suppose Mr. Holmes asked you to prepare this amendment?"

"Presumably because he intended to change the beneficiaries of his will."

I get right in his face. "Did he tell you who the new beneficiaries were going to be?"

"No."

"Any hints?"

"Objection. Speculative."

"Sustained."

"Did he tell you which of the beneficiaries were going to be replaced?"

"Yes. His wife."

"But if he proceeded in the manner that you've suggested, Mrs. Holmes stood to lose a substantial sum of money on the death of Mr. Holmes."

"Yes, she did."

I shift focus. "Could you please tell us what you know about the International Charitable Trust, Mr. Stern?"

He grimaces. "It's a charity organized in the Bahamas by Mr. Holmes."

"It does good things for mankind?"

"Yes."

"What sorts of good things?"

"The annual income of the trust is donated to various charitable causes. Schools, day-care centers, community centers, that sort of thing."

Prostitutes, drug dealers, that sort of thing, too. "And the charities that receive funding every year are called the income beneficiaries, right?"

"Yes."

"And the same income beneficiaries will divide the trust assets upon the death of Mr. Holmes, right?"

"No. Upon the death of Mr. Holmes, the remaining assets, or corpus, of the trust are divided among various designated individuals called the remaindermen."

"Could you tell us which charities received the most money last year?"

"I don't recall."

"Schools? Day-care centers? Community centers?"

"I'm not sure."

"Could you tell us the names of the remaindermen?"

"I'm afraid I don't know. That information was confidential. The trustee in the Bahamas was the only person who knew the names of the remaindermen."

"Mr. Stern, did you assist in setting up the trust?"

"Yes."

"Yet, you don't know the names of the income beneficiaries or the remaindermen?"

"That's true."

That's bullshit. "Why did you choose to set up the trust in the Bahamas?"

"Mr. Holmes enjoyed vacationing there. He became very involved in various causes over the years. Ultimately, he wanted to retire there. And, to be perfectly honest, the tax laws were favorable."

The accountant perks up. The lawyers look at each other.

"When you set up the trust, I'm sure you investigated the income beneficiaries very carefully, right?"

"Actually, the trust administrator in the Bahamas handled it," he replies. "I'm not involved in the day-to-day management."

He's tap-dancing around my questions. "I see." Rosie hands me another document. It has the seal of the Commonwealth of the Bahamas at the top. I hand copies to Skipper, the judge and Stern. I ask that it be introduced into evidence. Skipper doesn't object. "Mr. Stern," I say, "do you recognize this document?"

"Yes. It's the charter for the trust. It sets forth the rules for the governance of the trust. It names First Bank Bahamas as the sole trustee."

"It also names the income beneficiaries and the remaindermen, doesn't it?" I'm setting him up. I know the names of the income beneficiaries and the remaindermen are set forth in a confidential addendum which I've not yet seen.

"Well, no. That information is in a separate document. It's confidential."

"And do you now recall the names of the income beneficiaries and the remaindermen?"

"As I said before, I don't know."

Sure. "There are two individuals who serve as the so-called trust protectors, aren't there?"

"Yes. The trust protectors have the authority to take action on behalf of the trust and change the trustee. The trust protectors are Mr. Holmes and myself."

Now, we're getting somewhere. "As trust protector, Mr. Stern, I presume you would know the names of the income beneficiaries and the remaindermen of the trust?"

"I'm afraid not, Mr. Daley. As I said, that information is in a separate document. Under the laws of the Bahamas, it's confidential. I don't know."

Liar. "You mean to tell us the trust protector doesn't know who gets the money when Mr. Holmes died?"

"That's true. It was all handled in the Bahamas."

"So though you are the attorney who helped set this thing up, you don't know who gets the money?"

"Objection. Asked and answered."

"Sustained."

I glare at Stern. "Did you get a fee for acting as trust protector, Mr. Stern?"

"Yes."

"How much?"

"Objection. Relevance."

"It is relevant, Your Honor. Unless Mr. Stern wants to tell us that he doesn't know how big his fee is, either."

"That's enough, Mr. Daley. The objection is overruled. Answer the question, Mr. Stern."

"It depends," he says.

"On what?"

"On the value of the assets in the trust at any given time."

"You get a percentage of the value of the assets?"

"Yes."

"What percentage?"

"Your Honor," he implores. "This is highly confidential information."

"Answer the question, Mr. Stern, or I'll hold you in contempt."

"Five percent," he grumbles.

"Now, Mr. Stern, how much was your fee last year?"

He looks at the judge. She stares him down. "About four hundred fifty thousand dollars."

"Four hundred fifty thousand?" I repeat loudly. "If my high-school arithmetic is correct, this means the trust had about ten million dollars' worth of assets. Is that about right, Mr. Stern?"

"Yes," he says. "That's about right."

"Your Honor," Skipper says, "this is all very interesting. But I fail to see the relevance."

She turns to me. "Mr. Daley, are we going to see a point to this anytime soon?"

"Yes." Here goes. "Mr. Stern, isn't it a fact Mr. Holmes was unhappy about your fee?"

"I don't know what you're talking about, Mr. Daley."

"Let me be more specific. Isn't it a fact Mr. Holmes thought your fee was excessive?"

"No."

I turn to Rosie, who hands me three copies of a letter. I hand one copy to the judge, one to Skipper and the other to Stern. I introduce it into evidence. "Do you recognize this letter, Mr. Stern?"

"I don't recall."

"Let me refresh your memory. It's a letter dated September third of last year addressed to a Mr. Trevor Smith at First

Bank in the Bahamas. As you'll see, you were copied on this letter."

He studies it and shrugs.

"Would you please read the sentence I've highlighted, Mr. Stern?"

On go the reading glasses. " 'I believe that the fees paid to the trust protector are extravagantly high. I would like to terminate the services of Mr. Stern at the end of this year.' "

"Who signed the letter?"

He takes off the reading glasses and exhales. "Mr. Holmes."

"It appears that Mr. Holmes wanted to fire you. Isn't that about right?"

He clears his throat. "From time to time, he expressed some reservations about the amount of my fee. I don't believe he intended to implement the terms of this letter."

"You mean you don't think he would have fired you?"

"No. The trust was in place for many years. But he certainly could have done so if he wanted to."

I glance at the jury. I turn back to Chuckles. "What happens to your fee now?"

"It is paid until the trust is liquidated."

"When is that supposed to happen?"

"It will probably take two or three years."

"So, at half a million a year, the death of Mr. Holmes will result in your receiving an additional million or million and a half dollars. Isn't that right, Mr. Stern?"

"I have no choice, Mr. Daley. I have a contractual obligation to act as trust protector. When the trust was put in place, my fees were tiny. Over the years, the assets in the trust have grown considerably. It's not my fault that it turned into a very favorable contract for me."

"And if Mr. Holmes had lived, he would have terminated your deal, and you would have lost out on another million and a half dollars."

"As I said, Mr. Daley, I don't believe he intended to terminate my services."

Bullshit. "That's terribly convenient, isn't it, Mr. Stern?"

"Objection."

"Sustained."

Rosie hands me a thick legal-size document. I hand it to Chuckles. "Mr. Stern," I say, "you're familiar with this life insurance policy, aren't you?"

He puts on his reading glasses and glances at it. "Yes."

"It's what's called a key-man life insurance policy, isn't it?"

"Yes."

"It was taken out by the Simpson and Gates firm, wasn't it?"

"Yes."

"And the firm paid all the premiums, right?"

He looks over the top of his glasses. "Yes. That's how key-man insurance works. A business such as ours buys life insurance policies on the lives of important members of the firm. In our case, we took down this policy on the life of Bob Holmes. We had similar policies for all of our partners."

"I see. And would you mind telling us how much this policy was worth to the firm?" I've set the trap. At least I hope so.

He looks at Skipper. "Two and a half million dollars."

I pause. "Mr. Stern," I say, "I believe you've misread the policy value. Would you mind looking at the policy again?"

He flips open the policy. He adjusts his reading glasses. He stops stone cold. He takes off the reading glasses and looks at me.

"Mr. Stern? Would you mind telling us how much the policy was worth?"

Our eyes meet. "Twenty million dollars," he says quietly.

"Twenty million dollars," I repeat. "That's a lot of

money, isn't it? That's even more money than Bob Holmes had in that hokey trust you set up for him in the Bahamas."

"Objection."

"Sustained. Let's stop the editorial comments right now, Mr. Daley."

I don't stop. "Mr. Stern, if the firm had a twenty-million-dollar policy on Mr. Holmes, how come it had to file for bankruptcy protection?"

"The insurance company hasn't paid us yet. These things take time, Mr. Daley."

"And then all of the firm's financial difficulties will be worked out?"

"We think so, Mr. Daley."

"When was this policy issued, Mr. Stern?"

He puts on his reading glasses and glances at the cover page of the policy. "December fifteenth of last year."

"Mr. Stern," I say, "you've read this policy pretty carefully, haven't you? You were a partner in a big law firm, after all. So you read the fine print, right?"

There's only one possible answer. "Yes, Mr. Daley."

"Would you please turn to page six of the policy?"

He shuffles through the first pages. "Yes, Mr. Daley."

"Would you please read the heading on page six?"

" 'General Provisions.' "

I turn and face the jury. Without looking at Stern, I say, "Would you please read the title of the fifth paragraph in the right column of page six?"

" 'Ownership and Control.' "

I'm still looking at the jury when I interrupt him. "No, Mr. Stern. The following paragraph. It's entitled 'Suicide Exclusion.' "

His voice is barely a whisper. " 'If the Insured, whether sane or insane, dies by suicide within two years from the issue date, we will pay no more under this contract than the sum of the premiums paid, minus any contract debt and minus any partial withdrawals.' "

I turn and face Chuckles. "Mr. Stern, that section contains what is customarily known as a suicide clause, doesn't it?"

"Objection. Foundation. Mr. Stern isn't qualified as an expert on insurance."

"Overruled."

"It's a suicide clause," Stern says.

"And in layman's terms, what does it mean?"

"If the insured commits suicide within the first two years, the insurer doesn't have to pay."

"And, if it was determined Mr. Holmes committed suicide, what would it mean for the firm?"

"We wouldn't get the twenty million dollars."

I turn back to the jury. "Just so we're all perfectly clear on this, Mr. Stern, if the death of Mr. Holmes is determined to be a suicide, you guys will lose the twenty-million-dollar insurance payment."

"That's right," he says. His lips barely move.

"You might say the firm has twenty million reasons to hope the death of Mr. Holmes is not declared a suicide."

"Objection."

"Sustained." Judge Chen points her gavel at me. "I've already warned you about grandstanding in my courtroom, Mr. Daley."

I've gone far beyond the bounds. "No further questions." Thanks, Perry. I'll buy a million bucks of life insurance from you.

Skipper practically leaps out of his seat. First things first. Stern has placed Skipper at the scene that night. He must clear his name before he starts his cross-examination. It's as I had hoped. He's distracted. His reputation is on the line.

"Isn't it true that you saw me at the Simpson and Gates office at around one o'clock that night?"

"Yes."

"And we had a brief conversation, didn't we?"

"Yes."

"And I told you that I had returned to the office to pick up my briefcase, right?"

"Objection, Your Honor. Hearsay. Mr. Stern cannot testify as to what Mr. Gates said. If Mr. Gates wants to testify about what he said, we're perfectly happy to permit him to do so."

She can't resist a grin at Skipper. "Sustained."

Skipper gathers himself. "Mr. Stern, did you see me leaving the office with my briefcase?"

"Yes."

"Did I say anything to you?"

"Objection, Your Honor. Hearsay."

"Sustained."

Skipper frowns. This isn't going very well. "Mr. Stern, do you have any reason to believe that I was in the office for any purpose other than to collect my briefcase?"

"Objection. Speculative."

"Sustained." She certainly can't be faulted for going easy on him.

Skipper spends five minutes asking Chuckles perfunctory questions about the insurance policy and the firm's financial condition. Chuckles swears that the firm is in solid financial shape and doesn't need the proceeds from the policy to survive. He's unconvincing. The damage is already done.

We're back in my office at eight o'clock the same night. "You don't think it was Stern, do you?" Rosie asks.

"I don't know. I'd say he had about a million of his own

reasons to do it. And the firm had about twenty million reasons for him to do it." His memory lapses about the insurance policies and the trust made him look like a lying ass in front of the jury. I can understand his desire to keep the terms of Bob's trust confidential, but his testimony on the insurance policy was odd.

The phone rings. It's Pete. I tell him about our day in court.

"Listen," he says, "somebody wants to talk to you." The phone goes silent for a moment.

I punch the speaker button so Rosie can hear. A nasal male voice shrieks, "Who the hell is this?"

"Who the hell is *this*?" I bark back.

"Vince Russo. Who the hell are you? And tell this goon to let me go."

The line goes quiet. My mind races. A moment later, I hear Wendy's voice. "You'll never guess who we found down at the bank today."

"Elvis Presley?"

"Close." I can hear the smile in her voice. "We ran into Vince at Trevor Smith's office. I guess he decided to come down here to visit his money. Pete and I followed him back to his hotel. He's got a little cottage at the Graycliff. It's really very nice."

Indeed. The finest hotel in Nassau.

"Anyway," she continues, "it's a little tough finding a room down here, so Pete and I decided to bunk with Vince. He was just telling us all about his trip."

Jesus. "Wendy, listen to me. Don't hurt him. What you're doing may be somewhat illegal."

"Don't worry. We ordered room service. The foie gras is delightful. Pete takes off the handcuffs when he has to eat or pee. We offered to call the cops. Seems Vince is a little nervous about that. It kind of fouls up the part of his story where he wanted everyone to think he committed suicide."

Fabulous. Either we've just got the biggest break in the case or we're all going to jail. "You guys going to be there for a while?"

"Of course. We just ordered champagne." I hear a cork pop and she says thank you to Pete. "Say, Mike," she says, "are you doing anything this weekend?"

"I think I may need to take a little trip. The stress is getting to me."

"Anyplace in particular?"

"I understand the Bahamas are nice this time of year."

"Our cottage is called Yellow Bird. Tell the concierge you're with Mr. Kramer's party."

"Are they getting suspicious?"

"Probably. We told them we aren't to be disturbed."

"I'll be there as soon as I can."

I hang up. I look at Rosie. "I need you to go to Judge Chen tomorrow and tell her I was called out of town on an emergency. See if you can get her to put things off until Monday."

"What do you want me to tell her if she asks me what the emergency is?"

"Just tell her something came up."

At nine o'clock that night I'm on the phone. "Roosevelt," I say, "I need your help."

"I'm not supposed to be talking to you, Mike." He chuckles. "So, what do you need?"

"Got any plans for the weekend?"

"The usual."

"How would you feel about an all-expense-paid trip to the Bahamas?"

"Sounds pretty good to me."

51

"TECHNICALLY, YOU'RE DEAD"

"With long beaches, friendly people and perfect weather, the
Bahamas have been a tourist mecca for over two hundred
years."

—BAHAMAS TRAVEL BROCHURE

Fourteen hours later, at two o'clock in the afternoon
Bahamas time, Roosevelt and I get out of a cab in front of
the Graycliff, the dignified three-story Georgian colonial
mansion across the street from the Government House in
Nassau. No matter where I go, it seems to be raining. Our
connecting flights through Chicago and Miami were late,
and we flew through a hailstorm to reach the modern airport in Nassau. Air travel has never really agreed with me.
And I'm getting too old for all-nighters. I'm beat. Roosevelt
is holding up better. His stamina is remarkable. It comes
with the territory if you're a cop and you're interested in
living long enough to collect your pension.

The Graycliff was built as a private residence about two
hundred years ago. For the last hundred years or so, it's been
the finest hotel in Nassau. With only nine guest rooms in

the main house and four suites by the pool, it's a slice of nirvana in the middle of town. Although it's been a long time since the Beatles stayed here, it's still very popular among rock stars, businessmen and politicians.

When we walk into the lobby, our disheveled appearance immediately attracts the attention of the concierge. He stands and says with a clipped British accent, "May I help you, gentlemen?" He sounds like Sir John Gielgud and bears a striking resemblance to John Cleese.

"Yes, please," I say. "We're here for an important meeting with Mr. Rus—Mr. Kramer. I believe he's in Yellow Bird."

He eyes us suspiciously. "We've been instructed not to disturb Mr. Kramer and his colleagues."

"He's expecting us. If you'll explain to his assistant that Mr. Daley and Mr. Johnson from the San Francisco office have arrived, I'm sure they'll have you show us to his suite."

"One moment, please." He picks up the antique phone. He nods several times. I hope he's talking to Wendy or Pete and not to the local police. "Right this way, please," he says politely.

As we walk through the garden, I decide to speak the local language—money. "I trust you have access to a local banker," I say. "It may be necessary to set up an account here so we can wire some money to various locations around the world."

Roosevelt gives me the eye. I'm laying it on pretty thick.

The concierge keeps looking straight ahead. "It can be arranged, sir." He pronounces the word "sir" as "suh."

"Do you have a fax machine we can use? And I trust we'll be able to plug in our computers?"

"Of course, sir. The rooms have modems, sir. We can make special arrangements, sir."

I love people in this part of the world. They understand

their existence depends on tourists and maintaining their status as a tax haven. "Excellent. What did you say your name is?"

"Burton, sir. Duncan Burton."

Perfect. "Thank you for your assistance, Duncan."

"Of course, sir."

The Yellow Bird cottage is next to the pool where Winston Churchill used to swim. I can see that the drapes are drawn as Duncan leads us to the door. "Will you be staying with us tonight, sir?"

"I'm afraid not. Our business should be completed by the end of the day. We'll be taking the red-eye back to the mainland."

"Very good, sir."

I love this guy. "Duncan," I say, "we'll be in high-level negotiations all day. Would you please tell the hotel staff that we're not to be disturbed?"

"Of course, sir."

"Thank you, Duncan." I shake his hand and slip him three crisp hundred-dollar bills. The universal language. Good help is hard to find. "Remember, Duncan. We mustn't be disturbed."

He almost smiles. "Please let me know if there is anything we can do to assist you, sir."

As he leaves, I glance around the garden and knock on the door. Pete opens it immediately. "Come in," he whispers. He darts a quick look around the pool area before he shuts the door and fastens the bolt. "Anybody follow you?" He's still whispering.

Roosevelt shakes his head. "No, Pete. This isn't a James Bond movie."

He grins sheepishly. "I'm out of my element."

You could have fooled me.

The sitting room in the Yellow Bird is furnished with period pieces from the early Georgian era. An elegant blue sofa sits next to a comfortable tall chair with a paisley pattern. A ceiling fan circulates warm air. The window air conditioner detracts only slightly from the ambiance. A small TV and a fax machine in the corner are the only signs of the twentieth century. Trays containing the remains of dinner and breakfast sit by the door. An empty champagne bottle rests on the antique side table.

Wendy walks in from what I presume is the bedroom and smiles at us. "What took you so long?"

"We ran into a small hurricane. Where's our guest of honor?"

"Watching TV. He didn't want to miss his cartoons."

"Is he pissed off?"

"You could say that."

"How did you find him?"

"We got lucky. We saw him coming out of First Bank. We followed him here."

"How did you get in?"

Pete grins. "You don't want to know."

I glance at Roosevelt. "Has he said much?"

"Nothing you would repeat to Grace. He said he's going to kick our asses and sue us for everything we're worth. Fortunately, that isn't a whole lot."

Roosevelt turns serious. "You know, you guys could be arrested for kidnapping."

"I don't think he's going to complain," Pete says. "We offered to let him use the phone. He refused. He's gone to a lot of trouble to convince everybody he's dead. He'd have to call the cops to bring charges." Pete sounds pleased with himself. "It seems a couple of his investors are looking for him. They aren't as friendly as we are." He lowers his voice.

"In all seriousness, a couple of his investors from the Middle East are unhappy about some money they lost on one of his deals. He thinks his life may be in danger."

Roosevelt is silent.

"You didn't hurt him, did you?" I ask.

"Not really," Pete replies. "He tried to grab Wendy, so we got into a little shoving match. I just pushed him. Wendy was the one who kneed him in the balls. Lifted him all the way off the floor. He was doubled over for a couple of minutes."

"The asshole grabbed me," Wendy says. "He tried to put his hand over my mouth. I drilled him."

"Let's go see our little friend," I say.

We walk into the bedroom. The TV is tuned to CNN. The unshaven Russo is dressed in khaki pants and a maroon polo shirt. He's sitting at a small table eating a muffin and drinking coffee. I notice he's using only his right hand. Then I see his left hand is handcuffed to the table.

"Mr. Russo," I say, "my name is Michael Daley. I'm Joel Friedman's attorney. This is Inspector Roosevelt Johnson of the San Francisco Police Department. He's the lead investigator in the case involving the deaths of Robert Holmes and Diana Kennedy."

He doesn't look up. "Are you the one who sent this goon to kidnap me, Mr. Daley?" he barks.

"That goon is a licensed private investigator. He's also my brother. You're lucky that he found you before somebody else did. You're a popular guy. A bunch of bankers are looking for you. So are a few of your investors and a couple of bounty hunters." Probably a few ex-wives, for good measure.

"Assholes." He pushes the muffin away. "I have nothing to say." He strains to fold his arms before he realizes that he can't.

I hand him a short legal document. "This is a subpoena that requires you to appear at Mr. Friedman's trial." Roosevelt and I got Judge Chen to issue a subpoena on our way to the airport. It's a bluff. A California subpoena isn't binding in the Bahamas. "I may have to get some dispensation from the judge to get you to testify, however."

"Why the hell is that?"

"Technically, you're dead. But I think I can persuade the judge to the contrary."

"And if I don't cooperate?"

Pete hands him a card with English writing on one side and Arabic writing on the other. "This gentleman is looking for you," he says. "We saw him last night. He's asked us to call if we find you."

He stares at both sides of the card. "Read my lips. Fuck you."

"Mr. Russo," Roosevelt says, "I've come here to ask you to voluntarily return to San Francisco so that we can sort out this matter."

"Why the hell would I do that?"

"If you have nothing to hide, you shouldn't have any problem returning with us." He eyes him closely. "We'd be happy to buy you a ticket. You don't have anything to hide, do you, Mr. Russo?"

"Of course not."

"Good. Now, we can do this the easy way, or we can do this the hard way. The easy way means you'll get on a plane with us and we'll go back to San Francisco together."

"And the hard way?"

"I'll call the local police. They'll want to know why a dead man checked into this lovely hotel under an assumed name. I'll ask them to detain you. We'll begin extradition proceedings. You'll be spending a fairly long time in jail here in Nassau. I'll swear out a complaint that you're a flight risk. They'll keep you in jail until your extradition is resolved."

"Are you charging me with something?"

"Not yet. But you're a suspect. Which reminds me," he adds, "this would be a good time to read you your rights." He clears his throat and recites the Miranda warnings. "Mr. Russo," he says, "we're prepared to call your lawyer right now. He can meet us at the airport."

Russo looks at the TV. "I didn't do anything," he says. "It isn't a crime to go on a vacation."

"All the more reason for you to cooperate," Roosevelt says.

"I want to talk to my lawyer."

Wendy takes out her cellular phone. "Who do you want me to call?"

"Arthur Patton."

"Who the hell do you guys think you are?" Art Patton bellows at me through Wendy's cellular phone. "You can't detain him. It's kidnapping."

"He's here voluntarily," I reply. "I can call the local cops."

Silence. "Let me talk to Johnson."

I hand the phone to Roosevelt. He listens for a moment. He says "Uh-huh" a few times. Then he says, emphatically, "No deal. Look, if you're going to be an ass about this, we'll call the local cops. I'm sure they'd be delighted to make up a bed for Mr. Russo for the next six months while you argue about his extradition." He winks at me. "By the way, we're going to make sure all his assets down here are frozen. I think all his assets up your way are already frozen, so you may be doing his legal work pro bono." He listens for a minute. "Uh-huh. Okay." He has Pete unshackle Russo. He hands the phone to Russo and turns to me. "I think reason is about to prevail," he says.

I call the concierge. "Duncan," I say, "it's Mr. Daley. I need you to make some travel arrangements for us. Mr. Kramer, Mr. Johnson and I need to get to San Francisco as soon as possible. Yes, first class is fine. Just bill it to Mr. Kramer's credit card."

The line goes silent for a few moments. Then Duncan comes back. "We'll have all the arrangements ready within the hour, sir," he says.

"Thank you, Duncan." I wink at Pete. "Mr. Kramer's colleagues will need a place to stay for the next few nights. They have banking business on Monday. Would you make arrangements for them to keep Mr. Kramer's cottage?"

"Of course, sir."

"Thank you, Duncan. You may want to send a house-keeper up here. And some cold drinks."

"Very well, sir."

Our plane leaves Nassau at six o'clock Friday night. We connect through Chicago. When we get off the plane at O'Hare, we're met by three cops. At first, I think they're going to arrest Russo. Or me. Then I realize Roosevelt has called in a favor from a friend in the Chicago Police Department. He doesn't want to let Russo make a break through the mobs at O'Hare. With the help of Chicago's finest, we negotiate the United terminal. Naturally, our flight to San Francisco is delayed two hours.

Art Patton and three San Francisco police officers meet us at the gate at SFO. Art isn't taking any chances. He's brought Rita Roberts with him. As soon as we're off the plane, he turns to Rita's camera and demands that we release Russo.

Roosevelt looks at him. "Mr. Russo accompanied us voluntarily from the Bahamas."

"Then he's free to go?"

"After he's answered some questions."

Patton scowls. "I'm instructing him not to answer any questions until I've spoken to him."

"Fine," Roosevelt says. "You can accompany us to the Hall, where you can talk in the comfort of one of our consultation rooms."

I haven't ridden in a paddy wagon in years. My head is throbbing as Roosevelt, Russo, Patton and I sit in silence in the back of a van, with two other officers. Patton looks at Roosevelt. "You know," he says with a sneer, "he doesn't have to talk to you guys."

Roosevelt yawns. "I know. I'm sure he has nothing to hide."

"You got that right," Russo snaps.

Patton holds up his hands. "Vince, we'll talk about this when we get there. I don't want you to say anything right now, understood?"

Russo pouts. "Understood."

"Are you going to charge him?" I ask Skipper as we sit in a consultation room down the corridor from where Patton has been meeting with Russo for the last hour. Roosevelt drinks coffee. Marcus Banks is there too, sitting quietly and drinking a Sprite. Bill McNulty studies the sports section in the *Chronicle*.

"With what?" Skipper asks. "It isn't a crime to park your car at the Golden Gate Bridge. Last time I looked, it isn't a crime not to show up for a closing. It's still legal to travel to the Bahamas."

"How about murder?"

Roosevelt looks up. "How about murder, Skipper?" he repeats.

"On what basis? There's no evidence pointing toward Russo."

"Yes, there is," I reply. "He was at the scene. He faked his own suicide. He fled the country. He was traveling under an alias. What else do you want?"

"Where's the motive?" Skipper asks.

"He didn't want the deal to close. He had to create a diversion to get out of the country."

Skipper is skeptical. "If he didn't want the deal to close, he could have just said so. He didn't have to kill two people. Besides, there isn't a single shred of evidence he pulled the trigger. We can put him at the scene, but we can't tie him to the murder weapon."

I search for a retort. He's probably right. There isn't any physical evidence to convict Russo. I look at Roosevelt. "I need him to testify," I say. "You can't let him leave the country again. I'll put him on the stand on Monday."

There's a knock on the door. A uniformed deputy reports that Patton and Russo want to talk. "Mike," Roosevelt says, "I have to ask you to wait here. I'll tell them you want to speak to them."

"I understand."

I sit in the cramped gray consultation room by myself in the middle of the night. The lights are dimmed. The Hall has an eerie, deafening quiet at this hour. My body is overwhelmed by a combination of fatigue and jet lag. I sit in never-never land—not quite asleep, but certainly not awake.

My mind starts playing tricks on me. I see Grace's face. I'm at the Hall of Justice in the middle of the night. I should be home taking care of her.

I hear footsteps in the hallway and I see a uniformed

policeman walk by. I think of my dad. So proud of his uniform. So proud he put the bad guys away. A good cop. He did what he thought was right. Hard to think he's been gone for five years. So little time to know his first grandchild, Grace. He was so proud of her. And she'll never remember him. Sometimes, I think I never really knew him. Sometimes I think I knew him too well. He was a good dad, but somewhat distant. I think of my brother Tommy, who went to war to please him. And Pete, who became a cop to show him. And for a brief moment, I think of myself. I became a defense attorney to spite him. I think of my sister, Mary, who pleaded with him to take early retirement, just so she could stop worrying about him.

I think of my mom, who raised four kids on a cop's salary. How she'd stay up every night, waiting for him to come home. How she wouldn't sleep until she heard his car door slam. How she counted the days until his retirement. And how she had to nurse him when they discovered the cancer only a few weeks later. Five years of caring for him through all that pain. She worried about all of us. Now she lives half her life in a world of confusion that she doesn't understand and I can't imagine.

I think about Rosie, the only woman I've ever truly loved. And our mutual realization that we're utterly incapable of living together. I feel the pain of our separation all over again. I wonder whether I'll ever find the same kind of love again. I hope I'll never feel the pain again.

I worry about Grace. I wonder where she'll be in another ten years. Or another twenty years, for that matter.

I think about my friend and client Joel. I think about his less-than-perfect marriage. I think about his relationship with his father, and how it isn't all that different from my relationship with mine. I wonder whether he'll have a chance to repair the damage to his life that's been inflicted on him—and that he's inflicted upon himself.

I think about our special circumstances. It may be the fatigue or it may be the stress. Or it may be both. I realize I'm crying. And I wonder if it's all worth it.

"Mike?" Roosevelt stands in the doorway of the consultation room, his hands in his pockets.

"Huh? Sorry, Roosevelt. I must have dozed off for a few minutes."

"Patton and Russo want to talk to you."

"Are you going to arrest him?"

"No."

"Will he testify?"

"I think so."

"Keep it under your hat, Roosevelt."

"I will." He pauses. "I can't make the same promise for the DA."

"I understand." I look at him. "Roosevelt?"

"Yes?"

"Thanks."

52

"DID YOU HAVE A NICE TRIP?"

"In an unexpected twist, local financier Vincent Russo Jr. was located in the Bahamas. He will be called to testify at the murder trial of Joel Mark Friedman later today."

—KCBS NEWS RADIO. MONDAY, APRIL 13. 6:30 A.M.

The traffic on Bryant is terrible on Monday morning. The minicams are lined up two-deep. Word got out about Vince Russo's resurrection. The gallery is packed.

"The defense calls Vincent Russo Jr."

Judge Chen watches as Russo slithers into the courtroom in his dark blue suit. Russo is sworn in. He takes the stand. He's sweating. He gulps water from a Styrofoam cup. I can smell his aftershave. His diamond ring gleams. His cuff links look like gold golf balls.

Judge Chen says, "We weren't sure we were going to see you, Mr. Russo."

He glances at the clock. "I've been out of town."

"You may proceed, Mr. Daley," she says to me.

"May we approach the witness, Your Honor?" I want to get right in his face.

"Yes, Mr. Daley."

I button my jacket as I walk from the lectern toward Russo. I position myself directly in front of him and I turn slightly so the jury can see his facial expressions and mine. "Mr. Russo," I begin, "you were in the Simpson and Gates offices on December thirtieth, were you not?"

His slitty eyes wander. "Yes."

"And you were working on an important deal involving the sale of your company, right?"

"Yes."

"And the sale was supposed to close on the morning of December thirty-first, right?"

"Objection, Your Honor. He's leading the witness."

Indeed I am. "Request permission to treat this witness as hostile."

Judge Chen says, "All right, Mr. Daley."

"Thank you." It's okay to lead hostile witnesses. I turn back to Russo. "The deal didn't close, did it, Mr. Russo?"

"No, it didn't."

"Why not?"

"Because I didn't want it to. I didn't want Continental Capital Corporation to take over my father's company. It would have been disrespectful to his memory." He glares at me. "It didn't close because I said so." So there.

"So, Mr. Russo, instead of showing up for the closing, what did you do?"

"I decided to take a little vacation. Most recently, I was in the Bahamas."

I look at the jury and I grin sarcastically. "Did you have a nice trip?"

Skipper stands up, but doesn't say anything.

"As a matter of fact, I did," Russo replies. "Right up until this weekend when you insisted that I return to San Francisco." His expression is long-suffering.

All right, asshole. "Mr. Russo," I say, "let's talk about the night of December thirtieth."

Victim face again. "Whatever you'd like, Mr. Daley."

"The negotiations went into the night on December thirtieth?"

"Yes."

"In fact, you finished negotiations by about nine o'clock that night?"

"That's true." He tries to sound nonchalant.

"And then you went out for dinner with Mr. Holmes, didn't you?"

"Yes. We went to Tadich Grill. I'd recommend it."

"And you returned to the office around eleven-fifteen?"

"Yes."

"And everything was ready to go by about twelve-thirty?"

"Yep. Everything." He takes another swallow of water.

"You had a meeting with Mr. Holmes around twelve-thirty, didn't you?"

"Yes."

"What did you talk about with Mr. Holmes?"

"A lot of things. Our plans for New Year's. Our kids. His latest divorce."

"Did you talk about the deal?"

He turns his head at a slight angle. "Yes. I told him I wasn't going to proceed with the closing. I decided I would keep my company or take my chances in bankruptcy."

"Or go to the Bahamas. How did Mr. Holmes react when you told him?"

"He was pissed off. He said I should sell the company. And he told me if the deal didn't close, Simpson and Gates was going to go bankrupt." He smirks. "Of course, you can't run a successful business worrying about whether your lawyers are going to be able to pay their bills."

Or an unsuccessful business like yours, Vince.

"Mr. Russo, were you aware Mr. Holmes was going to receive a big bonus?"

"Yep. Three million bucks." The corners of his mouth turn up slightly.

"And you realize, of course, that by pulling the plug, Mr. Holmes was going to lose his bonus."

"Like I said, you can't spend your life worrying about how much money your lawyer makes."

Legitimate point.

"Mr. Russo, did Mr. Holmes look upset when you told him you weren't going to close?"

"Objection. State of mind."

"Your Honor, I'm just asking for an observation of Mr. Holmes's appearance."

"Overruled."

"Yes, he was very upset. Really honked off, if you know what I mean."

I know what you mean. "Was he upset about his divorce?"

"No, he wasn't."

Shit. I should have left well enough alone.

"Actually," he continues, "he was far more upset about the fact that his girlfriend dumped him."

Hello? "Really? And would that girlfriend have been Diana Kennedy?"

He chuckles. "No, Mr. Daley. It wouldn't. His relationship with Ms. Kennedy was long over. Old and cold. Dead as a doorknob."

We get the idea.

He looks at the jury. "He was upset because his new girlfriend dumped him."

I look frantically at Rosie. I'm going to have to break the cardinal rule of cross-examination and ask a question for which I don't know the answer. "Mr. Russo, do you know the name of this new girlfriend?"

"No. He wouldn't tell me. It was his little secret. He said

it was somebody we knew. He said he'd tell me when the time was right. He never did."

"Mr. Russo, did Mr. Holmes give any other indications that he may have been upset that night?"

"Objection. State of mind."

"Overruled."

"Mr. Daley," he says, "are you asking me if he was suicidal?"

"In a word, yes."

"The answer, in a word, is maybe. He was very upset about the deal. He was very upset about losing the money. And he was particularly upset about his girlfriend. But he wasn't that upset."

I had it coming. "Mr. Russo, what time did you leave Mr. Holmes's office?"

"Around one o'clock."

"Did you see Diana Kennedy before you left?"

"No."

"And Mr. Holmes was still alive when you left?"

"Very much so."

"So, Mr. Russo, just so we're straight on this, you didn't happen to kill Bob Holmes and Diana Kennedy that night, did you?"

"Of course not. Bob was still alive when I left him. I didn't see Diana."

"And you didn't see anybody else kill them, did you?"

"Nope."

"Did you hear any gunshots?"

"Nope."

"What time did you leave the building?"

"Around one-forty-five."

"After you left the Simpson and Gates office, you abandoned your car at the Vista Point at the Golden Gate Bridge, right?"

"I intended to retrieve it the next day." He looks up. "I was too tired to drive."

Right. "And you left your wallet in the car, didn't you?"

"I forgot it."

"And your keys."

"I forgot them, too."

"And you decided to leave the country."

"It isn't a crime to go on vacation, Mr. Daley."

"No, it isn't, Mr. Russo," I agree. "And where did you go?"

"First, I went to New Zealand. Then Thailand and Greece. Then the Bahamas."

"Where you were checked into a very fancy hotel under an assumed name."

"Yes. I always travel under an assumed name. I don't like to draw attention to myself. Wealthy Americans are often targets in other parts of the world."

"Mr. Russo, you realize that reasonable people might interpret your actions as an attempt by a desperate man to flee the scene of a crime?"

"Objection."

"Sustained."

"Come on, Mr. Russo. Let's put our cards on the table. Let's tell the truth today, for once. You killed Bob Holmes and Diana Kennedy, didn't you?"

He shakes his head. "No, I didn't."

"And you fled the country."

"No, I didn't."

"And you went to the Bahamas to collect a bunch of money that you kept hidden there."

"That's not true."

"Your Honor," Skipper interrupts. "Is this harassment of Mr. Russo really necessary?"

"Your Honor," I say, "this man is lying. It's evident to

everyone in this room that Mr. Russo killed Mr. Holmes and Ms. Kennedy and fled the country."

"Move to strike, Your Honor. Mr. Daley is out of order."

"Sustained. The jury will disregard Mr. Daley's last remarks." She stares at me. "Sidebar."

We approach the bench. She puts her hand over her microphone. "Mr. Daley," she says sharply, "if you're trying to get a mistrial, you'll be disappointed. Now finish your examination."

We return to our places. Judge Chen looks at me. "Anything else for this witness, Mr. Daley?"

I see Rosie close her eyes. "No further questions."

She looks at Skipper. "Cross-exam, Mr. Gates?"

"No, Your Honor."

She pounds her gavel. "Ten-minute recess."

Joel isn't overjoyed with my direct examination of Russo. "I thought you were going to nail him," he says.

"Did you think he was going to break down on the stand and confess?"

"Maybe."

"This isn't an episode of fucking *Perry Mason*," I snap. I catch myself. "I'm sorry. I gave it a shot. It was worth a try, but it's unrealistic to think that Russo is going to do anything but lie. He was better-coached than I thought. And he held up better than I thought he would."

"I want to take the stand," Joel says firmly.

"We'll talk about it after Patton testifies."

53

"WHAT DOES THE MANAGING PARTNER DO, MR. PATTON?"

"The managing partner of a major law firm is like the chairman of the board of a Fortune 500 company. Every big business needs leadership. And you have to have a vision."

—ARTHUR PATTON. *SAN FRANCISCO LEGAL JOURNAL.*
MONDAY, APRIL 13.

"You are the managing partner of the Simpson and Gates firm, aren't you, Mr. Patton?"

"Yes I am." After lunch, Arthur Patton has squeezed himself into the uncomfortable wooden chair in the witness box. He's dressed carefully today. The red suspenders are at home. His chins jiggle. His eyebrows form a straight line right above the tiny wire-rim glasses that sit against the bulbous nose and mask the tiny eyes.

"What does the managing partner do, Mr. Patton?"

He purses his dry, thin lips. "The managing partner of a major law firm is like the chairman of the board of a Fortune 500 company. Every big business needs leadership. And you have to have a vision."

"Your vision seems to have led the firm into bankruptcy, Mr. Patton."

"It was merely a protective filing," he assures me. "The

firm continues to operate and will remain fully functional while we are sorting out our obligations to our creditors."

I note that the accountant doesn't seem convinced. It's time to talk about something Art understands: money. "Mr. Patton, you are aware that the firm maintained a key-man life insurance policy on Mr. Holmes, aren't you?"

"Yes."

"And you knew the firm had a twenty-million-dollar policy on the life of Mr. Holmes?"

"Of course."

I face the jury. "And you knew, of course, that the policy had a so-called suicide clause, right?"

This is ticklish. If he admits he knew about the suicide clause, he admits the firm stood to gain twenty million dollars if he can show Joel killed Bob and Diana. It gives him incentive to set Joel up. If he says he didn't know, I'll have the pleasure of chastising him in open court for not having read the policy carefully—very unlawyerlike for an attorney of his stature.

In fact, he handles it pretty well. "Mr. Daley," he says, "it's a standard clause in every life insurance policy. Of course, I never thought about the suicide exclusion clause. I was much more concerned with the loss of Mr. Holmes. We'd certainly miss him and his contribution, but we're a large firm with many productive partners."

So there.

That didn't go very well. Now for some fun. "Mr. Patton," I say, "you have an ongoing social relationship with Elizabeth Holmes, don't you?"

"We're friends."

"Would it be fair to say your relationship is more than just friends?"

"Objection. Mr. Patton's social life is not at issue here."

"On the contrary, Your Honor, his social life very much is at issue here."

"Overruled."

"Mr. Patton, would it be fair to say that you and Mrs. Holmes are now 'an item'?"

"I don't know what you mean."

"I think you do. You and Mrs. Holmes have a romantic relationship, don't you?"

"That's not true. We're just good friends." He's starting to turn red.

"Mr. Patton," I say in a measured tone, "I'm prepared to introduce evidence that you and Mrs. Holmes have spent more than a few nights together in the last few months. And I'm prepared to introduce pictures of you and Mrs. Holmes together on a beach in Mexico." He's very unhappy. "I'll ask you again, Mr. Patton. Do you and Mrs. Holmes have a romantic relationship?"

"All right. We have a romantic relationship. What's the big deal? We used to be married."

"And how long has this romantic relationship been going on?"

He looks away from me. "For a couple of months."

I was hoping he'd say a couple of years. I move closer to him. "Mr. Patton, are you aware that there was a five-million-dollar life insurance policy on Mr. Holmes's life?"

"Yes."

"And are you aware that the policy named Mrs. Holmes as the beneficiary?"

"Yes."

"And your former brother-in-law, Perry Guilford, is the firm's insurance agent, right?"

"Yes."

"And he was the insurance agent for Mr. Holmes, right?"

"Yes."

"Mr. Patton, isn't it true that your former brother-in-law told you that Mr. Holmes was going to change his life insurance policy after he and Mrs. Holmes separated? And isn't it true that your girlfriend, Mrs. Holmes, was going to be removed as a beneficiary of that policy?"

"I haven't the slightest idea what you're talking about, Mr. Daley."

Sure. I'm convinced. "You're friends with your partner, Charles Stern, right?"

"Yes."

"And are you aware that Mr. Holmes had asked Mr. Stern to draft an amendment of Mr. Holmes's will when his marriage was on the ropes?"

He doesn't deny it. "Yes."

"And you were aware that as soon as Mrs. Holmes filed for divorce, she was going to be written out of the will, right?"

He takes off his glasses. "Once again, Mr. Daley, your jump in logic is nothing short of remarkable. I had no idea what the will said before Mr. Holmes died. It was none of my business. And if you're suggesting that I had some financial motivation to kill Mr. Holmes, you're crazy."

"That is exactly what I'm suggesting, Mr. Patton. If Mr. Holmes committed suicide, the firm was going to lose twenty million dollars. And you will be forever known in the legal community as the managing partner who presided over the dissolution of what was once the largest and most profitable law firm on the West Coast."

"Objection. Mr. Daley has started his closing argument a little early."

"Sustained."

"Mr. Patton, how much money will the firm get from the life insurance policy if they can pin this crime on Mr. Friedman?"

"Objection. Argumentative."

"Sustained."

I rephrase the question.

"Twenty million dollars."

"And how much money was your girlfriend, Mrs. Holmes, supposed to get under the terms of the will that Bob Holmes was about to change just prior to his death?"

"Objection."

"Overruled."

"Five million dollars."

"And how much money was Mrs. Holmes supposed to get from the life insurance policy that he was about to change just prior to his death?"

"Five million dollars."

"So, Mr. Patton, isn't it fair to say that you had about thirty million reasons to hope Mr. Holmes died? Especially if it was a murder, and not a suicide?"

"Objection. Argumentative."

"Sustained."

"Come on, Mr. Patton. You had all the incentive in the world. You had a chance to save the firm. You had a chance to help your girlfriend. You'd look like a hero. What more could you want?"

"Your Honor," Skipper wails. "Move to strike."

"Sustained."

Patton is starting to foam. "Look, you little jerk," he blurts out, "I'm going to haul you into court and sue you for slander. These preposterous, unsubstantiated charges . . ."

"Your Honor," I say calmly, "would you please instruct the witness that he is supposed to answer questions and not make speeches."

She pounds her gavel and looks at him. "Mr. Patton," she says, "please."

He manages to bluster, "Yes, Your Honor."

"Mr. Patton," I say, without looking at him, "what was your relationship with Diana Kennedy?"

"She was an associate at our firm," he says.

"Was she a good lawyer?"

"Yes. She got very good reviews."

"And did she get good reviews in bed, Mr. Patton?"

"Objection."

"Sustained. Mr. Daley, please."

"I'll rephrase. Mr. Patton, isn't it true that you thought Ms. Kennedy was very attractive?"

"Everyone at the firm would probably agree that Ms. Kennedy was very attractive."

"And isn't it a fact that you asked her out on several occasions?"

"No. That would have been inappropriate."

"Really, Mr. Patton? Your colleague Mr. Holmes apparently came out the other way on that particular moral dilemma."

"I wasn't privy to Bob's private life."

"But you were attracted to her, weren't you?"

"She was a professional colleague. Nothing more."

Sure. "Mr. Patton, isn't it true that you asked her to sleep with you at the firm retreat last year?"

Skipper leaps up. "Your Honor, for God's sake," he cries.

"Your Honor," I say, "it's a completely relevant question."

"Overruled. The witness will answer."

"No," Patton says. "I did no such thing."

"Isn't it true she left your party because you wouldn't leave her alone?"

"Absolutely not."

"Isn't it true you followed her back to her room and attacked her?"

"No."

"Mr. Patton, isn't it true the firm has had to pay four multimillion-dollar settlements to female associates who have accused you of sexual harassment?"

He glares at me. Then he looks helplessly at Skipper.

"Isn't it true, Mr. Patton?"

He mutters through clenched teeth, "The firm has settled various cases involving unsubstantiated charges. We decided we didn't want the publicity or the trial costs."

Right. I glance at the phone company supervisor. I get right back into Patton's face. "Isn't it true that Ms. Kennedy made a claim against you for sexual harassment? And that you were negotiating a substantial settlement with her?"

"No."

"Isn't it true she threatened to go to the newspapers if the firm didn't agree to her demands?"

"No."

"Mr. Patton, if you don't start telling the truth, I'll call witnesses who will."

He addresses the jury. "Mr. Daley's claims are entirely without merit."

"Mr. Patton, isn't it true that you killed Diana Kennedy because she threatened to expose your pattern of sexual harassment to the media? And isn't it true you killed Bob Holmes because he threatened you with expulsion from the firm because of your escapades? And so that the firm and your girlfriend could collect the insurance money?"

His response is concise, the tone incredulous. "No, Mr. Daley. That is not true."

Patton eyes the jury. I look at Rosie. She closes her eyes.

I look at the ceiling and exhale melodramatically. "No further questions."

54

I NEED HER TO CALMLY ASSASSINATE ALL OF THE PROSECUTION'S KEY WITNESSES

"The defense is still battling uphill. Mr. Daley has done a decent job so far."

—NEWSCENTER 4 LEGAL ANALYST MORTON GOLDBERG.
TUESDAY, APRIL 14.

"My name is Doris Charlotte Fontaine."

"What was your relationship to Robert Holmes?" I ask.

"I was his secretary."

At ten-thirty the next morning, Doris is dressed in her finest schoolmarm attire: a navy blue dress, a small, decorative pin and a minimal amount of makeup. Her glasses hang from a small gold chain around her neck. I want her to project the very embodiment of the voice of reason. In the simplest terms, I need her to calmly assassinate all of the prosecution's key witnesses. And I want Skipper to look like an arrogant ass if he tries to interrupt her.

"Ms. Fontaine," I begin, "could you please tell us how long you worked for Mr. Holmes?"

She smiles politely. Nice touch, Doris. "Twenty-two years. From the day he started."

"I see. You must have been very close."

Skipper starts to stand, then stops. Good idea. It's too soon to be combative.

"We were. We'd been through a lot together."

"It's unusual to see such loyalty." I remind myself not to let things get too thick. "Ms. Fontaine," I continue, "could you please tell us where you were on the evening of December thirtieth?"

"Of course. I was in the Simpson and Gates offices, assisting Mr. Holmes on a big closing."

"How many people were working on the deal?"

She bobs her head back and forth as if she's counting. "Probably about fifty," she decides.

"When did you go home?"

"Around eight o'clock. We were having a going-away party for Mr. Gates that evening." She looks at Skipper. "I stopped by for a few minutes. I live out in the avenues. I got home around nine."

She's hitting the right notes. The jury seems to like her. "Ms. Fontaine," I continue, "could you please describe Mr. Holmes's mood that night?"

"Objection," Skipper says. "State of mind."

"Your Honor," I say, "I'm not asking for a medical determination. I'm asking her to describe her observation of his mood, based upon her many years of experience working with him."

Judge Chen gives Doris a small smile. "Overruled."

Doris says Bob appeared extremely upset that night. The deal wasn't going well. "We weren't sure Mr. Russo would authorize us to proceed with the closing," she says. "He was worried about his bonus. Wouldn't you be upset?" she asks rhetorically. Skipper could object to her asking a question, but wisely chooses not to.

"Ms. Fontaine," I continue, "is there any other reason why Mr. Holmes may have been upset?"

"Yes. Mrs. Holmes served him with divorce papers." She says he was surprised and repeats that he was very upset.

"Do you know what caused the breakup of their marriage?"

"Mr. Holmes was seeing another woman. She threw him out."

"Do you know who that other woman was?"

"It was Diana Kennedy."

"You've testified Mr. Holmes was surprised and distraught when the papers were served. Shouldn't he have expected it? He was seeing another woman and his wife threw him out. Why would he have been surprised when Mrs. Holmes served him with divorce papers?"

"He tried to reconcile with his wife because Ms. Kennedy had told him she didn't want to see him anymore."

"Ms. Kennedy broke off their relationship?"

"Yes. Emphatically, I might add." She's doing better than she did in our rehearsals.

"So," I say, "after Ms. Kennedy dumped him, he tried to reconcile with his wife?"

"Yes. It didn't work out. In late December, Mrs. Holmes's investigator caught him with another woman."

"Was it Ms. Kennedy?"

"No. It was a different woman. That's when she decided to file the divorce papers."

A half hour later, we are still discussing Bob's love life. "Ms. Fontaine," I say, "are you sure Mr. Holmes and Ms. Kennedy were no longer seeing each other on December thirtieth?"

"Yes, Mr. Daley. I was always aware of the women in his life. From time to time, Mr. Holmes asked me to cover for him."

"You mean he asked you to make up stories so Mrs. Holmes didn't find out about his affairs?"

"Yes," she replies quietly.

"Can you identify the woman he was seeing in late December?"

"He never mentioned her name. He said he'd tell me when the time was right."

"Could it have been Diana Kennedy?"

"No."

I pause. "Was it Dr. Kathy Chandler?"

"I don't know."

"Let's switch gears," I say. "Were you aware that Joel Friedman and Diana Kennedy had been romantically involved at some point in the fall of last year?"

"No, I wasn't."

"It's been suggested Mr. Friedman and Ms. Kennedy were still involved in late December. Do you have any knowledge of that?"

"No."

"It's also been suggested that Ms. Kennedy informed Mr. Friedman on December thirtieth that she was seeing Bob Holmes. Do you have any knowledge of that?"

"No, sir, I don't."

"Well, Ms. Fontaine, would it surprise you to find out several witnesses in this courtroom have suggested Mr. Friedman killed Mr. Holmes because Ms. Kennedy dumped Mr. Friedman in favor of Mr. Holmes, and he was jealous?"

"Objection. Speculative."

"Overruled."

Doris tugs at her hair. "Yes, Mr. Daley, that would surprise me. Ms. Kennedy's relationship with Mr. Holmes was over. There was nothing for Joel to be jealous about. How many times do I have to say it? Diana broke up with Bob in the beginning of December."

"Thank you, Ms. Fontaine."

————

"Ms. Fontaine," I say a little later, "let's talk a little bit about Vince Russo's deal."

She explains that Russo wasn't happy about selling his father's business. "There was great doubt as to whether it would close," she says. "Ultimately, it didn't and Mr. Russo disappeared."

"Was Mr. Russo distraught on the evening of December thirtieth?"

"Objection. State of mind."

"Sustained."

"I'll try it another way," I say. "How long have you known Mr. Russo?"

"About ten years."

"Did he spend a lot of time at the S and G offices?"

"Yes. He was in the office at least twice a week."

"Based upon your knowledge as an acquaintance of Mr. Russo for about ten years, did it appear to you that Mr. Russo was distraught on the evening of December thirtieth?"

Skipper starts to stand, but McNulty stops him.

"Yes," Doris says, "he appeared very unhappy about selling his company."

"I see. And could you please describe Mr. Russo's behavior that night?"

"Erratic. At one point while I was standing outside the main conference room, Mr. Russo stormed out the door while he was screaming at Mr. Holmes. He was angry because he had been told that the purchase price for his company was going to be reduced by forty million dollars."

No reaction from the jury. "Is it fair to say Mr. Russo was extremely upset that night?"

"Yes."

Rosie nods. Time to move on. Judge Chen interrupts me to ask how much longer I'll be questioning Doris. I say a couple more hours. She decides to adjourn for lunch.

———

Rosie, Doris, Joel and I eat sandwiches in the consultation room. "So far, so good," Rosie says. "You've created a plausible argument for suicide. You've cast doubt on the jealous-rage theory. And you've established motive for Russo." She turns to Doris. "You're doing great."

Doris shrugs. "Let's see how it goes. It's easy with Mike asking the questions."

She's right. "We've got about another hour, Doris. I need you to slay one more dragon for me this afternoon. Just follow my lead and keep the answers short. Just the way we talked about it."

"You got it."

"Did you hear anything from Pete?" Rosie asks.

"I talked to Rolanda. He called and said the banker won't reveal the names of the income beneficiaries or the remaindermen of the International Charitable Trust. Wendy is looking for a judge."

Joel changes the subject. "When do I get to testify?" he asks.

"We'll talk about it later. If everything goes well today, we won't need you."

"But I want to."

"We'll talk about it later," I say again.

We begin the afternoon session at one o'clock. "Ms. Fontaine," I say, "are you acquainted with a man named Arthur Patton?"

"Yes. He is the managing partner of Simpson and Gates. I've known him for many years."

"Are you familiar with an incident involving Mr. Patton and Ms. Kennedy at the Silverado Country Club in October of last year?"

"Yes I am."

"How did you become aware of this incident?"

"The firm conducted an internal investigation."

"How did you become aware of the internal investigation?"

"My boss, Mr. Holmes, was in charge of the investigation. He told me about it. Mr. Friedman was interviewed in the course of the investigation. He told me about it, too."

"I see. And why didn't you come forward with this information when the police first questioned you?"

"They didn't ask me. And I didn't think it was relevant. It was a confidential, internal investigation. The matter was closed."

"Can you tell us about the nature of the investigation?"

Skipper stands. "Your Honor, I must object. Any testimony that Ms. Fontaine is about to give on this investigation is inadmissible hearsay." It's a legitimate objection. I glance at the jury. The phone company supervisor seems perturbed.

"Your Honor," I say, "rather than argue the merits of this objection, we would like to handle this issue in a different manner. We would like to introduce into evidence a memorandum prepared by Mr. Holmes which was dated December fifteenth of last year and was addressed to the Simpson and Gates executive committee." Rosie hands copies of a memo to Skipper and to the judge. "This memorandum sets forth the official findings of a special investigative committee appointed by the Simpson and Gates executive committee with respect to the so-called Silverado Incident."

"Objection. Irrelevant." Skipper is on his feet. "This is highly inflammatory. It is an internal memorandum that is privileged communication. Furthermore, we have no basis to verify its authenticity. Finally, this information has not been provided to us by the defense."

"We produced this memorandum several weeks ago,

Your Honor," I say. I don't mention that it was included with those eighteen boxes of S&G financial records that we never planned to introduce into evidence. Skipper glares at McNulty. Somebody on their side missed it.

"In addition," I continue, "if Mr. Gates is concerned about the authenticity of this memorandum, I am prepared to call Mr. Stern and the head of the firm's labor law department to verify that they got a copy of it. If Mr. Gates were permitted to testify, he would acknowledge that he has seen a copy of it."

Judge Chen pounds her gavel. "The bailiff will take the jury out. I want to see all the attorneys in my chambers. Now."

We meet in chambers. Skipper tries to sound incredulous. "What kind of stunt are you trying to pull?" Often, this isn't the right tone in chambers.

Judge Chen interrupts him. "Be quiet, Mr. Gates. Let me see that memorandum." She puts on her reading glasses. Skipper, McNulty, Rosie and I sit in silence. She scans it quickly and then studies it carefully. "Mr. Daley," she says, "where did you get this?"

I keep my tone professional. "From Ms. Fontaine."

"I see. How do you know it's authentic?"

"She typed it. She'll swear to it under oath."

"Your Honor," Skipper begins.

She cuts him off. "Shut up, Mr. Gates. It will be your turn to talk in a minute." She looks at the memo again. She turns to Skipper. "Mr. Gates," she says, "I happen to find Mr. Daley's argument persuasive on this point. Do you have anything to say?"

He glances at McNulty, then turns to the judge. "There is no foundation proving its authenticity. It could have been cooked up on Doris Fontaine's word processor. It isn't signed. We don't have an original. Before you destroy Art Patton's career, you should consider the ramifications."

I put both my palms on her desk and push myself up. "Your Honor, if he's accusing us of manufacturing evidence, he's crazy. Doris will swear under oath the document is authentic. I'll swear under oath we obtained it through legitimate means. If I'm lying, you can have my ticket to practice law right now. I will trot out everybody who ever saw this memo. If you insist, I will testify. Our request is legitimate and our evidence is good. And if Skipper thinks it's tainted, he can argue it to the jury. Let them decide whether we made this whole thing up. We'll take our chances."

"Your Honor, with all due respect to Mr. Daley and his ticket to practice . . ."

She holds up her hand. "Mr. Gates, have you ever seen this memo before?"

He swallows. He looks at McNulty, who raises his eyebrows. "I don't recall," he stammers.

Judge Chen shakes her head. "I've heard enough. The objection is overruled. The memo comes in. Now all of you get out of here."

Skipper sits on his hands and seethes the rest of the afternoon while Doris and I go through the memo in detail in front of the jury and destroy what's left of Art Patton's reputation. There is a lesson somewhere in this. The memo reveals Diana had, in fact, reported Patton's advances to the head of the firm's human-resources department, and had threatened to sue the firm for sexual harassment. According to witnesses, Patton had propositioned her at the party in his room. She rejected him and returned to her own room. He followed her. Diana said Patton then grabbed her from behind and pinned her to her bed. He tried to muffle her calls for help. She managed to free one of her legs and kicked him in the groin. She ran to Joel's room. About five minutes later, Patton knocked on Joel's door and found Diana there.

Patton claimed it was all a misunderstanding.

The report says Patton had been sued for sexual harassment on four occasions and that the firm settled all four lawsuits. The firm also received a dozen other claims that did not lead to formal legal action. In each case, Patton claimed he was misunderstood. In his mind, it was all a problem of perception.

The other members of X-Com ordered him to have counseling and fined him a hundred thousand dollars. His points were reduced. He was told he would be expelled from the firm if another incident ever took place.

"Ms. Fontaine," I say, "were there any other developments after this memorandum was issued?"

"The day before Christmas, Ms. Kennedy gave her resignation to Mr. Holmes. She had accepted a job in San Diego. She wanted a fresh start." I introduce the resignation letter into evidence.

"What does this have to do with Mr. Patton?"

"When she tendered her resignation, she told Mr. Holmes and Mr. Patton that she had retained a lawyer. She was going to sue the firm and Mr. Patton for sexual harassment. Mr. Holmes told me he was going to begin procedures to have Mr. Patton expelled from the firm."

"Did Ms. Kennedy ever initiate legal action against Mr. Patton?"

"No, Mr. Daley. She died before she had time to do anything."

"Ms. Fontaine, would it surprise you to know that Mr. Patton has testified that he had never propositioned Ms. Kennedy?"

"Yes."

"Was Mr. Patton telling the truth, Ms. Fontaine?"

"No," she says firmly. "Mr. Patton is a liar."

"No further questions."

Skipper asks a few perfunctory questions on cross. As Doris steps down, I write a note to Rosie. "Is it enough?" it says.

She whispers into my ear, "I think so."

That night, we spend two hours at Rabbi Friedman's house arguing with Joel about whether he should take the stand. The conventional wisdom says you never let your client testify unless you absolutely must. A good prosecutor will turn a defendant's story around in a nanosecond. In a circumstantial case such as ours, the entire case could turn on Joel's demeanor.

"Mike," he pleads, "I don't want to hide behind my lawyer."

"It's too risky. Skipper could tie you in knots."

"I'll take my chances. I'm not going to spend the rest of my life wondering if my testimony could have made the difference. I want to tell my story to the jury."

And maybe piss your life away. We spend an hour going over his testimony, just in case. As I'm leaving, he begs again for a chance to take the stand.

"Let me sleep on it, Joel. We'll make a final decision in the morning."

I spend the night consulting my most trusted consigliere. I'm inclined to put Joel on the stand for just a few questions. Rosie is dead set against it. Her instincts are usually better than mine. Randy Long, my mentor from the PD's office, says I should follow the conventional wisdom.

I decide to make a final phone call at eleven-thirty. "Mort, it's Mike."

"Long time no talk."

"How's life as a TV star?"

"Not all that it's cracked up to be. I have to be up in a few hours for the morning news."

"The price of fame."

"Beats working for a living." He chuckles. "What's up?"

I pause. "I wanted a gut reaction from you."

"My gut is listening."

"You think I should put Joel up on the stand tomorrow?"

Silence. I picture him sitting in his bathrobe, fingering a cigar. "That's a two-cigar question."

"I know."

I hear his asthmatic breathing. "The conventional wisdom says no."

"I know."

"The conventional wisdom isn't always right."

"I know that, too."

He pauses. "I'd put him on. But I'd get him off in a hurry. Just a few questions. Get a good, forceful denial and get him the hell off."

"Thanks, Mort. I'll be watching you in the morning."

55

"JUST KEEP EVERYTHING SHORT AND SWEET"

"In what court observers are describing as a reckless gamble, Joel Mark Friedman will take the stand in his own defense today in what might be described as the legal profession's equivalent of the Hail Mary pass. Michael Daley should be sued for malpractice."

— NEWSCENTER 4 LEGAL ANALYST MORGAN HENDERSON.
WEDNESDAY, APRIL 15.

"You ready?" I ask Joel the next morning. He's pacing in the consultation room.

"Yeah. I'm ready."

"You don't have to do this, you know."

"I know."

"And you understand my reservations?" A standard lawyerly CYA question.

"We've been through it a million times. I'm going to testify. It's my life."

It's your funeral. "Fair enough. I'll be with you all the way."

He stares at the wall. "What would you do if you were in my shoes?"

"I'd listen to my attorney."

He gives me a knowing smile. "I knew you were going to say that."

"Just keep everything short and sweet. Just the way we rehearsed it. I want you off the stand in no more than five minutes. Skipper can cross-examine you only on stuff that we've talked about. I don't want to open the whole case. I want you to tell everyone you're innocent, and sit down. Got it?"

"Got it."

The courtroom buzzes. The gallery is packed. Naomi sits between Rabbi and Mrs. Friedman in the first row behind us.

Skipper has given VIP passes to three big contributors from the Republican caucus. The gossip columnist from the *Chronicle* is here. It's the biggest local news event since the Niners were eliminated from the playoffs in January.

We rise as Judge Chen enters the courtroom. Harriet Hill brings in the jury. "Mr. Daley," Judge Chen says, "will this be your last witness?"

"Yes, Your Honor. The defense calls Joel Friedman."

Joel looks lawyerly. His hair has more gray than it did four months ago. His features are drawn, if not gaunt. Yet his eyes are clear. After four long months, he's going to tell his side of the story. I've told him not to drink any water unless he has to. It makes you look nervous.

"Mr. Friedman," I begin, "you were assisting Robert Holmes on a deal for Vince Russo on December thirtieth of last year?" I like to start with an easy, leading question.

"Yes, Mr. Daley."

I ask Joel to provide a brief summary of the deal. We talk about his dinner with Diana at Harrington's. He says she left because they got into an argument about the deal. He says he returned to the office and Diana went home.

"What did you do when you got back to the office?" I ask.

"I assembled all of the final documents for the closing. The papers were signed by twelve-thirty. I went to see Mr. Holmes. I explained to him that the escrow instructions that Ms. Kennedy was working on had not been completed and that I was going to finish them. Mr. Holmes was in the middle of a heated discussion with Mr. Russo at the time. Mr. Holmes instructed me to call Ms. Kennedy and tell her to come back to the office."

"And it was that telephone call from you to Ms. Kennedy that was tape-recorded on Ms. Kennedy's answering machine?"

"Yes."

I stop for a moment. "Did you see Ms. Kennedy after she returned from her apartment?"

"No."

"Mr. Kim, the custodian, testified that he heard you and Mr. Holmes having a rather intense discussion about twelve-thirty on the morning of the thirty-first. Do you recall that discussion?"

"Yes. Mr. Kim overheard us discussing the closing and certain issues involving my career."

"What career issues?"

"I was told on the thirtieth that I was not going to make partner."

"And were you upset about that?"

"Yes."

"And did you convey your feelings to Mr. Holmes?"

"Yes, I did."

"And what was his response?"

"Objection. Hearsay."

"Sustained."

I continue. "Let's try this another way. On the evening of the thirtieth, were you given an indication that you would be put up for partner the following year?"

Skipper stands. He's trying to figure out which objection to use. Before he can speak, Joel says, "Yes, I was promised that I would be put up for partner the following year."

"And did Mr. Holmes promise to support your election to the partnership the following year?"

"Objection. Hearsay."

Judge Chen looks perplexed. "I'll allow it this time, Mr. Daley. Then I want you to move on."

"He promised to support me," Joel responds.

"Mr. Friedman," I say, "could you please tell us what happened the following morning?"

Joel describes how he and Chuckles got the keys to Bob's office from Doris's desk. He says he got sick and went to the bathroom and threw up. When he returned, he opened the gun and took the three remaining bullets out. "I had shot the gun at the range," he says. "It was sensitive and unreliable. I disarmed it so that nobody would be injured. I thought it was the right thing to do."

"Could you describe your relationship with Diana Kennedy?"

"Yes. We were colleagues. And we were friends." He pauses. This is going to get tough. "And, for a very brief period of time, we were lovers. It's not something I'm proud of."

"How long did your affair with Ms. Kennedy last?"

"One night during October of last year." He looks at Naomi. "I'm embarrassed. I've let my family down. I've let myself down." He looks appropriately contrite. You could put a scarlet A on his chest right about now. "I'm sorry, Naomi," he says.

"Joel," I say quietly, "did you know she was pregnant?"

"Yes, I did," he whispers. "She told me in early December."

"And were you aware that you were the father of her baby?"

"No. She told me that I wasn't the father. I guess she was wrong."

"Were you aware that Diana had decided to move to San Diego?"

"Not until the night of the thirtieth."

"When did she tell you?"

"When we were having dinner at Harrington's."

Careful now. "You know, Joel," I say, "some people might think that your argument with Diana at Harrington's may have had something to do with the fact that you were the father of her baby and she was leaving town. Some might suggest that she dumped you and demanded support for the baby. Is that what really happened that night at Harrington's, Joel?"

He looks serious. He says, in a perfectly level tone, "No, Mr. Daley, that's not right. Diana and I were arguing about work. Our relationship was over long before the evening of December thirtieth."

"One final question. Let's put all of our cards right on the table. Did you kill Robert Holmes and Diana Kennedy?"

His words are perfectly measured. "No, Mr. Daley. I did not."

I glance at the phone company supervisor. No discernible reaction.

"No further questions."

Skipper can't wait. "Mr. Friedman," he begins, "do you remember having a conversation with Inspector Roosevelt Johnson on January eighth?"

"Objection, Your Honor. Mr. Gates is attempting to introduce into evidence matters that were not addressed in direct exam."

"I'll tie it together," Skipper pleads.

Judge Chen grimaces. "Overruled. But I want to see some direct relevance right away."

"Thank you," Skipper says. He turns back to Joel. "Do you remember the conversation with Inspector Johnson?"

"I had lots of conversations with Inspector Johnson."

Easy, Joel. Don't get cute. Just answer the questions.

"Well, Mr. Friedman, let me refresh your memory. According to Inspector Johnson's police report, you had an interview with him at the Hall of Justice. Do you recall the meeting?"

"Yes I do."

"And do you recall at that meeting Inspector Johnson asked you whether you had ever had a sexual relationship with Ms. Kennedy?"

"Yes, I recall that he asked."

"And how did you respond?"

Joel looks at me. "I told him we had never had a sexual relationship."

Skipper is pleased. "We later found out that you were the father of her unborn child, didn't we?"

"Yes."

"So, Mr. Friedman, when Inspector Johnson asked you about your relationship with Ms. Kennedy, you lied, right?"

It's pointless to object.

Joel casts his eyes downward. "Yes, I did," he says quietly.

"What other things have you lied about, Mr. Friedman?"

"Objection. Argumentative."

"Sustained."

I twist in the wind for the next forty-five minutes as Skipper cross-examines Joel. He gets Joel to admit the fight at Harrington's was a big one. He gets Joel to acknowledge his voice-mail message to Bob sounded ominous. He gets Joel to admit that he didn't tell the cops about his phone call to Diana until he was confronted with the tape. I object every three or four questions, just to break up Skipper's rhythm. The jury is riveted. Naomi stares at the floor. Rabbi Friedman sits with his hands folded. I second- and third- and fourth-guess my decision to put him on the stand.

Joel acknowledges his affair with Diana. His explanation is credible. When you're the father of two kids and the rabbi's son, you don't necessarily want to admit adultery. He explains his love-hate relationship with Bob.

After a seemingly endless string of questions, Skipper gets right in Joel's face. "Mr. Friedman," he says, "as Mr. Daley so eloquently said, let's put our cards on the table. Let's admit what really happened that night. We'll all feel better about it."

Here we go. Stay the course, Joel.

"Mr. Friedman," Skipper continues, "what really happened that night is that Diana Kennedy dumped you at Harrington's. She told you she didn't want to see you again. And she told you she was going to resume her relationship with Bob Holmes. Isn't that the truth, Mr. Friedman?"

"That's not true," Joel says evenly. He looks Skipper right in the eye.

"And," Skipper says, "you went back to the office that night and got into a big fight with Bob Holmes. Oh, it may have started out as a fight about business, but eventually it turned to a fight about Ms. Kennedy. Turns out she was two-timing you. She was sleeping with Mr. Holmes."

"That's not true, either," Joel says. He glances at Diana's mother.

"Come on, Mr. Friedman. We've seen you lie when things get tough. You lured her back to the office and you killed both of them with Mr. Holmes's gun. And you tried to make it look like a suicide. Except you got a little sloppy. You left your fingerprints on the keyboard. And you didn't realize your message to Ms. Kennedy had been recorded. Isn't that the truth, Mr. Friedman?"

"No, Mr. Gates, that is not the truth."

"You did it, Mr. Friedman, didn't you? You'll feel better if you get it off your chest."

Joel takes a deep breath. "It is not true. I did not kill Bob Holmes and Diana Kennedy."

"You're lying again, aren't you, Mr. Friedman?"

I leap up. "Objection, Your Honor."

"Sustained."

"No further questions."

My redirect is brief. I want to leave the jury with a final impression of a calm, collected Joel. I ask him to reiterate once more that he did not kill Bob and Diana. Then I sit the hell down.

At eleven-thirty Judge Chen looks at me. "Do you have any more witnesses, Mr. Daley?"

"No, Your Honor. The defense rests."

"We'll hear motions right after lunch and we'll begin closing arguments first thing in the morning. We're adjourned."

She pounds her gavel.

Late that night, Rosie and I are watching CNBC in her living room. "I can't understand why Daley put him on the stand," intones Marcia Clark.

"It was a terrible mistake," says Morgan Henderson, who has left the comfort of the NewsCenter 4 studio for an appearance on CNBC.

"I should have left well enough alone," I say to Rosie. "I never should have put him on the stand. It was too risky."

"He did okay. At least he got it all off his chest. That's good."

"I don't think the jury bought it."

"They're a tough group to read. I just can't tell."

"Want to hear my closing one more time?"

"Sure."

The following day, Skipper and I spend the morning engaging in the legal profession's version of hand-to-hand combat. We line up toe-to-toe and deliver our closing arguments. The commentators will describe it as a classic matchup: the charismatic DA against the eloquent defense attorney. Skipper rants for the better part of two hours. He pounds the lectern. He prances like a gazelle. He points at Joel as he describes each piece of evidence. The theatrics are effective. The jury follows his every move.

I speak for less than an hour. I try to keep my tone measured. I can't compete with histrionics, so I have to try for empathy. The courtroom is a blur of jurors' faces. I attack each piece of evidence. I plead with them to believe Bob killed Diana and then committed suicide. I remind them that somebody could have entered and exited the S&G suite by the stairs or the freight elevator without being seen on the security tape. Finally, I tell them that if they insist on concluding that somebody killed Bob, they have far better choices than Joel. With glib self-assurance, I try to deflect the blame toward Vince Russo, Chuckles Stern and, above all, Art Patton. I remind them Art had at least thirty million reasons to kill Bob.

At a quarter to twelve, I thank them and tell them that Joel's life is in their hands.

———

When all is said and done, I'm not a big believer that you win cases in closing arguments. If the jury isn't already predisposed to vote your way, your goose is probably cooked. We take a brief lunch break and Judge Chen charges the jury. At two o'clock, she pounds her gavel and sends them to the jury room.

After four long weeks of trial, it's out of my hands.

56

"I OVERREACHED. I JUST KNOW IT"

"We are very pleased with our closing arguments. We have great faith in this jury and we are confident Mr. Friedman will be acquitted."

—LIVE INTERVIEW ON CHANNEL 4 WITH DEFENSE ATTORNEY MICHAEL DALEY. THURSDAY, APRIL 16.

"I bombed, Rosie. I blew it. I overreached. I just know it." Rosie is driving us back to the office after closing arguments.

"Calm down," she replies, as she pulls onto Bryant and heads east toward our office. "You're overreacting. You did fine."

I'm looking for any wisp of comfort that I haven't just blown our case into kingdom come. Some lawyers walk out after closing arguments firmly convinced they were so good they could have persuaded the pope to convert to Judaism. I remember all the things I should have said differently, or didn't say at all. "You've got to admit I overreached a little." It's starting to drizzle.

"You did fine," she repeats. "They were listening and they were with you. I could see it."

"I hope you're right. You never can tell with juries."

"You got that right."

We park in the pay lot across the street from the office. A row of minivans line up on Mission Street. It looks like a taxi stand. I know most of the reporters by name. Rosie and I push through them. I mouth appropriate platitudes about the strength of our case.

Inside the door, Rolanda hands me a stack of phone messages. I sift through them quickly. One catches my eye. "Rosie," I say, "I've got to make a couple of calls."

I dial 1, 242, and the seven-digit number. You don't need to dial 011, the international access code, to call the Bahamas. The person answers in an elegant British accent. I recognize the voice of Duncan Burton, the concierge at the Graycliff. "Ms. Hogan has left for the airport," he says. "You can reach her at the following number." It's Wendy's cellular.

I can barely hear her when she answers.

"It's Mike. Where are you?"

"O'Hare. We just got in from the Bahamas. Our plane for San Francisco leaves in a few minutes. How are things?"

"It's up to the jury."

"You ought to go back to the Bahamas when you can spend more time."

"Maybe when I have a lot of money to hide. Did you find anything?"

There's a pause. "The good news is we finally got Trevor Smith to talk. We found out who gets the money from the International Charitable Trust. The bad news, I'm afraid, is the information won't help you much. If you were looking for a magic bullet, I don't think it's here."

"Try me. Who gets the money?"

"Bob's kids."

"That's it?"

"Yeah. And one other person. Jenny Fontaine."

"Really?" I stop for a second. Why would Bob leave money to Doris's daughter? But it makes sense, I guess. "Bob always had a soft spot for Jenny," I say.

"Kind of a thank-you to Doris."

"I suppose. Is it divided up evenly?"

"Not exactly. Jenny gets a third of the money. The other kids share the rest equally."

"Interesting."

"Yeah, I guess. Any of this going to help you, Mike?"

"I doubt it. It's too late to introduce any of it into evidence. I can't imagine Bob's kids or Jenny were involved."

"Yeah." Silent disappointment at the other end of the line.

"Look, Wendy, I didn't expect you to break the case. You really helped a lot, okay?"

"Yeah. I guess."

"When will you be home?"

"Tonight."

I look through the bars on my window. I hang up the phone as Rosie walks in. "Find out anything good from Wendy?" she asks.

"How did you know it was Wendy?"

"You have that look."

"What look?"

"The 'I wish Wendy would realize how big a crush I have on her' look."

"It's that obvious?"

"Uh-huh."

"You're not jealous, are you?"

"Nope." She's lying. At least I think so.

"You'll see. Nothing will come of it."

She smiles. "I may not give up my boy toy without a fight."

A few minutes later, Rosie and I sit in my office. My TV is tuned to NewsCenter 4. Morgan Henderson and Mort Goldberg are arguing about whether I should have put Joel on the stand. They've already declared Skipper the hands-down winner of closing arguments. Henderson is explaining to the world how I've botched Joel's defense and what a horse's bottom I am. "He never should have let his client get up on the stand," he says. "Friedman should have hired a real lawyer."

"Don't worry," Rosie says. "The only people whose vote counts right now are locked up in a closed room. And they're not talking to anybody but themselves."

"Thanks," I tell her. "I hope you're right."

At four o'clock Rolanda walks into my office. "They just called. The jury's in."

57

"WHAT SAY YOU?"

"It's a complicated case. The jury will be out for several days,
or maybe even a week."

—NEWSCENTER 4 LEGAL ANALYST MORGAN HENDERSON.
THURSDAY, APRIL 16.

"That's quick," Rosie says. The jury was out for less than two
hours.

"I don't like it," I say, more out of superstition than conviction. I know attorneys who never change their shoes
while a jury is out. My superstition is simple. I never predict
a positive outcome. Then again, I never predict a negative
one, either.

"You never can tell with juries, Rosie," I say yet again. I
turn to Rolanda. "What time?"

"Five o'clock. The clerk said they wanted to give everybody a little time to get back."

"I'll call Joel," I say.

"What do you think, Rosita?" I can't leave it. We're
in Rosie's car, driving toward the Hall. The radio news-

man solemnly intones that the verdict will be read at five.

"Too hard to predict. I'm too close to it." We turn onto Bryant.

"Me too." I look out at the auto-body shops and bail bondsmen. "I know I'll regret saying it out loud, but I just can't see how they can vote to convict." Even superstitious people have moments of weakness. And moments of wishful thinking, perhaps.

"Juries are funny," she says. "They make decisions for different reasons. I had one jury vote to acquit because they didn't like the way the prosecutor dressed. In this case, they might vote to convict just because Joel is a lawyer. Or they may not like guys who cheat on their wives. You just never know."

A dozen white TV minivans are parked bumper to bumper on the north side of Bryant in front of the main entrance to the Hall. At least two dozen TV reporters from the local and national media have staked out spots on the front steps and are broadcasting live. There's barely enough room for all of them. Mobile satellite transmitter trucks line the south side of Bryant. I heard that one enterprising bail bondsman is renting his tiny driveway to a cable station for a thousand bucks a day.

The horde surrounds Rosie and me as we walk through the police line toward the front door.

"*Mr. Daley, how do you think the jury's going to decide?*"

"*Mr. Daley, doesn't it seem like the jury was out for a very short time?*"

"*Mr. Daley, do you plan to appeal?*"

"*Mr. Daley, do you think your client got a fair shake?*"

"*Mr. Daley? Mr. Daley? Mr. Daley?*"

We push our way inside. Joel and Naomi are waiting

with Rabbi and Mrs. Friedman by the metal detectors. Naomi gives me a hug. "This is it," she says.

"Everything's going to be all right."

Rabbi Friedman and I shake hands, but we don't speak. We take the elevators. They seem even slower than usual.

We huddle outside the courtroom. "Listen," I say, "no matter what happens in there, we'll have no comment today. There'll be plenty of time to talk to the reporters."

As we're about to walk into the courtroom, Rosie touches my arm and motions down the hall with her eyes. "Check this out, Mike," she says.

I see Skipper and his entourage. McNasty is at his side. A few print reporters follow them. For some reason, Art Patton and Charles Stern are with him. Moral support from his old partners, I suppose. They look grim and I get an uneasy feeling in my stomach.

"What do you make of that?" she whispers.

"Beats me."

Skipper sees me and nods. Chuckles's face is unreadable. Patton looks daggers at me.

We walk into the courtroom. The bailiff escorts us to the defense table. Naomi and the Friedmans sit in the first row of the gallery.

"Mike," Joel says, "I guess this is it. What do you think?"

"They haven't been out very long. That's usually a good sign. Remember, the O.J. jury was out for only a few hours."

"And they made the wrong decision."

I don't respond.

"What's your gut?" he asks.

I look him in the eye. "Innocent." There's no point in telling him the truth. I just don't know.

We take our places. The court reporter is already seated. We rise for the judge. She recites we're on the record. She asks Harriet Hill to bring in the jury. Time slows down.

Joel looks at the jury as they walk in. They aren't looking at him. Not a good sign. Naomi is wearing her sunglasses. Rabbi and Mrs. Friedman hold hands. Rosie sits perfectly still. I'm glad she's here. My stomach churns.

Judge Chen turns to the jury. "Have you reached a verdict, Madam Foreperson?"

The phone company supervisor stands. "Yes we have, Your Honor."

We watch the ceremonial passing of the paper from the phone company supervisor to Harriet Hill to the judge. She looks at the verdict impassively. No discernible sign either way.

"Will the defendant please rise."

Joel, Rosie and I stand. So does Skipper. McNulty stays seated. Out of the corner of my eye, I see Naomi and the Friedmans. Their eyes are closed.

Here we go.

Judge Chen turns to the jury. "What say you?"

I can hear myself breathing.

The phone company supervisor takes a deep breath. Time stops. "Not guilty on all counts, Your Honor," she replies without emotion.

Pandemonium in back of me. Reporters sprint to the door. Joel falls back into his chair. Judge Chen pounds her gavel. "The jury is excused with the court's thanks. The bailiff is instructed to release Mr. Friedman at once. We're adjourned."

Joel turns to me with a bewildered look. "Does that mean what I think it means?"

"Yeah. It's time to go home, Joel."

When a client is acquitted, the defense lawyer becomes an extraneous observer in a matter of seconds. Joel, Rosie, Naomi and I get together in the front of the courtroom for what Grace likes to call a group hug. Naomi is sobbing. Then Joel climbs over the rail and hugs his parents.

The reporters have already left the courtroom. I give Rosie a big hug of her own. "Thanks," I manage to say. I barely notice the tears in her eyes. I feel the tears in mine. I pause for a moment before I gather my papers. "What the hell just happened?" I say.

"You won, Mike."

Skipper strides toward me, the three-million-dollar smile plastered on his face. He shakes my hand forcefully. "Nice job, counselor," he says.

"Yeah. Thanks, Skipper." Let's go out for a beer sometime.

He turns and addresses the gallery. "Obviously, we're disappointed with the result. However, we believe in the system and we must accept the jury's verdict. I'll be holding a press conference in my office in twenty minutes." I tune it out.

I turn and see Bill McNulty sitting at the prosecution table, shaking his head. He hasn't moved. He's looking straight ahead, and he's muttering over and over, "Jesus fucking Christ."

58

MY LAST CONFESSION

"We still have faith in the criminal justice system."
—SKIPPER GATES. *LARRY KING LIVE*. THURSDAY, APRIL 16.

There are no victory laps or trips to Disneyland for victorious defense attorneys. A few get interviewed by Larry King. Some get book contracts. Most are held up to universal scorn and are cited as the reason for the collapse of the justice system and, by extension, the moral fabric of our society.

I seem to be one of them. As Rosie and I drive from the Hall to Joel's house for an early-evening celebration, the Monday-morning quarterbacks on the radio are already proclaiming I'm a social pariah. "In local news, in a stunning conclusion to the trial of the decade, accused double murderer Joel Mark Friedman was found not guilty. District Attorney Prentice Gates expressed his disappointment with the verdict, but said he would abide by the result. Friedman's attorney, Michael Daley, said he was pleased and had no further comment. KCBS news time is six-ten."

Rosie turns off the radio. "Enough," she says. "This case will be held up as a textbook example of what's wrong with the justice system."

"And the American way of life," I add. "Actually, Rosie," I wax, "I doubt anybody will be thinking about it in a couple of days."

"You're probably right. By the way, did the judge have anything to say?"

"Skipper and I talked to her for a few minutes right after the verdict was read. She said it was the most disgusting display she had ever seen in a courtroom. It seems she isn't real fond of lawyers who hide evidence and bring witnesses back from the dead. It violates her sense of fair play." I smile. "She said she hopes she'll never see any of us again."

"You're running out of judges, Mike."

"I know. Well, you know the old saying. 'So many judges, so little time.' "

Rosie grins. "Actually, I thought she did a good job."

I agree. "She did. She's going to be a good trial judge."

"Did you interview the jurors?" After a trial is over, the lawyers are permitted to ask the jury about the case and how they reached their decision.

"Briefly. They thought it was a suicide. They didn't buy Beckert's theory that Bob was knocked unconscious."

"What did they think about you and Skipper?"

"They said Skipper was arrogant. And they thought I was whiny."

"Sounds about right," she replies. "What about Joel?"

"That's interesting. They were impressed that he had the guts to get up on the stand." I look out at City Hall. "And they didn't really believe a word he said."

"Why?"

I grin. "He's a lawyer."

"Got it." She chuckles. "Did you get anything out of Skipper or McNasty?"

"Not much. I talked to them after we interviewed the jurors. Skipper was extolling the beauty and wisdom of the criminal justice system. McNasty kept saying he couldn't believe it."

"He's such a jolly guy."

"You know, he may be a sourpuss, but at least he's an honest one."

"You're not going soft on prosecutors in your old age, are you?"

"I'd take a hundred Bill McNastys ahead of Skipper Gates anytime."

We drive in silence north on Van Ness and turn west on Geary and head toward Joel's house. We're reversing the route I took in January when I made my mad dash to the Hall of Justice the night he was arrested. It was only four months ago, but it seems like years.

We find a parking space in front of Joel's house. You know the stars are really lining up right when you find a place to park on the street on a weeknight. It's warm and the sun is still out. Winter may be ending.

The news vans are parked in every driveway on Joel's street. The neighbors will be furious. Rosie pushes me toward Rita Roberts. "Go ahead," she says. "Say something nice about Joel and your renewed faith in the criminal justice system."

Rita sticks the microphone in my face and asks me how it feels. I utter banalities about how pleased I am that justice has been served, that a good and innocent man was set free and how the criminal justice system worked. I also prattle on about how proud I am to be a lawyer. I take the obligatory gratuitous swipe at the press for attempting to try the case in the media. I make a plea that they respect Joel and Naomi's privacy and give them an opportunity to put their lives back together. Rita nods solemnly. To me, it sounds like "blah blah blah justice, blah blah blah legal system, blah blah

blah media, blah blah blah privacy." Rosie grabs my arm and we push our way toward the door.

The party is already in full swing when we enter. Joel gives me a big hug and puts a cold beer in my hand. Naomi kisses me. Alan and Stephen come running down the hallway. Alan leaps up and gives me a bear hug. Doris has a glass of champagne in her hand and we toast each other. High fives and more hugs. The owners of Shenson's deli on Geary are members of Rabbi Friedman's temple. They have sent over huge trays of corned beef, pastrami, roast beef and turkey. Naomi gives me a sandwich and I devour it. I'm hungry for the first time in weeks.

I see my mother in the living room. Her eyes sparkle. "I'm proud of you, Michael," she says.

I'm glad she's having a good day. "Thanks, Mama. It means a lot to me."

About thirty people jam into Joel and Naomi's living room to watch the early news. There's wild applause when the announcer gives the verdict. I get an odd feeling when I see myself on TV. Rosie screams, "Mike, you look like shit." Roars of laughter.

I see myself talking to Rita Roberts. Then I'm talking to the serious-looking Vietnamese reporter from Channel 5. The anchors on Channel 7 joke that I must be having a great day. I watch myself on three different channels. Then I catch Mort interviewing Skipper on Channel 4.

"So, Mr. Gates," Mort says, "do you feel like Marcia Clark?"

"I don't know what you're talking about, Mr. Goldberg. We're disappointed with the result, but we respect the process and the jury system."

Mort rolls his eyes. I watch him spar with Skipper for five more minutes before I leave the throng in the living room and make my way to the back porch, where I find Joel sipping a beer.

"Getting some air, Joel?" I ask.

"Yeah." He pauses. "By the way, thanks for everything. I don't know if I would have made it without you."

"You're welcome. You would have been okay, one way or another."

He looks unpersuaded.

I look out at the small patio. The garden has fallen into a state of disrepair. "Joel," I say, "if you wouldn't mind, I'd like to ask you something. Man to man, attorney-client, just you and me."

He takes another gulp of beer. "Sure."

"You don't have to answer if you don't want to."

"Fair enough."

"You probably know what's coming."

He nods.

"Well, here goes. Was justice served today?"

He takes a long draw from his Samuel Adams. He looks me in the eye and doesn't blink. "Yeah, justice was served today."

"I thought so. I just wanted to be sure." Then I ask, "How are you and Naomi doing?"

"One day at a time, Mike."

"Maybe you could get some counseling."

"That's probably a good idea."

"I know some people who might be able to help you."

"I thought I'd call Dr. Kathy Chandler." A pause. "Just kidding. Give me a few days, I'll call you."

I wonder if he will. I take a deep breath of the unseasonably mild air. "Thought about what you'd like to do next?"

"I haven't given it much thought. I've had a lot on my mind. I think maybe I'd like to try teaching for a while."

"You'd be good at it."

"Maybe. Naomi thinks I should write a book."

"Really? A law book?"

"Nah. I've always wanted to write a novel. Legal thriller. You know. John Grisham."

I laugh. "Forget it. It's harder than it looks. And every lawyer I know is writing a novel. It's been done to death."

He grins. "You're probably right." Then he says, "What about you and Rosie? You guys are so good together. You're more married than most married people. Why don't you try it again?"

Tough question. No good answer. "We talk about it every once in a while. I think we finally figured it all out. We work great together. We love each other very much. We have a great time when we're together." And, Lord knows, the sex is terrific.

He interrupts me. "There's a big 'but' coming, isn't there?"

"Yes. Do you know any people who are really nice, wonderful people, but when they get together with somebody in particular, they become obnoxious jerks?"

"Yeah."

"Well, the same concept sort of applies to Rosie and me. We're nice people and we get along great. But when we try to live together, we lose it. I can't explain it. We're fundamentally incompatible. And we take it out on each other. She's careful about money. I don't have a clue. I'm neat. She's not. She likes everything to be scheduled. I don't. We drive each other crazy."

"Maybe the status quo isn't so bad after all, Mike."

"I guess. One of these days, she's going to find a guy and I'm going to get really jealous."

"Maybe not for a while. You never know. People change."

Rabbi and Mrs. Friedman walk onto the back porch. They each give Joel a hug. Then, to my surprise, they each give me a hug.

"Michael," says Rabbi Friedman, "thank you for all that

you've done." He pauses to clear his throat. "I'm sorry I may have underestimated you. You're a fine attorney."

"I'm glad everything worked out, Rabbi," I say. We all go back into the house.

At seven-thirty, Wendy and Pete walk up the steps and enter to another round of wild cheers. They look bushed. Wendy comes right over to me and gives me a big hug. "You did it, Mike!" she shouts.

"*We* did it, Wendy. And we couldn't have done it without you."

Pete's beaming. "You son of a bitch," he says. "We heard it on the radio in our cab."

"How the hell did you get the banker to talk?"

Wendy says, "Pete's very persuasive. He held him by his ankles from the window of his office. It's on the tenth floor."

I look at her. She's a good liar. "You're kidding, right?" I ask.

She grins. "Yes, I'm kidding."

Pete tells me, "Actually, Wendy came up with the plan."

"Uh-oh," I say. "Wendy, you didn't sleep with him, did you?"

"Of course not, Mike. That would be crude. My methods of persuasion are far more sophisticated."

"So how'd you do it?"

"I offered to sleep with him."

"Really?"

She laughs. "No. It's Pete who had the really sophisticated plan."

Pete smiles. "Bankers don't like pain, Mike," he says.

Oops. "You didn't hurt him, did you?"

"Not much. No broken bones."

Jesus.

Wendy beams. "And Mike, there's one other thing.

Guess what? Pete and I have spent a lot of time together the last couple of months. We've decided to get married."

Jesus. Shit. Great. I think. How do you tell a woman her taste in men still leaves a lot to be desired? How do I tell my brother I had dibs on Wendy? I know these people too well. I feel too close to them. I know all their flaws. There's no purpose pointing them out now. Wendy shows me the engagement ring they bought in Nassau. "That's great, you guys," I say. "I'm very happy for you." I raise my hand and shout at the top of my lungs that Pete and Wendy have an announcement to make. Wendy holds up her ring finger and the room bursts into cheers. I see my mother in the corner of the room, her face glowing.

At eight-fifteen, I'm on the back porch. The sun has gone down and a cool breeze is beginning to blow. After two beers and a glass of champagne, I'm starting to get lightheaded.

"Hi, Mikey." Doris grins at me. "You did a helluva job. I knew you'd pull it out."

"I couldn't have done it without you, Doris. Like always."

"You're a helluva lawyer."

"Thanks. Now will you come work for me?"

"I'll have to think about it."

"I might be able to afford you now."

"I'll let you know."

We look out into the evening sky.

"So, Doris," I say, "let me ask you something."

"Anything, Mikey. It's your night."

"You won't get mad at me, will you?"

"Of course not."

"Good. Well, there are a couple of things I've been wondering about for a while now. Maybe you can help me piece them together."

She drinks her champagne. "Sure."

"Well, for one thing, could you explain how you managed to get back upstairs after you ran your security card through the scanner and made sure the security camera showed you leaving? That was the key, right? To be certain that you had witnesses who saw you leave."

There's a pause. She sets her champagne flute on the railing. Then she says, "I don't know what you're talking about."

I don't say anything. I feel my jaws tighten. I wait.

The silence finally gets to be too much for her. She fingers her glasses. "I could lie to everybody else, but I never could lie to you, Mikey," she says. "You figured it all out, didn't you?"

"I think so."

"When?"

"Just this afternoon. When I found out Jenny was going to get the money from the International Charitable Trust. Bob was trying to amend the trust. That's when I realized there was a big financial stake for Jenny in all of this. It gave you a motive."

"Are you going to turn me in?" she asks.

I take a deep breath. I think of the day she came by and gave me the hundred-dollar retainer check that's hanging in a frame in my office. "No, Doris. I can't. I'm your lawyer and you're my client. Everything we say is privileged." I look directly into her eyes. "It doesn't mean I'm happy about it."

She's trying to hold back tears. "Good," she whispers.

There's a big lump in my throat. I swallow hard. "You killed two people, Doris," I tell her.

"I know." Tears roll down her cheeks.

We stand in silence for a few minutes, staring at the trees

in Joel's backyard. I think of Doris's daughter, Jenny. I think of Diana Kennedy and her mother. I realize I'm standing next to a woman who has murdered two people, and there isn't a damn thing I can do about it.

The pain at the bottom of my stomach is excruciating. I'm speechless. I can't stop thinking about Diana's mother. And Joel. And Naomi and the kids. Lives forever changed. Finally, I manage to say, "But you framed Joel. How could you do that to an innocent man?"

She grimaces. "I didn't mean to. I didn't know I had. That's not what was supposed to happen."

I wait.

"It was such a perfect plan, Mike," she bursts out. "I'd really read up on investigative techniques, planned it all out so carefully. I thought of everything to make it look like suicide. Bob's fingerprints on the gun. A close shot, so there'd be residue from the gunpowder on his hands and shirt and tattooing around the entrance wound. Typing the suicide E-mail on his computer. I didn't miss a thing. And it *would* have worked, except for Joel. No way I could have predicted all the goofy things that pointed toward him."

True enough. "But you were willing to ruin his life for something he didn't do," I tell her.

"I know. I'm truly sorry about that—believe me. But I was trapped. Hell, if he hadn't made such an ass of himself when he called Diana that night, they probably wouldn't even have brought charges. And then he went and picked up that damned gun—how could I have guessed anyone would do something that stupid?"

She's right about that. I even think she means it when she says she's sorry. But it doesn't change anything, and I still can't put it together.

She's watching me uneasily. "Look," she says, "it was always supposed to be a suicide. That's the way I planned it. And even with Diana turning up, it would have worked if it hadn't been for Joel. It was such a standard script. She and Bob were sleeping together and he was a jilted lover. Plenty of reason for him to kill her and then himself."

"Were they sleeping together?" I ask.

"For a while. But she'd dumped him."

I need to backtrack. I've got the *how*—some of it, at least—but the *why* is missing. It doesn't make sense. No matter how much of an asshole and a bastard Bob was, Doris had endured him for twenty-two years. What in Christ could have brought her to decide on murder—cold-blooded murder? And it isn't as if she did it on impulse. She'd organized it like a military campaign: reading up on it, getting all her ducks in a row. Nothing can alter the atrociousness of two deliberate killings, but I think somehow it will help if I can only understand why.

That's going to take a while. I know Jenny's got to be at the heart of it but I'll wait on that. Best to begin with the timing.

I say, "How long did you plan all this?"

"For several months," she says. "I didn't pin down the time when I began, but I knew I had to do it."

"And that night Beth served Bob with the divorce papers, the time had come? You figured he might change his will? Maybe write Jenny out of the trust?"

"Yes." She's crying now.

Okay, I have the *when*. I decide to fill in the rest of the *how*. "How did you get back upstairs?" I ask again.

This time she tells me. "I took the freight elevator. There's no security camera there. After I made sure everyone saw me leave at eight, I went downstairs to the Catacomb and took the freight elevator up to the new construction area on forty-nine. I just waited there until one in the morning. I figured everyone else had probably left by then."

"How did you know Bob would still be there?"

"I didn't—I just took a chance he might still be finishing up on Russo's deal. If there was anyone else around, I wasn't going to do anything. I'd have just gone home."

"And after you went to Bob's office, then what?"

"I told him I came back to work on his bills. I started giving him a back rub, like I always do—did. Then I whacked him on the side of the head with one of those heavy Plexiglas bookends on the shelf behind his desk chair. You know: the ones with the scales of justice on them that say, 'Justice, Equality and Mercy.' I'd put on gloves so there'd be no fingerprints. He just sat slumped over in his chair after I hit him, quiet as a baby. Then I put the gun in his hand and brought it up to his right temple, and I was set to make him pull the trigger . . ."

"And Diana walked in."

I see her shoulders sag. "And Diana walked in and fouled everything up." She swallows. "She was just in the wrong place at the wrong time. It happened in a flash—I didn't even stop to think, I just aimed at her and shot. And then I went back and made Bob shoot himself."

The bloody photos of the bodies flash before my eyes. I shake my head trying to get rid of them. I can't. She's keyed up too, remembering. "I was shaking all over," she tells me. "I couldn't keep my hand under control. The gun was jiggling when I pressed his finger against the trigger. I wanted to get a clean fingerprint on it, but I didn't. I was too upset about Diana. I meant to press his finger on it again but I had to finish everything up—type the E-mail message with my gloves on, wash the bookend to get rid of any traces of blood—and I forgot about it."

The smudged fingerprint—I have all the *how* now, except for all the keyboard evidence that pointed toward Joel. "What about the keyboard?" I ask. "Was it Bob's?"

"How do I know? I assumed it was. It must have been."

"Then how did it get switched?"

She says she doesn't know. But Art and Charles were certainly eager to pin it on Joel, and even get him to confess before the case ever got to trial. "Maybe Charles switched them or got someone else to do it," she suggests.

"You didn't move it?"

"Swear to God, Mike."

"Well, you almost pulled it off," I say. "If it hadn't been for Joel . . ."

"Yes. If Joel hadn't screwed it up, it would have gone down as a murder and a suicide. And that's what I wanted: the suicide verdict on Bob." Then she says "Suicide" again, so emphatically that I'm startled. "That's what mattered most."

Well, sure, I think—that would have ended it then and there, unlike a charge of murder, which never closes until it's solved. But so what? Doris was never under suspicion. It was Joel who was the unwitting victim of that foul-up, but she was clean. Why *is* she so fixated on suicide? I'm at a loss.

"Doris," I say, "what difference does it make now? Sure, the official cause of death is murder and that means they can reopen the investigation at any time, but I don't think you're in any danger. I've told you everything we've said here is privileged."

"I know that." She sounds impatient. "You don't understand. That's not the reason the suicide verdict was so important."

I look at her blankly. Her eyes are on fire. "Don't you get it, Mike?" she asks. "It's the key-man policy. The suicide clause. I wanted Bob dead—Christ did I ever!—but I wanted the whole damn firm wiped out too. Just as dead as he was. Stone-cold dead."

I'm stunned. The venom in her voice is palpable. I don't understand it. Sure, Bob treated her like shit for years. And there's Jenny to protect. But killing two people because she hates him? Bringing down the firm because she hates him?

It doesn't make sense. All I can manage is a barely audible, "Why, Doris?"

"Because I hate them all—every last one of them. They're all scum. I knew they were in trouble. I wanted to be sure there was nothing to save them. I didn't want them to get the twenty million from the key-man policy. I hope they all go to the poorhouse and rot in hell."

I keep trying to bring some semblance of reason to all of this. I can't. I tell her she may get her wish about the firm—after the verdict, Skipper said Art told him they were going to shut down because they'd lost too many partners—but there's still a chance of their getting the insurance money. "The official cause of death is still murder," I remind her.

She holds up her hands. "It isn't a perfect world, Mike," she says. "They'll be fighting about it with the insurance company until hell freezes over, anyway."

I give up. "Doris," I say, "I still don't get it. Why do you hate them so? Even Bob—Jesus, you put up with his shit for more than twenty years. I know he treated you like dirt, but *murder*? Even to protect Jenny's share of the trust, how could that justify killing him in cold blood?"

"Oh, Mike," she says softly, as if she's spent. "It wasn't the money. I couldn't kill for money. You should know that. It's Jenny."

"Jenny?"

I see her take a deep breath. "Bob was sleeping with her, Mike."

Dear God. A married man more than twice her age preying on the daughter of his secretary. Bob was an even fouler bastard than I thought. But I still find myself thinking why the leap to *murder*?

"I begged him to stop." She's crying now. "I begged him over and over, and he refused." I can hardly hear her for the sobs. "Oh, Mike, I had to, don't you see? He was Jenny's father."

Jesus fucking Christ. "Did he know?" I ask softly.

"Of course he knew. From the very beginning. That's why he left all that money in the trust for her."

"And Jenny?"

"No. I never told her. I didn't think she had to know." She's trying to pull herself together. She takes a deep breath. "I asked him to stop and he wouldn't. He was infatuated. He wouldn't even acknowledge he was doing anything wrong. My God, I even went to Art Patton. He wouldn't believe me. He said I was making it all up. I got so furious I threatened him. I said I'd reveal things that would bring down the whole damn firm—and he . . . he *sneered* at me, Mike, as if I was a piece of dirt. He said he'd crush me."

She looks at me imploringly. "What was I supposed to do?" she asks. "What else could I do? What would you have done if it were Grace?" She takes a deep breath. "I did what I had to do, and I'd do it again. Twenty-two years ago I made a mistake when I slept with Bob. He controlled my life. I wasn't going to let him control Jenny's. Destroy it. No way. So I did it."

I realize Jenny was the new girlfriend that Bob talked about, the woman Beth's investigator had seen at the Fairmont. I know *why* now, and I feel sick. We stare into the backyard and hear the joyous voices of the party behind us.

"You going to turn me in?" Doris asks.

Actually, I'm prepared to shred my state bar card right now and lose my license. But I won't. "Nope. You're a client. I can't do it."

"Thanks, Mikey."

Jesus Christ.

———

"What are you thinking about, Mike?" Rosie asks.

At eleven o'clock the same night, Rosie and I are sipping champagne on her back porch in Larkspur. Naomi gave us a bottle as we were leaving. I glance at the full moon.

"Nothing, Rosie."

"You're a lousy liar."

"Oh, I don't know. Sometimes the legal system just sucks everything out of you. And sometimes, it just sucks."

She smiles at me. "Don't beat yourself up on this one. Your client is free. He didn't do it, and now he's back home with his kids. What's so bad about that?"

"Nothing, I guess. I'll probably get to fulfill my lifelong dream of being the first lawyer to grace the cover of a Wheaties box."

I get a chuckle. "You're upset, though."

"It's the way I'm drawn."

"Why do you always do this to yourself? The system got the right result this time. That's not so bad. Half the time it gets the wrong result and puts the good guys away or sets the bad guys free. This isn't like figure skating. You don't get style points. Your client ended up in the right place. So for once in your life, take what you can and enjoy it."

"Okay, Rosie. But just for tonight. Tomorrow I get to go back and be my usual guilt-ridden, tortured self."

"It's a deal." She drinks her champagne. "There's more to all of this than you're telling me, isn't there?"

I remain silent.

"He didn't do it, did he?"

"He didn't do it. That's all there is to it."

She grins. "It wasn't a suicide, was it?"

"I'm not talking."

"What's it going to take to get it out of you?"

"I'm not talking."

"I can be very persuasive."

"I know."

"Let's try this. I'd like you to become a full partner in the firm."

"Sounds pretty good so far. I'll have my people talk to your people and we can set up a meeting to discuss terms." We can use the settlement agreement from our divorce as the model form for our partnership agreement.

"Good. Oh, by the way, matrimony is out of the question in these negotiations."

"Absolutely."

"Now that we're partners, everything you say to me is completely confidential within the confines of our firm."

"I like the sound of that. Our firm."

"I thought you would. It's what we should have done from the start."

"I know."

"Now, about your little secret."

Well, you see, Rosie, my former secretary—the one I've been trying to get to come to work for me—murdered two people in cold blood and is going to get away with it—scotfree. She probably had a good reason to kill Bob, but she killed Diana just because she was in the wrong place at the wrong time. But, hey, don't worry—she hasn't killed anybody else in the last four months and she promised me—pinky swear—that she'd never do it again.

"It's going to take more than a partnership to get it out of me."

"What did you have in mind?"

She pours the rest of her champagne into my empty glass.

"If I didn't know better," I say, "I'd say you're trying to get me drunk and take advantage of me."

"You could say that."

Her dark brown eyes reflect the moonlight. I remove the elastic band that holds her hair in a tight ponytail. I pull her close. "Where's Grace?" I whisper into her ear.

She kisses me softly on the mouth. "Staying with her grandmother." Her warm breath smells like champagne.

"I see." I smile. "Well, a second ago you said that for tonight, I should just take what I can and enjoy the moment."

She shakes her hair. "After all, you won your big case, but you didn't get your trip to Disneyland." She begins to unfasten the buttons on my shirt.

"I've got another trip in mind."

"What do you suppose George Costanza would call it?"

"Victory sex?"

"Victory sex. I like that. It has a nice ring to it."

ACKNOWLEDGMENTS

During the day, I'm a corporate and securities lawyer. When I began to write a book about a murder trial, I realized right away that I needed a lot of help. I'm very lucky that I know many wonderful and generous people. I have to say a lot of thank-yous, so you'll have to bear with me.

To my extraordinary editor, Ann Harris, and to Irwyn Applebaum, Nita Taublib and the entire team at Bantam. Your thoughtful work and dedication helped make this book a lot better than the draft that found its way to your in-boxes. Thanks for everything.

To Margret McBride, the finest literary agent in the business, and the gang at the Margret McBride Literary Agency: Kris Sauer, Donna DeGutis, Sangeeta Mehta, Rachel Petrella and Faye Atchison. Thanks for all of your hard work. You've made my life a lot easier. You're the best. Special thanks to my colleague, Chris Neils, who introduced me to Margret.

To my generous and talented writing instructors, Katherine V. Forrest and Michael Nava. This book simply would not have happened without you.

To the Every Other Thursday Night Writers' Group: Bonnie DeClark, Gerry Klor, Peggy Stiefvater, Kris Brandenburger, Anne Maczulak, Liz Hartka and Janet

Wallace. Thanks for your thoughtful comments. I'll look forward to seeing your work in bookstores in the very near future.

To criminal-defense attorney David Nickerson, who helped me figure out the ins and outs of criminal procedure. If you ever get in trouble, David's your man.

To Inspector Sergeant Thomas Eisenmann and Officer Jeff Roth of the San Francisco Police Department, who helped me with police procedural issues. If Tom or Jeff arrests you, not even David will be able to get you off.

To Dr. Gary Goldstein and Dr. Dan Scodary, who taught me more about the anatomy of the human brain than I ever wanted or needed to know. If you ever get sick, they're your guys.

To my friends and colleagues at Sheppard, Mullin, Richter & Hampton, who have been wonderfully supportive of my literary efforts and who have relaxed the firm's stringent billable-hour requirements from time to time so that I could meet my publishing deadlines. I am proud to work with you and I'm glad you're my friends. Unlike the lawyers portrayed in this book, you embody all of the ideals that are honorable about our much-maligned profession. In particular, my heartfelt thanks to Randy Short, Bob Thompson, Joan Story, Lori Wider, Becky Hlebasko, Donna Andrews, Phil Atkins-Patterson, Julie Ebert, Geri Freeman, Jim Hodge, Kristen Jensen, Tom Counts, Ted Lindquist, Bill Manierre, Betsy McDaniel, John Murphy, Tom Nevins, John Pernick, Joe Petrillo, Maria Pracher, Ted Russell, Rick Runkel, Ron Ryland, John Sears, Mark Slater, Bill Wyatt, Bob Zuber, Aline Pearl, Terry Meeker, Kathleen Shugar, Sue Lenzi, Nancy Posadas and Donna Luksan. Special thanks to my secretary, Cheryl Holmes, who read every word of this book, helped me scout locations in San Francisco and has put up with me every day for more years than either of us cares to admit.

To my friends who read early versions of this manuscript, who (as we lawyers are fond of saying) include, without limitation, Rex Beach, Jerry and Dena Wald, Gary and Marla Goldstein, Ron and Betsy Rooth, Alvin and Charlene Saper, Angele Nagy, Polly Dinkel and David Baer, Jean Ryan, Sally Rau, Bill Mandel, Dave and Evie Duncan, Jill Hutchinson and Chuck Odenthal, Tom Bearrows and Holly Hirst, David and Petrita Lipkin, Pamela Swartz, Cori Stockman, Allan Zackler, Ted George, Nevins McBride, and Al and Marcia Shainsky. Special thanks to Maurice Ash, who quietly sat next to me on the Larkspur ferry for the better part of two years while I composed on my laptop, and his wife, Sandy, who was very supportive.

Thanks to Charlotte, Ben and Michelle Siegel, Ilene Garber, Jan Harris, Matz Sandler, Scott and Michelle Harris, Cathy and Richard Falco and Julie Harris. Family matters.

Finally, thanks to my wonderful, beautiful, supportive wife, Linda, the love of my life, my soul mate and my best friend, who reminds me every day that extraordinary things can happen when you believe in yourself. I'll love you forever and ever. And thanks for buying me the computer.

Last, thanks to the joys of my life, my twin sons, Alan and Stephen, who were very understanding when Daddy had to stay up late or miss a few days of vacation to edit his book. You make every day a celebration. And thanks for letting me use the computer.

ABOUT THE AUTHOR

SHELDON SIEGEL, a graduate of the University of California/Berkeley Boalt Law School, has been in private practice in San Francisco for over fifteen years, and specializes in corporate and securities law with the firm of Sheppard, Mullin, Richter & Hampton. He lives in Marin County with his wife, Linda, and their twin sons. *Special Circumstances* is his first novel.

Look for Sheldon Siegel's new legal thriller
from Bantam Books
INCRIMINATING EVIDENCE
available in bookstores in August 2001

1

"WE HAVE A SITUATION"

"The attorney general is a law enforcement officer, not a social worker."

—PRENTICE MARSHALL GATES III, SAN FRANCISCO
DISTRICT ATTORNEY AND CANDIDATE
FOR CALIFORNIA ATTORNEY GENERAL.
MONDAY, SEPTEMBER 6.

Being a partner in a small criminal defense firm isn't all that it's cracked up to be. Oh, it's nice to see your name at the top of the letterhead, and there is a certain amount of ego gratification that goes along with having your own firm. Then again, you have to co-sign the line of credit and guarantee the lease. You also tend to get a lot of calls from collection agencies when cash flow is slow. In this business, founder's privilege extends only so far.

Unlike our well-heeled brethren in the high-rises that surround us, the attorneys in my firm, Fernandez and Daley, occupy cramped quarters around the corner from the Transbay bus terminal and next door to the Lucky Corner Number 2 Chinese restaurant. Our office is located on the second floor of a 1920s walk-up building at 553 Mission Street, on the only block of San Francisco's South of Market area that has not yet been gentrified by the sprawl of downtown. Although we haven't started remodeling yet, we recently took over the space from a now-defunct martial arts studio and moved upstairs from the basement. Our files sit in what used to be the men's locker room. Our firm has grown by a whopping fifty percent in the last two years. We're up to three lawyers.

"Rosie, I'm back," I sing out to my law partner and ex-wife as I stand in the doorway to her musty, sparsely furnished office at eight-thirty in the morning on the Tuesday after Labor Day. Somewhere behind four mountains of paper and three smiling pictures of our eight-year-old daughter, Grace, Rosita Fernandez is already working on her second Diet Coke and cradling the phone against her right ear. She gestures at me to come in and mouths the words "How was your trip?"

I just got back from Cabo, where I was searching for the perfect vacation and, if the stars lined up right, the perfect woman. Well, my tan is good. When you're forty-seven and divorced, your expectations tend to be pretty realistic.

Rosie runs her hand through her thick, dark hair. She's only forty-three, and the gray flecks annoy her. She holds a finger to her full lips and motions me to sit down. She gives me a conspiratorial wink and whispers the name Skipper as she points to the phone. "No, no," she says to him. "He'll be back this morning. I expect him any minute. I'll have him call you as soon as he gets in."

I sit down and look at the beat-up bookcases filled with oatmeal-colored legal volumes with embossed gold lettering that says *California Reporter*. I glance out the open window at the tops of the Muni buses that pass below us on Mission Street. This is an improvement over our view before we moved upstairs. When we were in the basement, we got to look at the bottoms of the very same buses.

On warm, sunny days like today, I'm glad we don't work in a hermetically sealed building. On the other hand, by noon, the smell of bus fumes will make me wish we had an air conditioner. Our mismatched used furniture is standard stock for those of us who swim in the lower tide pools of the legal profession.

Rosie and I used to work together at the San Francisco public defender's office. Then we made a serious tactical error and decided to get married. We are very good at being lawyers, but we were very bad at being married. We split up almost seven years ago, shortly after Grace's first birthday. Around the same time, I went to work for the tony Simpson and Gates law firm and Rosie went out on her own. Our professional lives were reunited about two years ago when I was fired by the Simpson firm because I didn't bring in enough high-paying clients. I started subleasing space from Rosie. On my last night at Simpson and Gates, two attorneys were gunned down in the office. I ended up representing the lawyer who was charged with the murders. That's when Rosie decided I was worthy of being her law partner.

I point to myself and whisper, "Does Skipper want to talk to me?"

She nods. She scribbles a note that says "Do you want to talk to him?"

Prentice Marshall Gates III, known as Skipper, is the San Francisco district attorney. We used to be partners at Simpson and Gates. His father was Gates. He's now running for California attorney general. His smiling mug appears on billboards all over town under the caption "Mr. Law and Order." Two years ago, he won the DA's race by spending three million dollars of his inheritance. I understand he's prepared to ante up five million this time around.

I whisper, "Tell him you just heard me come in and I'll call him back in a few minutes." I'm going to need a cup of coffee for this.

Skipper is, well, a complicated guy. To my former part-ners at Simpson and Gates, he was a self-righteous, condescending ass. To defense attorneys like me, he's an opportunistic egomaniac who spends most of his time padding his conviction statistics and preening for the media. To the citizens of the City and County of San Francisco, however, he's a charismatic local hero who vigorously prosecutes drug dealers and pimps. He takes full credit for the fact that violent crime in San Francisco has dropped by a third during his tenure. Even though he's a law-and-order Republican and a card-carrying member of the NRA, he has led the charge for greater regulation of handguns and sits on the board of directors of the Legal Community Against Violence, a local gun-control advocacy group. He's an astute politician. It's a foregone conclusion that he'll win the AG race. The only question is whether he'll be the next governor of California.

Rosie cups her hand over the mouthpiece. "He says it's urgent." Her eyes gleam as the sunlight hits her face.

With Skipper, *everything* is urgent. "If it's that important," I whisper, "it can wait."

She smiles and tells him I'll call as soon as I can. Then her grin disappears as she listens intently. She puts the chief law enforcement officer of the City and County of San Francisco on hold. "You may want to talk to him," she says.

"And why would I want to talk to Mr. Law and Order this fine morning?"

The little crow's-feet around her eyes crinkle. "It seems Mr. Law and Order just got himself arrested."

"I'll take it in my office."

My new office isn't much bigger than my old one downstairs. My window looks out on a large hole in the ground that will someday evolve into a high-rise office building across the alley. At least I don't have to walk up a flight of stairs to the bathroom.

I stop in our closet-sized kitchen on my way down the hall and pour coffee into a mug with Grace's picture on it. I glance at the little mirror over the sink, which is filled with empty cups. My full head of light brown hair is fighting a losing battle against the onslaught of the gray. The bags under my eyes are a little smaller than they were a week ago. I walk into my office, where my desk is littered with mail. I log on to my computer and start scrolling through e-mail messages. Finally I pick up the phone, punch the blinking red button, and say in my most authoritative tone, "Michael Daley speaking."

"Skipper Gates," says a familiar baritone. "I need your help ASAP. We have a situation."

I haven't heard the euphemism "We have a situation" since I left Simpson and Gates. We used to refer to this as Skipper speak. When somebody else screwed up, Skipper called it a fuck-up. When he screwed up, it was a situation.

I try to keep the tone measured. "What is it, Skipper?"

"I need to see you right away."

Nothing changes. I'm still glancing at my e-mails. We aren't the best of pals. He led the charge to get me tossed out of the Simpson Firm and we've had our share of run-ins over the last couple of years. It comes with the territory when you make your living as a defense attorney. San Francisco is a small town. Everybody involved in the criminal justice system knows everybody else. We have long memories and unlimited capacity for holding grudges. "Where are you?" I ask.

"The Hall of Justice."

"Are you in your office?"

"No. The holding area. They're treating me like a prisoner."

"What happened?"

Silence.

"Skipper?"

I hear him clear his throat. "We had a campaign rally at the Fairmont last night." Skipper tends to refer to himself in the royal we. He's one of the few people I know who can get away with it. "It ended late," he continues, "so I decided to stay at the hotel. When I woke up this morning, there was a dead body in my room."

"How do you suppose it got there?"

"I don't know."

"What do you mean, you don't know?"

"Just what I said. I don't know. It wasn't there when I went to sleep last night."

With Skipper, the imaginary line between reality and dreamland is often pretty fluid. He isn't exactly lying. Well, not on purpose, anyway. He spends a substantial part of his waking hours in a parallel reality. This is a very useful skill if you're a lawyer or a politician.

I ask, "Do you know who it was?"

"Uh, no."

"Did you call security?"

"Of course. They called the cops."

"What did they say?"

"They arrested me." He may as well have added the words "you idiot."

I stop to regroup. "Skipper," I say, "why did you call me?"

"We need somebody to deal with this right away. We have to start damage control. This isn't going to help me in the polls."

I'll say. A dead body is serious. "You know how the system works. You should hire somebody you trust. There are a lot of defense attorneys around town. I may not be the right guy for you."

I hear him exhale heavily. "You *are* the right guy. Notwithstanding our history, I called you for a reason. You're a fighter. You have guts. You'll tell me what you really think."

He pauses and then adds, "And unlike most of your contemporaries in the defense bar, you won't try to cut a fast deal or turn this case into a self-serving infomercial."

I'll be damned. A compliment from Skipper Gates. "All right," I say, "You're on." I ask him a few more questions and agree to meet him at the Hall.

I glance at my watch. Five to nine. Rosie walks in. "So, did you get lucky?" she asks.

"Maybe. Looks like we may have a new case."

"No, dummy. Mexico. Did you get lucky in Mexico?"

Rosie. Ever the pragmatist. First things first.

"No," I say. "I didn't get lucky." I'm probably the *only* guy at Club Med who didn't get lucky. "I'm still all yours."

She's pleased. "Well, then you *did* get lucky, didn't you?" She glances at the notes I've scribbled. "What's Skipper's story?"

I take a long drink of coffee. "Nothing out of the ordinary. A dead body wandered into his room in the middle of the night. The cops think he had something to do with it becoming dead."

She takes this news in stride. "Do they know who the victim is?"

"No ID yet. The cops told him it may have been a prostitute."

"How did she die?"

"They think suffocation." I arch my eyebrows and add, "By the way, it wasn't a she."

2

THE ASSHOLE PREMIUM

"The Hall of Justice isn't a big tourist attraction."
—SAN FRANCISCO POLICE CHIEF. *SAN FRANCISCO CHRONICLE.*
TUESDAY, SEPTEMBER 7.

In San Francisco, the wheels of justice grind at a snail's pace in the Hall of Justice, a monolithic six-story structure that rises above the 101 Freeway at the corner of Seventh and Bryant. The criminal courts, DA's office, chief medical examiner and county jail jockey for position in this crowded testimonial to industrial-strength urban architecture. A modernistic new jail wing that opened in the early nineties adds little to the overall ambiance of the original gray building, which dates to the late fifties and looks as if it could withstand a nuclear attack. I park my eleven-year-old Corolla in the pay lot next to the McDonald's and walk quickly through the throng of reporters who are already camped on the front steps of the Hall. The news is out.

I glare into the nearest camera and invoke Skipper speak. "We have a situation. This misunderstanding will be resolved shortly and Mr. Gates will return to his duties at the

DA's office." I push through the heavy doors, nod to the guard as I pass through the metal detector and walk up the stairs to the sixth floor of the new jail wing, known as County Jail Number 9.

I present my state bar card and driver's license to Sergeant Jeff Dito, a mustached, olive-skinned sheriff's deputy who administers the intake center with a steady hand. He studies my bar card through deepset eyes. When I explain I'm here to see Skipper, he furrows his brow. " 'Mr. Law and Order' is in booking," he says. He punches some buttons on his computer keyboard and makes a phone call. "He'll be up in a few minutes."

It's early, but things are hopping. For historic bureaucratic reasons, the jail facility is run by the County Sheriff's Department. Deputies walk through the hallway. I nod to a couple of my former colleagues from the PD's office. I take a seat next to a man who is trying to persuade his parole officer that Jesus is talking to him. The parade of humanity resembles a flea market on a busy afternoon. Police, prosecutors, public defenders and criminals barter in the hallway. Instead of selling trinkets and other junk, the prosecutors sell trips to jail and probation terms. The defense attorneys do their clients' bidding. If you sit here long enough, it almost sounds as if you're listening in on a half dozen simultaneous time-share pitches for those condos in Mexico. When I was a PD, I used to make some of my best deals in the corridor just outside the old booking hub on the sixth floor of the Hall. That part of the facility is now used for hard-core prisoners. The new jail wing is a lot quieter.

Whenever I'm in the Hall, I think of my dad, who was a San Francisco cop. He died a few weeks after Grace's first birthday. He was beside himself when I decided to go to law school. He detested lawyers—even the prosecutors. He was appalled when I became a PD. He took it as a personal affront. Somehow, I still expect to see him walking down the corridor, chest out, cigarette in his hand.

Five minutes later, Sergeant Dito nods and a deputy leads me to an airless room just behind the intake desk, where I find Skipper pacing like a caged lion. Even unshaven and in an orange jumpsuit, he's impressively handsome, all trim six feet six of him. His charismatic public persona remains intact. Until now, I have never seen him dressed in anything other than a top-of-the-line Italian suit. He wags a menacing finger at me. "Somebody's ass is going to fry for this," he says.

Hopefully, it won't be yours.

"I'm going to kick the chief's butt all the way back to Northern Station for promoting McBride," he snaps. Inspector Elaine McBride made the arrest. She's only the second woman to make homicide inspector on the SFPD. She's tough. Her stellar reputation is well deserved. Skipper sits down in a heavy wooden chair. "This is preposterous," he says. "It's a publicity stunt."

This sort of thing isn't supposed to happen to God-fearing Republicans. In many respects, getting arrested is society's great equalizer. Even a well-connected, rich white guy like Skipper has been strip-searched, showered with disinfectant, given a medical interview and placed in a holding cell. There isn't much dignity left after the process is completed. I place a pad of white paper in front of me on the table. Most lawyers have stopped using those ugly yellow pads because they can't be recycled. I look directly into his eyes. "You're the DA," I say. "You know the drill. Tell me what happened."

He's indignant. "Nothing happened," he replies, emphasizing each syllable. He looks at the drab walls. On Friday, he was sitting in his opulent office on the third floor of the old Hall. Now he's sharing space with murderers, child molesters and pimps. "We had a kickoff rally for my campaign in the grand ballroom at the Fairmont last night. Fifteen hundred people showed up. It was terrific."

Particularly if your idea of a good time is paying a thousand bucks a head to the Republican caucus to eat rubber chicken and kiss Skipper's ass.

"The program broke up around eleven," he continues. "Then we had a summit conference upstairs."

"What about Natalie?" I ask. Skipper's long-suffering wife. Serious old-line money. Her great-grandfather was a Crocker. Her mother's family used to own the *Chronicle*, where her name appears regularly in the society column.

"She stayed for a few minutes and went home. She was tired." He sighs and adds, "I have no idea how I'm going to explain all of this to her."

I guess even self-centered guys like Skipper have to answer to somebody from time to time. "So you decided to stay at the hotel?" I ask.

"I do it all the time," he replies. "I had a breakfast meeting this morning." His eyes wander over my left shoulder. "I didn't want to go all the way out to the house."

This is odd. He lives ten minutes from the hotel. "May I assume, Skipper, that the dead man wasn't there when everybody left?"

"That's right."

"And he wasn't in your room when you went to bed?"

He looks a little too solemn. "I was by myself."

Uh-huh. "And when you woke up this morning, the dead man was in your bed with you?"

"He was in the bed," he explains. "I fell asleep in the chair. I was watching TV. I woke up when the room service waiter knocked on the door. That's when we found the body."

"You didn't hear anything?"

"Nope."

"See anybody?"

"Nope."

He's a sound sleeper. "Did anyone else have a key to your room?"

"Just the hotel staff, I suppose."

There you have it. He fell asleep in the chair in front of the TV. In the middle of the night, a body wandered into his room and plopped itself into his bed. Same thing happened to me in Cabo last week. "Skipper," I say, "did you know the guy?"

His eyes darted toward the door. "I'd never seen him before."

"Do you know how he died?"

"It looked like he had suffocated. His face was covered with gray duct tape. He was handcuffed to the bedposts."

I can confirm this from the police reports. "Did you touch the body?"

"Of course. I checked for a pulse. I pulled the tape off his face in case he could still breathe. I tried to release the handcuffs, but I didn't have a key."

"Then you called the police?"

"I called the hotel operator, who put me through to security. I told them to call the cops."

"You realize your story sounds just a tiny bit odd, don't you?"

He looks right at me. "I didn't do it."

It's his story and he's sticking to it. "For some reason, the police seem to think you did."

His eyes narrow. "It's no big newsflash that I'm not going to win any popularity contests with the SFPD. I'm making the cops work harder than they have in a long time."

They hate his guts. Although the public perceives Skipper as a champion of law-and-order, the police aren't as easily impressed. They think he ducks the tough cases.

"I did the right thing," he says. "I gave them my statement. Next thing I know, McBride decides to be a big shot and arrests me."

"What are you leaving out?"

"Nothing." Even in an orange jumpsuit, he is capable of sounding condescending. "It's a setup. I'm ahead in the polls. My political enemies want to embarrass me. That's the only plausible explanation."

Another plausible explanation is that he did it. On its face, that would seem pretty far-fetched. Politicians call each other names, lie, cheat and run attack ads. By and large, they don't commit murders in hotel rooms. And it seems unlikely that a murderer would spend the night in the same room as the dead body and hang around until the cops showed up.

I ask if he's spoken to Natalie.

"I talked to her for a few minutes right before I called you. She's terribly upset. Ann went over to try to calm her down."

"I'll go talk to McBride and the DA," I say. "The arraignment will be later this week. I'll need you to sign a client retention letter and I'll need a fifty-thousand-dollar retainer."

"Fifty thousand?" he says. "Seems a little steep."

If this case goes to trial, he'll spend at least a quarter of a million dollars on legal fees and another hundred thousand for experts, jury consultants and investigators. He's well aware of this. "Grace has to eat," I say. "If you're out of here as soon as you think, your money will be cheerfully refunded."

"We're a little tight on cash. We've put a bunch of our liquid assets into the campaign war chest. You know how it is."

Actually, I don't. "If you want me to represent you, I'm going to need a fifty-thousand-dollar retainer. If that doesn't work for you, you'll have to find somebody else to handle your case."

I hear him sigh. "Okay," he says, "fifty thousand it is. Bring along the letter this afternoon. I'll sign whatever you want."

It's not like he's going to read it.

"Good. And I'm going to need a check for a hundred thousand dollars."

He's unhappy. "I thought you said it was fifty."

"It was. The price just went up." Rosie and I refer to this as charging the Asshole Premium. We reserve such special treatment for our more difficult clients. "Is there a problem?"

The deputy knocks on the door. "We need to finish your client's paperwork," he says.

It's my turn to point a finger at Skipper. "Don't talk to anybody," I tell him. "I'll see if I can get this cleared up before things get out of hand."

"I didn't do it," he insists. "Somebody's going to pay for this."